Hawaiian Flames

Sheri Lynne

DORRANCE PUBLISHING CO
EST. 1920
PITTSBURGH, PENNSYLVANIA 15238

The contents of this work, including, but not limited to, the accuracy of events, people, and places depicted; opinions expressed; permission to use previously published materials included; and any advice given or actions advocated are solely the responsibility of the author, who assumes all liability for said work and indemnifies the publisher against any claims stemming from publication of the work.

This is a work of fiction. Names, characters, places and incidents are either the product of the author's imagination or are used fictitiously, and any resemblance to actual persons, living or dead, business establishments, events or locales is entirely coincidental.

All Rights Reserved
Copyright © 2022 by Sheri Lynne

Cover: Photo and Graphic Design by Dina Marie Photography
Dina.m.peek@gmail.com

No part of this book may be reproduced or transmitted, downloaded, distributed, reverse engineered, or stored in or introduced into any information storage and retrieval system, in any form or by any means, including photocopying and recording, whether electronic or mechanical, now known or hereinafter invented without permission in writing from the publisher.

Dorrance Publishing Co
585 Alpha Drive
Pittsburgh, PA 15238
Visit our website at *www.dorrancebookstore.com*

ISBN: 979-8-8860-4134-7
eISBN: 979-8-8860-4799-8

ACKNOWLEDGEMENTS

Hawaiian Flames is dedicated in honor of my brother-in-law, who served in the United States Army during the Vietnam War. Captain Greg Ross was a helicopter pilot and flew the UH-1C Huey Gunship, which was equipped with rockets and machine guns, and also the UH-1H Slick, a large transport helicopter that could transport troops in and out of the combat zone along with resupplies of ammo, food, water, and whatever the troops on the ground needed. While Greg was on a mission, flying a UH-1H Slick, he was coming up out of a hot Landing Zone, with North Vietnamese soldiers shooting at the helicopters, when his helicopter went down. Greg's back was crushed in the ensuing crash. His crew carried him to a rice paddy where his commanding officer flew in and rescued everyone on board the aircraft. Three weeks later, in Japan, he was very fortunate to have an excellent neurosurgeon, who was able to put his spine back together. With the excellent care he received, Greg was walking again three months after he was shot down. Greg, thank you for your service in the military and for fighting for our freedoms which we all hold so dear, and to Steph, his beautiful wife who shared how they first met. Both are retired now and live in sunny New Mexico. Although this book is a work of fiction, some of their early events are weaved into the characters in the book.

A special thank you goes out to First Lieutenant K. Rod and Lieutenant A. Stoner of the Michigan State Police, for giving me permission to use their first names in one of the characters in the book, for their support, and all the State Troopers who would patiently answer my questions. Thanks again to retired Detective Sergeant C. Goch for critiquing my work and guiding me in some of the crime scenes, and to my niece Melissa who reads my manuscript and keeps me on track. Also, to my daughter Wendy Janca, her husband Joe, and my beautiful granddaughter Madi for their continued support in writing the first two books!

Hawaiian Flames is the second book in the trilogy, staring Peyton TreVaine, the older brother to the twins Mike and Mark. My hope for all my readers is that this book will take you away to an island that's filled with twist and turns, and how Peyton and Detective Sergeant Stacy Rayland find love in the midst of incredible danger.

Sheri Lynne, author of *Hawaiian Dreams and Hawaiian Flames*

CHAPTER 1

Captain Peyton McManus TreVaine, serving in the United States Army, was flying over flooded land in Afghanistan, in a search-and-rescue mission to save any survivors caught in the flash flood. Flying a UH-60 transport helicopter, Peyton landed his team and the medics on board near the muddy waters where hundreds of homes had been destroyed and people were crying out for help. He shut down the chopper. The medic team was the first to exit the aircraft with supplies to treat the injured. They set up a makeshift tent to bring the injured in for treatment. Peyton, with his rescue team, and his military dog, First Sergeant Justice, gathered to decide where to begin their search for survivors. More army helicopters were on their way in the effort to save as many lives as possible. They pulled out the inflatable boat from the back of the chopper and pulled the cord. The boat was equipped with a boat motor and oars. Peyton and his team placed the boat in the muddy water and set off towards a large building protruding out of the water. The building was covered in water halfway up the sides of the building. Justice was riding in front of the boat, and was on high alert, ready for the command from his handler. As they neared the building, Peyton and his team heard the screams and cries for help inside. As they pulled up alongside the building, looking inside the window they saw women and children hanging on for dear life from the beams inside an orphanage. Peyton and his team broke the window. Lieutenant Rick Fielding, who could speak the language, spoke to the women and children, whom they were there to help, and would soon have them out to safety. Lieutenant Fielding and Sergeant Rowling put life jackets on and entered the building via the window. One at a time, they started to bring the children first, to the window where the boat was secured to the building. They handed them off to Captain TreVaine and his two other teammates. First Sergeant Justice, his black lab, started barking. Looking out over the water, he saw, near the corner of the building, a little boy barely hanging on. Peyton gave the order to Justice. The black lab dove in the water, swimming towards the little boy. The boy caught hold of Justice's life jacket and the dog brought him back to the boat. Peyton lifted him out of the water along with Justice. When all was evacuated, they headed back to shore where the victims were treated by the medics.

Looking back on that mission, it had been a long week. Unfortunately, not everyone made it out of the muddy waters. The death toll and injuries of the Afghan people were substantial, and it broke his heart every time he saw a body floating in the water that he and his team couldn't save. His dog Justice was the best military dog in the army, in his opinion. He could go where they couldn't and drag the bodies back to the boat or to shore.

Peyton was headed back to the States. He had served his country over twelve years in the army. He was ready to get out. He spent ten years in the special ops division in Afghanistan, and his last year with search and rescue. When the army issued Justice to him, a black Labrador retriever, he instantly fell in love with him. He and his dog trained together for a couple of months and worked as a team for the rest of his tour. He hated leaving the men who served with him, especially Justice, who was by his side day and night. His heart ached when he passed him on to a new handler. When he left him with Sergeant McGinnis and walked away, he could hear his cries and barking. He hoped he was doing well. As soon as he arrived back in the States, he was going to petition the army to bring him back to live with him. Justice had a few more months before the army would retire him, but Peyton would try his hardest to get his dog back home where he belonged, with him.

Looking out the window of the military aircraft, he could see in the distance Joint Base Pearl Harbor-Hickam where they would soon be landing. He couldn't wait to touch his feet on American soil again and see his twin brothers, Mike and Mark, where they lived on the island of Oahu. His brothers were co-owners of a successful restaurant called the Hawaiian Lanai. He was eager to see them and catch up with what was happening in their lives.

He felt the plane touch down on the landing strip. When it came to a stop, he and the other soldiers gathered up their duffle bags and exited the plane. When Peyton stepped down onto the tarmac, he looked up and gave thanks to the Lord for his safe arrival, and everyone else on board. As he walked toward headquarters, he looked out over the blue waters of the Pacific Ocean and felt the tension leaving him. He checked in, asked if he could hitch a ride with a soldier, and it wasn't long before they pulled up in front of the restaurant.

When he got out of the military jeep, he thanked the soldier and looked around. He didn't see very many cars around and wondered if they were closed. When he walked up to the front door of the restaurant, he could hear voices and laughter coming from the lanai. He pulled on the door; thankfully, it was opened. He walked in through the bar and stood in the doorway of the lanai. He saw his brother Mike, one of his identical twin brothers. He was a tall man with broad shoulders, sandy blond hair, and the same deep blue eyes as his twin and him. When they were younger and people would see all three of them together, they would often be mistaken for triplets. He was talking to a group of people with a pretty brown-eyed brunette standing beside him. She caught his eyes and was just about to nudge Mike when Peyton put his finger to his lips. She gave him a pretty smile and nodded as he walked toward them. Mike felt a hand on his shoulder. "Can anyone join this party?" Mike, surprised, turned to see his brother Peyton by his side.

"Peyton," exclaimed Mike. He gave his brother a big bear hug. "Damn, did you just get in?" he asked. Before he could answer, Mike yells over to his twin. "Mark! It's Peyton, he's home!"

Mark, who was the spitting image of Mike, was over talking to Sasha's parents when he heard his brother yell over to him. He took one look and excused himself to run over to his older brother and give him a fierce hug. "Peyton, my God, you're finally home! When did you land? Are you home for good this time?"

"Whoa, slow down! Can a man get a drink around here?" Mike motioned over to Megan. Megan came over to them and noticed the excitement in her bosses over the handsome, rugged man in the camouflage uniform that resembled them both.

"Megan, this is our brother, Peyton. He just got home from overseas while serving in the army, and we are all hoping that this time is for good! Peyton, this is Megan, one of our top waitresses," Mark beamed.

"It's very nice to meet you, Peyton. And I want to thank you for your service for defending our freedoms in this great country of ours."

Peyton smiled at the pretty blonde with her hair done up in a ponytail. His eyes gave her a slow appraisal. She had green eyes, and a body with nice curves and long legs. "You're welcome."

"What can I get you to drink?" she asked.

"Can your bartender make a good martini?"

"He's the best!" she replied.

He chuckled. "Okay, fix me up!"

Megan turned to go, when Mark stopped her and said, "Thanks, Megan," and gave her a wink. Megan blushed and went to get Peyton's drink. Peyton watched the exchange and decided she was hands off. Damn! He didn't want to infringe on what might be his brother's woman.

Jenna, who was watching the exchange with Mike and his brothers, was feeling a little left out. As she talked to her parents, she was wondering if she would ever get introduced to Mike's older brother. As she studied him, conversing with his brothers, she saw that he was a handsome man, in a rugged sort of way. He had the same deep-blue eyes as his brothers, same color hair. His chest and shoulders were a little broader than the twins. The muscles in his arms showed in the short sleeve camouflage T-shirt. With his matching twill trousers and the army boots he wore, it gave him a look of authority. But he looked tired and worn after his long trip back to the States.

Mike turned to Jenna. "Jenna, love, come meet my older brother. Bruce and Margaret, please, come."

Jenna and her parents came up beside Mike. "Peyton, meet my beautiful fiancée Jenna Hathaway, and her parents, Bruce and Margaret Hathaway."

Peyton shook hands with her parents and then with Jenna. "It is so nice to meet you, Peyton. I've heard a lot about you from your brothers."

He chuckled. "I hope it was all good."

"Oh yes! We are all very proud of you and your dedication to serving our country. Thank you so much! May I ask you if this was your last tour?"

Peyton could see how his brother was head over heels in love with this woman. It showed in his eyes when he introduced her to him. Her brown eyes greeted him with warmth that shone along with her friendly smile. "You're welcome, and the answer to your question is yes, this was my last tour and I am home for good!" Everybody cheered and clapped their hands. Peyton, a little embarrassed, was glad when Megan came back with his drink. He smiled and said thank you. He took a drink and nodded his head. "Very good! Tell your bartender great job!" He turned back to his brothers and Jenna. "What are we celebrating today?"

Mike put his arm around Jenna and gave her a squeeze. "We are celebrating Jenna receiving her BA degree from the University of Hawaii."

"Wow!" said Peyton. "What was your course of study?"

"CPA, I am actually starting to work here in the finance department helping Mark with the accounts payables. I met your brothers when I did my internship here at the restaurant this last semester, and fell madly in love with this guy." She looked up with love in her eyes as he bent and gave her a seductive kiss. Peyton and Mark watched the exchange between the two.

Mark nudged his arm and said quietly, "Ever since they became engaged, they're all over each other." They both chuckled.

Palani came out and informed them that the food was ready and all were welcome to start helping themselves at the buffet table set up in the bar area. They all filed in and enjoyed the wonderful Hawaiian dishes Palani and his helper had made, which featured Kalua pork, grilled chicken in a sweet Hawaiian sauce, corn, cooked green cabbage, cooked rice, a fruit bowl with a mixture of pineapple, kiwi, and strawberries, and to top it off, Palani's famous Haupie pie.

Peyton sat down next to his brothers and thought he had died and gone to heaven as he took his first bite of the Kalua pork. He hadn't had a good meal in months, so this was monumental. When he finished eating, "Man, guys, that was excellent!" he said appreciatively. "How long has Palani been with you?" he asked Mark.

"Almost from the beginning. We hired him in a little over a year after we opened. He is a great chef and an asset to this company. He runs a tight ship, and the kitchen staff love working with him. We are very fortunate to have him. You need to go and get a slice of his Haupie pie before it's gone. It's one of our favorite desserts we offer here. Customers rave over it."

"Okay, I think I will." Peyton came up out of the booth and met his brother Mike at the buffet table. "Mark said I need to try this pie."

Mike turned to his brother and smiled. "And he is absolutely right. You don't want to miss it."

While Peyton was getting a slice of pie, Mike studied his brother. Something was off. "Hey, Peyton, how are you doing, I mean really doing. Are you sure this is what you want, civilian life? Not that I don't want you home with us, but I sense something is bothering you."

"Mike." He sighed. "This is definitely what I want. The only thing that kept me going this last year was when I transferred to the search-and-rescue team out of the special ops division. When the army gave me my military working dog, Justice, I instantly bonded with him, and it tore my heart out when I had to turn him over to a new handler. I want to petition the army to bring him home to live with me. I just wish I knew how he was doing." Mike could see he was having a rough time with this.

"Is there any way you can find out?"

"I need to get to the army base and see if they can tell me anything. I will feel better if I know he was accepting his new handler. When I left, I was afraid to look back with him barking and whining."

"I'm sorry, bro. If you need help, let me know. General McCall is an Air Force general, but he might be able to pull some strings to get him home."

"Thanks, Mike, I will let you know."

"Not to change the subject but was there a reason you left the special ops division?" inquired Mike.

"Shortly after I started my last tour, my team and I were at one of the NATO training centers and it was hit by a car bombing. One of my teammates was killed, and one seriously injured. We had to fight like hell against the Taliban insurgents to get the men who were injured to the hospital and to safety. Shortly after that I decided to transfer to search-and-rescue. It is still dangerous work, but my dog Justice helped me get through the loss. He never left my side. It was like Justice knew what I was going through. Now, let's get back to the table, my taste buds are dying for this pie!"

Mike followed his brother back to the table. He wanted to hear more about his brother's experience but would wait till they had more privacy. He could see he was hurting. He would talk to Mark and see what they could do to reunite him with his dog.

After everyone enjoyed the food and dessert, they thanked Mark and Mike for a wonderful dinner and headed home. Mike walked Jenna and her parents to the door. Mike shook Bruce and Margaret's hands and said he would see them in the morning to take them to the airport. He took Jenna's hand and pulled her close for a hug. He whispered in her ear, "Are you doing okay?" Ever since her ordeal with Ralph, he worried. She pulled away from him and looked up into his eyes.

"Yes, I still get anxious at times, but it will get better in time. I love you. And thank you for all this, it was wonderful. I will see you in the morning."

He bent and gave her a kiss. "It was my pleasure, sweetheart. I love you. Be safe going home."

"We will." He watched them go. Even though he enjoyed having her parents here with them, he missed being alone with her. He headed back to the booth where Mark and Peyton were sitting.

Mike asked if either of his brothers would like anything else to drink before he sat down. "No, I think Peyton and I are going to head out. Peyton's had a long flight, and he's going to bunk with me till he finds a place of his own," said Mark.

"Okay, you two get out of here and I'll lock up." Mark and Peyton came out of the booth.

Peyton shook Mike's hand. "Hey, thanks for today."

"You're welcome, bro." He gave his brother another hug. "Glad you're home."

After they left, Mike went to check out the kitchen. Palani and his helper were just leaving. "Goodnight, Palani. Goodnight, Greg."

"Goodnight, Mike!"

Mike went through the restaurant to make sure it was ready for tomorrow. He turned the lights out, locked the door, and headed home. He smiled. It was a nice surprise: his brother Peyton was finally home for good. It saddened him about his dog. He would make sure to help his brother bring Justice home.

CHAPTER 2

Two days later Peyton was at the army base to see if he could find anything out about his dog and how he was doing. The sergeant on duty checked into the computer and looked up Sergeant McGinnis and First Sergeant Justice but didn't have an update on how they were doing working as a team. Peyton thanked him, gave him his card, and told him to contact him if he had any updates for him. He then asked the sergeant if he could have the paperwork to fill out so he could petition the army to adopt Justice and bring him home. He handed the paperwork to Peyton. "Just so you know, Captain, it is really hard to bring a dog home when he has not been retired by the army yet. Even if he doesn't respond well with Sgt. McGinnis, they will try another soldier till they find a match."

Peyton felt his spirit drop. He looked the sergeant straight in the eyes and said, "I have to try. He was my lifeline this last year when I was stationed in Afghanistan. He means more to me than life itself."

"Well, I wish you luck, and I will do my best to find out how he is doing," replied the sergeant.

"Thank you."

Peyton left the building and climbed into his used SUV he just purchased yesterday. It was a 2017 black Explorer with low mileage and would be great for his hunting expeditions. His love for hunting stems back to when he was growing up in Michigan, when his father taught him and his brothers how to hunt wild game. He was sixteen when he shot his first deer, a seventeen-point buck; it was the biggest one taken that year. The picture of him and the buck landed on the front page of the local newspaper. His dad couldn't have been more proud of him. He smiled remembering. He would check out when the hunting seasons were for wild game here on the island. He also loved to snorkel and scuba dive. You can't beat catching fresh lobster when it is in season. Maybe he would hire a charter boat and do some deep-sea fishing. It would keep him busy until he decided what he wanted to do with his life, and keep him from worrying about what was happening with Justice. He would talk to Mike to see what his general friend could find out for him.

It was late in the afternoon when he pulled up in the side parking lot of the Hawaiian Lanai restaurant. When he went in, the restaurant was already busy. People were waiting to be seated. He looked around for either Mark or Mike, and found Mark coming in from the lanai after seating a group of people. Mark greeted him, "Hey, Peyton, how did it go today?"

"Not as well as I wanted, but I picked up the paperwork to petition the army to bring Justice home. It's a longshot, but I've got to try."

"I know that Mike has already spoken to General McCall. He said he would see what he could do. He also said he would need specifics of who the dog was assigned to and where he is stationed."

Peyton breathed a sigh of relief. "I will be happy to give him all the information he needs. Just let me know when I can speak with him."

"Mike is busy interviewing prospects for a general manager position here at the restaurant. He should be done in a couple of hours. Are you planning on having dinner?" asked Mark.

"Yes. I want to look at some of your specialty items on your menu. I'm hungry for a good steak!" replied Peyton.

"If you're looking for a good steak, we have the best Hawaiian steak on the island. Come this way, I want to introduce you to a couple of detectives from the police department."

"Lead the way!" Peyton followed Mark through the bar and over to a booth by the window where two men were sitting having a beer.

"Detectives, I would like to introduce you to my brother Peyton, who just finished his last tour in Afghanistan. Peyton, this is Detective Sergeant Zackary Williams and Detective Sergeant Craig Jenson." Both men rose to shake hands with Peyton. Zack, who stood a little taller than Craig, with black hair cropped short and liquid brown eyes that could turn to steel when he interrogated a suspect, shook his hand first. Craig, who was extremely handsome, with sandy blond hair and vivid blue eyes, shook his hand next. Both men kept themselves in shape and could turn heads wherever they went.

"Good to meet you, Peyton."

"Do you mind if I join you?" asked Peyton.

"No, not at all, please, have a seat."

"Thanks."

"So, you just returned home from overseas?" asked Zack.

"Yes, this last tour was a long one. I'm glad to be home and done with the military. It was time."

"I was in the army for a couple of years and went directly into the police academy when I got out. I came over to the island after graduating from the academy and fell in love with it. Been here ever since," said Zack.

"How about you, Craig, did you ever serve in the military?" asked Peyton.

"No, I never served. My parents moved over here when I was a boy. I always saw myself as a police officer, even when I was young, and here I am today. I love what I do," answered Craig.

Megan came up to their booth and asked Peyton if he wanted a drink. "I'll have a glass of your best beer on draft."

"How about you, Zack?" asked Megan.

"I'll have another beer."

"Craig?"

"The same," he replied.

"I'll be right back with your drinks."

When she left, Peyton wanted to know what the hunting was like on the island. They discussed the different wildlife that people hunted, and when the season started for each animal and the cost associated with them. Megan came back with their drinks, set them down on the table, and asked if they were ready to order.

"Mark tells me you have the best Hawaiian Steak on the island."

"And he is so right," Megan replied, smiling.

"I'll have that with my steak prepared medium rare, red potatoes and a salad with your Hawaiian dressing," said Peyton.

"Zack?" ask Megan.

"Give me the fried cod and fries."

"How about you, Craig?" she asked.

"I would like the fried shrimp and fries," he answered.

"Excellent! I'll just go and put your order in and it will be out shortly."

Peyton smiled up at the pretty waitress. "Thanks, Megan," he returned.

Mark came up to their booth. "Mike is just finishing up his last interview and will be out to join you in a bit."

"Will you be able to join us, Mark?" his brother asked.

"Later, when it slows down a bit." Mark turned and looked over at the hostess station and saw Marco Manchez and his wife waiting to be seated. "Excuse me. I need to go and seat this couple." As Mark left, Zack looked over and locked eyes with Manchez. Manchez glared at Zack as Mark came up to greet them.

"Hi, Marco, Mille, how are you this evening?"

"Fine, fine," he replied. "I see the detectives are in tonight. Is there a new detective on board?" He noticed when he came in that someone he hadn't seen before was sitting with them. Marco liked to keep tabs on the police force. He didn't like surprises. Mark looked back and noticed all three were looking this way. He turned back to Marco.

"That's Peyton, he just returned from a tour overseas. Are you ready to go to your table?" asked Mark. Marco nodded, took Millie's arm, and followed Mark to the Hawaiian Room, but not before he gave a warning glare back at the three men sitting in the booth.

Peyton could feel the hostile energy coming off Zack and Craig as they looked at the couple waiting to be seated, and wondered what was going on and if he should even ask. He lost his chance to inquire when their food came, and all three of them dug in.

While they were eating, Peyton decided to lighten the mood by asking questions about the tourist attractions on the island, if they knew when lobster season was, and if either of them enjoyed the sport.

Craig piped in, "Oh man, I love it. There's nothing like fresh lobster to eat. The season is closed from May first through August thirty-first. After that, it's open season. You can take a charter boat out and scuba dive for them, but I like to go out at night in about one to four feet of water and catch them when they come in to feed. Hey, if you ever want to go out, let me know. It's a lot of fun and I know the best place to find them."

"Thanks, Craig, I might just take you up on that sometime." They finished their meals, and Megan came up to take the plates away. She asked if they would like anything else, just as Mike came up to join them.

"Hey, guys, how was everything?" asked Mike.

"Mike," answered Peyton, "that was the best steak I have had in a long time!"

"I'm glad you liked it."

Megan took the dishes to the kitchen and came back to the booth. "Mike, can I get you a drink?"

"Bring me my usual, on the rocks. How about you guys?" he asked.

"I'll have another beer," said Peyton.

"I'm all set," said Zack.

"Me too," said Craig.

"Could you bring us our checks?" Zack smiled. "We need to get going."

"Sure, I'll be right back," she answered in return.

Mike turned to the detectives and asked, "How is the case coming along? Have you found out anything else regarding Ralph's murder?"

"No," answered Zack. "We know Ralph was working for Manchez in his loan shark business. When you and Ralph got into that fight at the bar, you messed him up pretty good. We know through Jason that Manchez gave Ralph two weeks off. My guess is Manchez was getting nervous about Ralph when he started drawing attention to himself and had him followed. When he broke into Jenna's apartment and tried to assault her, the guy Manchez hired took him out. The autopsy report showed a clean shot straight to the heart. But we can't prove a thing. We do know the name of the person Manchez hired, and what he looks like, but nobody saw a man with that description around at the time of the murder. The guy is good at what he does, which makes him very dangerous."

Peyton, sitting back listening to this conversation, was wondering what the hell was going on. Megan came back with their drinks and the checks for the detectives. The detectives pulled their wallets out, threw some bills on the trays, and handed them back to Megan. Zack smiled. "Thanks. Megan, keep the change."

She smiled back. "Thank you!"

When she left, Mark came up to the booth and leaned down with his hands on the table. "Listen, guys, Manchez will be coming out of the Hawaiian Room soon. I think it might be a good idea not to be sitting together when he comes out. He's already asked about Peyton, wondering if he's a new guy on the force."

"We were just getting ready to leave."

Mike and Peyton came up out of the booth to let the detectives out. They shook hands.

"It was nice meeting you, Peyton." said Zack. He turned to Mike. "We'll keep you up to date if anything new develops."

"Thanks. Be safe out there," returned Mike.

When they left, Peyton talked with his brothers while he finished his beer. "Listen, guys, I'm going to head out. Do you two know a good bar where I might meet up with a woman? It's been a while, and I'm feeling an itch that needs to be satisfied."

The two brothers looked at each other and grinned. "There are several bars on Kalakaua Avenue. One in particular is the H-Bar and Grill. It's fairly new and draws a crowd," answered Mark.

"There is also a new club at the Rock Inn on Waikiki Boulevard if you like dancing and letting loose."

Peyton grinned. "Uh, I don't know about that, but I think I'll try out the bar."

As he turned to leave Mike stopped him. "Hey, if you run into any trouble, give one of us a call."

"Will do, bro, but I'm a big boy, I'll be just fine. Thanks for the dinner and the beer."

Mike and Mark watched him go. "What do you think, Mike?" asked his brother.

"You heard him, he's a big boy. Trouble at a bar would never top what he dealt with in Afghanistan. Do you have time to sit and have dinner? I would like to go over the interviews I had this afternoon."

"Sure, just let me make sure the staff can handle things. Hey! Order me a cheeseburger with the works!" Mike shook his head as he headed for the kitchen thinking, *Him and his cheeseburgers!*

Marco Manchez and his wife came from the Hawaiian Room. They were passing the bar to head out, when Marco hesitated to see if the detectives were still sitting in the booth. Everyone was gone, including the guy called Peyton. He would see what he could find out about this Peyton. If he was a new one on the force, he needed to know. He never liked surprises, especially where his businesses were concerned. Millie nudged her husband. "Is there something you needed to talk with Mike or Mark about?"

"No, let's go."

Peyton found the bar that his brothers had mentioned. He went in and took a seat at the bar. Next to him was a tall Texan with a black Stetson hat perched on top of his head. The bartender came up to Peyton and asked if he wanted anything to drink. "Can you make a good martini?"

"Sure!"

"Okay. Bring me one!" he replied.

Mick was studying the man who just sat down next to him and thought he looked familiar. He introduced himself and extended his hand, "Hey, I'm Mick Southerland. You look so familiar to me. Have we met somewhere?"

"No, I don't believe so," he answered, as he shook his hand. "I'm Peyton TreVaine. I just got out of the army after serving over in Afghanistan."

"You're Mike and Mark's brother!" exclaimed Mick.

"Yes, I am, but how do you know them?"

"I ran into Mike at their restaurant several months ago. We got to talking about our service days and he mentioned you were in the special ops division."

"I was, but I transferred to the search-and-rescue team shortly after I started my last tour. I lost one of my teammates in a car bombing and had a rough time with the loss. When I transferred, I was teamed up with a military dog, and we bonded immediately. He got me through some rough times."

"I was in the army for fourteen years, eight in the special ops division. I can attest to what you're going through. I still have nightmares!"

"Me too!" replied Peyton.

A couple of hours passed as they swapped war stories. Mick looked at his watch. "Well. Peyton, I need to get going. I have a long day ahead of me tomorrow."

"I'm glad I ran into you. Maybe we'll bump into each other again," he said as he shook Mick's hand again.

"Look forward to it," replied Mick. After he left, Peyton

finished his drink and asked for his tab. He paid his bill, and headed back to Mark's home. It was good to talk to someone who went through some of the same trauma and bullshit he went through while serving in the armed services. He didn't regret serving his country, but there were times when it just tried a man's patience and physical ability to do the job. If Mark was still up, he wanted to know about the conversation Mike and the detectives had earlier. Especially the fight!

Detective Sergeant Stacy Rayland was an undercover cop for the state police department, working out of Los Angeles. They were given a tip that a large drug deal was going down here on the island, headed for LA. She, her partner Fred Zealand, and Lieutenant Kevin Andrew were sent to the island to uncover who was behind the drug deal and find out where in LA it was going to be delivered. They checked in with the sheriff's department, where they received the tip. Captain Jim Bowen went over the information with them and they came up with a plan. Their suspect was a prominent business owner whose office was located on 10th Avenue in downtown Honolulu. Fred was to check out his sporting goods stores, while Stacy went undercover inside the owner's business. Her undercover name was Helen Gray. Her assignment was to work as his receptionist. She had yet to uncover anything pertinent to the case. He had her calling in these rough-looking characters who only stated their name. He had a soundproof office, so she could never hear anything said. He never allowed her in his office, unless he called her in, and then it was only briefly. Helen tried to keep a low profile when she was working. She wore her long blond hair in a tight bun on top of her head and no makeup. Large dark horn-rimmed glasses, perched on her nose, covered most of her pretty face. She always dressed in a straight skirt, blouse, and suit jacket. She wore a shoulder harness with her nine-millimeter Glock in the holster under her jacket, ready to defend herself if she needed to. But at night, that was a different story. She let her beautiful blond hair down, enhanced her pretty hazel eyes with dark mascara and eyeliner. She only needed lip gloss to cover her pink lips, shaped like a bow. Dark skinny jeans and a T-shirt showed off her nice curves.

She and a friend from the sheriff's department were sitting at the H-Bar and Grill, having a drink and enjoying an appetizer, when she noticed a tall man with broad shoulders and a nice build come into the bar. He was dressed in a dark tee, camouflage pants, and army boots. He was handsome, with facial features that were strong and clearly defined. Her heart skipped a beat as she watched him take a seat next to a man with a cowboy hat on. Her friend motioned her. "How is the case going?"

She glanced back at her friend. "Not good, Gwen. My partner and I have yet to uncover anything that would tie this guy to drug trafficking. I'm hoping we'll get a break in the case soon."

Gwen was a police officer for the sheriff's department. They met when she arrived on the island and instantly formed a friendship. She mainly patrolled the highways, but sometimes her work brought her into the city.

"Hang in there," she said. "I'm sure something will come down soon."

"I hope so, Gwen. I have to confess, it's a little boring sitting there all day looking at figures on the computer and answering the phone. I need some action!" And speaking of action, she focused on the hot, rugged man sitting at the bar. She wouldn't mind getting some with him! It's been a long time since she was in a relationship. They finished their appetizer and wine while Gwen filled her in on all the local tourist attractions in the area. Her eyes kept glancing over to the man sitting at the bar and she wondered if she should get up and introduce herself. She watched as the man with the cowboy hat got up and left. *This is my chance*, she thought, *I just need to get up off this chair and go over to him.*

Gwen nudged her arm when she noticed Stacy wasn't paying attention to what she was saying. "Who are you staring at?" asked Gwen.

Stacy looked back at her friend. "There is a very hot-looking guy sitting at the bar over there," nodding her head in that direction.

Gwen looked over at the bar but didn't see any hot guy sitting there. "Where?" she asked.

Stacy turned her head back toward the bar. He was gone! Damn! She missed her chance! "He was right there! Oh, Gwen, I so wanted to meet him!"

"Maybe you'll run into him again."

"Maybe." She sighed. "Come on, let's get out of here. We both have to work tomorrow, and after I finish with my job as a receptionist, I have a meeting with my partner and our boss, Lieutenant Andrew. It's going to be a long day. Not looking forward to it."

CHAPTER 3

The next morning, Helen sat down at her desk and turned on her computer. She checked her calendar to see what appointments her boss had this morning and at what time. As she scanned his appointments, he had several with his top men in the company, and one in particular with Mick Southerland at ten. She had some suspicions about Mick and also the man called Victor. Marco Manchez owned several legit businesses in downtown Honolulu, and a marina on the north side of the island near Waikiki Beach. Her partner, Fred Zealand, has been checking out his sporting goods stores to see if he could uncover any evidence that would help lead them to the drugs in the case they were working on. She would find out tonight if he had any luck. She pulled up the accounting records for the sporting goods stores that she had been going over for the last several weeks. She needed to go over this final one, but didn't think she would find anything that would lead them to the drug smuggler.

The elevator door opened, and a tall Texan with a black Stetson cowboy hat perched on top of his head came up to the desk. She knew who he was as he had come in several weeks ago. He was tall, dark, and handsome, with steel gray eyes that could see right through a person. He had a beard which he kept trimmed close to his face, and if she was interested, which she is not, she would bet he could have any woman he wanted. But after admiring his physic and those hard muscles of his, something inside of her told her not to trust him. When he reached her desk, he gazed down at the woman sitting behind the desk. She was kind of a plain-looking woman, with her blond hair pulled up in a tight bun on top of her head. The large dark horn-rimmed glasses covered most of her face, but he could see she had pretty hazel eyes through her glasses. She was dressed in a black suit jacket and underneath she wore a pale blue blouse. He couldn't see beyond that. The first time he saw her was when he was with Ralph and another time when the boss called him in. The vibe he got from her was not of physical attraction, but something else. He couldn't put his finger on it, but he would keep a sharp eye on her to make sure she wasn't the type to blow his cover if she ever found out who he was really working for. "Mick Southerland to see Mr. Manchez," he stated.

"One moment, please," said Helen. She pushed the intercom button.

"Yes, Helen," replied Manchez.

"Mr. Southerland is here to see you."

"Send him right in."

She glanced up to steel gray eyes. "You can go in now, Mr. Southerland," directed Helen. She watched him go into Mr. Manchez's office and close the door. Suddenly it hit her that he was the man sitting next to the guy she wanted to meet last night! She only saw his back side and not his face. She had no idea it was him! She looked at the door again and noticed it was slightly ajar. Unless you looked at it just right, no one would notice it. She looked around her office, stood up, and walked over to the door to see if she could hear anything.

Mick walked up to Manchez, stood in front of his desk, feet apart with his arms crossed. As he stood and stared at Marco seated behind his desk—he was a big man, with a balding head and beady black eyes, who carried himself off with an air of authority—he asked, "You wanted to see me?"

"Yes, have a seat, Mick." Mick took the chair in front of his desk, placed his arms on the arms of the chair, with his hands folded, leaned forward. "I wanted to tell you I'm impressed with the job you have been doing with the loan business. I want to move you up to my other business. There's a shipment of boi"—referred to as heroin—"coming into the island in ten days, and I need you to make sure it goes into my warehouse, and then placed on another ship bound for LA."

"Where is this warehouse located?" inquired Mick.

"I own a marina on the north side of the island. The warehouse sits back a little ways from the water."

"Who's going to run the loan business?"

"You let me worry about that," answered Manchez.

"When you worked for Lopez, you said you handled this sort of thing. I trust you will be able to take care of it?"

Manchez gave him a look that bore right through him to see if there was any hesitancy in his body language. Mick didn't give an inch and stared right back. "I can handle it. Just tell me the exact date it's supposed to arrive, and when it gets loaded on the boat. I'll make sure everything is handled discretely."

Manchez continued to watch Mick. He didn't want any screw ups. The street value was over a million dollars. It was one of the largest drug deals he had ever handled. Mick sat there and waited.

"Okay," Manchez instructed, "I will give you a call the day before the shipment arrives and give you instructions. As an extra precaution I am having several of my guards watching the warehouse inside and out to make sure everything goes as planned. Victor will be one of them."

Mick continued to study the man behind the desk. He was sharp, he'd give him that. The heroin had to be worth hundreds of thousands of dollars of revenue for him. "How will I know who the other guards are? I have only met Victor," inquired Mick.

"When you go to the warehouse, and before the shipment arrives, I will have Victor introduce you."

"Okay, let me run this by you, to make sure I have this straight. You will call me the day before the shipment arrives and let me know the time and how it is to arrive. Then it is to be stored in the warehouse, at which time you will let me and the guards know when the boat will arrive. The drugs are then to be placed on the boat headed for LA. Is that correct?" asked Mick.

"Correct."

"How will I know what the drugs will be placed in?"

"There will be a crate marked 'sporting goods.' Look for a star stamped on the crate. Mick, you do this job, and do it without any problems, there will be a big bonus in it for you."

Mick nodded his head, rose from his seat, and headed for the door.

"Mick." Mick turned back and looked at Manchez. "Heed my warning. I have a lot on the line here. Make sure it goes smoothly."

"You can count on it," he returned.

Helen, with her head glued to the crack in the door heard the door handle turn. She hurried back to her desk as Mick came out and shut the door behind him. He nodded at Helen and waited for the elevator to open. When the door opened, he turned and looked right at her. With his steel gray eyes burning right through her, the door closed and headed down to the main lobby. That look gave Helen the chills. She needed to check him out to see who Lopez was, when he worked for him, and where. From what she heard, it sounded like there was going to be drugs moved for a deal in LA. This might be the break they have been looking for. She couldn't wait to get with her partner and the lieutenant tonight.

Going down to the main lobby, Mick got that vibe again that the receptionist couldn't be trusted. He saw her scurry to her desk when he came out of Manchez's office. The sign on her desk said "Helen Grey." He'd get Zack and Craig on it to see what they could find out.

As soon as Mick left the building, he went to his car and pulled out onto 10th Avenue. He pulled up Zack's number. When he answered, "Hey, Zack, did you get all that?"

"Yes. Sounds like a hand off will be taking place to secure a drug deal in LA," said Zack.

"You got it. Listen, when I came out of Manchez's office, I noticed his receptionist hurrying to sit behind her desk. The door was slightly ajar when I came out of the office, and my guess is she was listening in. It might be a good idea to have her checked out."

"Right, what's her name?" asked Zack.

"Helen Grey," he responded.

"I'm on it."

"Good, I'm heading over to the marina to check out this warehouse and I'll give you an update later."

"Be careful," answered Zack.

"Always," he returned.

Mick pulled into the marina and saw where the warehouse was located. He pulled his car into the parking lot and got out. He looked around to see if anyone was around. There were a few people on the docks, so he thought he would play it safe and take a walk along the pier. As he walked, he looked for anyone suspicious or watching the building before he headed back to the warehouse. He walked up and tried to open the door, but it was locked. He went around the side to the back of the building. He looked inside the window. On one side, he saw a lot of crates with what he assumed were extra stock for Manchez's sporting goods stores. On the other side were spaces for boat rentals. There were a couple of nice yachts stored in the area. On the left side of the back of the building was a large garage door to bring the boats in and out, along with trucks bringing in the extra inventory for his stores. He didn't see anyone working inside the building. He walked up to the garage door to see if he could get inside. There was a coded panel on the wall next to the door, same as the front door. Damn! He would need to get a code to get in. Mick went back to his car and got in. He took out his cell phone and pushed Zack's number.

"Detective Williams," he answered.

"Hey, Zack, I'm out here at the warehouse. There doesn't appear that anyone is around. I checked out the entrances and both are locked. You need a code to get inside. Looking inside through the window, it appears he rents out space for yachts, and he has a space for his inventory. I am going to sit here and watch to see if anyone goes into the warehouse. Maybe I can get inside."

"Right, just watch your back," he said with concern. "I don't need for you to get killed."

"Don't worry, I don't want that either." He ended his phone conversation and sat there for several hours with no activity. He decided to go and get something to eat and come back later. Maybe he would see some action tonight.

Mark and Peyton were having coffee at the counter in Mark's home, when Peyton wanted to know more about what was going on with a case the detectives were discussing at dinner last night, and why his brother had been in a fight. "Hey, Mark, I'm curious, last night when I had dinner and Mike was able to join us, Mike asked the detectives how the case was going. The detectives mentioned that Mike was in a fight and messed the guy up pretty good. Can you tell me about it?" he asked.

Mark looked at his brother, took a moment to think about it, and decided he needed to tell him what had been going on in their restaurant these last couple of months. "Yes, I think you need to know what we have been dealing with, to give you a better idea about the case Mike and I and the detectives have been working on. First, Mike and I discovered that a couple of our employees had been stealing liquor out of our restaurant. Jenna, an intern from the university I brought in, pointed out a number of times when the sales and inventory reports didn't match up." Mark smiled. "Mike fell head over heels in love with her the first moment he saw her. Anyway, Mike and I, along with the detectives, put in a security system one night after we closed. When we discovered who it was that was stealing from us, we decided to find out the why before we took any action against them. Found out their mother was dying of cancer, and to cover her medical expenses, they borrowed money from a loan shark. The loan shark worked his business through his enforcer's, and when they got behind on their payments, he upped their interest rate. It made it impossible for them to pay back the loan," informed Mark.

"I've heard it's quite a racket, this loan shark business," said Peyton.

"Yes, it is. Too many people are taken advantage of, especially those who are financially stressed."

"So what about the fight Mike was in?" he asked again.

"Let me back up a bit. The detectives brought in an undercover agent out of Waco, Texas, to set up this enforcer, and get the two people out of the loan. The loan would be passed off to the undercover agent, so he could get inside the loan shark's business. Turns out its Marco Manchez, a regular customer of ours," Mark said with disgust.

"You mean the guy that the detectives were glaring at last night?"

"That's him," replied Mark.

"You could feel the tension between them as soon as he walked in. But that still doesn't explain about the fight."

"Before it all went down, Mike and I along with Detective Williams came into the back parking lot in a van, to watch and listen and be Jason's back up if he needed it. We saw Jenna having a conversation with this Ralph character. When he got into her face and was just about to hit her, Palani opened the back door when he heard arguing outside the entrance. Thank God he did, or Jenna could have been seriously hurt. A week later, Sasha, a good friend of Jenna's, wanted her to go to a bar after they had dinner at the restaurant. Mike was beside himself. Jenna was hesitant on going with her friend, but Jenna made him promise to join them after we closed down the restaurant. I went with Mike, and when we got there, I saw Jenna being assaulted by Ralph. When Mike saw what was happening, he saw red, and the rest is history. Mike messed him up pretty good, but he had it coming. When Marco Manchez saw how beat up he was, he told Ralph to take two weeks off. That pissed him off. He went after Mike and Jenna. He hired someone to follow them, only it ended up being me and Jenna. Mike was on a trip to LA to speak with an investor about franchising our restaurant. Zack had a police officer spend the night outside Jenna's apartment, and when I left to go home, I was hit from behind. The next night, Mike was due home around seven thirty and went straight to Jenna's, only to find Ralph had broken into her apartment. He could hear Jenna screaming, but when he went to open the door, it was locked. He broke down the door and found Jenna with her dress torn, and a knife to her throat! Jenna's cat Cuddles jumped up on Ralph's neck and proceeded to scratch and bite the hell out of him, which gave Mike time to get the knife out of his hand. He pulled back to slug him when a shot was fired. Ralph dropped dead right in front of them. Mike turned to see who fired the shot, but he was gone."

Man. He couldn't believe what he was hearing. "And this all started a couple of months ago?" asked Peyton.

"Yes. Trust me, bro, we have never had to deal with this kind of trauma since we opened the restaurant eight years ago!"

Peyton sat back in his chair, stunned at what his brother had just told him.

"Just so you know, Peyton, what I have told you, and what I am about to share with you, is to be kept in strictest confidence. The detectives are pretty sure that Manchez had Ralph taken out. They can't prove it, and that's why Jason is undercover inside Manchez's business. He is also suspected of drug trafficking, along with other homicides in the city. In case you run into him, his undercover name is Mick Southerland."

Peyton sat forward with a look of shock on his face. "I met the guy last night! At the bar you and Mike suggested I go to! We hit it off right away. Found out he was in the special ops division in the army, same as me. It was good to talk to someone who had similar circumstances that I did while serving our country." Peyton looked at his brother with concern. "Hey, if you need any help catching this guy, let me know. I'd be glad to help. Too bad Justice isn't here with me. He is the best dog when it comes to sniffing out drugs."

"Thanks, Peyton. We just may need more hands, if you know what I mean. What are you doing tonight?" he asked.

"A couple of my buddies are in for the weekend and we thought we would hit a couple of the bars in Honolulu, maybe if we're lucky hook up with some women. I've been on a long dry spell." He definitely needed to get some action, and soon.

"Mike, Jenna, and I are hitting the Rock Inn after we close the restaurant tonight. If you and your buddies would like to join us, we should be there around eleven."

"Thanks, bro, we might just do that," he returned.

"Good!" Mark slid off his barstool and took his mug and breakfast dishes to the sink. "I need to get ready for work. Friday nights are always crazy busy! What are your plans for today, Peyton?" he asked.

"Just going over to the army base to see if they have any news on Justice," he replied.

"Make sure you get with Mike. General McCall may be able to connect with someone in the army to get Justice home for you."

"I will. Thanks, Mark. I'll stop by the restaurant later this afternoon."

"Good, I'll see you then."

Peyton finished his cold coffee and decided to get moving. He'd go over to the army base and then take a cruise around the island, maybe check out some of the tourist attractions in the area.

CHAPTER 4

When Peyton checked in at the army base, only to find out they still didn't have any information to give him about how Justice was doing with Sergeant McGinnis, he left feeling deflated. He decided he didn't want to cruise the island and instead went into Honolulu to check out some men's clothing stores. He didn't have much in the way of civilian clothes, so he thought he would stock up. He pulled up to a stoplight on 10th Avenue. He watched the people crossing the street. There was a woman in particular who looked like Miss Prudence. Dressed in a plain black straight skirt, light-blue blouse, and black suit jacket, she looked like someone who worked in a library. Her hair was pulled straight up on top of her head, and her dark horn-rimmed glasses covered most of her face. She turned her head and locked eyes with him. Something hit a nerve in him. She looked away the same time he did. What the hell! He glanced back as she disappeared into the crowd. The light turned green. Peyton pushed on the gas. That was the weirdest feeling he had ever had looking at a woman! He couldn't possibly be attracted to her. Definitely not his type! He pulled into a parking space in front of the clothing store. He needed to get her off his mind and on to other things, like having the time of his life with his buddies tonight, and possibly getting laid!

Helen hurried into her office building after grabbing some lunch up the street. Her heart was still pounding after she locked eyes with the one guy she wanted to meet! What were the chances of him seeing her in her undercover garb! What must he think! She hoped she would run into him again, but only when she looked hot! Not some plain Jane in a business suit! She sat down at her desk to get a grip. She tried to focus back on the meeting with Lieutenant Andrew and her partner last night. The lieutenant had sent her an email this morning on the information he had on Mick Southerland. *But those eyes! Whew!* Helen sighed and clicked on the email. Reading the message, Mick Southerland had worked for a Ray Lopez out of Dallas, Texas. He had been dealing in drug trafficking and loan sharking. He got busted, but Mick was out of town when it went down, and never got caught. *Hmm… interesting*, she thought. She would talk to the lieutenant to see about putting someone on to tail him. *He may be able to lead us to the drugs that would be going to LA.*

Peyton came into Mark's home laden with shopping bags. He immediately started ripping off price tags and throwing the clothes into the laundry. While they were washing, he went in to take a shower. Instead of shaving, he decided he would grow a beard and shaved his neck and cheeks. He felt he needed to make some changes in his life to fit into civilian life, this was one of them. When he had finished showering, he went and threw the clothes in the dryer, then went and made coffee. He poured himself a cup and sat down at the counter to wait until his clothes dried. While sitting there, he thought back to that day in his life when circumstances took a bad turn. He was in a NATO training center. He and his team received word that the Taliban insurgents were in the area and to be on alert. The days grew into a week. He and his team thought it was a false alarm. Then one night a Taliban soldier drove a car bomb into the building. Taliban insurgents stormed the building and shot down one of his teammates and wounded another. Two other soldiers lost their lives in the fight. But they were able to push back the Taliban, killing several while the rest ran for their lives. When it was over, he rushed to his teammate's side, but it was too late. He was already dead. He left a wife, a young boy, and two little girls. Every time he thought about it, he felt sick to his stomach and wanted to crawl into a hole. He went over and over in his mind what he could have done differently to save his life. Justice, his military dog, was the only thing that kept him from going insane. He heard the dryer buzz and came out of his thoughts. He went to pull his clothes out and get dressed. He was looking forward to spending some time tonight with a couple of his army buddies and letting loose. It was a long time coming. He hopped into his SUV and drove over to the restaurant to see Mike and what he needed to do to get Justice home.

Mike was in his office when he arrived. A beautiful redhead greeted him at the door and took him back through the restaurant to his office. Peyton knocked on the door. "Come in," replied Mike. Peyton opened the door as Mike glanced up.

"Peyton!" he said in surprise. Mike came up and around his desk to shake hands. "How are you doing? Are you getting settled in over at Mark's?"

"Yes, I just went out and bought me some new clothes and feeling a little more comfortable in civilian life," answered Peyton.

"Good, have a seat." Mike motioned to the chair in front of his desk, then went and sat down in his chair. Peyton sat down. "Mark mentioned you have some paperwork that General McCall wanted filled out to see if he could bring Justice home."

"Yes."

Mike pulled some papers out of his top desk drawer and handed them to his brother. "He needs to know what date you were discharged from the army, when you turned Justice over to a new handler, the name of the handler, and where he is currently stationed at in Afghanistan. He also wants to know why you want to be reunited with this dog. He knows a Colonel Rayland at Fort Sill Garrison that might be able to help us out."

"I've heard of the colonel. Fort Sill Garrison is one part of the military where they train working military dogs. I will get this filled out and back to you."

"Do you have time to fill it out now and grab a bite to eat? I'm just finishing up these reports and should be out on the floor in about twenty minutes," said Mike.

Peyton looked at his watch. He was supposed to pick the guys up at six thirty at the army base. It was five. "Yeah, I can do that. I'll go get a booth in the bar. Will you be able to join me?"

Mike smiled. "Sure, Jenna and I will both be joining you along with Mark. Mark may already be out on the floor," he replied.

"Would you like me to put in an order for all of you?" he asked.

"Yeah, Mark's got us hooked on cheeseburgers. Order three with the works, done medium well, and we'll be out shortly."

"Got it!" As he left the office and headed out into the restaurant, he found a corner booth in the bar and sat down. One of the waitresses came up and asked if he wanted anything to drink. Peyton smiled up at the waitress, a cute little thing with light brown hair and amber eyes. "Could you bring me a glass of your best beer on draft?"

"Sure thing." She smiled in return. "I'll be right back!"

When she left, he looked at the paperwork in front of him and realized he didn't have a pen. When she came back with his beer, he asked if she had one. She handed him hers and smiled. When he looked surprised, she said, "I can get another one."

"Thanks! Oh, can you put in an order for four cheeseburgers, medium well with the works, and a large plate of fries?" he asked. "Mark, Mike and Jenna will be joining me shortly."

"No problem, I'll put it right in," she answered. When she turned to place the order, he noticed she had a cute little ass and a nice set of legs.

Man, TreVaine, he thought, *you got it bad*. Peyton shook his head and refocused his thoughts on filling out the forms.

He was just finishing up, when Mark came up to him. "Hey, how'd it go this morning?"

"Still no news," he answered. "I just finished the paperwork for General McCall and we'll see what he can do. I just ordered cheeseburgers for all of us. Mike and Jenna should be out soon."

Mark slid into the booth. "Good, we have a packed house tonight, and half the time we're not able to eat until after nine. It will be nice when we decide on a general manager to relieve some of the stress."

"How's that going?" asked Peyton.

"We have it narrowed down to two individuals. We're making our final decision on Monday." Mark looked out over the bar area and saw Mike and Jenna, hand in hand, heading this way.

Peyton looked up, just as Jenna and Mike slid into the booth. Jenna gave Peyton a brilliant smile. "Hi, Peyton! How are you?"

"Hey, Jenna. I'm fine. How are you?" he asked.

"I'm good except for these two slave drivers who keep me buried in reports!"

Everybody chuckled.

"So, when's the big day?"

"August twenty-eighth, less than two months away, and I don't mind telling you I have no idea how we are going to be ready!" exclaimed Jenna.

Mike reached up and placed his hand on her cheek and gently turned her head towards him. He looked lovingly into her eyes. "Hey, everything will be beautiful, but if I have to whisk you away and elope, we will be married on that day." He bent his head and gave her a gentle kiss. Their food came, and the kiss was broken.

Tammy set the food down on their table and asked if she could get them anything else. They gave Tammy their drink order. "Be right back." She smiled and left to get their drinks.

As they dug into their food, "What are your plans for this evening, Peyton?" asked Mike. Tammy came back with their drinks and placed them on the table. "Thanks, Tammy," Mike said with a smile.

She returned his smile. "You're welcome." She turned and left to serve other customers.

Peyton glanced over at his brother. "I'm meeting a couple of my army buddies over at the army base. They're here on a short furlough. I went online today and found a popular tiki bar on Saratoga Road and thought I would take them there first, maybe hit a couple of other bars later," answered Peyton.

"I've never been to the tiki bar on Saratoga, but I've heard they have excellent barbeque pulled pork sliders," added Mark.

"We are all headed over to the Rock Inn after we close. They have a club there if you and your buddies like music and dancing. When I was there with Jenna, I noticed there were a lot of single women there," suggested Mike.

Jenna tuned and looked at Mike. "Oh, you did, did you? I thought you had eyes only for me that night!" She poked him in the ribs.

"Oh!" He grabbed his side. "I forget you have a feisty side to you! You know I had to canvass the place before I could find you. But when I did, it was you, and only you, from that day forward." Mike gave her that look that melted her heart.

"Okay, you're out of the doghouse for now."

They all laughed.

"Mark had mentioned the Rock Inn to me earlier. I'll see what the guys want to do and we may see you there." Peyton looked at his watch and pulled out his wallet. "I've got to get going." He threw some bills on the table to cover his bill. He picked up the paperwork and handed it to Mike. "This is all filled out. Let me know what he finds out and if he needs anything else from me."

"Will do, bro. Have fun, and stay out of trouble!"

Peyton just laughed and left to pick up his buddies.

The tiki bar was a definite hot spot on the island, lots of people milling around the outdoor bar and having a good time. His buddies ordered some Hebrew hotdogs cooked in beer, smothered in chili sauce, and some beers, while Peyton ordered a martini. They hung out for a couple of hours, catching up on what was going on in the military since he got out.

"Hey, Peyton, do you know of a place where we could meet some women?" asked Matt.

"Well, since I'm new to the island as a civilian, I don't know of a lot of places, but my brothers suggested the Rock Inn. They said there was a club that opened up a while back that has music, dancing, and I quote, *lots of single women*. Are you game?" he asked.

"Let's go!"

Stacy was sitting in her apartment looking over some files of the case she was working on when her phone dinged with an incoming text. It was her partner, Fred Zealand. *Hey Stacy, Gwen and I are headed over to the Rock Inn. Wondered if you would like to join us?* Stacy read the text and didn't feel like going out tonight. She had planned on staking out this warehouse that Manchez had mentioned over the weekend, to get an idea of where it was and how it was laid out.

She sent back, *Sorry, I'm working on the case this weekend, thought you were too.* She set her phone back on the desk and returned to the files.

Her phone dinged again, *I am, but wanted to cut loose before I put in a long weekend. Come on out and have a drink with us. We can discuss how we can break this case wide open.*

After she read the text, she thought for a moment, *I may not get another chance to go and have fun until after this case is solved.* They were just starting to get some good leads.

She sent a text back, *Okay, what time?*

8:00, we are meeting at the club inside the Inn.

I'll see you and Gwen there. She sent the text and looked at her watch. It was six thirty. She shut down her computer and went to get ready. When she was dressed, she looked at herself in the mirror. With a pair of black dress jeans and a white knit sleeveless top, the outfit showed off her nice curves. She put on a pretty gold rope necklace to accent. Stacy applied her makeup and finished it off with a light-pink lip gloss. With her beautiful blond hair flowing down her back and shoulders, she felt pretty and ready to take on the town. Her hazel eyes glowed in anticipation of a fun-filled night. She bent down, slipped on the ankle holster, put her small revolver inside the holster, and put on her dress boots. One could never be too careful. She left her bedroom, picked up her purse, and was off to meet Gwen and her partner. She texted Kevin and asked if he would like to join them.

At the club, Stacy looked around and found her friends at a table in the middle of the room near the dance floor. They saw her and waved her over. Stacy walked up to their table and took a seat. "Hi, guys!"

"Hi!" said Fred. "Glad you could join us!"

Stacy noticed they already had drinks in front of them. "I texted the lieutenant, he should be here shortly; have you ordered anything to eat?" she asked.

"Not yet, we were waiting for you," replied Gwen.

Stacy picked up the menu on the table and gave it a look. The waitress came up to the table and asked if she wanted anything to drink. "I'll have a glass of white wine." When she left, "Have either of you eaten here before?"

"I haven't," replied Gwen.

"I've had their burgers, they're pretty good," said Fred. She looked over at her partner, a blond-haired, brown-eyed chic magnet, who could always get a date when he wasn't working on a case with her, or in his off time, and wondered when he had come here to have burgers!

As she looked over the menu, the fried halibut sandwich and fries sounded good. She glanced up and saw Kevin at the door. She waved him over. Lieutenant Kevin Andrew was a handsome man. He was six feet in height. Broad shouldered, and he carried himself with an air of authority. He was in his early forties. His jet-black hair had a light dusting of grey at his temples, and he had the lightest blue eyes she had ever seen. Whenever she watched him interrogating a suspect, she felt those eyes could see right through the person. When she was first hired in at the Post, she secretly had a crush on him, but he was madly in love with his wife-to-be. They now have two boys and a darling little girl. He's been with the force for a while now, and a great boss to work with. He headed over to their table.

The waitress came back with her drink and asked if they were ready to order.

"Can you give us a minute? We have another one joining us."

Kevin came to their table and sat down. "Hi guys!" He smiled up at the waitress. "I'll have a draft beer." He turned back and picked up the menu. "What's good on the menu?" he asked.

"Fred said the burgers were good," Stacy answered.

"Sounds good." Kevin set his menu back on the table, just as the waitress came back with his beer. They each gave her their order.

When she left, they turned back to each other. Gwen wanted to know how the case was coming along, and if there were any new developments since they talked last. Fred started in and gave Gwen the updates, while Stacy turned to Kevin and asked, "Did you find anything else about Mick Southerland?"

"Nothing more than what I gave you this morning. I think your suggestion to tail him is a good idea. I talked to the captain at the sheriff's department and he said he would put one of his detectives on it."

"Good, he's involved with Manchez. Through him, we might be able to find out when the drugs arrive and where they are to be delivered in LA," she replied.

"Also," Kevin leaned in and said with concern, "when I was at the sheriff's department today, I noticed one of the cops hanging out, trying to listen in on our discussion. It gave me a bad feeling. We need to keep an eye out and watch each other's back."

"What did he look like in case either one of us happen to run into him?"

"He's about five-nine, head shaved, brown eyes, a little pudgy around the middle."

Stacy nodded and looked over at Gwen. She also had a feeling about Gwen. Could she be trusted? She was a good cop and a good friend, but when they were together, first thing she wanted to know was what was going on with her case she was working on. Gwen was a tall, slender woman, with short black hair, brown eyes, and an olive complexion. She had a great personality and they always got along, but lately… She turned back to Kevin. "Maybe you should talk to the captain and let him know of your suspicions. He could have him watched, or check out his emails to see if he is doing something he shouldn't be."

"That was my thought as well. I'll get a hold of him in the morning. I'll send you and Fred an update in a text message after I speak with him." Their dinner came and everything looked delicious! As they ate, the conversations went in other directions. When they finished eating, the waitress came up to their table, asked how everything was and if they wanted anything else. Kevin asked for his check; everyone else ordered another round of drinks.

Stacy sat back in her chair and looked around. The flame lighting along the walls and the lighted dance floor set the mood. When the music started up, couples walked out on the dance floor and danced to the music of the nineties. Kevin paid his bill, said goodnight, and headed out. As she watched him leave, her eyes shifted to three gorgeous men standing in the entrance looking for a table. One stood out in blue jeans and a black tee. Her eyes got big when she recognized who it was! He locked eyes with her briefly, turned to his friends, and started walking her way. Stacy started to get goosebumps as he and his buddies walked by their table, close enough to touch. He locked eyes with her again as he walked by, and the electric energy she felt was powerful. They took a seat at a table directly behind them.

At the door of the club, Peyton, who was feeling no pain from the martinis he had at the tiki bar with his buddies, looked around for an empty table. He spotted one, just on the other side of a table with a pretty blonde sitting there. As he walked by, he locked eyes with her and felt a strange energy come over him.

The men waved a waitress over and they gave her their order. His buddies ordered beers, while Peyton stuck to his martini. He looked over at the table in front of them and glanced at the blonde sitting there with another man and a woman. She was stunning. Her back was to him, but he could tell she had nice curves, and with her long blond hair flowing down her back, it made him itch to run his fingers threw it.

When he got another drink or two in him, he would ask her to dance.

Fred was asking Stacy something. He nudged her. "Hey, are you still with us?"

Stacy jumped out of her trance. "Sorry, Fred, what were you saying?"

"What were you and the lieutenant talking about?"

Stacy looked over at Gwen and noticed her leaning forward to hear. "Nothing important, said he missed his wife and kids. Was anxious to solve the case and get home." Gwen leaned back in her chair and rolled her eyes. She would mention to Fred when they were alone not to divulge any more information to her. An upbeat song came over the sound system. Fred and Gwen got up to dance. Stacy, sitting alone, sipped on her wine. She sensed a pair of eyes on her and glanced back. Taking a drink from his glass, he set it on the table, smiled, and winked! Stacy turned back around. She was sure she was red from head to toe!

Peyton couldn't resist. "Guys, it's time for me to go meet a woman!" His buddies roared as he got out of his chair and walked up to her. "Hi, beautiful, would you care to dance?" He held out his hand to her.

Stacy looked up to the hottest man she had ever seen. His deep blue eyes smiled down at her. His shadow beard gave him a rugged, sexy look. For a moment she could only stare. She could tell he had a little too much to drink, but she didn't care. Hell yes, she wanted to dance with him! She took his hand and followed him out on the dance floor.

They danced a couple of fast-moving sets. Peyton, watching

her dance, was enthralled with her body moving to the beat of the music. Stacy wanted the music to slow down, so she could get close and move her body next to his. As if by magic, the music slowed. He took her in his arms and pulled her close. Stacy felt the lean muscles against her body and shivered. The electrifying energy she felt was heart stopping. She put her head on his chest and swayed with him to the music.

This woman felt so good in his arms. He hadn't held a woman in a very long time. There was some chemistry between them that he had never felt with other women before. He had a flash back from this morning, when he was at a stoplight and locked eyes with Miss Prudence. He quickly got that thought out of his head! He pushed her back and twirled her. When he brought her back, he looked into her pretty hazel eyes, and feeling her soft body next to his, there was no way it could be her! He smiled down at her and pulled her closer to him.

The music stopped and Peyton slightly pulled away. "Can I take you back to my table and buy you a drink?" he asked.

Looking into those blue eyes, she smiled. "I would love that."

They headed back to the table. She noticed that Fred and Gwen had left. She grabbed her purse and followed Peyton to his table. When the waitress came by, "What are you drinking?" asked Peyton. Stacy had already had two glasses of wine, and since she was driving, she ordered a cola. His buddies ordered another round of beers, while he ordered another martini. "Are you sure you don't want something stronger?" asked Peyton.

"Oh no, I have something I need to do tomorrow, and I have to leave early in the morning."

"You know, pretty lady, tomorrow is Saturday. No one works on Saturday."

Stacy gave him a sly look. "And what do people do on a Saturday?" she asked.

With mischievous eyes, he grinned. "Well, if you must know, after a night of passionate lovemaking, they sleep in!"

Stacy had goosebumps from head to toe just imagining what it would be like to sleep with him! She stared back at him. "Well, I wouldn't know, I haven't slept with a man in a long time."

His eyes turned to hunger that sent tingles down into her mid-section when he said, "I haven't slept with a woman in a long time." They continued to stare into each other's eyes.

When she heard the music start up again, she smiled and said, "Um, I think we need to get up and dance."

At the entrance to the club, Mark, Mike, and Jenna were looking for a table. Jenna nudged Mike. "Look out on the dance floor." She pointed in the direction where his brother and a beautiful blond woman were dancing.

Mike nudged Mark. "Looks like our brother is having a good time!"

Mark grinned. "He also looks like he's a little wasted!"

"Hey, there's a table open, over in the middle of the room, next to the dance floor," Jenna suggested pointing over to the table.

Mike took her hand and grinned. "Let's go grab it!

They settled in at the table. A waitress came up and asked

what they wanted to drink. Jenna ordered her usual, a glass of white Moscato, while the guys ordered beers. They watched as Peyton and the young woman laughed and danced to the music. Their drinks came, and Jenna took a sip of her wine. When the music slowed, Mike came out of his chair, took Jenna's hand, and pulled her out onto the dance floor. They came up next to Peyton. He was so into the woman he was dancing with he didn't even notice them.

Mike pulled Jenna close, leaned down, and asked, "Do you think we should interrupt?"

She looked over at the couple. "Absolutely not!"

He grinned. "I think we should."

"No, we shouldn't," she returned.

"You're in an argumentative mood tonight," he teased.

She put her arms up around his neck and smiled. "Only because you are."

He laughed and bent to give her a kiss. "I love you, you little minx." He pulled her close as they swayed to the music. The music turned upbeat, and Jenna and Mike danced the next two songs. When they returned to the table, Mike didn't see his brother or the woman he had been dancing with. He asked Mark, "Did you see where Peyton and the blond woman went?"

"He just walked out the door with her. I am assuming she had to leave. Just between the three of us, he should not be driving when he leaves here. He didn't even see me sitting here."

Mike looked over at the entrance to the club and saw his brother staggering in. They all watched as he walked right by their table.

"Hey, Peyton!" yelled Mark. Peyton turned and almost lost his balance.

He staggered up to the table, placed his arms on the table, and slurred, "Hey, guys, how long have you been here?"

"We've been here for a while. Who was the blonde you were dancing with?" asked Mike.

"I don't know, I never got her name," he slurred.

Mark rolled his eyes. *He's really gone*, he thought. "Peyton, I hope you are not planning on driving," said Mark.

He swayed as he stood up from the table. "Nope!"

"How are your buddies? Are either one of them able to drive?"

Peyton looked over at his buddies, laughing and having a good time. "I don't know, I'll go ask." He stumbled over to their table. "Hey, guys, are either one of you able to drive? 'Cause I sure as hell can't!"

"Well, damn, we've had as much to drink as you have. Let's have one more drink and we'll call an Uber."

When Mike, Jenna, and Mark listened to the conversation, they were all slurring their words! Mike looked at his brother. "You have the bigger car. I can't get them all in my Corvette."

Mark took a deep breath. "I hope they don't all get sick in my car, or in my house for that matter!" They got up out of their chairs and walked over to Peyton's table. "Hey," said Mark, "Let me drive you back to my house. None of you should be driving."

Peyton's buddies looked up and asked who he was.

"Sorry, guys, these are my brothers, Mike and Mark, and

this is Jenna, Mike's fiancée. Guys, this is Rob and Matt." They looked up at his brothers and squinted.

Rob piped up. "Man, you two sure look alike. If I didn't know better, I would think I was seeing double!" he said. They all laughed.

"Do you mind if we join you for one last drink?" asked Mark. "Then I will drive you back to the base, or you are welcome to stay at the house," said Mark.

"Sure, grab a seat!" They ordered another round. Jenna had to laugh. She has never seen so many drunks in her life! The rest of the evening should be interesting.

CHAPTER 5

Peyton opened his eyes and closed them again. He wasn't sure what day it was. It must be daylight he thought, because even with the blinds closed it was still too bright for him. He opened his eyes again and wondered how in the hell he got here. He tried to sit up, but with his head feeling like a sledgehammer was pounding in his head, he lay back down. He grabbed his head and groaned. Mark must have heard him. He opened the door. "How are you feeling this afternoon, bro?"

Peyton groaned again. "Do you have to talk so loud?"

"Sorry, I think you're going to need my special drink for your hangover. I'll be right back." He left the room.

Peyton thought he would have to die to feel better. Whatever his brother was bringing him, he was sure he would puke it up! He vaguely remembered last night. The last thing he did remember was having a drink with his brothers, Jenna, and his buddies. After that, it was a loss. He wondered what happened to Matt and Rob.

Mark came back into the room carrying a glass of what appeared to be tomato juice. "Can you sit up, bro?" he asked.

Peyton looked at his brother and then at the glass he was carrying. "My head is busting, and if I try to drink what you are holding, I will probably puke all over the place."

Mark put the glass on the nightstand. "Trust me, it will help." Mark helped his brother in a sitting position.

"Oh God," cried Peyton, "I feel like my head is going to explode!"

Mark had to refrain himself from laughing. "Try taking a sip of this tonic I made."

Peyton looked up and was sure he saw two Mark's. "I don't think I can." He groaned.

"Sure you can, it will make you feel better."

Peyton took the glass from his brother with shaking hands and took a sip. He scrunched up his face as he swallowed the potion. He waited to see if it was going to come up. Luckily it stayed down. He drank the rest and handed the glass back to his brother. Mark handed him two pain pills and went to get a glass of water out of the bathroom. When he came back, Peyton downed the tablets with the water. He lay back down on the bed and prayed that his head would feel better. "Try to go back to sleep. I'll check on you in a couple of hours."

Several hours later, Peyton woke up. He sat up and was amazed that the pounding in his head was gone! He went to use the bathroom and to take a shower. He looked in the mirror. Man, he looked bad! He took his shower, put some clean clothes on, and headed out into the kitchen. He heard voices in the living room. It sounded like Matt and Rob were watching a game on TV. He put coffee on and waited while it brewed. When the coffee was ready, he poured himself a cup and went to see what the guys were watching on the TV.

Matt and Rob greeted Peyton when he walked in, "Hey, the man awakes!" said Matt.

"Hey, guys. Sorry, I guess I had one to many martinis last night! I didn't mean to leave on your own."

"Don't worry about it, man. Your brother took care of us," said Rob.

"Where is my brother?" he asked.

"He had to go into the restaurant. He said to feel free to relax and hang out. We were waiting for you to get up so we could order something to eat. What do you feel like eating?" asked Matt.

"Doesn't matter to me. What sounds good to you guys?"

"Mark said there was a good pizzeria just down the road. He left the number on the counter. Order one with the works."

Peyton strolled over to the counter, pulled his cell phone out, and dialed the number. Once the pizza was ordered he went back to join his buddies.

As Peyton drank his coffee, he asked, "What game are you watching?"

"The Tigers and the Cubs game," said Rob. "So far, the Tigers are down by one at the bottom of the seventh."

"I hope they can pull it out, that's my team!" exclaimed Peyton. "Can I get you guys some coffee or anything to drink before the pizza arrives?" he asked.

"Has your brother got any colas in the fridge?"

"I'm sure he does. I'll be right back." Peyton grabbed three colas out of the fridge and headed back to the living room. He was just setting the colas down on the coffee table when the doorbell rang. He went to get the pizza and brought it back to the table. They opened the box and dug in.

"Man, this is good!" said Rob.

"Hmm, excellent!" said Matt.

They scarfed down the pizza and colas while they watched the game. The Tigers won 4–3, pulling it out in the ninth inning with two home runs! They all cheered! Peyton shut the TV off.

"What do you guys want to do tonight?"

"Well," said Rob, "after last night, I sure as hell don't feel like going out tonight!"

"Does your brother have a– deck of cards? We could play a couple rounds of poker," asked Matt.

"I don't know, let me text him." Peyton pulled out his phone. *Hey bro, do you have a deck of cards somewhere?* He pushed send and waited.

Mark was sitting in a booth with Mike, discussing which candidate they should hire for the general manager's position when he heard his phone ding. He pulled it out of his pocket. He smiled. "Looks like Peyton is feeling a lot better. He's asking for a deck of cards." Mark started laughing remembering this afternoon. Mike started chuckling.

"What?"

"I don't mind telling you, our brother looked like death warmed over when I took my special drink for hangovers into him. I think he was still seeing double!"

Mike laughed with him. "You know, bro, we shouldn't laugh. We sure have had our share of them."

Still chuckling, "You're right, bro." Mark sent a text back, *In the top drawer, next to the fridge, you'll find a couple decks of cards.* Mark received a "thumbs up" sign, and placed his phone back into his pocket. "After we close, maybe we should join them," suggested Mark.

Mike shrugged his shoulders. "Jenna is working on the wedding plans with Sasha tonight. I'm game if you are," he said.

"Sounds like a plan. Let's start closing up. I haven't played poker in a long time," Mark said with a chuckle.

"We'll show them how it's done." Mike laughed,

"You better hope we don't get our asses beat, bro!"

Peyton, Matt, and Rob had just finished their second round of poker when Mark and Mike came in from the garage. "Hey, guys, who's winning?" asked Mark.

"Not me, that's for damn sure!" answered Peyton.

"May we join you?" asked Mike.

Rob and Matt looked at each other and grinned, turned back to the twins and said, "Have a seat."

"Before we get started, I have some chips and pretzels in the cupboard along with some beers in the fridge. Who wants some?" asked Mark.

"Here, here!" they all yelled. Mike went and helped his brother bring out the chips and beer. They set them on the table, placed a beer by each one of them, and took a seat.

Rob shuffled the cards, placed the deck in front of Peyton. Peyton cut the deck. Rob picked up the cards and began dealing one card at a time until each player had three cards. They each picked up their hand and took a look. Everyone tossed in a chip. Peyton drew a card off the top of the deck. He studied the cards in his hand. It wasn't great, a pair of tens. He threw another chip in. To his left, Matt drew a card. He held three of a kind. He, too, threw another chip in.

Mark drew a card and asked, "Hey, Peyton, what do you remember about last night?"

Peyton glanced over at his brother. "Not a whole hell of a lot. Last thing I remember was having a drink with all of you and Jenna. After that I don't remember anything."

Mark threw in a chip.

Listening to the conversation, Mike drew a card. "How about the blonde you were dancing with?" he asked.

Peyton took a drink of his beer and looked at Mike. "I was dancing with a blonde last night?"

"Oh, come on, TreVaine," said Rob, "you gotta be shitting me! You don't remember the exceptionally hot woman you were dancing with?"

Peyton sat there, and for the life of him, he couldn't remember even dancing with someone last night. "Describe her to me."

"She had long blond hair, somewhat petite, pretty face, and killer curves. She sat at our table and had a drink with us."

Peyton tried to remember the woman they were talking about. "I'm sorry, guys, but I don't remember much about last night, or the blonde you just described to me. I wish I did. Sounds like she would be someone I'd like to get to know."

Mike shook his head. "Brother, the way you were dancing and having a good time with her, I can't believe you don't remember her!"

Peyton shrugged his shoulders. "I'm sorry, I guess I had one too many martinis."

"You got that right," said Mark.

Mike threw a chip in and it went to Rob. Rob drew a card and threw in a chip. Rob looked at Peyton. "Well, TreVaine, there is always a possibility that you might run into her again," he said. "It's your call."

Peyton looked at his cards and took one off the deck. Peyton placed a ten of diamonds in his hand, which gave him three of a kind. He also threw in a chip. "Yeah, maybe," he said. *Damn!* He had no idea how that could happen when he couldn't even remember what she looked like! The game closed out, with Mark winning the pot. Rob and Matt sat there in shock that one of them didn't win!

"Where did you learn to play poker, Mark?" asked Rob.

"When I was in the service, we had a regular poker night once a week in the barracks." Mike got up from the table. "I'm heading out. Jenna and I are going to church and then hiking in the afternoon."

Mark grinned. "Are you going to the cave?" he asked.

"No." He chuckled. "Jenna's scared to death of bats! Last time I took her there, one come flying out at us and Jenna completely lost it. I thought she was going to run right off a cliff before I could catch up with her! Don't tell her I told you this or she'll have my head!" They all laughed.

"Your secret's safe with us," replied Peyton.

Mike shook hands with Rob and Matt, invited them to visit their restaurant the next time they were in town, and left.

"What do you say guys, one more round?" asked Matt.

"I'm in," said Mark.

"Me too," said Rob.

"Deal the cards," said Peyton.

Stacy, sitting with her partner Fred in a rented black SUV, was staking out Manchez's warehouse. It was dark out, and the SUV was parked a ways away from the building but close enough to be able to see clearly anyone coming or going out of the warehouse. As they watched the building, Stacy turned to her partner. "This might be none of my business, Fred, but I noticed last night that you and Gwen left at the same time. When I got back to the table, you were both gone," she inquired.

He glanced over at Stacy and shrugged his shoulders. "Yeah, she offered, and I obliged. We went back to her apartment and filled a need we both were feeling."

"Before you get in too deep with her, I want to go over what the lieutenant and I discussed at dinner last night. I don't know what all you have told Gwen about the case we are working on, but I think we should both keep it quiet until the case is solved."

"Don't worry, Stacy. I didn't give out any names pertaining to the case. I got the same feeling about her when she kept drilling me for answers last night," he returned.

"Good. As you know, we are checking out a Mick Southerland who is working for Manchez and hope to get the information we need to see where the drugs are going in LA. The lieutenant informed me that there was a cop at the sheriff's department lurking around when he and the captain were discussing the case. As you know from his text, Kevin spoke with the captain this morning, and they are putting a man on it. After being around Gwen a while, I would hate to think she was part of it, but we can't take any chances."

Fred nodded his head. "I agree. You don't have to worry about me."

As they both looked over at the warehouse, they saw headlights heading into the parking lot. Stacy and Fred slid down in the seat. They watched as a man got out of the car and walked up to the door. He looked around, punched in a code on the panel, opened the door, and walked in. They saw lights go on in what appeared to be the office. Stacy and Fred got out of the SUV, looking around as they crept up to the window with their guns pulled. They scrunched down and peered inside the window. Stacy checked out the man who was sitting behind the desk through the blinds, while Fred kept a look out. Her eyes got big as she realized it was a man who fit the description of the cop who Lieutenant Andrew described last night! She watched as he checked into the computer. He glanced down at some papers on the desk and proceeded to type the information into the computer. When he was finished, he placed the papers in a folder and put them in a file drawer. He logged out, got up from the desk, and went to turn out the lights. Stacy whispered, "He's coming! Let's get out of here!"

Both Fred and Stacy ran to the side of the building as the man was coming out of the warehouse. He looked around and headed for his vehicle. They watched him drive off. Stacy turned to her partner. "I'm pretty sure that was the cop that the lieutenant described to me last night!"

"If it is him," returned Fred, "he's not doing his dirty work at the station. Which means he's working for Manchez."

"Agreed," said Stacy. "There's nothing more we can do tonight. The door will be locked, and you need a code to get in. I will see what I can do about getting the code from Manchez's office. Let's head out. I'll make a call to the lieutenant and give him an update."

"Sounds good, we'll take this up again on Monday," he said. They got into their vehicle and Fred dropped her off at her rental.

"See you Monday, Fred," she said.

"Right," he replied. As he drove off, she walked into her rental, kicked her shoes off, and called the lieutenant.

The next day, Peyton and his buddies stopped at a Hawaiian coffee shop in a little town just a few miles from the base. The shop offered a selection of pastries and rolls along with different blends of coffee and espressos. While they were sitting at a table, having their coffee and a sweet roll before Peyton had to have his buddies back to the army base, a pretty blonde with her hair up in a ponytail and shades to cover her eyes from the sun came into the shop. Rob watched her come in. She was wearing light blue jeans, a white tank top, a navy-blue dress jacket, and two-inch navy wedge shoes.

"Hey, Peyton." Rob nudged him on his arm. "Take a look at the blonde that just walked in. I'm pretty sure she is the one you were dancing with Friday night."

Both Peyton and Matt looked over at the woman who was waiting in line to give her order. Matt piped in, "That's her all right, I'm sure of it!"

Peyton studied the woman. He wished he could remember something about that night. How could his buddies be sure it's her? "I don't know, guys. Are you sure she was the one I was dancing with? I would hate to embarrass myself if it's not her."

"I'm positive," confirmed Matt. "Take the shades off, let the hair down, and she's the one!"

"You need to go and introduce yourself. This may be your only chance," exclaimed Rob.

Peyton hesitated. He watched as she placed her order and moved down the line. She was a beauty. She kind of reminded him of Miss Prudence. If she had her hair on top of her head and wore a straight skirt instead of the jeans, she would be her. Peyton sat back against his chair. Why does that woman keep popping up in his head? He shook himself. He continued to watch as she picked up her coffee and started to walk out the door. Rob and Matt sat stunned, as they too watched her leave!

Rob took one look at Peyton and stated, "Well, you blew that, TreVaine!"

Peyton glanced back at his friend. "Maybe not. Let's go!"

All three rushed out of the coffee shop, climbed into Peyton's SUV, and proceeded to follow the blonde in the red Charger.

Stacy was on her way to the army base. Her dad, who was a colonel in the army and stationed at Fort Sill Garrison, had flown in this morning for a meeting scheduled for tomorrow morning with a General McCall. Her father had called late last night and asked if she could meet him there this morning.

As she sipped on her coffee, she looked back on her life as an army brat. She traveled the world with her parents. Two years in the States and two years overseas. It was hard growing up at times. She would just get comfortable where they were living, make friends, and they would have to leave again. When she graduated high school, she enrolled in a few online courses. She later set her sights on law enforcement and decided to settle in LA. She enrolled in the police academy and has been there ever since. She liked being settled in one place. The job could get pretty intense at times, especially arresting someone who had a history of drug abuse or criminal assault, but she loved her job. The men and women on the force were like a second family to her. Her parents were not crazy about her choice to go into law enforcement, but they came to terms with it and accepted that she knew best about what she wanted to do with her life. She pulled up in front of the office building where her dad said to meet him. She shut the engine off and started to get out of the car. A black SUV rushed up beside her. When she got out of the car and closed the door, she looked inside the SUV and her heart started to pound. It was the men she met at the club the other night! The hot man she danced with came barreling out of his car and ran right up to her.

Peyton stared at the beautiful woman in front of him and didn't quite know what to say. He ran his hand across the back of his neck and looked back at his buddies who were encouraging him with hands and facial expressions through the window of the SUV. He turned back, took a deep breath, and held out his hand. "Hi, I'm Peyton TreVaine. I'm not quite sure how to say this, but I think you might be the woman I danced with Friday night, at the club."

Stacy hesitated just for a few seconds. She was sure he didn't remember her. He was pretty wasted that night. This was her chance to officially meet him. Should she tell him her real name, or her undercover name? In a split-second decision, she gave him her undercover name. When the case was solved, she would tell him the truth and hoped he would understand. She took his hand. Instantly she felt the tingles go throughout her body, the same as when he held her in his arms. "Hi," she said breathlessly, "I'm Helen Gray. It's nice to meet you, Peyton. I enjoyed dancing with you the other night at the club."

Peyton felt the energy as she shook his hand. His heart beat a little faster as she smiled up at him. He released her hand. "This might be a little forward of me, but would you like to go out and have coffee or dinner with me sometime, maybe tonight?" he asked.

Inside, Stacy was ecstatic but held her emotions in check. "I would like that. Where and when?"

"I'm not familiar with a lot of the restaurants on the island. I would take you to my brother's restaurant, but they are closed on Sundays. Here's my phone; if you could put in your information, I will text you the time and where we can meet." He handed her his phone.

Stacy put her name and phone number in and handed it back to Peyton. Peyton took his phone, took a look at the number, and placed it back in his pocket.

Stacy smiled. "I'll look forward to your text."

Stacy turned and walked into the building, leaving Peyton staring after her. He got a big grin on his face. He went back and got into his SUV. He looked at his buddies. "Guys, I think I just landed me a date!"

Both men started jumping in their seats and yelling. "Nice work, TreVaine!" exclaimed Rob.

Matt, who was sitting in the back, sat forward and asked, "Was she the one?"

"Well, she said she enjoyed dancing with me, so I guess you guys were right. It was her!" he answered.

"I told you, man!" said Rob, chuckling.

Peyton started his vehicle and drove his buddies over to the barracks. They all piled out of the vehicle. Peyton helped them with their duffle bags, shook their hands, and said good-bye.

"Hey, thanks for the great time," said Rob.

"You're welcome. I'll say a prayer for you both, for the Lord to keep you safe when you arrive back in Afghanistan."

"Thanks," they returned.

"Hey Peyton." Matt grinned. "We have one for you!"

"What's that?" he asked.

"That you score!" Peyton laughed and hopped back into his SUV, said a prayer, and drove back to Mark's. He needed to search the internet for a good restaurant to meet Helen at. Maybe Mark could help him out.

Stacy walked up to the office where her father said he would be. At the age of twenty-seven, she still felt like a little girl instead of a grown woman. She took a breath and knocked on the door. "Come in," her father answered. Stacy walked in. She walked up to her father and gave him a hug. "I see you're wearing your armor," said Carl.

"Sorry, Dad." She smiled. "When I'm working on a case, I never go anywhere without being armed and ready for anything that might come up. How's Mom doing?" she asked.

Carl, even though he gave his blessing on her career choice, still worried about something happening to her. He sighed and gave his daughter a slight smile. "Your mom is good. She would have flown over here with me but she had a meeting in the morning with the women's auxiliary. She told me to tell you she loves you and misses you. Hell, I miss you! You don't come home often enough, Stacy!"

"I'm sorry, Dad. It seems like I just finish solving one case, and they put me on another. I will try to get home more often in the future," she said sincerely. She felt bad about not getting home as much as she wanted, but her job kept her so busy. Being a detective on the force, she could be working day and night, especially if it was a homicide.

"Well, I'm glad we had this opportunity to see each other. Let's have a seat over here and catch up." She followed her dad over to the couch along the window of the office and sat down.

"So what case are you trying to solve here on the island?" her dad asked.

"Well, Dad, you know I'm not at liberty to discuss an ongoing case, but I can tell you it has to do with drug trafficking. We've just had some good leads this past week, and I'm hoping we can get this case wrapped up in a couple of weeks. I do have some vacation time coming; maybe you and mom could come over to the island for a week and we could spend it together. It's so beautiful here. We could relax on the beach. Mom would love it!"

Carl thought a moment. "Maybe we can. I'll talk to your mother about it. Keep me posted and I will see what we can do."

"I understand that you have a meeting with a General McCall tomorrow?" she inquired.

"Yes. Daniel McCall is a retired general from the Air Force. He has a friend who requested his help to bring back a military dog that served with his brother while he was in Afghanistan. I'm here to see if there is anything I can do to release the dog from active duty. He has a few more months before the army will retire him. Once I find out how the dog is doing with his new handler, I will determine whether or not I will retire him early. General McCall has the information on the soldier that wants to adopt him. I will be going over the specifics with him tomorrow morning."

"I've heard that a soldier and their dog can have a close bond to the point that the dog doesn't respond well to a new handler," she said.

"Yes, we will have to see, and then I will make my decision."

Her dad was well known in the field of training military dogs. She smiled. "Whatever you decide, I'm sure it will be the right one, Dad."

They talked for another hour to catch up with each other's lives. Her dad looked at his watch. "I need to check into my hotel. Any chance we could have dinner tonight?" he asked.

"I'm sorry, Dad, but I have plans tonight. Are you still going to be here on the island tomorrow night?"

"Actually, I will. My flight doesn't leave until Tuesday morning. Let's plan on having dinner then."

"Sounds good," she said. "They have a nice restaurant in the hotel, why don't we meet there, say at eighteen hundred hours?" he asked.

"Okay, I'll see you there," replied Stacy. Her dad gave her the address of the hotel he was staying at. She and her dad left the office and gave each other a hug before they got into their cars. As she backed her car up, she waved to her father. She started to head back to her rental, when suddenly she decided she needed to go shopping. She wasn't sure where Peyton was going to take her, and she wanted to look her best. Who knows what the night might bring! It gave her goosebumps just thinking about it!

Peyton was focused on the internet when his brother Mark and his nephew Cameron came into the house. "Hi, Uncle Peyton, whatcha doing?" His nephew came up beside him and was looking at the computer with him. His nephew was the spitting image of his dad, a towhead with deep blue inquisitive eyes, and the curiosity to go with them. At age seven, he was smart as a whip.

"Hi, Cameron." Peyton lifted him up on his lap. "I'm trying to find a good restaurant I can take someone to."

"Do you have a date?" he whispered.

"I do!" he whispered back.

"Uncle Peyton, I know a really good restaurant you can take your date to."

Peyton looked surprised. "You do? Where?" he asked.

Cameron looked up at his uncle. "My dad and Uncle Mike's!" he said enthusiastically.

Peyton chuckled. "I thought of that, Cameron, but remembered your dad and Uncle Mike's restaurant is closed today."

"Oh yeah, sorry, Uncle Peyton." He sighed.

"That's okay, Cameron. I'm sure I'll find something here on the internet I can take her to."

Mark was listening to the conversation his son and Peyton were having. He had to smile. His son was full of questions and would always try to come up with a solution to a problem. He wanted to know who he had a date with. "Who is the lucky gal you have a date with?" asked Mark.

"You're not going to believe this, but my buddies and I saw the woman I danced with at the club Friday night at a coffee shop near the base. She left before I had a chance to introduce myself, so we followed her. We ended up at the very base I needed to drop by buddies off. I had no idea if she was the one I danced with when I got out of the car to meet her, but she confirmed it was! So now I want to take her to a nice place so we can get to know each other."

"Is she pretty, Uncle Peyton?" asked Cameron.

Peyton smiled down at his nephew. "She's very pretty."

Mark chuckled. "Have you had any luck, Peyton?" he asked.

Peyton looked up at his brother. "No, not so far. Just bistros and coffee shops."

Mark got a grin on his face. "Hey, Cameron, how would

you like to help your dad give your uncle Peyton and his date a nice restaurant to go to?"

Cameron jumped off Peyton's lap and ran to his dad. "Yeah! How are we going to do it, Dad?" he asked, jumping all around.

"Let's see... I'll send a text to your uncle Mike, to see if he and Jenna can help. Peyton, you send a text to your date to meet at the Hawaiian Lanai at six thirty." Mark sent a text to his brother. When he received a "thumbs up" sign, he turned to his son and grinned. "Okay, son, let's put this plan into motion!"

CHAPTER 6

Mike and Jenna were halfway up the mountain of Diamond Head when he heard his phone ding. He was surprised there was service this far up. He pulled his cell out of his pocket and checked the message. Jenna, beside him, asked, "What is it? Is everything all right at home?"

Mike looked down at his soon-to-be wife and grinned. "I know this is the second time we have tried to make it up to the crater, but would you be interested in helping out my brothers this evening?" He handed his phone to her so she could read the text. *Hey Mike, Peyton ran into the woman he was dancing with at the club, and has a date with her tonight. Would you and Jenna care to help out? If so, meet us at the restaurant at 5:30.*

Jenna looked up at Mike and grinned. "Oh, I am so in!"

Mike sent back a "thumbs up" sign, picked Jenna up and kissed her. Before he got too carried away by the passion that always happens between them, he slid Jenna down his body and lifted his head. "I love you. Maybe we can continue this when we get back to the house?" he asked, wiggling his eyebrows.

"Maybe," she said with a sly grin. "If we have time."

He took her hand, "Let's go!"

At the restaurant, everyone gathered to go over what each one was responsible for to make this night special for Peyton and his date. Mike, in black dress pants and a white shirt, was ready to attend bar. Mark, in a chef's outfit, was ready to cook. Jenna and Cameron were to be the servers. Both were dressed in navy-blue dress slacks and light blue shirts. They each wore a black bow string tie around their necks. Jenna wore her dark hair up in a ponytail and only had a light dusting of makeup on to enhance her features. They set a table up in the Hawaiian Room in one of the pagodas. All was ready, and it was just about time for Peyton's date to arrive.

Peyton, who was nervous as hell, went to the entrance of the restaurant and waited for Helen, who was on time for their date. He held the door open for her. He watched as she walked toward him. She was beautiful. She was dressed in a light-green sundress, with thin straps and a low neckline, showing just enough cleavage to entice him. The dress hugged her bodice, with the skirt flowing down just above her knees. Her long blond hair was down and curled around the ends. The two-inch heeled white sandals gave her some height and complimented her legs and ankles. When she came up to him, looking into a pair of hazel eyes, he was blown away. His heart started to pound as he breathed out a "Hi, welcome to the Hawaiian Lanai." *Peyton*, he said to himself, *that was the dumbest thing you ever said to a woman*!

Stacy was trembling as she looked into his eyes and remembered the other night, dancing so close in his arms. He was so handsome in his dark dress slacks and beige short-sleeve shirt, opened at the collar, showing off part of his chest. She itched to put her hands on his skin. She shook herself. "Hi." She looked around. "Is the restaurant open? There's nobody around."

He put his arm out. "It is for us. Shall we?" She took his arm, and they entered the restaurant.

They were greeted by a little boy who carried menus in his hands. "Hi, I'm Cameron, and I'll be your host for tonight."

Stacy grinned; he was adorable. "It's very nice to meet you, Cameron."

"Thanks, and this is Jenna; she will be your server tonight."

Stacy glanced over at the young woman as she was giving Cameron a "thumbs up" sign. Jenna turned back to the couple. "Welcome to the Hawaiian Lanai. Cameron, would you like to show them to their table?" she asked.

"Yes! Follow me!"

As the couple followed Cameron into the Hawaiian Room, Jenna looked over at the two men standing behind the bar, grinning from ear to ear as they watched the performance. Jenna grinned back, gave another "thumbs up," and went in to wait on her customers. When they stepped into the Hawaiian Room, Stacy was in awe. In the center was a pond with different-colored fish swimming around in the water. There were five pagodas around the room, with bridges crisscrossing to each pagoda. She looked around at the lush green plants and colorful tropical flowers in and around each pagoda. In the center pagoda stood a single table covered with a white linen tablecloth. In the center of the table was a single candle burning, with pretty orchids placed around it. The glassware sparkled, and the china gleamed in the soft light.

At the table, Cameron was pulling out a chair. "Come on, guys!"

Peyton smiled down at Helen. "I think our host is getting a little impatient."

She smiled back up at him. "I think you're right. This is so nice. Thank you, Peyton."

They walked along the bridge to the table where little Cameron was waiting by the chair. Stacy sat down and scooted up to the table. Peyton sat down, just as Jenna came up to the table.

Jenna smiled. "Can I start either one of you off with a drink?"

Peyton couldn't hold back any longer. He chuckled. "Helen, I would like to formerly introduce you to my future sister-in-law, Jenna Hathaway, and my nephew, Cameron TreVaine. Jenna, Cameron, this is Helen Grey. They along with my brothers Mike and Mark helped plan this night for us. Mike and Mark are the owners of this establishment."

Jenna held out her hand. "It's so nice to meet you, Helen. We all wanted to make this night special for you and Peyton."

Stacy shook her hand. "Thank you, this is such a surprise!" She looked around the room, then turned back to Jenna. "This room is so beautiful!"

Cameron pulled on his uncle's arm. Peyton bent down. "You were right, Uncle Peyton. She is pretty!"

Stacy blushed as they all laughed.

"What can I get you to drink?" asked Jenna.

"I'll have a glass of your white wine," answered Stacy.

"Make that two," returned Peyton.

When Jenna and Cameron left to get them their wine, Peyton glanced back at this beautiful woman sitting across from him and wished he could remember dancing with her the other night. He wanted to remember the feel of her in his arms as he held her close. Maybe he would get a second chance tonight. He smiled. "So, let's say we get to know each other. Hi, I'm Peyton."

Starring back at him, "Hi, I'm Helen."

"What do you do for a living Helen?" he asked.

Helen hesitated, she couldn't tell him she was a cop. "Well, it's not very exciting. I work at MM Financing as a receptionist. It's actually very boring. But I just moved to the island not too long ago and needed a job. I took the first job that came along to pay the bills. I'm keeping my eye out for a better job. How about you, Peyton? What do you do for a living?" she asked, smiling.

"Currently nothing, I was just recently discharged from the army and haven't decided on what I would like to pursue in the job market. I've thought about going into aviation. I flew the UH-60 transport helicopter over in Afghanistan where I was stationed. It was dangerous and exciting at the same time. I was in the special ops division for most of my tour. My last year I spent in Afghanistan, I was in search and rescue."

As she listened to Peyton, she had a thought. "Have you considered flying for a corporation or a company? I bet they need pilots."

"I hadn't thought of that. Thanks, it gives me something to check out."

Jenna brought out their wine glasses, with Cameron following behind, holding a bottle of wine with a white linen napkin wrapped around it. Jenna set the glasses down in front of them and turned to Cameron. She took the bottle of wine from him and filled each glass, then set the bottle on the table. She smiled at them both. "Are you ready to order?"

Peyton glanced over at Helen. "Do you mind if I order for us?" Jenna had to keep from laughing. Their dinner was already preplanned.

Helen, surprised, "No I don't mind," she said.

"How do you like your steak?" he asked.

"Medium," she replied.

"We'll have two of your sirloin steaks, one medium, one medium rare, baked potatoes and salads."

Cameron stepped up to Helen. "I hope you don't mind, it's the only thing on the menu that my dad can cook!" They all laughed. Peyton shook his head. You never know what is going to come out of the mouth of a seven-year-old!

Jenna took Cameron's hand. Chuckling, she said, "We'll be right back with your salads."

She led Cameron out of the Hawaiian Room. He ran up to his dad. "Start cooking, Dad, they're ready!"

Mark picked his son up and grinned. "Okay, son, let's go cook!" They all went into the kitchen and started to prepare dinner for the special couple.

When Jenna set their salads down, with a selection of

dressings, Peyton turned back to Helen and asked, "What do you like to do in your free time, Helen?"

Helen looked into his eyes and was mesmerized. His eyes were such a deep blue. His beard had grown out since she last saw him. She wanted to touch it and feel the roughness against her hand. She wanted to lean forward and kiss that chiseled mouth of his! Her thoughts were running away from her. She shook herself and answered, "Um, not much of anything. I go out with friends on occasion."

Peyton stared back and wondered how soon it would be appropriate to take her to bed. Looking into those hazel eyes of hers, and then to her breasts, already had him aroused. Peyton switched his thoughts to keep from imagining what it would be like to have her under him, caressing her body and kissing the fullness of her breasts. As they started in on their salads, "Do you have any hobbies or sports you enjoy?" he asked.

"Well, when I have time, which isn't very often, I like to hunt wild game."

Surprised, Peyton set his fork down, looked into her eyes and asked, "Really?"

"Yes, really." She grinned. "I know it's probably not common for a woman to hunt, but some of us like the sport."

Amazed, Peyton replied, "I have been hunting since I was in my teens. If you're game, let's plan a time when we can go out together." Their eyes locked.

Stacy started to melt as his eyes devoured her right there in the restaurant. She shivered. "I'd like that," she said breathlessly.

Peyton's thoughts ran away with him, *Out in the forest, hunting for wild game, with a gorgeous woman by his side, kissing those perfect lips of hers.* They might not get much hunting done, but thoughts of making love to her out in the wild already had his heart racing. They were interrupted when Mark brought their steaks out, followed by Jenna with their side dish, and Cameron with rolls and cinnamon butter.

Mark set everything out on the table. "Let me know if your steaks need to be cooked longer, I'm not the best cook in the house, but I can cook a pretty good steak," explained Mark.

Both Stacy and Peyton cut into their steak. "It's perfect, thank you, Mark. How is yours, Helen?"

She cut a little more into her steak. "Perfect," she answered as she smiled up at Mark.

"Oh, Mark, this is Helen, Helen, this is my youngest brother, Mark," said Peyton.

Mark extended his hand. "Nice to meet you." He smiled.

"Nice to meet you too." She smiled back. "And thank you for all this. You have a beautiful establishment here."

"Thanks." He turned to Jenna and his son. "Let's let these two eat, and we'll go have our dinner."

"Okay, Dad!" exclaimed Cameron, who ran out of the room followed by Mark and Jenna.

Both Peyton and Stacy laughed. "I'm now wondering if it would have been better to meet you at a bistro."

"Oh no, I wouldn't miss this for the world!" she exclaimed. "This is great, and the steaks look delicious!"

While they were eating their dinner, they discovered that

they had a lot in common. They both liked to fish and scuba dive, as well as various other sports. "Hey," said Peyton, "I met a detective last week that loves to catch lobsters. Open season will be starting in a couple of months. He said he knew the best place to catch them."

Stacy instantly became alert. "What is his name?"

"Craig Jensen. He and his partner are working on a case that involves this restaurant."

"May I ask what it is about?" she asked.

"Well, I know a couple of their employees got involved with a loan shark and it got pretty sticky. My brothers have a couple, who are regular customers of this restaurant, whom the police department feel may be the ringleaders."

"Do you know the name of this couple?"

Peyton sat back and caught her eyes. Mark warned him not to disclose any information about the case. He didn't know Helen well enough to trust her. "No, I don't," he said. "They're keeping it under wraps for now."

Peyton saw the disappointment in her face as she answered, "Oh, I'm sorry. I shouldn't have asked." Stacy felt the excitement drop when Peyton wouldn't answer her question. She wondered if they might be related to the case she was working on. He didn't trust her, that was for sure. She needed to change the subject. She could see it was upsetting him.

Mike came to their table at the right moment. Picking up the plates, he asked, "Can I get you two anything else, maybe some more wine?"

"Oh, no thank you, Mark, I am so full. It was delicious by the way." Stacy moaned, holding her stomach.

Mike extended his hand. "I'm Mike." As she extended her hand, surprised.

Stacy had never seen two men look so much alike! Both men were striking with the same facial features, same hair color, only Mike's, as she studied him, was lighter. Looking at Peyton, all three men had the same deep blue eyes. She shook his hand. "I'm Helen. Nice to meet you."

"Same here." He smiled. He turned to his brother. "Peyton?" he asked.

"Oh no, everything was great by the way," he said, smiling up at his brother. "Thank you, Mike, for doing all of this for us."

"You're welcome. I will leave you two alone to finish up your wine."

After he left, Peyton refilled their wine glasses. As they were sipping their wine, soft music started to play over the sound system. Peyton gazed into her eyes and smiled. "I'm a little embarrassed that I can't remember dancing with you the other night. I'd like to make it up to you." He set his glass of wine down, held out his hand. "May I have this dance?"

Stacy smiled and took his hand. She came up from the table and into his arms. Stacy shivered as she felt the chemistry between them. His arms were strong around her as he pulled her close against his body. *Does he feel this too?* she wondered.

Peyton was in heaven as he felt her body move with his to the slow rhythm of the music. It felt like she belonged in his arms. He gazed down into her pretty hazel eyes. He couldn't resist, he bent his head and gave her a soft kiss. He touched her lips again, and the kiss grew more passionate. Stacy wrapped her arms up and around his neck and kissed him back. She grew weak from wanting this man. She hardly knew him, but thoughts of making love with him already made her tingle throughout her body.

Peyton could feel her trembling as he deepened the kiss. His heart was racing as he pressed her soft body closer to his. The chemistry he felt with her was astounding him. He lifted his head. "What do you say we get out of here?"

As she gazed up into his eyes filled with passion, she smiled. "I would say that is an excellent idea."

Before they left the restaurant, he thanked his brothers again for making this night special for the both of them.

Cameron came up to the couple. "Are you going to marry her, Uncle Peyton? 'Cause Uncle Mike is going to marry Jenna. We could have a double wedding!"

Mark came up to his son. "Cameron, I think it's a little soon to be planning another wedding," he scolded.

"But, Dad, they kissed!"

Both Helen and Peyton looked embarrassed.

"Sorry," Mark apologized. "My son gets a little ahead of himself. Cameron, come with me and we'll start getting things cleaned up."

"Aww, Dad!" he cried.

"Now, Cameron!" He followed his dad into the kitchen, leaving Mike and Jenna with Peyton and Helen.

"Don't mind our little nephew, Helen. He always says what's on his mind without thinking," said Mike.

"No worries, Mike. You and Peyton have an adorable nephew, and I totally enjoyed meeting all of you, plus the food was fantastic!"

Mike put his hand out and shook hands with her. "You're welcome, Helen. We hope to see you again soon."

Jenna smiled at Helen. "It was so nice to meet you, Helen. You and Peyton have a good rest of your night." The couple said goodnight and left the restaurant. Jenna smiled up at her husband-to-be as Mike put his arms around her and held her close. "I like her."

Mike leaned down and gave her a soft kiss. "Me too. Let's go help get things cleaned up and get out of here. We didn't have our time together this afternoon and I'm suffering because of it."

Jenna placed her arms up round his neck. "Oh, you are, are you? I'll have to see what I can do to relieve your suffering," she said, with a gleam in her brown eyes that told him everything he wanted to know.

He squeezed her tight against him and kissed her hard. He lifted his head with hunger in his eyes. "Let's hurry and get this done before I devour you right here on the spot!" Hand in hand, they went to help Mark and Cameron in the kitchen.

Outside, "I'm sorry for that, he can be a little outspoken at times," he apologized.

Helen laughed. "No worries, I thought it was cute!"

"Where would you like to go?" he asked.

She gazed into his eyes and smiled. "I have a bottle of wine chilling at my place."

His eyes shone with thoughts of what it would be like with her. "I'll follow you."

They both got into their cars, and it wasn't long before

they were pulling up in front of a small bungalow that looked out over the Pacific Ocean. The sun was just starting to go down, and the colors in the sky were magnificent. Peyton followed Helen up the steps, onto a front porch. There was a table and two chairs sitting to the left of the door. "Would you like to have our wine out here?" she asked.

"Sure, do you need any help?"

She smiled. "No, I think I can manage. I'll be right back."

Peyton took a seat in one of the chairs, while he waited for Helen to come back out. He was watching the sun set when Helen came out with a bottle of white wine and two glasses. She filled their glasses and sat down in the other chair. They sipped on their wine while they both relaxed and watched the sun go down. It was so peaceful, just sitting there, enjoying each other's company, not having to think of something to say. *Nice*, thought Stacy.

Peyton looked over at Helen and wondered, "Have you ever been in a relationship, Helen?"

Surprised by the question, she glanced over at him. Did she even want to get into this when all she wanted to do is feel his skin next to hers? She decided to humor him with the boring details of a lost relationship. She looked back out over the ocean and slightly smiled. "Yes, a long time ago. We were together for a couple of years, but we found we just didn't have that zing that two people in love should have. We left on good terms, and we stayed friends, nothing more." Looking back, she had been with the force for a year when she met Brandon. They were both troopers at the time. She thought she was in love, and they had a lot in common, but as they continued the relationship, in time she found that there was just something missing. "How about you, Peyton? How many relationships have you had?"

He chuckled. "The last long relationship I had was in college. I thought I was in love. It only lasted a year. I've served in the army for twelve years and that was not the life she wanted. I've been with women, Helen, but was never interested in starting a relationship. They satisfied a need inside of me, that's all."

She knew what he meant. She did the same at times. She found as she got older, though, she wanted to find someone who she could spend a lifetime with. She looked back at Peyton. Could he be the one to fill this need inside her? She definitely felt some serious chemistry when she was near him.

Peyton turned and locked eyes with her. He saw a hunger there that needed to be satisfied. "Helen, come here."

She didn't hesitate. She put her wine glass down on the table as she came up out of her chair and walked up to him. He pulled her down on his lap and wrapped his arm around her. He placed his other hand on her soft cheek and brushed her hair back with his fingers. When he touched his lips to hers, it was like an explosion going off in his chest. He traced his tongue along her bottom lip and she opened for him. He deepened the kiss. His hand came down over her breast and he felt her hard nipple under her dress. He was so aroused. He needed to get her inside so he could feel all of her next to him.

Stacy was beyond aroused. She kissed him back as she felt his hands on her body that sent her hormones into overdrive. She started unbuttoning his shirt and placed her hands on his chest. She ran her hand down to his stomach and around his waist. Peyton reacted and kissed her harder. When he lifted his head, "Let's go inside," he breathed as he rained gentle kisses down her neck and onto her breast. Stacy groaned. She came up off his lap, led him into the house, and back to her bedroom.

Stacy saw the hunger in his eyes, and with hunger of her own, she was impatient to rip off all his clothes. She wanted to see and feel all of him. With his body exposed to her, she gazed at him openly. He was all muscle. She felt a surge of energy go right through her. Peyton let her undress him, and now it was his turn. Stacy placed her hands on his chest. She gazed up into those blue eyes of his as he unzipped her dress. With his hands so gentle, he slid his hands under the straps of her dress and let it fall to the floor. Peyton caught his breath as she stood before him, in her lacy bikini panties and her heeled sandals. He couldn't move as he explored her body with his eyes. Her body was tan, and her breasts were full, just right to fill his hands. He pulled her into his arms and proceeded to devour her mouth with his. He lifted his head. "Open for me, Helen," he whispered. When she opened for him, his kiss went deep as his hands roamed her body.

Stacy groaned. "Peyton, I'm not going to be able to hold out much longer. It's been so long since I've had sex. I need you now!"

Peyton, kissing her neck and down to those beautiful breasts of hers, murmured, "Be patient, I'm getting there." He laid her down on the bed and kissed her tenderly from her breasts down to her stomach. Stacy had goosebumps as he went lower. He traveled down her thigh and reached for her sandals. He slipped them off. He came back up, kissing her all the way up to her neck and then those tender lips of hers. Stacy thought she was going to go insane with want for him. She decided she needed to speed things up a bit. She started to caress his chest and back, down his hips and to his arousal. She got the response she wanted. Still, with his lips on hers, he reached down and removed her panties with a little help from her. He broke the kiss long enough to grab a condom out of his wallet, put it on, and, with one hard thrust, entered her. Stacy responded, bringing her hips up to match his slow pace till neither one of them could stand it anymore.

"Peyton, now, I can't hold out any longer!"

In response, Peyton took them both on a ride of ultimate bliss! When they were both able to breathe again, Peyton lifted himself up on his arms and brushed away the stray hair from her face. He smiled down at her. "I don't know how it was for you, but that was explosive for me."

She touched his face with her hands and felt the roughness of his beard. "It was mind blowing. I've never had it this good. And I mean that, Peyton. You were incredible."

He bent down and kissed her once, then twice. He felt himself getting aroused again as he continued to kiss her lips, her neck, her shoulders. Then he was lost, lost to the feelings this woman brought out in him. They made love into the night, and when they were spent, he held her in his arms, and promptly fell asleep.

CHAPTER 7

Stacy woke to her alarm on her watch. She looked over and realized Peyton had left. She felt the emptiness. She got out of bed and went into the shower to get ready for work. It was probably a good thing he left, so he wouldn't see her in her undercover clothes, let alone the gun she wore under her jacket. When she was dressed, she went to the kitchen to make a pot of coffee. As she passed the island, she noticed a note on the counter. She picked it up. *Helen, coffee is ready to go, hated to leave you this morning. I will text you later, Peyton.* She smiled remembering their night together. She sighed; she hated deceiving him. Maybe she should have come clean about what she did; otherwise, this would never work. She pushed the start button on the coffee pot. She put a couple slices of toast in the toaster and waited. When all was finished, she poured herself a cup of coffee and buttered her toast. She sat down at the counter and wondered how she was going to explain being a cop to Peyton. When the case ended, she would be going back to LA. If they both decided they wanted a relationship, how could it possibly work? *I would* *be in LA, and he would be here.* Long-distance relationships were never a good idea. She finished her toast and coffee, shut the coffee pot off, grabbed her purse, and headed to work. She was filled with anticipation on trying to find the code to the warehouse. They needed to get inside to see what the cop from the sheriff's department typed into the computer. Fred was good at figuring out the security codes. Maybe it could lead them to where the drugs are to be delivered. In the meantime, she would anxiously wait for Peyton's text.

Peyton got a call from his brother Mike while he was having coffee with Mark at his home. "Hey, Mike, what's up?" he asked.

"I just got a call from General McCall. Colonel Rayland flew in yesterday and has requested a meeting with you to discuss the issue of your dog you served with while overseas. Can you meet him at one at the army base?"

As he listened, Peyton sat forward. "Yes!" he said enthusiastically. "Did he find out how Justice is doing with Sargent McGinnis?"

"Sorry, bro, he didn't tell me but wishes to discuss the matter with you personally. You're to meet him at the message center," informed Mike.

"I'll be there, thank you, Mike."

"You're welcome and good luck!" he returned.

Peyton ended the call and glanced over at Mark. "I have a meeting with Colonel Rayland this afternoon. He may have some information on Justice!" he announced.

"Well, that's good news! Maybe you will get reunited with your dog soon."

"Maybe," he answered. "Or at least have information on how he is doing. When I left, it was hard leaving my best friend behind. He was my lifeline and my companion."

Mark could see in his brother's eyes that he truly missed Justice. He sure hoped that the army will retire the dog early and release him to his brother.

"Not to change the subject on you, but you came in early this morning. How did it go with your date after you two left the restaurant?"

Peyton smiled. "Let's just say it went very well. She's quite a woman." Peyton, remembering their night together, still felt the rush of making love to her. After his meeting with the colonel, he would text her to see when they could get together again.

"Sounds like you two hit it off," he said.

"We did. Listen, it's after eleven, I'm going to get cleaned up and head over to the base."

"Okay. After your meeting, stop by the restaurant and let us know how it went," insisted Mark.

"I will." Peyton got up from his chair, put his cup in the sink, and headed for the shower, "I'll see you this afternoon."

Peyton drove into the army base and pulled up in front of the message center. He suddenly realized that this was the exact same place he and his buddies had followed Helen to. He didn't think about it at the time but was now wondering what she had come here for. He shrugged, got out of his SUV, and entered the message center. He walked up to the desk. "Captain Peyton TreVaine to see Colonel Carl Rayland," he stated.

"Do you have an appointment, sir?" asked the sergeant on duty.

"Yes," answered Peyton. "At thirteen hundred hours, sir."

"Have a seat, sir. He'll be right with you."

Peyton sat down in one of the chairs and waited while the sergeant informed the colonel his appointment was here.

A few minutes went by before the colonel stepped out of the office. Peyton rose from the chair and saluted the colonel. He returned the salute and walked up to Peyton with his hand extended. As they shook hands, "Captain TreVaine, thank you for meeting me on such short notice. Come this way."

Peyton followed the Colonel into the office and waited while Colonel Rayland took a seat behind the desk. "Have a seat, Captain." As Peyton sat down, "I understand that you would like to adopt a military dog that was commissioned to you while serving over in Afghanistan."

"Yes sir, the black lab, First Sergeant Justice. He and I worked well together, and we had a bond between us that I feel can never be broken. He got me through some hard times. I realize he has a couple of months before the army will retire him. I filled out the paperwork to adopt him when he is released from active duty. My main concern now is how well he is doing with the new handler. I have not been able to find out anything at this point, sir."

Colonel Rayland smiled and answered Peyton's concerns. "Yes, I checked on the dog, and he is doing okay with Sergeant McGinnis. The sergeant states that Justice does his work, but when he's done, he doesn't engage in any down time activity and seems depressed. I want to give it another week to see if he improves. If he doesn't, I will release him from active duty and the dog will be yours."

Peyton breathed a sigh of relief. "Sir, you don't know how much this means to me."

"I think I do," he replied. "I've seen it before, when a soldier and his dog bond so close, that neither one of them are the same until they are reunited. Your paperwork to petition him for adoption appears to be in order. So we will wait and see." Colonel Rayland leaned back in his chair and asked, "How are you dealing with civilian life? You were in the army for a little over twelve years, most of it in the special ops division, has it been hard for you to adjust?"

Peyton stared back at the Colonel and wondered if this was part of the adoption process. He shrugged his shoulders. "Well, if you are asking me if I am suffering from PTSD, I would have to say that yes, on occasion. I have trouble at times, accepting what happened over in Afghanistan while serving my country. My team was caught in a car bombing at one of the NATO training facilities and one of my teammates was killed, along with another one seriously injured. I still have nightmares. Justice helped me get through the loss. I have twin brothers who live on the island, and they have been very supportive. They actually own a restaurant over on Waikiki Boulevard. It has a great view of the ocean, and the food is excellent," he said.

"I talked with your brother Mike this morning. He was the one who had General McCall contact me. He sounds like a good man."

"They both are. They both served in the Air Force and went in as a twin enlistment. They were stationed over at Joint Base Pearl Harbor-Hickam. They fell in love with the island and never left. Say." Peyton leaned forward. "What are you doing for dinner tonight? You should check out their restaurant. You won't regret it."

"I'm having dinner with my daughter tonight. She's here working on a case," he answered. He leaned forward. "But you know, after eating dinner at the hotel last night, I think I'll take you up on your offer. I'll text my daughter and let her know where to meet me. Can you give me the address?"

After Peyton gave him the address, he asked, "What does your daughter do for a living?"

"She's a cop. Not the career choice I would have wanted for her, but from what I've heard, she's a good one," the colonel answered.

"I'm sure she is." Peyton got up from his chair and held out his hand. The colonel came up from his chair and shook his hand. "Colonel, I won't take up any more of your time, it was nice meeting you, and thanks for letting me know how Justice is doing."

"You're welcome, Peyton. Listen, if you need to talk to someone about what you went through over in Afghanistan, I know a good therapist here on the base. She helps get soldiers through the trauma of war so they can transcend into civilian life."

"Thank you, Colonel Rayland. I will keep that in mind," Peyton returned.

"Will I see you tonight?" he asked.

"What time?"

"Eighteen hundred hours," he stated.

"I'll be there, and I look forward to meeting your daughter." Peyton nodded his head and left the office.

Colonel Rayland sat back down at the desk and thought, *Now there's a good soldier. I might just go ahead and release the dog and bring him home to be with his master.* That thought gave him a good feeling inside. He picked up the phone and made a call.

At the police department, Detectives Zack Williams and Craig Jenson, along with Lieutenant Ray Fillmore, were on a conference call with Jason Hague (alias Mick Southerland). Jason was out in a semi-remote park having a discussion about the case. "What did you find out about Helen Grey?" asked Jason.

"Well, we couldn't find out much about her. She was living in LA when she lost her job as an office manager for an insurance company. She moved here a few months ago and landed a job with MM financing, which we all know Marco Manchez owns," replied Zack.

"There must be something more. Why would she try to listen at the door if she was just the receptionist?" Jason asked.

"We'll keep digging. In the meantime, we got a bead on the cop in the sheriff's department that has been feeding Manchez with information. His name is Officer Ben Gillard. He's being watched. We'll keep you informed on his movements in the case."

"Good," answered Jason.

"Have you heard any more about when the drug shipment is to arrive?" asked Lieutenant Fillmore.

"No, but from what I was told before, my guess it will be on Monday of next week."

Mick looked in his rearview mirror and saw a black sedan pulling up behind him. "Look, guys, I've got company. I'll call you back."

"Jason!" exclaimed Zack. "Damn! He hung up! Can you track his phone, Lieutenant, to give us his location?"

The lieutenant punched in Mick's cell number and turned on the GPS tracker. "He's at a park just outside of Honolulu on the northside," answered the lieutenant.

Zack looked over at Craig. "Let's go!"

Jason watched as a big, burly man in a black suit, with his long black hair tied behind his thick neck, get out of the car. He knew instantly it was Victor, Manchez's hit man. *What in the hell is he doing out here?* he asked himself. *And how in the hell did he find me? I hope they haven't found me out*, he thought. *Or I'm a dead man.* He got out of the car as Victor was walking up beside the back of his car, ready to defend himself if he needed to.

"Victor! What brings you out this way?" asked Jason.

"I have a message from the boss. He's been trying to reach you all morning."

"Sorry, since I'm not handling the loan business anymore I find I have time on my hands and took a drive. I was talking to my sister back home; she's due to have a baby any day now." *Which is the truth, so a little white lie.* "Do you know what he wanted?" he asked.

"You're to call him on his cell immediately," he answered.

"I'll get right on it." He waited till Victor got back into his car and took off. Mick slid into the driver seat, brought Manchez's number up on his cell, and tapped his phone.

Manchez picked up. "Mick! Where the hell have you been? I've been trying to contact you all morning!" he yelled into the phone!

"Mr. Manchez," Mick returned sternly, "I was on the phone with my sister, who is due any day now with her first child. What do you need from me?"

"We have a problem," he answered.

Mick sat forward in his seat and asked, "What kind of problem?"

"The drugs are coming in earlier than was planned. I need you at the warehouse on Friday afternoon. The guards and Victor will be there as well. It will be coming in late Friday night, and the drugs will be put on board a ship early Saturday morning. I need this to go like clockwork. Understood?"

"Understood," replied Mick.

"Keep your phone open for any new developments."

"Got it, I'll be there," said Mick.

"Good," said Manchez, and hung up.

Just as Jason was about to call back the police department, he heard another car pull up behind him. He looked in his rearview mirror and saw Zack and Craig get out of the car. They walked up to his window. "Are you okay Mick?" asked Zack.

"Yes." Jason put a finger to his lips and got out of the car. He motioned for the detectives to follow him. They walked a ways away from their cars. "Hey," said Jason, "I was just about to call you. It was Victor who pulled up behind me."

"Manchez's henchman," said Craig.

"Yes. He had a message for me to call the boss. Now, I understand how you found me, but I don't know how Victor found me. I think my car has been bugged, or a GPS device has been put on it."

"Let's go check it out," said Zack, as they all walked up to Jason's car.

They looked inside doors and underneath the frame of the car. Craig was the first to find the small device back underneath the rear bumper. "Here's the culprit," he said.

Jason and Zack came up to Craig. Jason took the device from Craig, threw it on the ground and crushed it with his boot. "This pisses me off! And it's going to piss Manchez off knowing I found it!" exclaimed Jason.

"What did he want?" asked Zack.

"He wanted to inform me that the drugs are coming in sometime late Friday night and are to be put on a ship heading for LA early Saturday morning. We need to get a plan in motion to intercede. But there's one big problem," explained Jason.

"What's that?" asked Craig.

"There are going to be four to six guards on duty, two in the warehouse, along with Victor and me, and four outside. As I mentioned before, the entry door and the back garage door need a code to get inside. I'm not sure if Manchez is going to give me the code until Friday, when I arrive at the warehouse."

"Okay, Craig and I will head back to the police department and get with the lieutenant. With the information we have so far, I'm pretty sure we can set up a sting operation to catch these guys during the drug heist. We just need to figure out a way to get Manchez there without him suspecting the police are involved," explained Zack.

Jason, looking out over the park, replied, "I'll think on it. He's sharp as a tack when it comes to protecting his interest. We only have a few days to set this up." He turned back to Zack. "I'm heading back to Manchez's office. I'm sure by now he knows the device isn't working. I will need to cover my tracks."

"Be careful how you approach him," Zack said with concern. "He's put down a few of his men when he thinks they might be turning on him."

"Don't worry. I've dealt with this before. I don't think he'll try anything at his office," said Jason.

"That's not what I am worried about. He's already put a tracking device on your car, which means he wants to make sure he can trust you. Keep an eye out for anyone in and around your rental. Better yet, I will talk to the lieutenant about having one of our other detectives in an unmarked car keeping your place under surveillance at all times. We don't want to take any chances. The stakes are too high," stated Zack.

"I agree," Jason returned, "I'll call you as soon as I leave Manchez's office."

"Right, we'll be waiting for your call." All three men got into their cars and exited the park.

Sitting back into a wooded area, a man in a black charger watched as Mick sat in his car talking on the phone. A car pulled up behind him. The guy got out of the car, spoke with Mick, and left. Several minutes later another car pulled up behind him. Two men got out of the car and approached him. As he watched, Mick got out of the car. All three men walked a ways from their vehicles. They went back to Mick's car and appeared to be searching for something. They huddled again, got into their cars, and left. He pulled out and followed the man called Mick out onto the highway.

Mick stepped out of the elevator and walked up to Helen Grey. It still bothered him that the detectives couldn't find out anything about her. Why was she trying to listen in on my conversation with Manchez last week? He smiled as he had a thought. "Mick Southerland, to see Mr. Manchez."

Helen looked up from what she was doing. "Do you have an appointment, Mr. Southerland?" she asked.

"No, but it's important that I see him."

"Give me one moment." Helen pushed the intercom button.

"Yes, Helen!" he yelled.

Oh, he was not in a good mood. "Sorry to interrupt. Mr. Southerland is here to see you."

"Mick?" he asked.

"Yes," she answered.

"Send him in."

Helen felt Mick's eyes on her the whole time she talked with Mr. Manchez. She glanced up into steel gray eyes. "You can go in now."

He gave her a sly smile. "Thank you, Helen." Mick walked around her desk, opened the door to Manchez's office, and slightly closed it. She looked at the door and noticed it was ajar, just like the last time. She got up from her desk and placed her ear along the door edge, to see what she could hear.

Mick walked up to Manchez. "Is this some kind of joke?" asked Mick.

"I beg your pardon?" Marco asked in return.

"The GPS device I found on my car? You don't trust me, do you, Mr. Manchez?"

"Now, hold on, Mick—"

Mick interrupted. "No, you hold on! Ray Lopez trusted me explicitly, and I never let him down. It was just a bad rap that he got caught. If you can't trust me to handle this, then you'll have to find someone else to work your drug deal!" Mick said scathingly and loud enough for Helen to hear.

Marco sat back in his chair in shock and stared at Mick. He has never had anyone in his company talk to him that way. No one was ever brave enough to. He actually kind of liked that in him. Showed him he had leadership abilities. Mick turned to leave. "Mick, wait!" cried Marco. Mick turned back, glaring at the beady-eyed man with balding black hair seated behind the desk. "Have a seat, Mick," Marco said calmly. Mick hesitated only for a moment. He walked up to one of the chairs in front of his desk and sat down. "Listen," he began. "It's not that I don't trust you. I like to know where my people are."

"Mr. Manchez, I understand that it's important to you to make sure everything goes smoothly, but I've been doing this a long time. I'm a man of my word and I follow through with what I say. You can trust me to handle things."

Marco watched the man sitting across from his desk. He took a deep breath. "Okay, Mick, you've got my trust, but make sure you don't give me a reason to break that trust. It won't go well for you."

"Understood," he returned. Mick got up out of his chair, walked out of the office, and made sure the door was closed.

Just as he thought, Helen was just pulling herself away from the door. This time he confronted her. "Look, Helen, or whoever you are, I don't know what game you are playing, but I am going to find out. Why were you listening at the door?" he demanded.

Helen stood there in shock and embarrassment being caught listening in. "I, uh…"

"Don't have anything to say, Helen?" he questioned. "Mark my words. You keep your mouth shut about what you heard. It's only going to be a matter of time before I find you out." Mick turned away and pressed the elevator button. The door opened. Mick walked in, turned around, and glared at her one last time as the door closed, leaving Helen with her mouth open and shaking uncontrollably.

Once she got her nerves to settle, she texted Lieutenant Andrew to see if he could meet with her right after work. He texted back, *Where?*

There's a coffee shop over on Waikiki Boulevard near the restaurant where I am supposed to have dinner with my dad this evening, she sent back.

What's the address? he returned.

She texted him the address, just as Marco Manchez came out of his office. She quickly put her phone down. He walked past her with his head down, saying, "I'm going out for a while, Helen. I'll be back this afternoon. Take any messages for me and put them on my desk."

"Yes, sir," said Helen. She watched him get into the elevator, take a deep breath, and look up at the ceiling as the door closed. She could tell he was not happy about the discussion he had with Mick. He was the one who was always in control. She sent a text to her partner to find out his location. *Hey Fred, what's your twenty?*

I'm out here in the parking lot outside your office building, he returned.

Good, Manchez is on his way down. Can you follow him?

I'm on it!

She couldn't believe her luck! Now was the time to go see if she could find that code! She entered his office and looked around in each corner of his office to see if there were any hidden cameras. So far so good. She approached the desk. *Now in what drawer would he put the code to the warehouse?* she asked herself. She looked in the top side drawer and shuffled threw the papers. Nope, not in there! She tried the other side, with the same results. She pulled on the center drawer, locked! Damn it! She hurried out to her desk, grabbed her purse, and pulled out a leather pouch. Just as she was heading back in, her phone buzzed. Fred was sending her a text. *Hey, Manchez is heading back towards the building from the parking lot, just wanted to give you a heads up*! Stacy quickly pulled out the lock pick and headed back into the office. She figured she had about five minutes. She put the lock pick in and opened the drawer. Low and behold, there was the code sitting on top of some papers. She quickly memorized the number, shut the drawer, made sure it was locked, and hurried out of the office. Just as she sat down at her desk, her eyes focused on the computer, the elevator door opened. Her heart was still racing when she looked up. "Mr. Manchez! You're back so soon!"

"Just forgot something, Helen," as he barreled into his office.

He was so angry with himself! He forgot the damn code to his own warehouse! He hated getting old. It doesn't bode well when he can't remember a simple code. Maybe he should retire after this drug heist. It would set him and his wife up for life. They could settle on a secluded island somewhere in the Pacific Ocean. He was getting too old to be doing this kind of work anymore. He unlocked the drawer, pulled out the code, re-locked it, and headed out of his office. He said goodbye to Helen for the second time and headed down to the lobby in the elevator.

Helen breathed a sigh of relief. She wrote down the code on a piece of paper, stuffed it in her purse along with the lock pick. She texted her partner, thanking him for the tip and that she would see him after work at the coffee shop.

Jason left the building totally pissed! He would do his own investigation into Helen Grey. He needed to find out what she was about. He would be back here at five and follow her where she went. It might give him some idea as to what she was up to. Jason called the station to let Zack and Craig know what transpired after talking with Manchez. He informed them that he found Helen listening in at the door again, and he was going to follow her when she left work.

"Okay, Jason, let us know if you find out anything," replied Zack.

"Will do," he returned. He turned out onto Kalakaua Avenue and made a right on 10th. He looked into his rearview mirror and saw a black Charger behind him. He noticed that the same car drove by him when he pulled into the parking lot to go in to talk to Manchez. He traveled down 10th for a short way, then made a left into another parking lot and watched in his rearview mirror as the car drove by him. He did a quick turn around and waited till the Charger was out of sight. He pulled back out on 10th, turned left on Kalakaua Avenue, and followed it down to 9th Street. He took a right and then another right into a grocery store and waited. He sat and wondered who in the hell was following him. After ten minutes, he didn't see any sign of the black Charger, so he headed out. He would talk to Zack about issuing him another car.

Fred watched as Manchez came out of the building for the second time. He waited until Manchez got into his car and drove off. He put his SUV into drive and followed him out of the parking lot. He kept himself at a distance, which took him to a bistro on the north shore of the island. He drove passed the bistro and turned around. He got out of his car and entered the building. The bistro was pretty busy with patrons seated at tables and people waiting in line to place their order. After Fred purchased his coffee, he turned around and saw

Manchez sitting with a big man with long black hair tied in a ponytail behind his neck. Unfortunately, he couldn't get close enough to hear what they were discussing.

Manchez looked across at Victor. "Mick found the GPS on his car."

Victor, surprised said, "I can always put another one on his car, sir."

"No, he was pretty upset. I'm going to trust him to handle this, but if you suspect anything amiss on the handling of this deal at the warehouse, you know what to do. And do it discreetly. I don't want any cops around. Understand?" he asked.

With a sly look in Victor's eyes and a slight smile on his lips, he responded, "Understood."

"I need to go check on things out at the warehouse, I'll be in touch."

Victor nodded his head as Manchez rose from his chair and left the bistro. Fred watched as Manchez walked out the door of the building. He looked over at the man sitting at the table. He, too, came up from the table and left. He noticed that their exchange was brief. Fred hurried out the door to try and catch Manchez and follow him to his next destination, but he was too late. Manchez was gone!

When Manchez arrived at his warehouse, he went inside to his office. He opened up the computer to check and see what was typed into the computer over the weekend. As he read the report, he smiled. *Ben is proving to be quite an informant to me.* He closed out the computer, came out of his office, locked it, and headed back to his corporate office. After reading the report, he relaxed knowing the drug heist was well underway and his bank account would soon be overflowing. He smiled and sighed at the same time and thought, *Life is good!*

Later, Jason, sitting in the parking lot across from Manchez's building in a dark-blue sedan, waited for Helen to come out. It wasn't long before he saw her exiting the building and walking to her car. He slid down in his seat so she wouldn't see him and watched as she got into a red Charger. As she pulled out of the parking lot, Jason started his car and followed her out. He followed her down Kalakaua Avenue and watched her turn off on Waikiki Boulevard. A few miles down the road, she pulled into a side parking lot and stepped out of her car. He pulled into the parking lot across the street and parked. Helen walked into a coffee shop. She came out with a cup of coffee and went directly to a table where two gentlemen were seated at a table in the outdoor lanai. Jason took his cowboy hat off, ran his fingers through his hair, put some shades on, and stepped out of his car. He walked across the street and entered the coffee shop. He ordered a coffee, grabbed a local newspaper, and walked out into the lanai. Fortunately, a table was opened directly behind her. He went over, took a seat, and pretended to read the newspaper.

Lieutenant Andrew was the first to speak. "Okay, what do you have for me?" he asked.

Helen went first. "First, Mick Southerland came into the office to speak to Mr. Manchez. From what I was able to hear, Manchez had someone in his organization put a GPS finder on his car. Mick totally reamed Mr. Manchez out and threatened to quit. I wish I could have seen the look on that man's face. It would have been epic!" She chuckled. "Also, I was able to get the code to his warehouse."

"Excellent!" Kevin replied.

"What about you, Fred? Where did Manchez go when you followed him?" he asked.

"I followed him to a little out of the way bistro on the north shore of the island. He was sitting with a man who looked like a sumo wrestler. Big burly guy, with his long black hair tied behind his neck. I couldn't get close enough to catch the conversation without them becoming suspicious. But they didn't talk long before they both got up and left. Sorry, Lieutenant."

Jason, listening in on the conversation, was struck with the knowledge that these people were cops, but from where? It sounded like they were working on the same case as him and the police department. He knew the sheriff's department wasn't involved with the case. At least not that he was aware of. He would have to get with Zack, to see if he knew anything. Helen, or whoever she is, has the code to Manchez's warehouse. He continued to listen.

"We need to devise a plan on when we can go over to the warehouse and get inside his office," explained the lieutenant.

"I can head over there after I have dinner with my father tonight. Fred, can you back me up?" she asked.

"Yeah, just call or text me when you head over there."

Kevin glanced over at Stacy. "Let me know if something happens and you're not able to get over there tonight," he said. "It looks like we are finally making some headway on the case. As soon as we can get a location on where the drugs are going to be delivered in LA, we can notify the troops and head back."

Peyton came to mind as Stacy thought about going back to LA after the case was solved. She would talk to the lieutenant about taking some time off. She had some vacation time coming. She really wanted to get to know him, to see if a relationship would work between them. He was so hot. She had never felt the kind of chemistry with any other man than she had with him. Stacy was broken out of her thoughts when she heard Fred say, "Let me know, Stacy, if you are able to get over there. I've gotta run. I'm having dinner with a sweet redhead tonight."

Kevin shook his head as Fred got up from the table and headed out. "That guy can always get a date no matter where he is."

"Tell me about it," answered Stacy. She looked at her watch. She would have just enough time to get over to the restaurant and meet her dad. "Sorry, Kevin, I need to get going as well. I will let you know later how it went."

"Good. Be careful, and don't try to do this on your own. It's too dangerous. If you can't get ahold of Fred for some reason, call me."

"I promise," she said as she got up to leave. "I'll make sure I have back up."

The lieutenant watched her go. He knew she had a tendency to go off on her own. She would get a good reaming out if she didn't follow orders on this case. He looked at his watch and decided to head back to his hotel. He would check in with his wife and see how she and the kids were doing. God, he missed them! He couldn't wait for this case to be wrapped up and they could head back to LA!

Jason watched as they left the restaurant. He waited until they were out and on their way. He got up from the table and headed for his car. He made a call to the detectives and gave them an update. "Detective Williams," answered Zack.

"Hey, Zack, we've got a problem," he said.

"What's going on?" asked Zack.

"We've got some state troopers here from LA working on the same case as we are, Helen included. She's working undercover in his office. She also has the code to the warehouse. Other than Ben Gillard working for Manchez, have you heard anything about the sheriff's department getting involved with the case?"

"No. Other than keeping an eye on Officer Gillard, they are not involved in trying to catch Manchez. I'll give a call to the captain and see what I can find out about the state troopers being called in."

"From what I overheard," stated Jason, "they are here to find out where the drugs are to be delivered in LA. Once that's done, they're heading back. I don't think they are intent on catching the people suspecting of doing the drug heist here in Honolulu. Sounds like they want to catch the people involved on their end."

"Right, let me touch base with the captain at the sheriff's department and see exactly what's going on. I'll get back to you."

"Good, I'm going to stake out the warehouse tonight. I may need back up," returned Jason.

"Make the call and we'll be there," Zack fired back.

"Okay, I'll be in touch."

CHAPTER 8

Stacy, walking up to the Hawaiian Lanai where she was to meet her dad, was checking her phone to see if Peyton had texted her. She found she had one from him, explaining he had plans tonight, but could they get together tomorrow night? She stopped and sent a text back that she would have to let him know. She opened the door of the restaurant and realized she was still in her undercover clothes. She didn't have time to change, let her hair down, or even put on a little makeup! She sighed as she walked into the restaurant. She was met by the hostess on duty, a pretty redhead, with Tonya written on her name tag. "Hi, welcome to the Hawaiian Lanai. Do you have a reservation tonight?" she asked.

"No, Tonya, but I'm meeting my father, Colonel Carl Rayland, for dinner tonight. He should be here," said Stacy.

She checked the reservations. "Oh, yes! He's seated out in the lanai. I'll take you to him."

Stacy followed Tonya out into the lanai. As she passed the bar, she didn't realize when she was here last night with Peyton what a prestigious establishment this was! The bar was done in dark wood paneling with a wraparound bar. The indirect lighting gave it a warm look, and the upbeat music coming from the state-of-the-art sound system left you feeling energized and happy. The room had booths along the windows looking out into the lanai. Tables and chairs were placed around the center of the room. The bar area was already filling up with customers getting out of work, wanting to grab a bite and relax before going home. She stepped out into the lanai and felt she was transported to another dimension. There was another pond with all kinds of goldfish swimming all around. Tables and chairs were placed around the pond, with tropical shrubs and flowers weaving in and out around the tables. The colorful umbrellas were up to shade the patrons from the sun. Along the wall of the restaurant was a waterfall gushing down into a reservoir, adding to the atmosphere of a tropical paradise. The view of the Pacific Ocean was magnificent, with the sun gleaming down on the water. She spotted her dad sitting at a corner table in the lanai. She stopped. She glanced over at a man seated at the table next to her father. As she stared at Peyton, she wondered how and when did Peyton meet her father! Her heart started racing as she began to panic. Would he recognize her as Helen when her dad introduced them? Maybe she should turn tail and run while she had the chance! Too late, her dad saw her. He stood up as she approached the table where they were sitting.

Peyton watched the woman who followed the hostess to their table. He couldn't believe it! *Miss Prudence was Colonel Rayland's daughter?* Damn! What are the odds of this happening? He watched as she gave her dad a hug. He turned to Peyton. Peyton stood up from the table. "Peyton, this is my daughter, Stacy. Stacy, this is Peyton TreVaine. He is the soldier I am working with, to reunite him with the military dog he wants to adopt."

Stacy nervously turned toward Peyton. He extended his hand. When she shook his hand, she instantly felt the tingles flow throughout her body. *Can he feel me shaking?*

Peyton felt the electricity as he took her hand in his. Shocked, he dropped her hand. "It's very nice to meet you, Peyton." *Can he hear my voice shake?*

"Same here," Peyton answered in return. They all took a seat at the table. Thank God the waitress came to their table. "Hi, I'm Megan, and I'm going to be your waitress tonight. Can I get anyone a drink from the bar?" she asked.

"Stacy?" asked the colonel.

"I'll have a vodka and tonic with a lime wedge." She definitely needed alcohol to calm her nerves.

"Peyton?" he asked.

"Bring me your best bourbon on the rocks."

"And I will have a scotch on the rocks," requested the colonel.

"I'll have your drinks right out to you." Megan smiled.

"Thank you, Megan."

The colonel turned to his daughter. "How is your day going?" he asked.

"It's been busy," she replied nervously.

"Have you and your partner made any headway in the case you're working on?"

"Actually, we have, but still need quite a bit more information before the case is solved."

Stacy could feel Peyton's eyes on her the whole time she was talking with her dad; she should have been upfront with him from the beginning.

Peyton, watching her, tried to figure this whole thing out. How can he be attracted to two different women, who looked different but had similar features and a perfect body, at least from what he could tell under that jacket and straight skirt she wore! He felt the chemistry with her, and also with Helen. Remembering last night with Helen already had his heart pounding. "So, the colonel mentioned you're a police officer," he inquired.

She turned and caught his eyes. Her heart was racing as she answered, "Yes, I'm a detective for the state police department out of LA."

Wow, that was not how he pictured this woman when he first saw her walking across the street!

"Three of us were brought in on a tip from the sheriff's department about drugs being shipped to LA from here."

Peyton, looking through a pair of large dark-rimmed glasses, sees the same hazel eyes as Helen's. *Could she be one and the same? Take the glasses off and let her hair down, and that's Helen. If it's her, why couldn't she have been straight with me last night?*

"What happens when you find out?" he asked.

"We notify the troops back in LA to catch the smugglers with the drugs when they come in, then we head back," she answered.

Megan came back with their drinks and set them on the table. "Are you ready to order?" she asked.

Stacy stirred her drink, picked it up, and took a long draw on it. She hoped it would kick in soon and relax her nerves. This was not how she thought her evening would go. "I'll have the New York Strip steak, done medium, with red potatoes, and a salad with French dressing," answered the colonel.

"Peyton?" she asked.

"Give me the Hawaiian Chicken with your mixed vegetable, and a salad with your Hawaiian dressing."

Megan glanced over at Stacy. "And for you?"

"I will have your grilled shrimp salad with ranch dressing."

Megan picked up the menus. "I'll put this right in for you," she said, smiling.

Peyton noticed that Stacy had her drink half gone already. He had a feeling. He sat back in his chair and eyed her curiously. "So," he asked her, "how do you go about getting the information you need to solve the case?"

Stacy downed the rest of her drink. She might as well get this over with. If he's pissed, he's pissed. When Megan brought out the salads, she ordered another drink. She turned back to him. "We go undercover into the person's business that's a suspect, to see if we can uncover any information that would tie him, or her, to the drug deal. Unfortunately, that is all that I am at liberty to tell you."

Megan brought out her drink and set it down in front of her. She stirred it up and took another drink. Peyton sat forward with his arms pressed on top of the table. If she didn't slow down with the alcohol, she would be drunk soon. With a sly smile on his face, he asked, "When you go undercover, do you use a fictitious name, or do you use your own?"

Although the alcohol was starting to relax her, she was dreading answering his question. She glared back at him and instantly knew he knew who she was. She might as well get this over with and take the fall. "We use fictitious names."

Continuing to stare at each other, he asked, "Can you tell us yours?"

She glanced over at her dad who was sipping on his scotch, and looked as if was enjoying the conversation between her and Peyton. She looked back over at Peyton, took a deep breath, and answered, "Helen Grey."

Peyton sat back in his chair and was relieved that he wasn't going crazy but was a little pissed that she wasn't honest with him last night. Their dinners arrived and conversations went in other directions, thank God!

After they finished eating, "What time is your flight in the morning, Dad?" Stacy asked.

"I decided to stay a couple of more days," he answered.

Surprised, she asked, "Really?" "Yes, uh, the general wanted me to go over some military maneuvers and asked if I could stay a little longer."

"That's great, Dad! Maybe we can get together one more time before you go."

"I would like that, Stacy," he replied. "Just let me know when you are available."

Listening to the conversation, Peyton needed to get out of there and away from Stacy. The more he thought about it, the angrier he got. "Listen, I'm going to cut out and let you two catch up." He got up from the table and extended his hand to the colonel. "Again, it was nice meeting you, and thank you for all your help in letting me know how Justice is doing, and for dinner."

"You're welcome, Peyton. Enjoy the rest of your evening," returned the colonel.

He turned to Stacy. "Good luck with your case...Helen."

"Thank you," she returned. When he left, she could tell he was angry. She could only hope he would forgive her for deceiving him.

Peyton walked into the bar and saw his brothers sitting with one of the detectives in the corner booth. He walked up to them looking like he wanted to punch something. "You guys mind if I join you?" he asked gruffly.

"Bro, you do not need to ask that question. Have a seat. You remember Zack."

Peyton nodded. "Zack, how are things going with the case you and your partner are working on?"

"It could be better," Zack said, frowning, "We just keep running into bumps in the road concerning this case."

"Sorry about that," he said with little enthusiasm.

Mike watched his brother and knew something was off. "How was dinner with the colonel and his daughter?"

Peyton glanced back at his brother and grunted. "It was fine."

"Well, you don't sound like it was fine. What happened?" he asked, concerned at his brother's attitude.

"Well, if you must know," he said disgustingly, "I found out his daughter is a cop out of LA, alias Helen Grey. Her real name is Stacy Rayland. The one thing that bugs me the most is she wasn't honest with me last night when we were together."

Mark, listening to the exchange, piped in, "That little knock-out is a cop?"

"Yes, I couldn't figure out how I could be attracted to two different women. I saw her several days ago, obviously in her undercover clothes, and had a reaction to her. I thought it was strange since she wasn't the type that I would go for. When I was introduced to her and shook her hand I had the same reaction that I did with Helen last night. The chemistry was instant. Now I find out she is one in the same. I feel like a fool."

Zack perked up and leaned forward on the table. "Listen, Peyton, when she is here under cover, it's best if she doesn't give out her real name. This is a small island, and word gets around quick. Her life could be in danger if the suspect even has a hint that she might be a cop. Mick, who is working undercover for us, never reveals his real name."

Peyton sat up with his heart starting to pound. He didn't want to imagine anything happening to her even though she deceived him in the beginning. With his heart pounding even faster, impatiently he asked Zack, "What about having dinner with her dad? He introduced her as Stacy Rayland."

"We're going to hope that no one overheard the conversation that could be connected to the case. Mike, can we go back to your office? We need to talk privately."

"By all means, yes," answered Mike. They all got up from the table.

Mark stopped his brother. "Listen, I'm going to stay out here and keep an eye out."

"Okay, let us know if you see the colonel and his daughter leaving."

Mike led them back to his office. They all took a seat. "I'm going to be honest with you, Peyton. Mick followed Helen to a coffee shop because he suspected Helen wasn't who she said she was. Listening in on the conversation she had with her cohorts, he discovered they were state troopers out of LA. She's working undercover in Manchez's office. You better tell me what was said at dinner, and we'll try to figure this whole mess out."

Peyton went on to explain that she admitted she was a detective out of LA, and they were here due to a tip from the sheriff's department about a drug deal that was supposed to go to LA. "They are only here to find out where the drugs will be taken once they arrive in LA. After that, they alert the troops in LA to intercept and hopefully catch the drug dealers on their end. That's all I know. She didn't give out any names," explained Peyton.

"Sounds like the troopers have no idea that the police department here on the island has been working on this same case. Thanks, Peyton, we'll need to get ahold of them and discuss the next step."

Zack, impatient to get back out to the bar, said "Let's go out and see if the colonel and his daughter are still here."

They left the office and headed back out into the restaurant. Mark came up to them. "Just wanted to let you know Helen and her father are still in the lanai."

"Good," answered Zack. "Let's go sit down and wait. I have a feeling something is going to happen tonight."

Her father watched Peyton leave. He looked back over to his daughter and asked, "I felt some nervous tension between you and Peyton tonight. Can you tell your dad what's going on?"

Stacy met his eyes, took a deep breath, and sighed. "I met Peyton this past weekend at a club. He was a little drunk and didn't remember me. His buddies and he came into a coffee shop that I stopped in before I met with you this past Sunday morning. His buddies recognized me. When I left the coffee shop, they followed me to the base, and there I officially met him. When we introduced each other, I gave him my undercover name. He asked me to dinner that night. After dinner, we had some wine at my place and got to know each other better." She wasn't going to tell him she had already been in the sack with him. Some things you just didn't discuss with your parents, especially sex! Her eyes pleaded with her dad. "I wasn't sure what to do. If my cover is blown, I could be in serious trouble with the suspect involved in the case."

Carl studied his daughter. "Stacy, I don't begin to understand all that you do when you are involved in a case. I realize that you do have to protect yourself. If you felt that you needed to give your undercover name, I'm sure when you explain why you needed to do it, Peyton will understand. He's a good man and was a hell of a good soldier when he was serving overseas."

"Thanks, Dad," she said, relieved. "I needed to hear that." She anxiously looked around the restaurant. She hoped her cover wasn't blown already! She leaned forward and said in a low voice, "But from now on, you need to refer to me as Helen Grey."

"No problem, Helen." Talk about worry! Now he won't rest until this case is solved and knew she was safe. He wished she had told him sooner about the name change. He never would have introduced her as Stacy. They went on to discuss how her mom, careful not to mention any names, if she was okay with him being gone a few more days and other topics.

It was getting dark by the time they finished catching up. Helen was getting anxious about getting over to the warehouse. "Listen, I've enjoyed spending this time with you, but I have to get going. I'm sorry, but I'm supposed to meet someone in an hour."

Her dad gave her a big smile. "I understand, duty calls. Be safe out there." She came up out of her chair, bent and gave her dad a peck on the cheek. "I'll call you before you leave."

"I'll look forward to it. I love you!"

"Love you too, Dad!" And she was off! Carl watched as she walked out of the lanai and prayed that God would watch over her just as a gentleman came up to him, nice-looking man with similar features as Peyton, and knew it had to be his brother Mike whom he spoke with this morning.

Stacy hurried out of the restaurant to make a phone call to her partner. Peyton and Zack watched as she quickly walked past them and out the door. Zack looked over at Peyton. "Do you want to go for a ride?" he asked.

"Hell yes! Let's get out of here!"

Mike glanced at Helen as she flew by him. He could see where his brother could have easily been confused. He came up to the colonel and extended his hand. "Hi, Colonel Rayland?"

As they shook hands, "Call me Carl."

Mike smiled. "I'm Mike, Peyton's brother."

"I thought you might be. You look a lot alike."

Mike chuckled. "Wait till you meet my twin brother Mark! How was everything?" he asked.

"Mike, it was the best steak I have had in a long time, and I'm not just saying that. You and your brother have a beautiful restaurant here."

"Thank you, we appreciate the compliment. I hope I'm not imposing, but I was wondering if there was a possibility that you would retire Justice early?"

The colonel smiled. "Well, if you can keep a confidence, yes, I am. I didn't want to say anything to your brother, but if you could have him at the army base the day after tomorrow, I might just have a surprise for him." The colonel's eyes glittered as he revealed to Mike what he was hoping for.

Mike breathed out, relieved that his brother would soon have Justice by his side once again. With a grin on his face, he expressed, "Thank you, Carl. You don't know how much this means to all of us."

"Glad I could help, but keep it quiet," he said sternly.

"I won't say a word," affirmed Mike.

"Good!" he returned.

Mike spent a little time talking about his service days and working for General McCall, what the colonel did, and how they trained military dogs. Mike looked at his watch; it was getting late. Mike came up from the table and extended his hand. Carl also rose and shook Mike's hand. "It was good to meet you, Carl. I forgot to ask you what time you needed us at the base."

"It most likely will be in the afternoon. I will give you a call as to the time on Wednesday morning. The dog will need to be checked out with our vet before I can release him. I'll walk out with you. I need to get going as well."

Mike walked the colonel to the door, wished him goodnight, and said he was looking forward to his call. As Mike turned to start the closing process, he grinned. He couldn't wait to see the look on his brother's face when he would finally be reunited with Justice.

Stacy went back to her bungalow to change before she went out to the warehouse. She sent a text to Fred, her partner, to meet her out there in half an hour. She slipped into some dark jeans, paired with a black T-shirt. She let her hair down, then pulled it into a ponytail and slipped it under a ball cap with the logo "CSPD" embroidered on the front. She put her gun holster on and slid her nine-millimeter Glock inside. Her small revolver was safely tucked inside her boot. She grabbed one of her sweatshirt jackets and her flashlight. She checked her phone as she was heading out the door. No word from Fred yet. Well, she wasn't going to wait around. She sent him another text and left for the warehouse.

Zack and Peyton were sitting in a dark-blue van parked in the back area of the parking lot. They had a clear view of the warehouse. Zack had texted Mick. He was already parked in his dark-blue sedan farther down in the lot. Peyton glanced over at Zack and asked, "How do you know if Stacy is going to show up here?"

"According to Mick, she has the code to get inside the warehouse. She doesn't know that Mick is an undercover agent working for us on this case. My guess is her and her partner want to get into the computer in the office to see if there is any information that will lead them to the drugs destination. They have no idea yet that the drugs will never leave the island."

Zack and Peyton were alerted to car lights coming down the road. They eased down in their seats and watched as a red Charger pulled into a parking space two cars down. Peyton motioned to Zack. "That's her car."

"Nice, now let's see how Mick handles this. If he needs help, I'll back him up."

Zack and Peyton quietly watched as Helen got out of her car, looked around, and walked up to the door of the warehouse. She clicked on her flashlight and pointed it at the box to the right of the door, which lit up the numbers on the door lock. She lifted her hand to punch in the code when she heard a deep voice murmur, "Hoping to get some information out of the warehouse, Helen? Or should I say, Stacy?" Stacy froze. She knew that voice. How did he get her real name? Her heart started pounding as the rush of adrenaline coursed through her. Her reaction was instant. She turned and pulled her gun out at the same time facing Mick. Mick's reaction was quicker, as he expected her tactic. He grabbed her wrist and shoved it above her head against the wall. The gun dropped out of her hand. She fought him and swept her leg across his legs as he fell to the ground. Like lightning, she bent and grabbed her revolver from her boot and pointed the gun at Mick. On the ground Mick raised his hands.

"Don't move! Or you will regret it," she said with determination.

Helen felt a gun to her back. "Detective Zack Williams, from the police department. Drop it, Helen!"

Helen dropped her gun and raised her hands. Mick quickly got up and retrieved her guns. "Nice move, Helen, for a cop." Mick smiled.

Shocked, she asked, "How do you know I'm a cop?"

"Why don't we go inside and have a little chat; we're not going to hurt you. We just need to clear some things up."

Stacy lowered her hands. "Well, I guess I don't have a choice, now, do I?"

Zack placed his gun back into his holster.

Peyton, watching what was happening, couldn't stay in the van a minute longer. He got out just as Stacy turned and punched in the code to the door. The door opened and they all went in. Stacy turned on her flashlight. "Okay, now that we are all in here, explain," she said tersely.

"Look, Stacy—"

"How do you know my name?" she interrupted.

"Well, if you would let me explain, I will tell you!" Mick said sternly.

"Sorry, go ahead."

"I followed you to a coffee shop and overheard you and the two other gentlemen you were with discussing the same case the police and I are working on. I figured out from the conversation that all three of you are detectives for the state police working out of LA."

She stared at Mick in disbelief! "You're a cop?" she asked in surprise.

He put his hand out to her. "Special Agent Jason Hague out of Waco, Texas."

She hesitated before she took his hand and shook it.

"I've been working undercover with the detectives here at the police department for the last several months in Manchez's organization." He handed back Stacy's guns. "We already know when the drugs are going to arrive. They are never going to leave the island. What do you say, since you and the two other detectives are here, we work together and put this guy and his organization away?"

Peyton, standing by the door in the dark, saw light passing through the bottom of the door. "Hey, guys! Someone just drove in!"

"Peyton," Stacy said in surprise, "what are you doing here?"

"Yes, what are you doing here?" Mick asked impatiently.

Before he could answer, "He's with me," said Zack. "I'll explain later. Right now, we have a visitor we need to deal with."

Stacy turned her flashlight out. They all took flight and hid behind a boat or crate that was in the warehouse. Quietly, and on edge, they waited. Fred parked his car next to Stacy's. He looked over into her car. She wasn't in it. *Damn it all to hell!* he silently swore. He didn't see her text earlier. He should have known she wouldn't wait for him. She will get a good reaming out by the Lieutenant. Damn, he hoped she was okay. He got out of his car and looked around. No one seemed to be around. He pulled his gun, walked up to the door, and placed his ear next to the door. "Helen, are you in there?"

Stacy heard her partner's voice and breathed a sigh of relief! "It's my partner." She hurried to the door to let him in. Fred entered the building. He stopped. With his gun still raised, he saw several men in the background. "Put your gun away, Fred. We are all cops in here. Well…" She looked over where she thought Peyton was. "With the exception of one." Fred put his gun back in his holster. Stacy introduced him.

Mick spoke up, "Listen, I hate to break up this party, but we need to get out of here before someone else shows up. Stacy and I will continue to be undercover. The rest of you need to meet back at the police station and get a game plan together. Zack, get their phone numbers. He will then let you know when to meet. He also has the details when the drugs are going to arrive. I will keep him updated as we go along. Stacy, continue what you are doing. Be careful not to give anything away. If he senses at all you're not who you say you are, he'll have you taken out. Keep an eye out for Victor and watch your back. We're going to pray we all get out of this alive," expressed Mick. While Zack was getting their phone numbers and setting up a meeting time, Mick walked up to Peyton. "Sorry I was short earlier, Peyton. You took me by surprise."

"Hey, I understand," said Peyton. "When we have time, I'll give you all the sordid details."

"The way this case is going, it may have to be sooner than later."

"Just give me a text and I will meet you wherever," Peyton returned.

"Good, if you're game, I may need your help."

"Just say the word, and I'll be glad to help." Mick turned back to Zack. "Hey, Zack, are you all set?"

"Yes, we're ready to go."

"Okay, let's get out of here," said Mick.

They all carefully exited the building. Each one drove away, while Zack and Peyton stayed behind. "Is there a reason we are still here?" inquired Peyton.

"Yes," returned Zack. "I want to make sure no one followed us here."

They sat there for fifteen minutes and didn't see anyone else leave. Zack started the engine, pulled out, and took a left down through the parking lot. Based on what Mick had told him earlier, he wanted to make sure. "I don't mean to sound stupid, but what are we looking for?" asked Peyton.

"I have a hunch. And if I'm right…" He looked to his left as they passed a black Charger. "Bingo!" He drove up and turned his van around. By the time he righted it, the Charger pulled out and sped off. Zack slammed on the gas pedal and surged forward. He got close enough to get a license number. Zack tried to keep up, but when the driver hit the highway, he punched it and was gone. Zack got on the radio. "This is Detective Williams. We are on a high-speed chase down Highway Seven, heading south. I'm not able to keep up. The car is a 2018 black Dodge Charger, license number H10869. Be on the alert, the man may be armed!"

About fifteen miles down the road, several police cars had the black Charger surrounded. When Zack and Peyton pulled up behind the police car, they were just pulling the guy out of the car and frisking him. "Hey," he yelled, "I'm a cop! I work for the sheriff's department! My badge is in my wallet!" They took his wallet out of his pocket, while still holding him against the car. Zack came up behind him and showed the police officers his badge.

"Detective Williams, I made the call earlier. May I have his wallet?"

The officer turned over his wallet to him. As Zack looked inside, he found his badge and ID number, with his name Officer David Beckman of the sheriff's department. He folded it, nodded to the officer to let him go. He handed the wallet back to him. "Okay, Officer Beckman, I have a few questions for you. What were you doing out at the warehouse, and why did you take off the way you did when I passed your car?"

"I was put on to follow a Mick Southerland. I was told he could be mixed up with a drug deal that is going down here on the island. I followed him to the warehouse. I parked a ways down the road but was able to see him and you, and several others go into the warehouse. I pulled in with my lights out so no one would suspect I was following him. When you all came out and drove off, I didn't see the blue van leave. I waited, then when you drove past me I took off. I didn't know if you were one of the drug dealers, and I didn't have back up," he answered.

Zack shook his head. *Of all the damn things that could go wrong in this case, this one takes it*, he thought. "What were you supposed to do with the information?" he asked curtly.

"I was to report back to the captain, and he was to inform the troopers who are here from LA working on the case."

Suddenly Zack got it, three different departments working on the same case. "I will call your captain in the morning. You, and he, will meet me at the police station at ten a.m. tomorrow morning. We are going to need to unravel everything that's been going on with this case." With that said, Zack left and got in the van where Peyton was waiting.

"How'd it go?" asked Peyton.

Zack huffed and glanced over at Peyton. "In all the years that I have been on the police force, I have never been on a case where three departments are all involved, and none of us knew it until just now. I've set up a meeting with all the police officers involved, and with any luck, we'll figure this whole thing out and how to proceed going forward."

"Well, for what it's worth, I'm glad you found out now and not later. Mick mentioned he may enlist my help. Just let me know and I will do anything I can to help," he said with determination.

As Zack pulled out on the highway, "Thanks, Peyton, I appreciate the offer. When I enlisted your brothers to get Mick in Manchez's organization, they were a big help, and still are, considering that Manchez and his wife are frequent patrons at their restaurant. We'll see what kind of game plan we come up with and let you know."

"Just say the word, and I'm there."

Zack pulled up beside Peyton's SUV. As he was getting out, "Be safe going home, Peyton. We'll be in touch."

Peyton nodded and shut the door. As he watched Zack pull out, Peyton thought, *What a night*! He climbed into his SUV and started down the road to Mark's. He had no idea his night was going to turn out like this. Finding out Helen was a cop, and watching her in action, took his breath away. The police were involved in some pretty heavy stuff. He saw it for himself when he was working undercover for the special ops division in the military. The drug lords will stop at nothing to protect their property. He didn't like the thought of anything happening to Helen or any of the officers involved with the case. He needed to get in touch with her. He was sure she was capable, but he would do all he could to protect her if the need arose.

CHAPTER 9

The next morning at the police station, seven men were seated around the conference table, Lieutenant Ray Fillmore, Detectives Craig Jenson and Zack Williams of the police department, Lieutenant Kevin Andrew and Detective Fred Zealand out of LA, and Captain Jim Bowen and Officer David Beckman from the sheriff's department. Lieutenant Fillmore called the meeting to order.

"Thank you all for meeting us here at the station this morning. There seems to be a little bit of a mix up on the case the police department has been working on for the past several months and we want to clarify what has been going down on this particular case. Captain Bowen, you received a tip that a drug deal was going down on the island. Can you tell us where the tip came from?"

"Yes, it was from an anonymous caller. He called in to the department. It was very short and to the point. He informed us that a drug deal was going down and was headed for LA. I wasn't able to track the call due to the fact the message wasn't long enough."

"Is that when you contacted the LA police?" asked Lieutenant Fillmore.

"Well, at first I hesitated wondering if this was a legit tip. But several days later he called again. He said, 'Don't wait on this, time is of the essence.' So, that's when I called the troopers in LA to investigate," he replied.

"Lieutenant Andrew, what were you sent here on the island to uncover?" asked Ray.

"We were sent here to get information on when the shipment of the drugs were to arrive in LA. At which time we would intercede and confiscate the drugs and the perpetrators involved. We were able to get Detective Rayland undercover in the suspect's business as his secretary, hoping to get any information on the case," he answered.

"And what have you found out so far?"

"So far, Helen was able to get the code to the warehouse, plus"—he glanced over at Captain Bowen—"you have an officer in your sheriff's department who is suspected of working for Manchez. Fred and Helen were out at the warehouse over the weekend and saw him in the office putting information into the computer. When Helen got the code yesterday, she and Fred went to see if they could find out any information where the drugs were headed in LA last night. And as you know, so were most of you there," said the lieutenant, looking around the table.

Zack spoke up, "The officer in question is Ben Gillard. We had gotten a tip from one of Manchez's enforcers that he had an inside cop feeding him information on any of his new hires to make sure none of them were in law enforcement through our undercover agent, Mick Southerland. This man, Marco Manchez, will stop at nothing to protect his interest in his illegal drug trafficking and loan sharking businesses."

"Are you able to get any more information from this enforcer?" asked Detective Zealand.

"No, he's dead," said Lieutenant Fillmore. "Manchez had him taken out when he started screwing up. His hitman shot him right through the heart when he attacked a young woman. Her boyfriend turned to see where the shot came from, but the guy was gone. We have a description of the man who we feel did the shooting."

Zack got up, picked up a folder on the table, pulled out pictures of Marco Manchez and the man called Victor, and set each one in front of each officer. Lieutenant Fillmore went on to inform them, "The picture on your left is Marco Manchez, who we have been trailing for quite some time now. He is our suspect for illegal drug trafficking and loan sharking. The picture on your right is Manchez's hitman. His name is Victor Makaha. Mick has encountered him twice. He's very good at what he does and is considered very dangerous. Several homicides in the city, which we feel are connected to Manchez, have occurred, but we are not able to prove because we don't have enough hard evidence to arrest him. Zack, why don't you take it from here and explain what we are up against and see if between all of us we can come up with a game plan to nail this guy and his organization."

Zack stood up. "Okay, this is what we know so far through our undercover agent Mick Southerland. We discovered Manchez is involved with loan sharking and charging astronomical interest when they get behind on payments, which makes it hard for the victims to pay off the loan. We have witnesses that will testify to this. We know that drugs are being smuggled in and will be arriving at Manchez's warehouse sometime Friday evening to be placed on a ship early the next morning, headed to LA. He will be putting several guards on the outside of the warehouse, and two inside, along with Mick, who is to oversee the drug delivery and placement on the ship. Victor we know will be with Mick to make sure everything goes as planned. He's the one I'm most concerned with. Over the next several days we need to keep a close watch on Mick and Helen to make sure nothing happens to them. Manchez has a bead on every cop in the city. We have three men who have volunteered to help if we need them. Their names are Mike, Mark, and Peyton TreVaine. All three are experts in self-defense, and Peyton was a special ops ranger in the army. He may be able to give us some insight due to the fact that on several missions he went undercover to fight the drug cartel in Afghanistan. Now, what do you say about putting our heads together and figuring out how to intercede the drugs coming in and taking out the enforcers, then Manchez."

Everyone agreed and started working on a plan.

Peyton was out jogging along Waikiki Beach. He needed to clear his head after the night he had last night. He wanted to see Stacy again, but after he found out she was a cop and would be heading back to LA when the case was solved, he wasn't sure he should, and yet there was this attraction he had for her. She made him feel something he has never felt with a woman before. *Could there be a chance that we can work out a relation-*

ship with me being here and her in LA? he wondered. He really needed to talk to her. Tell her he understood why she had to deceive him in the beginning and not blow her cover. After seeing her in action last night, he smiled; she was one badass cop. He wondered what other moves she had up her sleeve. It made his heart start pumping just thinking about them. He remembered his night with her. She was so soft and vulnerable in his arms. He wanted more of that. He decided he would text her when he got back to Mark's. He was coming up on a petite brunette. As he approached her, he recognized it was Jenna.

"Hi, Jenna!" he exclaimed.

Jenna turned to see Peyton jogging up next to her. "Hi, Peyton," she answered out of breath. She slowed to a walk and Peyton followed suit. "How's it going?" she asked.

"Well, other than finding out Helen is a cop last night, I'm hanging in there."

Surprised, "Helen is a cop?"

"Yes, a detective out of LA, working on the same case as the police department. Mike didn't tell you?"

"I haven't seen Mike since yesterday afternoon. I had a dress fitting and went directly to my apartment after. That must have been a shock. So, her real name isn't Helen Grey?" she surmised.

Peyton looked around. He didn't see anyone around as he answered her. "No, it's Stacy Rayland. She's Colonel Rayland's daughter. At first I was a little pissed that she wasn't up front with me the other night, but I can understand why she did it. From what I have learned of the case so far, I'm worried about her safety."

"You have every right to be. This guy Marco Manchez will take out anyone, even his own men if he suspects foul play. He had his hitman take out Ralph right in front of your brother and I; it was the worst night of my life. I truly thought I was going to be raped or killed. If Mike hadn't showed up when he did…" Jenna shuddered.

Peyton stopped her. "Hey." He pulled her in for a brotherly hug, "Mark told me about what's been happening at the restaurant and that creep Ralph who assaulted you. We are all thankful, even though it was Manchez's hitman that took him out, that you are safe from him ever hurting you again! As far as I'm concerned, he got what he deserved."

"Thank you, Peyton. It still affects me at times. Even though I know he's gone, the nightmares come back to haunt me."

"I know what you are going through. I still have nightmares concerning my time in the military over in Afghanistan. It doesn't seem to go away."

"Was it hard to serve our country over there?" she asked.

He looked out over the distance, not really seeing anything when he answered, "There were days when I just wanted to give up, and then there were days when my team and I fought the Taliban and felt we were doing the best we could in keeping the freedoms we hold so dear to our hearts."

"I can't imagine, Peyton, what it must have been like over there, but know that your time spent serving our country was not wasted. I thank all the military men and women serving our country, fighting to keep us safe," she said sincerely.

"Thank you, Jenna. That means a lot."

"You're welcome." She smiled up at him. "I need to head back and get ready for work."

"I'll jog back with you." He smiled back. "I need to come up with a game plan for getting back in Helen's good graces. I'm afraid when I left her last night I was a little pissed at finding out who she was and wasn't able to talk to her later that night."

Jenna laughed. "Good luck with that!"

Helen, sitting behind her desk, starring at the computer, wondered what she was going to do about the situation with Peyton. She didn't have a chance to talk to him last night when they broke to leave. He didn't text her either, like she was hoping. Was he still upset with her? *Probably*, she answered herself. He didn't look happy when he found out she was a cop. And an out-of-state cop at that. Maybe she should text him, invite him over for dinner? There wasn't much they could do on the case until they came up with a plan. The lieutenant and Fred had a meeting this morning reviewing the case with two other police departments. She should know later on today what they came up with. Remembering when they made love together the other night left her tingling down in her lower abdomen. She wanted more of that before she left the island and beyond. Would there be a chance for a relationship? Just as she was thinking about texting him, the elevator door opened. Victor stepped up to her desk.

"Victor Makaha, to see Mr. Manchez," he stated. Helen peered up at the big, burly man, with his long black hair tied behind his thick neck, and the blackest eyes she had ever seen. When he had come into the office on several occasions, his body language always came off as daunting to her.

Helen looked down at her computer and opened up the appointment calendar on her computer screen. She scanned Marco's appointments for the day and didn't find his name. Her eyes went from the calendar on the screen to him. "I'm sorry, Mr. Makaha, but I don't see your name on his appointment calendar. May I ask what this is concerning?"

His body went ridged and his black eyes bore into her. "No you may not! I need to speak to him now!"

Well, okay… she thought irritably. She pushed the intercom button.

"Yes, Helen," Marco answered. "Mr. Makaha is here to see you. He's not on your appointment calendar." She looked up into those angry black eyes that kept staring at her. "He says it's important."

"Victor?"

"Yes, sir," she answered.

"Send him right in," Marco instructed.

She smiled. "You can go in now." Victor gave her a scathing look, turned, walked around her desk and into Marco Manchez's office, and slammed the door!

Marco glanced up from his desk as Victor came in looking like he wanted to kill somebody as he sat down in one of the chairs in front of his desk. "You really need to do something about that secretary out there! She is always giving me the third degree when I come in and I don't like it!"

Marco sat back in his chair and wondered what the hell has his hackles up. "Well, Victor, that's her job. I've instructed her to check the calendar to make sure there is an appointment or someone I have called in that's not on it. I don't know why that should upset you."

"There's just something about her that irritates me. She asks too many questions for my liking."

Marco leaned forward on his desk and took a deep breath. "What is so important that you needed to see me?" he asked sternly.

Victor knew he'd better calm himself. It wasn't a good idea to upset the boss. He blew out a breath and felt himself relax. "I have the information on this man you wanted checked out."

"Oh, yes," Marco answered. "What did you find out?"

"His name is Peyton TreVaine. He's an army vet and was deployed over in Afghanistan. He was just discharged recently and has no affiliation with any of the police departments. He is also Mark and Mike TreVaine's older brother."

"Ah, I thought he looked familiar. Good job, Victor. Is there anything else?" asked Marco.

"No, just wanted to keep you informed, sir. He doesn't impose a threat."

"Thanks, Victor. I'll be getting back to you later in the week."

Victor knew he was being dismissed. He got up, nodded his head, and exited out the door. When he saw Helen busy at her desk, he felt his muscles tighten. He may just do a little investigation on his own into Helen Grey, without the boss's permission!

Peyton was busy on the computer looking up aviation schools. He wasn't sure what he wanted to do with his life. He felt whacked out since becoming a civilian. He loved to fly, but he only flew helicopters in the army. Which gave him a thought, *Is there a need for helicopter pilots in the medical field?* His last tour took him, his team, and the medic team all over Afghanistan in search-and-rescue missions. He would look into it. He clicked on job opportunities in the area. He was amazed at all the jobs listed. He searched down through until he came to medical listings. When he saw the job for a helicopter pilot for the big island of Hawaii's hospital, he jotted down the number and the contact information and made the call. He wasn't able to get in touch with Dr. Sawyer but left his contact information with a brief outline of what his skills were and prayed he would get in touch with him soon. He needed something to do with his life; he hated being idle.

He thought of Stacy. Should he call her? Would she even talk to him after last night? He missed holding her and running his hands all over her beautiful, soft body. Just thinking about her aroused him. He decided to send her a text and hoped she didn't reject him. To be safe, he sent it via her undercover name: *Helen, we need to talk. Would you be willing to have dinner with me tonight, or go have coffee somewhere? Peyton.* He pushed send and set his phone back on the desk. He decided to get up and make himself a sandwich while he waited for her response. He hadn't eaten since breakfast, and it was well after three o'clock. He just bit into his sandwich when his phone dinged. He went over and picked up his phone to check his message,

My place? she responded.
What time?
7:00.

Perfect, I'll be there. Can I bring anything?

No, just you, she returned. Peyton smiled and sent her back a "smile emoji" sign. As he finished his sandwich, his thoughts wandered as to how the night might end. He couldn't wait.

Stacy finished what she needed to do on the computer and signed out. She was to meet the lieutenant and Fred shortly and needed to pick up a few things at the market for dinner tonight. She was looking forward to spending time with Peyton again. She decided to text Lieutenant Andrew to see if he would meet her and Fred at the International Market Place to discuss what happened in the meeting this morning. After the way Victor responded to her earlier, she felt this would be a safe place in case he decided to follow her. She would keep a close watch out for him. She texted Fred, *Hey, I texted Kevin and told him to meet at the International Market Place. After the exchange I had with Victor this afternoon, he may follow me.*

He responded, *I'm already on it. Sitting out in the parking lot. Was told he drove a black sedan, haven't seen him so far.*

She sent back, *Good, he was pretty angry at me when he left after speaking with Mr. Manchez. I'll be out shortly.*

He sent back a "thumbs up" sign.

Stacy gathered up her things and headed for the elevator. Marco Manchez came out of his office and locked his door. "Hold the elevator for me, Helen. I'll ride down with you."

Helen pushed the hold button and waited for him to join her. They both entered the elevator and the door closed. "Have you got any plans for this evening, Helen?" he asked.

"Nothing special, it's been a long day. Just want to pick up something for dinner and crash! How about you, Mr. Manchez? Any special plans for you?" she asked in return.

"I'm taking my wife Millie to our favorite restaurant for dinner tonight."

"Oh, where's that?"

"The Hawaiian Lanai. Have you heard of it?" he inquired.

"I have, I hear it is a very nice restaurant, and the food is excellent!"

"That it is!" he replied.

The elevator door opened, and Helen stepped out, with her boss directly behind her. They went out the door onto the busy sidewalk. "Well, goodnight, Mr. Manchez. You and your wife enjoy your dinner."

"Thank you, Helen. Goodnight."

Helen turned to cross the street and into the parking lot, where her car was parked. She saw Fred's car a few cars down from her. She nodded to him, opened her door, and slid in behind the wheel. She started the engine, backed up, and pulled out into the traffic. Fred waited ten minutes and watched for a black sedan in the area. When he didn't see one, he headed over to the marketplace to meet his partner and the lieutenant.

When Helen arrived at the marketplace, she picked up a basket and started strolling through the different vendors. Kevin was the first to arrive, followed by Fred a short time later. When they came in, they each picked up a basket, while Helen continued to look at the different fruits and vegetables the vendors had to offer. Helen had picked up a few items here and there when they met up by the tomato stand.

"How did it go this morning?" Helen asked nonchalantly.

"It went good," answered Kevin. "Went over a lot of information. Actually too much to discuss here. Can you meet us at my hotel in the morning around seven?"

She looked over at him with concern. "Were you and the other departments able to formulate a plan?" she asked.

"Yes, but it's going to require some outside help. Fred and I will fill you in tomorrow morning."

"Okay, I'll be there."

"Good, we'll see you then." They each finished up their shopping and checked out. Helen said goodnight and hurried back to her cottage to prepare dinner for her and Peyton.

When she arrived, she changed into jeans and a T-shirt, combed out her hair so it flowed down her back and shoulders. Took her glasses off and applied a lip gloss. She said the heck with the make-up and went into the kitchen to prepare their meal. She decided to make something quick and simple. Spaghetti, salads, and garlic bread should do. She put on a pot of water to boil when the doorbell rang. She rushed over to answer the door. When she opened it, there in the doorway stood Peyton, dressed in blue jeans and a dark T-shirt, handsome as ever holding a bottle of white wine. "Hi!" she greeted him breathlessly.

"Hi." His eyes devoured her as he continued, "My mother taught me to always bring something when you are invited to dinner."

She continued to stare at him. His eyes took her in, dressed in a V-neck T-shirt and jeans, her feet bare of any shoes, she couldn't look sexier if she tried. He raised his eyebrows and smiled. "May I come in?"

Helen came out of her trance. "Oh, I'm sorry. Please, come in." He stepped into the cottage and handed her the wine. She took it into the kitchen and placed it on the counter. She then went and took two wine glasses out of the cupboard and placed them next to the bottle of wine. When she found the corkscrew, she handed it to Peyton. "Would you do the honors?" she asked.

"Of course!" he replied. He took the corkscrew from her and proceeded to open the bottle, then poured them each a glass. He handed hers to her.

She took a sip. "Hmm, excellent!"

"Is there anything I can do to help with dinner?"

She set her wine down on the counter. "Well, I have the water boiling for the spaghetti. If you could put a couple of salads together and get the garlic bread ready for the oven, that would be a big help. Everything you'll need is in the refrigerator. I will throw the spaghetti in and get the meat sauce ready."

He grinned. "Sounds like a plan." They got to work, laughing and talking about different situations that happened over the course of their lives, and within an hour, they were sitting down at the table enjoying a traditional Italian dinner.

"This is really good, Helen." He stopped. "I'm sorry, what would you like me to call you when we are not out in public?" he inquired. "And I would also like to apologize for being a little put off when I found out who you really are."

She smiled as she gazed into his eyes; she couldn't get over how deep blue they were. She could tell he was being sincere. "I prefer that you continue to call me Helen for the time being. And I don't blame you for being angry with me. I should have been upfront with you from the beginning. It's just that you never know who could be listening. We don't know who all is involved with the case, and we must take all precautions."

"I understand. I have a meeting with Zack, along with my brothers, in the morning to go over the plan they want to implement. We will do all we can to help."

"I also have a meeting with the lieutenant and Fred in the morning. We were not able to discuss the plans tonight. I am anxious to find out how it will play out. If we only knew who the other guards are, it would help. We only know what Victor looks like, and by the way, Victor was pretty upset with me this afternoon. It's leaving me feeling a little uneasy."

Peyton took a sip of his wine and set it back down on the table. As he studied her, "What got him upset?" he asked.

"He came in to talk to Mr. Manchez, but he didn't have an appointment. So, I asked him what it was concerning, and he blew a nut! I let him back to see him, but he wasn't happy. He's Manchez's hitman. He can be a little intimidating to say the least," she explained. "I know if he were to come at me physically, I wouldn't be able to take him down on my own."

"Oh, I don't know, Helen. You did a pretty good job of handling Mick last night." He grinned.

She laughed. "Mick's a pretty big guy, but Victor has another fifty pounds on him! I know my capabilities. Not going to happen, not without backup."

As he listened to her, he was also concerned. He hadn't got a look at Victor, but from what he was hearing, he was big, and when he took out a hit, he could become stealth-like, and disappear with no one the wiser. He was a dangerous man. It left him feeling a bit on edge as well. "Well, we should both know more in the morning. How about we don't talk shop and enjoy the rest of our evening."

"Sounds good to me. Would you like some coffee if I made it?" she asked.

"I would drink a cup, but don't make it just for me. I'm happy with the wine."

"Okay, just let me clear these dishes away and we can relax in the living room." Helen got up from the table and started picking up the dishes to take to the sink.

Peyton followed suit. "Let me help you. The quicker we get this done, the sooner we can relax." It didn't take them long before they had everything cleaned up and put away. They picked up their wine glasses and the bottle of wine and headed for the living room.

Peyton refilled their glasses and set the bottle on the coffee table. They both sat down on the sofa. "Have you had any luck deciding on what career path you'd like to take?" asked Helen.

"Funny you should ask that question. I was on the internet this afternoon, in the want ads section, and came across a job listing for a helicopter pilot for a hospital on the big island of Kona. I wasn't able to speak to the person in charge but left a message with my contact information. It sounds like something I would enjoy, so I'm hoping to hear from him soon."

"Wow, that's great, Peyton. I wish you luck!"

"Thanks."

"What about you, Helen?" he asked. "What are your plans when this is all over? Are you going to have to head back right away, or is there a chance you might stay a little longer?" He really wanted her to stay, to see if there was anyway a relationship between them would work. Staring into her hazel eyes with questioning eyes of his own, he found himself holding his breath as she answered him.

"I do have some vacation time coming. I mentioned it to my dad that he and Mom should come over to the island and we could spend some time together. I haven't run it by the lieutenant yet. He may want me to go back to LA after the case is solved. I would like to stay and get to know you better, but how would this work, Peyton? My job is in LA."

"Somehow it will work out." Peyton looked into her eyes with growing passion. He set his glass down on the table and patted the seat next to him. He wanted her in his arms again.

Helen couldn't look away. She was mesmerized by those eyes of his, filled with intensity she couldn't describe. She wanted to get close, but should she? She didn't know yet if she would be leaving after the case was wrapped up, or if she would be able to stay a little longer. Peyton could see she was hesitant. "Helen, I know what you are feeling. We both know you will be leaving sometime in the future. Let's just take this one day at a time and see where this leads. I'm attracted to you, and no other woman has made me feel the way you do when you are in my arms."

Helen could feel herself melt. She didn't want to resist him. More than anything she wanted those arms around her, holding her close. She could easily fall for this man, but could she walk away as she became more involved with him? Her brain is telling her to stop before it's too late, but her heart is telling her to go for it and see what happens. When she came up next to him, he pulled her down onto his lap, wrapped his arms around her, and just held her. She laid her head on his chest. "Peyton."

"Hmm?"

"I'm not sure this is a good idea…" She lifted her head and gazed into his eyes, and her heart stopped. He bent his head to kiss those soft lips of hers, then another. He trailed his lips across her cheek until he reached the sensitive spot behind her ear. Then she was lost. He came back to her lips. His kisses became more passionate, and she returned those kisses with her own pent-up passion. His hands started roaming her body till he found her hard nipple through her T-shirt. His thumb circled and teased until Helen groaned and started her own exploration. Her hand went under his shirt to his hard chest. She could feel his heart thundering underneath her hand. Peyton broke the kiss long enough to pull his shirt off and then hers. He unclasped the lacy bra, which opened in the front, brushing it aside. His eyes took in the fullness of her breasts. His hand went up to cup one of her breast and then the other before his mouth came down to suckle each one. "Peyton…" she whispered; her fingers wove through his hair, holding him there as he continued to give her the pleasure she was seeking. His hand moved down her belly to undo her jeans. He slid his hand around her hips and the jeans and panties came off. His hand roamed her body and touched her sensitive areas till she could stand it no longer. She wanted him inside her now!

He raised his head. "Do you want to finish this here or in the bed?" he groaned.

"It will be more comfortable in the bed," she breathed. He raised her up and carried her back to the bedroom. He laid her down on the bed and quickly finished undressing. He pulled a condom out of his wallet and slipped it on. His eyes devoured her as he gazed from her pretty hazel eyes to her abdomen. Helen explored his body with her own eyes and couldn't wait for him to be inside her. She needed to feel his hard muscles on top of her. "Now, Peyton," she breathed.

He arched one eyebrow and smiled. "You are an impatient one, aren't you?"

"Yes." She raised herself up and pulled him down upon her. With her heart beating wildly, "I'm impatient for you." She pulled his head down and ran her tongue over his lower lip, and he opened for her and kissed her deep. He finally gave her what she wanted, but not before he tortured her with his lips and hands. He entered her with one deep thrust and took them on a ride of shear ecstasy that neither one of them had expected. With their hearts beating wildly they both cried out when they climaxed. Peyton shuddered as he came down to rest on her soft body. When they were both able to catch their breath, he rose up on his arms and gave her a gentle kiss.

"You are one incredible woman," he said softly. "You light a fire in me."

"And you are one extremely hot man whom my body burns for," she whispered softly. As she looked into his blue eyes, she knew without a doubt she was falling for him. *How will I be able to leave him?* she wondered.

"I need to get up, I'll be right back," he said and gave her a quick kiss.

When he got up to take care of himself, Helen lay there and tried to think of what she should do. She didn't think long when she thought she heard a noise outside her window. As she lay there listening, she heard it again. She quietly got out of bed, and since her clothes were out in the living room, she went to her dresser drawer and pulled out some panties, a T-shirt, a pair of sweatpants. She quickly got dressed. Peyton, coming out of the restroom, was surprised that she had dressed. He was just about to say something when she put her finger to her mouth for him to be quiet and pointed over to the window. He went to grab his boxers and jeans and slipped them on. As he was getting dressed, they both heard the noise again. Stacy grabbed her gun from the nightstand and silently walked over to the window. Peyton was right behind her.

Helen pulled the curtain slightly back. She couldn't see anything. There it went again! It sounded like something rustling in the bushes outside the window. Peyton moved her slightly so he could take a look. He looked down toward the ground, when suddenly a mongoose came out of the bush and scurried off toward the road. He breathed a sigh of relief! "It's all right, it was only a mongoose."

Helen, relaxing, said, "Oh, thank God! For a minute there I thought Victor might be out there spying on us."

After the ordeal she had with him this afternoon, it

wouldn't surprise her. Peyton turned her around to face him. "No worries, but just in case, I'm going out to take a look around and make sure he's gone."

"Okay, let me know if you see anything else," she replied.

"Can I borrow your gun?" he asked.

"I'm not able to give you this one, but I have a small revolver in the drawer you can take." She went to retrieve it and handed it to him. "The safety is on," she informed him.

"Got it." He wasn't familiar with the layout of her bungalow since he had only been in the kitchen, living area and her bedroom, so he asked, "Where is your back entrance?"

"Come, I'll show you." They walked out of her bedroom, with Peyton following her past the kitchen. Down the hallway, was a laundry room on the left with the back door straight ahead. "Stay inside, I'll be right back. Lock the door." When he went out, she locked the door behind him.

Outside, Peyton stood for a moment to let his eyes adjust to the darkness. When he was in Afghanistan, he was used to finding his way in the dark when he was on secret missions. He crept around the side of the house where the mongoose had come out of. He kicked at the bushes to make sure there wasn't another animal in there. All was clear. He crept up to the side of the porch and took a look around the front yard and across the street. Off the side of the road, there sat a black sedan. He got down on his haunches and watched. He couldn't see if anyone was sitting in the car due to the dark tint on the windows. He got up and crept around the back to the other side of the bungalow. He didn't see anyone lurking about. He went back to the door and knocked softly. Helen let him in and relocked the door. She was just about to say something when he put his fingers to his lips. He went over to the counter, where he pulled a pen and paper out of the drawer and scribbled something on to it.

Helen's eyes got big as she read what was written. She looked up at him and mouthed, *Victor?* After their heated encounter this afternoon, it could very well be him. Peyton grabbed the paper and scribbled something else. He handed it back to her. She nodded her head yes. They went throughout the house and shut off all the lights.

"You go on back to bed. I'll sit by the window and keep watch," he whispered.

"No way. I will sit by the other window and keep watch with you," she whispered back. "Do you have your cell phone?" she asked.

"Yes, it's in my pocket." He pulled it out. "I'll text Mark and let him know what's going on. Maybe he can get ahold of Zack to send a car out."

She nodded her head yes. While Peyton texted his brother, Helen went over to the window, slightly pulled the curtains back, and peered out to see if there was any movement outside. Peyton was right. The black sedan was sitting directly across the street, off the side of the road. She didn't know if he could be legally parked there. If Zack could send out a patrol car, it might scare him off.

Mark was relaxing in front of the TV watching a game, drinking a beer, when he heard his phone ding with a message. He pulled his phone out and saw it was from his brother. As he read the message, he instantly became alert. *Mark, I* am over here at Helen's. There is a black sedan parked across the road in front of her house. We think it might be Victor but not sure. Can you alert Zack and see if he can send a patrol car out to cruise the area? Do not come out! We are both fine. We will keep watch. Peyton.

Mark immediately pulled up Zack's number and made the call.

"Detective Williams," he answered.

"Zack, we have a problem."

"What's going on?"

Mark explained Peyton's text.

"Can you confirm her address?"

Mark swore. "No, but I will get it and text it right back to you," he anxiously replied.

"Good, I'll have a car waiting." Mark ended the call and texted Peyton back requesting the address. When it came back, he forwarded it to Zack. He sent another text to his brother, *Please keep me informed. I don't want anything to happen to you or Helen.*

No worries, I'll keep in touch, returned Peyton.

Peyton slipped his phone back into his pocket. He glanced over at Helen, who was still standing by the window, peering out. He walked up to her. "Have you seen any action yet?" he whispered.

"Not yet. Did you get ahold of your brother?"

"Yes. He was able to get ahold of Zack and they're sending a car out."

"Good, let's hope they're quick!" Stacy continued to watch. The black sedan had dark tinted windows which made it hard to see if anyone was still in the car. Maybe it was someone visiting in one of the other bungalows and they were stressing for nothing. Peyton strolled back over to the other side of the room. He pulled the curtain back slightly so he could take a look at the situation. He immediately became alert when he saw the car door open and a man come up out of the car. He looked around before he started walking towards the door. Peyton raised the revolver near the window, ready to defend them if needed. He glanced over at Helen who was also poised to take him out. Just as he reached the door, a police car with his lights on came up behind his car.

Son of a bitch, Victor silently swore. He turned around and walked up to the officer who was getting out of his car.

"Are you the owner of this car?" ask the officer.

"Yes, sir."

"Can I see your driver's license and registration please."

"Yes, sir." Victor pulled out his wallet and gave the officer his license. He climbed into his car, where he pulled the registration out of the glove box and handed it to the officer.

"Stay in your car, I'll be right back." The officer returned to his car and typed in Victor Makaha's name and license number into his computer. The guy came back clean. The officer came out of his car and walked up to the window of the sedan. He handed Victor back his license and registration. "Mr. Makaha, you are illegally parked."

"I'm sorry, officer. I was just coming from some friends of mine's home. I wasn't parked here long."

"Well, however long it was, you shouldn't park on the side of the road," he said sternly. "I'm going to let you off with a warning this time, but if I see your car here again, you will be ticketed."

Victor breathed a sigh of relief. "Thank you, officer." Victor started his car and slowly drove off.

The officer waited till his taillights were out of sight before he turned his police lights off. He pulled into Helen's drive, got out of his car, and walked up to the door. He knocked. Helen pulled the door open, with Peyton right behind her.

"Hi, I'm Officer Brown. I got a call from Zack to come out to check on the black sedan sitting out off the side of the road. His name is Victor Makaha. Do either of you know this man? He said he was a friend of yours."

"Officer Brown, why don't you come inside and we will explain everything to you," suggested Helen.

Officer Brown came inside and took a seat at the end of the couch. Helen and Peyton sat down across from him and explained who Victor was. "I'm afraid I upset him this afternoon with questioning him."

"So, this Victor, he works for Marco Manchez?" asked Officer Brown.

"Yes, he's Marco's hitman. My lieutenant, partner, and I have been working on this case. We are very close to breaking this case wide open. We don't need anyone in his organization to suspect I'm a cop working undercover."

"I understand. I am somewhat familiar with the case. I was called to watch a woman and her friend one night several months ago. From what I've heard, I'm pretty sure that this Victor character took the man out that was harassing her," he returned.

Peyton spoke up, "Yes, that was my future sister-in-law, Jenna, and her friend Sasha. My brother was there the night Ralph was killed. It's all connected to the case the department is working on as we speak."

"Yes, from what I have heard, this man is extremely dangerous. When I ran his information through the computer, he came back clean. I had nothing I could arrest him for. I'm sorry. I wish I could have been more help."

"Just getting here as quickly as you did was a big help. I'm sure he wasn't expecting a cop to come around or he wouldn't have risked coming here tonight," answered Helen.

He had to smile as he rose to come up off the couch. "I need to file this report. I'm working the night shift tonight. I'll swing by this area several times on my shift to make sure he doesn't come back around. Try to get some sleep." As he headed for the door, he turned. "I'll make sure Zack is informed as to what took place tonight."

Peyton and Helen followed him to the door. As Helen opened the door for him, "Thank you again, Officer Brown, for getting here so quickly," she said sincerely.

"You're welcome." He nodded his head and left.

"That was close. Victor was definitely going to try and break in. What do you think he wanted to accomplish with both of us here?" she asked Peyton.

"Well." He sighed. "With the lights out, he might have wanted to bug the place to try and get information on you. Speaking of which, we need to canvass this place to make sure it hasn't already been done, plus your car." Helen and Peyton got to work. They didn't find anything in the bungalow, but they did find a GPS device underneath her back bumper. Peyton took it off.

"Let's go back inside and decide what we need to do."

Helen led the way, and when they were inside, "Well," he said, "finding this device on your car means he definitely wants to track you. He's going to be pissed when he finds out it's no longer there. Which could come back and bite us."

"You're right, Peyton. If he is trying to find out who I am and what I'm doing after work hours, it will raise his suspicions about me if it's not there. Let's put it back on my car. I will only drive it to work and back. Do you think you can take me to my lieutenant's hotel in the morning and drive me back here? Then I will go into the office."

"What time do you need to meet in the morning?" he asked.

"At seven a.m."

"That should work out. I'm meeting my brothers and Zack at ten."

"Perfect."

Peyton went outside and placed the device back on Helen's car where they found it. He checked his car just to be safe. When he came back inside, Helen had a concerned look about her. "I need to let the lieutenant know what happened tonight."

"Look, Helen, it's late. You have an early morning meeting with the lieutenant and your partner, and I have a meeting with Zack and my brothers. We can let them know then. Let's take the officer's advice and try to get some sleep. I'll bunk on the couch so if he comes back and tries to break in, I'll be sure to hear him."

"Okay, you're right." She went back to her bedroom to find a pillow and a blanket. She came back out and handed them to him. "Are you sure you want to do this?" she asked. "I'm not sure how comfortable this couch is. I doubt Victor will be back tonight. With him getting caught outside my rental, I don't think he'll take that chance."

Peyton came up to her, took the pillow and blanket from her, and set them on the couch. His eyes told her that on no uncertain terms was he leaving. "I'm staying. I'm not going to leave you alone with the chance that he might be back, especially when he would just as soon shoot you as look at you. Go to bed. I'll be fine. I've slept on worse, trust me."

Helen came up to him and gave him a kiss on the cheek. "Thank you for being here with me." She searched his eyes as he bent his head to touch his lips to hers. The kiss soon turned to passion. Before he went too far, he lifted his head. He smiled.

"You're welcome. Now get to bed."

She grinned. "Yes, sir." Something caught her eye as she turned to leave for her bedroom. She bent down to pick up her bra that was halfway under the couch. She dangled it in front of Peyton. She laughed. "Do you think Officer Brown saw this?"

Peyton laughed with her. "I think that might be a strong possibility!"

CHAPTER 10

The next morning, Peyton dropped Helen off at the hotel. "I'll text you when I'm ready to be picked up. It shouldn't be more than an hour to an hour and a half."

"Okay, I'll head over to the coffeehouse we passed by on our way here. Would you like me to pick you up something?" he asked.

"Just a cup of strong black coffee would be great." She got out of the car and headed for the entrance to the hotel. Peyton watched as she entered the hotel where the lieutenant and her partner were staying. When she was safely inside, he turned the car onto the street and headed for the coffeehouse.

When he entered, the coffeehouse was already busy with customers lined up to have their order taken. While he stood in line, he looked around. At one of the tables, there was a woman that looked very familiar to him. She had a little girl sitting with her. She had the same light brown hair and amber eyes as her mom. It suddenly dawned on him that it was Tammy, one of the waitresses that worked at his brother's restaurant. He moved on down the line. The waiter took his order. When it was ready and paid for, he stepped over to her table. "Hi, Tammy. I don't know if you remember me. I'm Peyton TreVaine, Mike and Mark's brother."

Tammy looked up surprised. "Yes, I remember you, I waited on you!" She smiled. "I remember I gave you my pen to use."

He grinned. "Yes, you did. And who is this pretty little lady?" he asked, smiling down at the little girl.

She looked down at her daughter and back up to him. "This is my daughter, Bethany. We always come here to have breakfast before we head to school."

Bethany grinned up at him. "I like their hot chocolate and bagel with cream cheese. It's really good. You should try it!"

"Well, that sounds like a good choice." He noticed that she was missing her two front teeth when she smiled. "Next time I'm here I'll be sure to order it! Well, I won't take up any more of your time. It was nice seeing you again, and meeting you, Bethany."

"Thank you. We hope to see you again!" cried Bethany.

Peyton went over to one of the empty tables that were available but not before he heard, "He's a nice man, and so handsome," she said to her mom.

Surprised, her mom looked down at her six-year-old and wondered that her child would even notice whether he was handsome or not. She gazed down at her daughter. "Yes he is, sweetie." She smiled back.

Peyton had picked up a local news magazine to read, then sat down at the empty table while he waited for Helen. He was just into an article and enjoying his pastry and coffee when a shadow fell over him. He looked up to a large man with a balding head and beady black eyes and knew he was staring into the eyes of Marco Manchez.

"Good morning, Peyton."

Instantly alert, *How did he know my name?* he wondered.

Marco held out his hand to shake. "I'd like to introduce myself. I'm Marco Manchez. My wife and I are frequent patrons of your brother's restaurant."

Peyton shook his hand.

"Do you mind if I join you?" he asked.

Peyton shook his head. "Have a seat, Mr. Manchez."

As he took a seat, "Call me Marco. Mr. Manchez is so formal."

"Okay, Marco. Can I ask you something?"

"Shoot," he replied.

"How do you know me? I don't remember either one of my brother's mentioning you to me." Peyton decided to play dumb and see what kind of information he could get from this guy.

He stumbled a little bit when he answered. "I was in your brother's restaurant last night. Mark and I got to talking and he mentioned that you had recently been discharged from the army. So, you served over in Afghanistan. It must have been a hard tour."

"It wasn't easy." *Still didn't answer my question. Did he see me with my brothers' to recognize me?*

"I can't imagine. I never served in the military. I wished I had. It might have changed my perspective on life. Made me a better man."

"You don't see yourself as a better man?" asked Peyton.

Marco shrugged his shoulders. "I don't see myself as a bad man, but I might have done things a little differently."

"What do you do for a living, Marco?"

"Oh, I'm into a little bit of everything. I own two sporting goods stores and a marina. I also have a finance company," he replied.

"Sounds like you keep yourself pretty busy."

"Yes, but I'm considering retiring. You don't know of anyone who would like to buy a couple of sporting goods stores and a marina, do you?"

Peyton chuckled. "Sorry, Marco, I don't. But if I hear of anyone interested, I'll be sure to let you know." Peyton's phone dinged with an incoming text. He pulled it from his pocket and read the text. "I'm sorry, Marco, I have to run." He slipped his phone back into his pocket and came up out of his chair. He extended his hand to Marco. "It was nice meeting you, Marco. Have a good rest of your day."

Marco shook his hand. "You do the same."

Peyton left the coffeehouse feeling a little bit on edge. First, Victor shows up at Helen's last night. Then this morning, Marco just happens to come into the very coffee house he was at? Were they being followed or was it just a coincidence? It bothered him that he knew his name, and his time serving in the army. He would ask his brothers in the meeting this morning if what Marco told him was true.

Peyton pulled up in front of the hotel when it hit him: he had forgotten Helen's coffee. Helen was outside, ready to get into the SUV. She opened the door and slid in. She looked over at him. "Sorry. The meeting lasted longer than I thought. We're going to have to hurry if I am to be to work on time. Um, did you remember my coffee?" she inquired, looking around the coffee cup holders in the SUV.

Peyton started to pull out, but not before he canvassed the area for the black sedan he saw last night. All was clear so far as he pulled out into the traffic. He kept watch in his rearview mirror as they headed for Helen's bungalow. "I'm sorry, Helen. I ran into your boss this morning. When I got your text, I hurried out and completely forgot it," he apologized.

Helen glanced over at him surprised. "Marco Manchez? You're kidding, right?"

"Nope. I was sitting at a table, enjoying my coffee, when he came right up to me and introduced himself. The odd thing is, I've never met the guy, but he seemed to know a lot about me."

"What are you thinking?" she asked.

"I don't know, Helen. I'm concerned. He told me him and Mark had a conversation about me. The only reason I recognized who he was is I was sitting with the detectives one night when he and his wife came into the restaurant. I was never introduced to him. It leaves me wondering. I'll be talking with my brothers this morning to see if his story holds."

"I'd be interested in hearing what transpires. I have a feeling you've been checked out. Just a heads up, I don't have time to go into all the details of the sting operation, but you and your brothers are involved. As you know, Zack will be filling you in on all the details."

Peyton pulled into Helen's driveway and put the vehicle in park. He turned to Helen. "Just so you know, we will do all we can to put this guy and his organization away. I know you're a good cop, and you've had your share of dangerous cases, but know that along with the rest of the law enforcement, I'll have your back. I care about you, Helen. I would like to explore a relationship with you, if it's even possible in this crazy world we live in."

Stacy stared into his eyes and wanted nothing more than to do the same, but she just didn't know. After her meeting with Lieutenant Andrew and her partner this morning, this was going to be one of the most dangerous missions they have ever been on, bar none. "Let's get through this, then we'll talk. I like you a lot. You make me feel things I haven't felt in a long time." She leaned in and gave him a sweet kiss. "I need to get going. I'll see you after work?"

"Just text me to let me know what time, I'll be there."

She opened the door and quickly got out and into hers. She gave a wave and was off. He watched her drive away until she was out of sight. He sighed. He put his SUV into drive and headed for the police station. He would see what it's going to take to lock this case up.

At the station, Peyton was greeted by one of the sergeants on duty. "Are you Peyton TreVaine?"

"Yes, sir."

"Follow me," he stated. The sergeant led him back to a conference room, where Zack, Lieutenant Fillmore, and his brothers were seated around the conference table. Peyton greeted the men, then went and sat down next to his brother Mark. Lieutenant Fillmore started the meeting. "Thank you, gentlemen, for coming down to the station this morning. As you know, we've been working on this case for quite some time, and it's now coming to a head. If you're willing, all departments involved have come up with a plan. We would like to incorporate you three men to help in the sting operation. I'm not going to lie to you, It's going to be dangerous. We're dealing with men who are experts in sharp shooting. One in particular is Victor Makaha. Peyton, I know from you serving in the special ops division that you as well are an expert shot."

"Yes, sir. I've taken out several hits while on missions overseas, but I'll be honest, I never felt good about it."

"Do you own a gun?" asked the lieutenant.

"I own a rifle, which I purchased shortly after arriving here on the island for hunting, but not a handgun," he answered.

"How about you guys?" the lieutenant glanced over at Mike and Mark.

Mark spoke up, "We both have a concealed weapons license for our handguns. I can't speak for Mike. We leave the restaurant late at night, and with the crime rate, I personally keep it with me at all times."

"Mike?" he asked.

"I keep it in my glovebox in the car. Probably not the smartest thing to do, but I tend to handle things with my fists." He smiled. They all chuckled.

"Yes, well, from what I've heard from your encounter with Ralph, you are very good with your fists, but how are you two at shooting your guns?" asked the lieutenant.

"We are both out at the gun range when we get the chance. You don't have to worry, we'll hit our target," answered Mike.

"Good. Peyton, you'll need to get a handgun. Bring it to the station and get it registered. With the plan we want to implement, you will all have to be armed and ready, due to the fact that the suspects will all be armed as well and considered extremely dangerous," informed the lieutenant. "Zack, why don't you take it from here and explain what we are up against."

Zack took a folder from the conference table and opened it. He handed two pictures to each of the three brothers. "The picture on your left is Marco Manchez, whom all of you know. The one on your right is Victor Makaha, one of Manchez's hitmen. He and several others, along with Mick Southerland, our undercover agent, will be at the warehouse on Friday to intercept the drugs and place them on a ship headed for LA."

Peyton spoke up. "Sorry, I don't mean to interrupt, but you know, this guy Victor was staking out Helen's last night."

"Yes, Officer Brown gave me an update as soon as he left Helen's place."

Mike felt his phone vibrate and pulled his phone out of his pocket. When he saw who was calling, he rose from the table. "Sorry, I've been expecting this call. Please excuse me for just a moment." Mike stepped out of the conference room and answered the call.

Back in the conference room, Zack turned to Peyton. "Just so you know, Peyton, we have an officer on surveillance at her place until this is over."

"Good. Also, I don't know if this means anything, but I ran into Manchez this morning at a coffeehouse near where Lieutenant Andrew and her partner Detective Fred Zealand are staying. I had dropped Helen off at the hotel because we found a GPS device on the back of Helen's car. After Officer Brown left, we searched the house for bugs and then her car. We're pretty sure Victor placed it there."

"What did you do with it?" asked Zack.

"We put it back. I was going to destroy it, but we both thought to leave it. Victor was pretty upset with Helen when he left the office yesterday. Helen is only going to drive the car to work and back so he can't track her every move. I'm pretty sure that's how he found out where she lived."

"I'm guessing you're right," replied Zack.

"What did Manchez have to say when you ran into him?" asked Lieutenant Fillmore.

"Well, I was sitting there having coffee when he came right up to me and introduced himself. He knew my name and the time I served overseas." He turned to his brother Mark. "When I asked him how he knew me, he said you and he talked when he was in the restaurant for dinner last night."

Mark shook his head and shrugged his shoulders. "I seated him and his wife Millie at their table, but I never mentioned you to them."

He looked back at the lieutenant. "Helen was right, he had me checked out, but why?"

"Hey, I just remembered something."

Peyton turned back to his brother, "When you were with the detectives a few weeks ago, Manchez and his wife had come into the restaurant, and I remember he did ask about you, if you were new on the force. I just told him your first name. That you had just got back from overseas, nothing else."

"That could be why he had me checked out," answered Peyton. It still left him on edge.

Mike came in from answering his phone call and took his seat. "Did I miss anything?"

"No, we'll fill you in later. Just a personal matter," informed Peyton.

"Let's get back to our discussion and the plan we want to implement to intercept the drugs, and finally put Manchez and his organization away. This isn't going to be easy, and it has to go like clockwork or we could all lose our lives. If after we go over the plan with you three men and you feel it is too risky to be involved, we'll understand," stated Zack.

"Let's hear it," answered Mike.

Zack and Lieutenant Fillmore went over everything involved with the plan, then looked in the eyes of all three men. "Well, men, what do you say? Are you in?" asked the lieutenant.

All three brothers looked at each other, turned back to the lieutenant, in union they all said, "I'm in!"

When the meeting broke, Mike pulled Peyton aside. "Hey, bro. The call I took this morning was from Colonel Rayland. He has some news about Justice that he wanted you to know."

Peyton's heart started to pound. He hoped nothing happened to his dog. "Did he say what it was about? Is Justice okay?"

Mike saw the fear in his brother's eyes and felt bad about not letting his brother know what was about to happen. "He didn't say, but he also didn't sound like anything bad had happened. He needs you to meet him at the base at one o'clock today. Is that possible?"

"Yes, Mike, yes! I'll meet him there. I just hope he doesn't have bad news for me. I was so hoping that Justice would be home with me soon."

"Try not to worry, bro. I'm sure Justice is fine."

"I hope so. He still has a few months before the army will retire him. I hope he wasn't wounded or killed in the line of fire...."

Mike put a hand on his shoulder. "Hey, if it would have been bad news, the colonel would have told me. Try not to stress until you meet with him. I have to meet Jenna at a bakery for a cake tasting. You wouldn't want to tag along, would you?"

"No thanks, bro. I'm going to head back to Mark's. I applied for a helicopter pilot's job on the big island of Kona for the hospital there. I need to see if Dr. Sawyer responded to my email."

As they were walking out of the police station, "That sounds like a job right up your alley. I'll send up a prayer for you to land it. Let me know how it goes with the colonel this afternoon."

"I will. I'll stop into the restaurant after I meet with him and let you know what's going on."

"Good. And in the meantime, try not to stress!"

Jenna and Mike sat at a table looking at five selections of cake. "I don't know which one to try first! They all look delicious!" Jenna exclaimed.

"Let's try the Swiss chocolate, that's one of my favorites," commented Mike. Mike cut a small piece and placed it in Jenna's mouth. Then he took a bite.

"Hmm, this is good." Jenna nodded her head yes while chewing her piece. "Let's try the lemon supreme next," offered Jenna. They both took a bite. It was okay, but not what they wanted. They tasted the next three, and decided the vanilla bean was the best choice for the wedding cake and the Swiss chocolate would be the groom's cake.

After they picked out what they wanted for the cake designs, Mike looked at his watch. "I think we better head over to the base. We need to be there a little bit before Peyton gets there. Mark said he would meet us over there."

As they left the bakery, Jenna took Mike's arm and looked up into those blue eyes of his and grinned. "I can't wait to see the look on your brother's face! It'll be epic!"

Peyton, sitting in front of Mark's laptop, *I really need to get one of my own*, was checking out the email he had sent yesterday for the job at the hospital on the big island. Dr. Sawyer had indeed responded and wanted to set up an interview as soon as possible. He returned his email and stated he would be available anytime except for Friday, which is when the sting operation would take place. He got up to make himself some lunch while he waited to see if he would get a response back from him. He had about an hour before he had to head to the base to meet the colonel. He prayed it was good news and not bad. He quickly ate his sandwich and drank down a cup of coffee. He went back to the computer to check the email he had sent. Dr. Sawyer responded with a two p.m. appointment for the next afternoon. Peyton sent back a reply that he would be there. With that sent, he headed over to the base to see what news the colonel had on Justice.

Mark, Mike, and Jenna were talking to the colonel while they waited in anticipation for Peyton to arrive. Mike turned toward the Colonel. "I'm afraid I might have given my brother a scare when I told him to meet you here," he said, chuckling.

"Well, it won't be long, your brother should be here any minute," he returned. "The airman has had a time with Justice this morning. After the vet checked him out, he has been full of nervous energy. I think he senses something is about to happen."

"I can't wait to see him!" cried Jenna.

"Don't look now," responded Mark as he was looking out the window of the message center. "Here he comes now."

Colonel Rayland took out his phone and sent a text. "Okay, let's go meet your brother."

Peyton pulled up in front of the message center and climbed out of his SUV. As he was walking up to the door, he was literally shaking inside, wondering what the colonel was going to tell him. As he neared the door, out came Mark, Mike, Jenna, and the colonel. Now he was panicking! With a look of surprise and fright on his face, he asked, "What are all of you doing here? You have bad news, I know it!"

The door opened behind them and out came Airman Burkhart, with a very impatient black lab on his lead, wagging his tail, his front paws prancing up and down, with his whole body moving at the sight of his master. He barked and whined for the airman holding him to let him go.

Peyton stood in shock for a moment. With tears in his eyes and a big grin breaking out on his face, he yelled, "Justice!" He got down on one knee, held out his arms, and cried, "Come here, boy!"

The airman unlatched his lead, and Justice was off! He landed in Peyton's arms, where they both fell back, with Justice licking his face and Peyton fiercely holding on to him.

Everyone stood and watched as Peyton and Justice were reunited for the first time since he left the military. "Okay, boy." He laughed. "We need to get up." The airman brought the lead over and attached it to his collar. He pulled him off as Peyton stood up. He handed the lead to Peyton. He gave the signal for Justice to sit. Justice immediately obeyed.

The colonel stepped up to Peyton. "I'm sorry if I gave you worry over Justice. I wanted to surprise you. He did well on the flight over here but has been full of nervous energy since he arrived here at the base. I'm sure he could sense you were near. After seeing you two together, I made the right decision in retiring him early. Captain Peyton TreVaine, Justice now belongs to you." He held out his hand to shake.

Peyton grabbed his hand. "Thank you so much, Colonel Rayland. I will take very good care of him."

"I know you will. Now, I need to finish up some paperwork. I know your family is anxious to meet him." Peyton looked down, gave Justice a signal, they both saluted the colonel. Colonel Rayland saluted them back. He grinned, bent down, and ruffled his hand over the dog's head. "Welcome home, Justice." He chuckled as he turned and walked back into the message center.

His brothers and Jenna rushed up to Peyton's side. Jenna bent down beside Justice. "Will he let me pet him?"

Peyton bent down beside his dog, "Justice, this is Jenna."

With his tail wagging, Jenna placed her hands along his head and gently petted him. "You are so handsome, Justice! And you were such a good boy traveling back to the States! Oh, Peyton, he's wonderful!" They both stood back up. She went and gave her future brother-in-law a hug. "I'm so glad you have Justice back by your side."

Peyton hugged her back. "Thank you, Jenna. It all seems so surreal to me."

As she pulled away from him and went over to Mike, Peyton eyed his brothers sternly. "You two are in trouble!" They both grinned.

Mark piped in. "Sorry, bro, but we were told to keep this confidential, and we never break a confidence. We are very happy the two of you are together again. We, unfortunately, have to get back to the restaurant. Our new general manager is starting his first day out on the floor tonight and we need to go over the training he has done so far."

Peyton looked at his brother with concern. "How do you feel about having a dog in your home until I find a place?" he asked.

"Are you kidding me?" Mark grinned. "Justice is more than welcome at my home, and Cameron has been off the charts with excitement waiting to meet him."

"Thanks, bro. Well, Justice, let's go for a walk along the beach and get you familiar with the area, then back to Mark's." He and Justice went to his SUV. His brothers and Jenna watched as Justice jumped in the back seat. Peyton opened the driver's side door, gave his brothers and Jenna a wave, and headed out.

Jenna glanced over at Mark, then up to her future husband, and grinned. "That was epic!"

Mike grinned back, as he placed his arm around her to give her a squeeze and a quick kiss. "That was totally epic!" With that, they headed back to the restaurant.

Peyton decided to drive over to the marina, to take a look during daylight hours, to get a feel for the area. He only saw it in the dark. After the plan that the police departments rolled out to him and his brothers this morning, he needed to scope it out. He took the exit off the highway into the marina. When he came into the parking lot, he parked his SUV down at the far end of the lot. Peyton climbed out and opened the door to the back of the vehicle. He took Justice's lead and led him out. Justice, alert, looking around and sniffing the area, was already pulling on the lead, ready to get going. "Hey, Justice!" he exclaimed. "You're retired now. We're just going for a walk." He decided to walk along the beach first, then he would stroll back to the warehouse to see if any activity was going on.

They walked quite a while, Peyton admiring the blue waters of the Pacific Ocean with the sun gleaming down, while Justice was prancing and sniffing through the surf coming up on the shore. Peyton noticed some surfers head out into the ocean to catch some waves. He stood and watched as they turned their boards and waited. He saw the first big wave come in and lift them up. At the same time, they jumped up on the board to ride it in. It always amazed him how they could keep their balance on such turbulent waters. He never tried surfing but knew his brother Mike loved to body surf. Maybe one day he'd try it.

Justice was pulling on his lead, ready to get going again. They walked down a little farther and decided to turn around. As they were walking back, Peyton looked for anyone around or near the warehouse, located back behind the docks. He didn't see anyone, but people could be working in the warehouse. He looked over to where the boats were moored. "First, let's go take a walk along the docks, Justice. Maybe one of these boats will be taking the drugs to LA." There were a lot of boats sitting in the water: sailboats, charter boats, and yachts of all sizes, bobbing up and down. As they walked along there were people milling about, sitting in their boats having a drink or getting ready to go out into the bay.

When they walked by this one yacht, Justice's ears perked up. He immediately went on point. He sniffed the air and the hair on his back stood up. He let out a low growl. Peyton bent down and placed his hand on his back. "Easy, boy. What is it?" They both watched. Peyton took his phone out of his pocket and took a picture. When he stood up, someone from behind him asked, "Is there someone you are looking for?"

Peyton turned around to stare into the eyes of a large man, dressed in worn jeans and faded T-shirt. His green eyes showed his anger as Peyton responded, "No, sorry, I was just admiring this yacht. Is it yours?"

"No, I just work on it. I would appreciate you deleting the picture you took of it. My boss don't like tourists taking pictures of his boat," he said gruffly.

"Sorry." Peyton took his phone and deleted the picture. He glanced over at the man. "Picture deleted." Justice let out another low growl.

The man looked down at his dog, "Your dog don't like me," as he backed away. Peyton heard Justice's low growl at the man. When he gave Justice a signal, he relaxed, then sat down beside his master.

"Sorry, he's very protective of me. Well, we'll be on our way. Come, Justice," he commanded. They walked past the man, but not before they gave each other a leering glare. Peyton put his phone back in his pocket and smiled. *Good thing I took two pictures!*

The man watched Peyton and his dog walk back down the dock, turn, and head down the stairs. He didn't like him snooping around. He'd keep a watch out for him and his dog if they ever stepped near his boss's boat again. He turned and boarded the yacht to get some work done before his boss and his dinner guests come aboard later tonight.

Peyton and Justice stepped down off the steps and wandered over to the warehouse. Justice, with his nose to the ground sniffing all around, while his master was looking for any activity going on in and around the warehouse, approached the door as a man was coming out. "Excuse me, sir." The man turned towards Peyton. "I was looking for the owner of this marina. I was told that he was interested in selling. Is he available?"

With anger in his eyes, the man glared straight at him. "Look, I don't know who you are, but the boss ain't interested in selling this place. I don't know where you got your information from, but I suggest you leave and never step foot on this property again!"

Surprised by his reaction, "Sorry, man," Peyton responded. "Must have been misinformed, I'll be sure to let my friend know it's not on the market. Come, Justice, let's head back." Peyton and Justice started walking to his SUV. He stopped, turned slightly, and watched the guy get into his truck and pull out of the parking lot. Peyton watched until he was out of sight. When he first drove into the marina, he saw a forest behind the warehouse. "Okay, Justice, let's go check out the woods behind here. I need to see how far back it goes." They headed past the warehouse and into the woods. It was pretty dense with bamboo trees, hardwoods, and tropical plants and palm trees. It took them a while, but they finally came out the other side to another road. Peyton and Justice followed the road to the left, where it led them back to the parking lot of the marina. "Okay, boy. I think we've seen enough for today. Let's head over to the store so I can get you some chow and a bed before we head back to Mark's."

Peyton stopped at one of the pet stores on the island. He picked up several toys he knew Justice liked, along with a nice big bed and his favorite dog food. Once back at Mark's, Peyton led Justice into the house. He let him go to sniff and get used to his surroundings. He brought everything in the house so he could set up his dishes with food and water. He took and put the dog bed in his bedroom. It wasn't long before Justice found his food and gobbled up every bit in just a few short bites! "Whoa, boy, slow down!" He chuckled. Peyton bent down to pet his head and back. "You're such a good boy. I'm so happy to have you by my side again."

Justice responded by licking his face and snuggling up against him. He gave him a hug. He rose to grab a tablet of paper and a pen from the kitchen drawer. As he headed over to the couch, Justice followed him, plopped down beside him, and went to sleep. Peyton wrote down the plan that the police departments wanted to implement in their sting operation, but after scoping out the marina and the warehouse, he had some ideas of his own. He set about devising a backup plan should the police departments fail. He would run it by Zack and Lieutenant Fillmore in the morning.

He was just finishing up, when he heard the garage door opening up from where he was sitting. Cameron came barreling in, with Mark right behind him! "Uncle Peyton! Is he here?" he shouted. Cameron rushed up to his uncle and got his answer. Justice sat up, curious to know who the intruder was.

Mark rushed up behind him. "Cameron, hold on! I'm not sure how Justice will react!" He turned to his brother. "What do you think, bro? Will Justice let Cameron pet him?"

Peyton put his hand on Justice's head. "What do you say, boy?"

Wagging his tail, Justice looked from his master to the little boy. "Okay, Cameron, come stand in front of me. Now, put your hand out for Justice to sniff it. It will help him get used to your scent. Sometimes military dogs can be unpredictable until they adapt to a new environment." Cameron did as he was asked, while Mark looked on. Justice sniffed his hand and started licking his fingers.

Cameron glanced up at his uncle with a big grin on his face. "I think he likes me!"

"I think he does, Cameron! Now, gently pet the top of his head."

Cameron gently touched the top of his head, then ran his hand down his neck and back. Justice started to nuzzle up against him. They instantly formed a bond. As he continued to pet him, "Do you think he will play with me, Uncle Peyton?"

"There are some toys over by the counter. Go grab one and see if he will."

Cameron ran over to the counter and picked up a thick rope. He came over to Justice and shook it. Justice looked up at his master, and then to the rope. "It's okay, you can go play," commanded Peyton.

Justice went and followed Cameron out into the living room. Justice latched onto the rope as the game of tug of war began. Cameron laughed as Justice pulled him along. Peyton and Mark watched as his son and Justice played together like they had known each other all their lives! "Looks like they each have a new friend," grinned Peyton.

"Yes." Mark grinned back. "Yes, it does."

"Are you home for the night?" asked Peyton.

Mark sat down across from his brother, "Yes, Mike said he would start working with our new general manager. Jenna was going to work on the wedding plans, and Cameron has been chopping at the bit to come and see Justice, so he told me to go home. I don't mind telling you, I need the break. I've been running on empty for a long time now."

"You and Mike have been putting in some long hours. It will be good for you both to have some free time," Peyton commented. "Along with this case we're working on with the police departments it can't be easy for either one of you."

"No, it hasn't been. We both have been dealing with burn-out for a long time." Mark laid his head back against the high back chair and closed his eyes.

Peyton hated to ask. His brother looked tired and worn out, but he really needed his thoughts on the picture he had taken. See if they matched up with his. "Would you be up for going over something with me?" asked Peyton.

Mark sat up and looked over at his brother. "Sure, what's up?"

"After our meeting this morning"—he grinned—"and getting the surprise of my life, I drove over to Manchez's warehouse to scope it out. I took Justice out, and we walked along the beach. When we came back, we walked along the docks to look at some of the boats anchored there. We came across this one." Peyton pulled out his phone and showed his brother the picture he took of the yacht.

"This is nice, bro, but what are you getting at?"

"When we approached the yacht, Justice went on point and he started to growl." Peyton looked over at Cameron and his dog. They were still playing with each other. He said in a low voice, "He only does this when he smells drugs or some type of bomb."

Alert, he asked, "Do you think this could be the boat the drugs will be shipped out on?"

"I don't know for sure but take a look at the name of the yacht."

He enlarged the back of the boat, and Mark read, "*The Millie Ann Dream.*" Mark looked back at his brother, shocked. "Millie is the name of Manchez's wife! This could very well be the boat that takes the drugs to LA! You need to get this to Zack, and Lieutenant Fillmore ASAP!"

"I intend to. I will send this over to him before I head out to Helen's. I'll have Helen get with Lieutenant Andrew and Detective Zealand and we'll do a three-way call. They can inform the sheriff's department. They can also get on intel communications to check out who the yacht actually belongs to."

Cameron came up to his dad, followed by Justice. "I'm hungry."

Mark picked his son up and placed him on his lap. He smiled down at him. "Okay, I'll get some dinner going." He glanced back at his brother. "Are you staying, bro?"

"No, I need to get over to Helen's. I'm sure she's wondering where I'm at."

"Can Justice stay here?" asked Cameron.

Peyton looked over at Justice. With his ears perked up, it looked like he was asking too! "It's up to your dad."

"Do you think Justice will be all right without you for the night?"

"I think so. What do you say, boy?"

Justice let out a big woof!

"Looks like he agrees!" cried Cameron. Both Peyton and Mark chuckled.

Mark placed his son back down off his lap and got up off the chair. "Let's go make some dinner." He turned back to his brother. "Let me know how it goes. I would be curious to know if that is indeed Manchez's yacht."

"As soon as we find out, I'll let you know. I'm going to head out." He went over to Justice. "You, be a good boy for Mark and Cameron. I'll see you in the morning." He gave his dog a pat on his head, then headed for the door.

As Peyton opened the door, Mark, concerned, said, "Be safe."

"Always," he returned.

Helen looked at the clock. It was well after seven o'clock. She thought Peyton would have been here by now. She had picked up some Chinese food on her way home from work, but she ended up putting it in the fridge and sent a text off to him. *Were you still planning on coming over tonight?* She hadn't received a response and wondered if he decided not to come, when the doorbell rang. When she opened the door, she was relieved to see him standing outside on her porch. She ran into his arms and hugged him tight. "I thought you weren't coming!"

He gave her a hug back, then, pulled away. "I'm sorry. I was on my way over here when I received your text. I thought I would wait until I got here to explain why I was running late. Let's go inside." Peyton followed her in and shut the door. "I noticed a black Camaro down in a parking lot along the beach when I came by."

Helen turned back, "Yes, Kevin, my boss, filled me in. He's from the police department. He's keeping watch over the next couple of days until we get through this sting operation."

"Good. That makes me feel a little better. I didn't see the black sedan anywhere in the vicinity when I drove over here. Hopefully, Victor will stay away and not try to do anything stupid."

"Amen to that! Have you eaten dinner?"

"No, I wanted to wait to see what you wanted to do," he returned.

"I picked up some Chinese food after work. We just need to heat it up." She walked into the kitchen, with Peyton following behind.

"Sounds good, what can I do to help."

"If you want to get some plates out of the cupboard and push the start button on the coffeemaker, I'll get the food out and we'll heat it up in the microwave."

Peyton went over and started the coffeemaker. Then pulled two plates from the cupboard and handed them to Helen. When the coffee was ready, he poured them each a cup as Helen was bringing over hot plates of Chinese food to set on the counter. They both sat down and ate in silence. Peyton with thoughts of what he had discovered out at the warehouse and Helen with thoughts of the sting operation. She wondered, after going over the plans that the police departments wanted to implement, if they would make it out alive or not. When they had finished eating, Helen suggested they have their coffee in the living room.

When they sat down, Helen asked, "You seem a little preoccupied tonight. Is everything all right?"

Peyton turned to her and smiled. "Your father gave me the surprise of my life this afternoon. I now have Justice by my side again, and I can't tell you the joy I feel inside just having him home with me."

"Oh, Peyton, that's wonderful!"

"It is. Which leads me to tell you what I came upon this afternoon out at the warehouse," he explained. He pulled his cell phone out of his pocket.

Helen scooted up next to him to have a look. He pulled up the picture and handed it to her. She glanced at the picture. "Nice yacht!"

"Not just any yacht. It might just be Manchez's yacht. Read the inscription on the back of the yacht."

She enlarged the picture and read, *"The Millie Ann Dream."* She shrugged her shoulders. "How does this connect with Manchez?"

"Mark informed me tonight when I showed him the picture that his wife's name is Millie. It could very well be his."

"But what makes you think it is? There could be any number of women with the same name."

"I don't, but when Justice and I came upon this particular boat, Justice went on point and started growling. He only does that when he senses drugs or a bomb. He was trained to search out bombs and drugs in the military. He also didn't like the guy we ran into. He said he worked on the boat when I asked if he was the owner."

"Are you saying that this boat could be the one that will be taking the drugs to LA?" she asked.

"It's possible. We won't know for sure until we have it checked out. I sent this over to Zack so they could start searching intel to find out who the boat belongs to. In the meantime, we need to call Lieutenant Andrew, and your partner, to do a three-way call to fill them in."

Helen got up to retrieve her phone off the counter. "Come over here and I'll pull up the lieutenant's number."

Peyton came up beside her as Kevin answered the phone. "Lieutenant Andrew."

"Hi, Lieutenant. Helen here. I'm going to put you on hold till I get ahold of Fred. Hold on!" She pushed the hold button and dialed up Fred's number. She hoped he wasn't on a date or in bed with somebody!

He answered, "Detective Zealand."

"Fred, I have the lieutenant on the other line. Hold on." She pushed the button. "Kevin?"

"I'm here, what's going on?"

Helen put the phone on speaker. "Now that we are all on the call, Peyton is here with me, and he wants to share some information with you both, regarding the case." Peyton went on to explain what he had discovered when he was out at the warehouse.

"So, you think this could be the boat that will carry the drugs to LA?" asked Kevin.

"It's possible." Peyton returned.

"I'm not sure that this Manchez, even if it is his boat, would use it to transport the drugs. I would be surprised if he did. I wouldn't think he would want any evidence to implicate him to the drugs. Most of these guys stay as far away as possible when the deal goes down. When will we know if the boat is his?" asked Kevin.

"We should know by tomorrow morning. The police department is working on it as we speak."

"Good. In the meantime, how about you and Fred head out there to check out this boat and see if you can find out any information that could help us out?"

"I'm on it" answered Fred.

"We'll pick you up at your hotel, Fred. We don't need to have two vehicles going out there. We'll be there in twenty minutes," stated Helen.

"Right, I'll be waiting," he returned.

"Keep me informed. If you need backup, call me."

"Will do, Lieutenant." Helen ended the call and glanced over at Peyton. "You've canvassed the area. Can you take us out there?"

"It would be my pleasure. In case anyone is out there, I have a back way to get in. It will require going through a forest. If you have your boots, it would be a good idea to wear them. Text Fred to do the same. Do you have any infrared flashlights?" he asked.

"I have one in my car. I'll let Fred know to grab his." As she was texting her partner, she went to her bedroom to grab her boots. She put on her ankle holster and slipped her revolver inside. After she put on her boots, she went over to the nightstand to take her gun out of the drawer. She put on her shoulder harness and slipped her gun inside. She grabbed her jacket and headed back out to where Peyton was waiting.

"All set?" he asked.

"Yes, I just need to grab the flashlight."

Peyton opened the door for her, made sure it was locked behind them, and followed her over to her car. She grabbed the flashlight, then followed Peyton to his SUV and climbed in.

Fifteen minutes later they were pulling up to the hotel. Fred was waiting outside when Peyton pulled up. He climbed into the back. "Hey, guys, are we ready to do this?" he asked.

"As ready as we'll ever be," answered Peyton. Peyton drove through the parking lot and out into traffic. He took a quick turn to his left that would take them out onto the highway. He took an exit that Helen wasn't familiar with when they came out here to investigate before.

"Where are we going?" she asked Peyton.

"When I was out here today with Justice, we took a little walk through the woods behind the warehouse. This road will take us behind the woods, and no one will be able to see us from the boats moored at the docks or the warehouse. With the infrared flashlights, we will be able to see where we are going, but no one will see us."

"Excellent!" replied Helen.

Peyton pulled into an opened area of the woods where there weren't a lot of trees. He killed the engine and shut his lights off. He opened his glovebox and pulled out his flashlight. He turned back and glanced at Fred, then at Helen. "Ready?"

"Ready!" they both said in unison. They exited the SUV and proceeded to walk through the dense woods till they came to the edge where the warehouse was located. All three went down on their haunches and watched. The garage door was open, and they had a clear view inside the warehouse. Three men were working. One on a forklift moved crates around, while the other two opened crates and checked out the merchandise inside. A truck pulled in and backed into the building. The man on the forklift waited for instructions. Two men waved him over and instructed him as to which crates needed to be loaded on the truck.

After an hour, "It's getting late. Let's wait till morning to deliver the goods."

"Sounds good to me," one of them replied. "My wife's holding dinner for me," they heard them say as Peyton, Helen, and Fred continued to watch as the men closed the garage door, shut the lights off, and exited out the front entrance.

Peyton turned to Helen and Fred. "Let's wait ten minutes to make sure they're gone." They both nodded their heads yes. Minutes later, "Let's head over to the left of the building and away from the security light," instructed Peyton. "With the trees in that area there will be less of a chance of being seen."

Helen and Fred pulled out their guns and followed Peyton around the building, across the parking lot, and near the docks. So far, so good, there didn't appear to be anybody around. Peyton took them near the stairway, which led up to where the boats are moored and went under the stairs. With their hearts pounding all three looked around; still clear. Peyton glanced over at Helen and Fred. "You two stay here. I'm going up," he whispered.

"Look, Peyton," Helen whispered back, "one of us should be the one to go up. The lieutenant specifically asked us to investigate."

Peyton was taken aback. He wasn't sure if anyone was up there, but after the encounter with the man who worked on the boat this afternoon, he didn't trust him. She could get hurt. But he had to let go of the fear. This was her job. He had to trust that she knew what she is doing. "Okay, but Fred, you be her backup. I'll stay and keep watch."

With guns still pulled, both Fred and Helen headed out. Peyton said a prayer for Him to keep them safe. With his heart pounding, he watched as Fred and Helen started up the stairs. Halfway up, they heard voices with footsteps heading towards the top of the stairs. Both Fred and Helen crept back down and hurried to hide back under the stairs. Helen grabbed Peyton's arm and pulled him back as far as they could go. All three scrunched down to keep hidden.

Listening, "Looks like you have it all under control, Rodrick. If this deal goes south, there won't be a shred of evidence to tie us to the drug deal."

"Always aim to please, Marco. Never hurts to be prepared for the worst. But I don't see any problems with the plan, so it should go smoothly," he stated.

"Good, we don't want to have any lose ends."

"No, sir, I'll make sure it goes as planned on my end."

"See that you do." Marco nodded his head and started down the stairs, with Victor trailing behind. When they got to the bottom…Peyton, Helen, and Fred covered their heads and held their breath. Both Marco and Victor headed for their vehicles. All of a sudden, Victor stopped. He felt the hair on the back of his head stand up. He turned back and looked all around. He didn't see anything or anyone lurking around. He shook himself and followed Marco to his car. He made sure Marco was secure and watched him drive off. He took another look around before he entered his own car and took off. All three breathed a sigh of relief.

"We'll wait just to make sure he doesn't come back around," whispered Fred.

When all was clear, they headed back the same way they came and were soon climbing into Peyton's SUV.

As they headed back to the hotel, Fred asked, "What do you think the plan might be?"

"I have no idea," answered Peyton. "We didn't get a whole lot of information." But in his gut he did have a feeling, and it wasn't good!

Helen and Peyton came back to her bungalow after dropping Fred off at the hotel. "Would you like a cup of coffee or a glass of wine?" she asked as she headed for the kitchen.

"I'll have a glass of wine if you will."

"Of course!" she exclaimed. She went to pull two wine glasses from the cupboard, the wine from the fridge, and poured them each a glass. She brought them into the living room, where Peyton was relaxing on the couch. She handed him his wine. "It's too bad we didn't get the chance to investigate the boat," sighed Helen.

"It would have been too risky. Maybe we'll get another chance before Friday," he replied.

"Maybe," she returned. As they sipped their wine, they both got caught up in their own thoughts. Peyton put his wine glass down on the coffee table and glanced over at Helen. She read his thoughts and suddenly felt the goosebumps coming out over her skin. "Are you staying tonight?"

"Yes, but I need to be up early. I've got to buy a handgun and take it to the police department to have it registered. I will go over what we have uncovered with Zack and Craig along with the lieutenant. Then I have to catch a flight over to the big island to meet with Dr. Sawyer at two."

"Wow! That was quick!"

"Yes, he sounded very excited about interviewing me. Hopefully, I will come back with a job in hand."

Helen put her wineglass on the table, came up from the couch, and took Peyton's hand. "Then I think we need to get to bed." She smiled and led him back to her bedroom. They both undressed and slid under the covers. Helen snuggled up to Peyton as he ran his hand slowly down her back and hips. They kissed, and soon the passion took over. Two hearts beating wildly as they made love into the night.

CHAPTER 11

Peyton was up before dawn. While Helen was still sleeping, he dressed, and set the coffeepot up for her. He left a note for her on the counter that he would be in touch. Peyton climbed into his SUV to head over to Mark's. He wanted to see how Justice did last night before he went shopping for a gun. He pulled into Mark's driveway and came into the house. All was quiet. He checked his bedroom but didn't find Justice there. He went to check his nephew's room. When he opened the door, he smiled. Justice and Cameron were snuggled up together in his nephew's bed. Justice raised his head when the door opened, took a look, and laid his head back down. Well, he had worried for nothing. His dog was in good hands. Peyton shut the door and headed toward the kitchen. He put on a pot of coffee and took a Danish out of the fridge to warm up in the microwave. When the coffee was done, he sat down at the counter to enjoy his breakfast. While he ate his Danish, thoughts of this case were swarming in his head. He did the same thing when he served overseas in the special ops division. He handled some dangerous missions, and if it didn't go right, he would have been dead a long time ago. This was no different. If the police departments didn't handle this right, it could all blow up in their faces. What worried him most was how Justice reacted when we got close to the yacht. It was either drugs, or a bomb. He hoped it wasn't the latter. He had to deactivate the ones in Afghanistan, but not all bombs are built the same. He would run it by the detectives and the lieutenant this morning, along with his backup plan.

Thoughts of Helen came back into his mind as he finished up his coffee. She was one powerful woman. His heart beat a little faster just thinking about their lovemaking. He knew he was falling for her. He sighed. He needed to pray that if their relationship was meant to be, somehow it would work itself out. He couldn't see himself in LA. He hated big cities. Mark walked into the kitchen. "Hi, bro. You're back early."

"Hi, I'm sorry, did I wake you?"

"No, I went to bed early." He smiled. "I've had more sleep in one night than I have had in a long time. Is there any coffee left?"

"Yes, help yourself."

Mark went and pulled a cup out of the cupboard and filled his cup. "Can I warm yours up?"

"Sure."

After he warmed his brother's coffee, he came around the counter and sat down. "How did it go when you informed the police department of your findings?"

"Well, Zack was going to get on intel communications to see who exactly the yacht belongs to. We should know something this morning. When I spoke with Lieutenant Andrew and Helen's partner Fred last night, the lieutenant said that it was unlikely that if it is Manchez's yacht, he didn't think he would use it to transport the drugs."

"So you think another boat is involved?"

"Possibly. We actually went out to the marina to see if we could uncover anything, but we didn't get very far. Helen and Fred were heading up the stairs to check out the yacht when we heard voices. They rushed back down. As we listened, I was surprised to hear Manchez's voice talking to a guy named Rodrick. I'm assuming that he was the guy I ran into on the docks yesterday. Said the plan was set, and if the deal goes south, the police wouldn't have a shred of evidence to indict any of them. So my gut is telling me that the yacht indeed belongs to Manchez. Whether he has another boat that will transfer the drugs is still up in the air."

"You've dealt with some of this stuff in special ops Peyton. What do you think is going to go down?"

"Mark, I hope I'm wrong, but my gut is telling me they could have set a bomb, but I just don't know where. The way Justice reacted yesterday, I would say it was Manchez's yacht. But it could also be drugs. There doesn't have to be a lot on the boat for Justice to detect it."

"Then someone is going to have to go undercover on the docks that knows how to deactivate a bomb just in case!" exclaimed Mark.

"Yes." Peyton got up from his chair and went into the living room to grab his notebook. He came back to the counter and opened it up. He showed the plan he came up with last night to his brother. "I don't mind telling you, bro, I am a little concerned about the plan the police departments want to implement. After Justice and I canvassed the area, I came up with this one."

Mark read over the plan his brother wanted to set in motion. "I can see where you are going with this. Are you going to show this to Zack?"

"Yes. I have to go buy a handgun this morning and take it over to the police department to have it registered. I will go over it with everyone concerned then."

"Good. What are your plans for the rest of the day, after you register your handgun?" he asked.

"I have an interview for a pilot's job at the hospital on the big island of Kona. Dr. Sawyer wants to meet at two o'clock. Also, later this evening I'm going back out to the marina to see what I can uncover about that yacht."

"That's great news about the job offer, bro! What time are you planning on going out to the marina?" he asked.

"After midnight," he answered.

"Do you mind if I join you? I'd like to get a scope on the area myself. I'm sure Mike would too."

"If you two are game, I think it would be a good idea to get familiar with the area before it goes down tomorrow night."

"Good. I'll let Mike know, and if you can meet us at the restaurant after we close, say, around eleven? We can go over a plan to get on board that yacht."

"Sounds good." Peyton came up from his chair. He went over to the sink to rinse his cup and dish and placed them in the dishwasher. "I'm going to go get showered and head out. If I don't see you before, I'll see you and Mike tonight."

"Okay, bro." Mark watched as Peyton left to go get cleaned up. As he went over in his mind about the two plans, he preferred Peyton's over the police departments'. Both were risky. But he could see himself making it out alive with Peyton's.

Later, Peyton walked into the police department with a gun in hand to get it registered. While he was filling out the paperwork, Detective Sergeant Craig Jenson came into the lobby. He extended his hand to Peyton. "Hi, Peyton. I see you purchased a gun this morning."

"Yes, just getting it registered. Hey, is Zack here this morning?"

"He's out working on a case but he should be back soon. Lieutenant Fillmore is here, along with Lieutenant Andrew. They're in a meeting right now."

"Would there be any way I could speak to them when I finish this up?"

"Does this have to do with the case?" he asked.

"Yes, it's important."

"I'm sure it will be fine." Craig turned to the sergeant on duty. "Sergeant Dobbs."

"Yes, sir."

"When you finish up the paperwork on Peyton's gun, send him back to the conference room."

"Yes, sir," he answered. Craig left to inform the lieutenants of Peyton's arrival. When the paperwork was done, Sergeant Dobbs led Peyton back to where the lieutenants were waiting.

When Peyton entered the room, both lieutenants and Craig were sitting at the table. "Sorry to interrupt, but I need to run something by you regarding the case." Peyton sat down, opened his notebook, and handed it to Lieutenant Fillmore. While he was going over Peyton's notes, Peyton turned to Lieutenant Andrew. "I'm sure Helen informed you what we uncovered last night when we were out at the marina."

"She did," he responded.

"Do you know who the yacht belongs to?" inquired Peyton.

"We do. We confirmed that the yacht does belong to Marco Manchez. We were just discussing the conversation that took place with him, and we're assuming his first mate," Lieutenant Andrew responded.

"Did either of you come up with anything regarding the conversation?"

Before Lieutenant Andrew could answer, Lieutenant Fillmore glanced up from the plan Peyton devised and remarked, "This looks good," as he slid the notepad over to Lieutenant Andrew to take a look.

"Thanks. I have some concerns, though."

"What are your concerns?" he asked.

"Well, my take on the conversation, and how Justice responded when we approached the yacht, is that Rodrick could have planted a bomb on the boat. I may be wrong, but my gut is telling me it's a strong possibility."

"So, you think we need a bomb squad available in case we need to deactivate one?" asked Lieutenant Fillmore.

"It wouldn't be a bad idea. I've deactivated them when I was overseas, but not all bombs are set up the same."

Lieutenant Andrew spoke up, "I like this plan," as he

handed the notepad to Craig. "We should bring up both plans and see which one would be the most advantageous to apprehend all who are involved in the drug heist."

After Craig read over Peyton's plan, he looked up. "I agree. This is good, but with a possibility of a bomb threat, we need to take a closer look to make sure we have the right plan in place. Do you have time to stay and discuss?" asked Craig.

"I have about an hour and a half. I have to catch a flight over to the big island for a job interview," he returned.

Zack walked into the conference room. "Hi, Zack," greeted Lieutenant Fillmore. "Take a seat. We were just discussing the Manchez case and looking over Peyton's alternative plan to take him and his organization down."

Zack pulled out a chair, sat down, folded his hands on the table, and leaned in. "Shoot."

Mike and Jenna were working on a financial report, when Mark came into the office. "Hi, you two, how's it going?"

"Good," answered Mike. "Just finalizing this report to give to the auditors on Monday."

Mark took a seat. "I wanted to run something by you, bro," he hesitated. He wasn't sure Mike had time to go over with Jenna on what was going down tomorrow night.

"What's up?" asked Mike.

He took a breath. "Peyton is going out to the marina to check out this yacht tonight." He looked over at Jenna, then back to Mike. "I wondered if you would like to join us. I think it would be a good idea."

Mike looked over at Jenna who was returning his look with questioning eyes. He glanced back at his brother. "I'll have to let you know. I haven't had time to discuss it with Jenna."

Determined to find out what was going on, "Discuss what?" she asked. Mike glanced back at his brother, upset that his brother brought this up in front of his future wife. "Could you leave us alone, Mark, and shut the door on your way out."

Mark got up from the chair and left the office. As he shut the door, he could hear Jenna say, "What's going on?"

Mike looked over at Jenna and knew she was concerned at the question Mark asked him.

"Mike, you're keeping something from me, what is it?"

"Jenna—" he began.

"Mike," she interrupted, "Pastor Kingsley said we shouldn't keep secrets from each other. Please tell me what's going on."

"Well, if you will listen to me, I will tell you," he said abruptly.

Jenna, taken aback by his response, replied, "I'm sorry, Mike. I didn't mean to interrupt. I think I have the wedding jitters and my nerves are on edge."

Mike came up from his desk, walked around, and took Jenna's hand in his. He pulled her up and led her over to the couch. He sat down and pulled Jenna onto his lap. With his arms around her, he gazed into her pretty brown eyes. "Jenna, sweetheart, I would never, ever keep secrets from you. With hiring and training a general manager, I haven't had time to bring this up to you, so I will tell you now." He took a deep breath. He had a feeling she wasn't going to like what he was about to tell her. "Peyton, Mark, and I, are going to be part of the sting operation that is going to take place tomorrow night."

Jenna broke free of Mike's arms, stood up, and stared with frightened eyes into his. "Mike, no! It's too dangerous! You could be killed; you all could be killed! We're going to be married in less than six weeks! I don't want to lose you before we even get started on our lives together!" Tears started forming in her eyes as she tried to come to grips with what he just told her. Her nerves have been frayed over the past several weeks getting ready for their wedding. She was so overwhelmed, and now this!

Mike rose and tried to take her in his arms, but she pulled away and walked towards the door. She turned back towards him. "Mike, please don't do this."

"Jenna, I have already committed to helping the police put Manchez and his organization away. Please understand." With pleading eyes he searched hers but only found anger and confusion in them.

"What about your commitment to our relationship? Is your commitment to the police department and risking your life more important than us?"

When he didn't answer, she turned and opened the door as tears slid down her cheeks. "I'm sorry, Mike, I need to leave. Please tell Mark I will see him tomorrow." As she walked through the door, she heard Mike yell out her name, but she just kept moving until she was out of the restaurant and on her way to her apartment. Mike watched as she left his office and out the main office door. He would have run after her, but he felt it wouldn't do any good. She needed some time to cool off. He left his office and walked over to his brother's.

Mark looked up as he opened the door. "I take it that it didn't go too well?" he asked.

"No, it didn't!" Mike started pacing, then turned toward his brother. "Mark, I wish you had waited to ask me about going out to the marina. I was going to tell her about the sting operation when we had dinner tonight." He sighed. "I guess I would have gotten the same reaction from her even if I would have waited till dinner. She's really upset, and I can't blame her. I know how I felt when she went to the bar that night! I was beside myself." He took a seat in one of the chairs in front of the desk and ran his hands through his hair.

"Sorry, bro, I thought you might have told her. Let her cool down. Then give her a call or go see her. In the meantime, I want to go over a few things before we head out to the marina tonight."

Mike glanced back at his brother. "Let's hear it."

As Mark went over the information from last night, and Peyton's alternate plan to nail Manchez and his organization, he finished up with, "Peyton is at the police station going over his plan he wants to implement. We should know tonight what plan they are going with."

Surprised, he asked, "So, there's a possibility that a bomb has been placed on the boat?"

"It's a possibility. Peyton wants to go out there after midnight with Justice to see if indeed there is one. But we need to come up with a plan to get the guy named Rodrick off the boat so he and Justice can get on. Peyton will be meeting us here at the restaurant."

"What time?"

"Eleven," answered Mark.

Mike nodded and took a deep breath. "Okay, I'm going to cut out early tonight and see if I can smooth things over with Jenna. Jack is catching on fast, so I don't think you will have any problems tonight." Mike came up out of his chair and headed toward the door. He turned back and glanced at his brother. "I'll meet you and Peyton back here at eleven."

"Good, I'll see you out on the floor in just a bit. I need to get these cash drawers counted and get a deposit made before the bank closes," he returned.

"Jenna left for the day. She said she would be in tomorrow. I'll be in my office if you need me."

"Okay, bro."

Mike opened the door and headed back to his office. He sat back down at his desk. He hoped he could make things right with Jenna. He hated being on the outs with her. She has been a bit touchy lately. Maybe there is something to this bridezilla thing that the guys were mentioning. He shook his head and started concentrating on this report he had to finish for Monday.

Jenna walked into her apartment, slamming the door behind her. Sasha was in the kitchen making a protein shake before she had to get ready for work. She watched as Jenna stormed into the kitchen, opened the fridge, and grabbed a soda. "Hey, what's up with you? Did you have a bad day at work?"

Jenna popped the tab on her soda and sat at the counter, stewing. Sasha watched her best friend take a drink of her soda, set the can back down on the counter, not saying one word. "Okay, Jenna, spill it. You are obviously upset about something, and you're home early. Tell me what's going on."

Jenna turned to her friend, with tears starting to fall from her eyes, she cried, "Mike just informed me that he and his brothers are going to be part of a sting operation tomorrow night. They're going to try and stop the drug heist and arrest all who are involved. I told him I didn't want him to do it, but would he listen? No! Sasha, I am rethinking about marrying this man."

"Jenna, you don't really mean that, do you?"

"Oh yes, Sasha, I think I do. Do you know we are supposed to be married in less than six weeks! Of course you do. Sasha, my brain is fried, and I don't even know if I'm coming or going lately. And then he hits me with this!" Jenna was getting hysterical as the tears came down her cheeks.

Sasha came and put her arms around her friend and let her cry it out. When the tears stopped flowing, Sasha gave her some Kleenex to dry her eyes.

"I'm sorry, Sasha, I didn't mean to cry all over the place. I'm just so scared. What if something happens to him, or his brothers? I don't know if I could go on without him."

"Listen, Jenna, don't you think you are jumping the gun a little?"

With red eyes she glanced over at Sasha and sniffed. "What do you mean?"

"Did you hear him out when he told you what he was going to do?"

She looked away. "No, I told him how I felt and walked out."

"Don't you think he is worth listening to, to see how this plan of theirs is going to play out? I'm sure they have plenty of backup to keep everyone safe."

Jenna looked back at her friend. "And who's side are you on?" she asked.

"I'm on both your sides! Jenna, you love him, and he loves you. You need to talk this out with him. If he is hellbent on being a part of this sting operation, you need to be behind him on this. If you let this put a wedge between the two of you, he may not be able to concentrate on his part in it."

"So you think I should just give in?"

"No, that's not what I'm saying. You need to listen to him. I'm sure Pastor Kingsley has gone over with you and Mike about how listening to each other is an important part of a strong marriage."

As she listened to Sasha, she started to regret her behavior with Mike, as Pastor Kingsley's message came into her mind, *Don't keep secrets, and always listen to each other, even if it is something you don't want to hear.*

"You're right. I need to go talk to him." Jenna reached over and gave her friend a hug. She was going to miss her when she went off to medical school after the wedding. She was her maid of honor and had been a tremendous help with the wedding plans. She was a beautiful Polynesian woman, with long black hair and dark eyes. She has always been able to help Jenna see things from a different perspective.

"Thank you, Sasha, for being such a good friend and helping me see things differently. I'll go and talk to him, but first, I'm going to take a shower, and get into some comfortable jeans and a T-shirt, before I go back to the restaurant. Are you working tonight?"

"Yes, and I need to get ready as well."

They both came up from their chairs and headed to their bedrooms. Cuddles, Jenna's black-and-white tuxedo cat, came running down the hallway to greet her, meowing and rubbing up against her ankles. Her beautiful green eyes looked up at her, as Jenna picked her up and gave her a hug. She placed her hand on top of her head and ran it down her back. "Oh, Cuddles, are you hungry? Let's get you fed."

While Sasha went to her room, Jenna took her cat into the kitchen and placed her on the floor. She went to the cupboard to get her favorite food and placed some in her dish. She gave her some fresh water and Cuddles quickly started feasting on her food. Jenna looked around their apartment. It saddened her at the thought of leaving this place. It was such a nice apartment. She and Sasha had their own bedroom and bathroom. The living room and kitchen were connected with a counter. There was a lanai off the living room, where her and Sasha spent endless hours studying or just relaxing after a long day. She would always treasure the memories. Life is full of changes, but she was looking forward to moving into Mike's beautiful home and starting their life together. Enough reminiscing, she needed to get going if she was going to settle things with Mike. Her last thought when she hit the shower was, *You need to listen to him, Jenna.*

Peyton hurried into the hospital and up to the information booth. An older woman greeted him with a big smile, "Can I help you, sir?"

"Yes, can you direct me to Dr. David Sawyer's office?"

The woman looked down and checked her directory. Peyton looked at his watch. He was already a few minutes late. His patience grew thin while the woman looked over every page. "Oh, here he is!" She glanced back up at Peyton and smiled. "His office is on the second floor, marked Administration, office number 205."

Peyton returned her smile. "Thank you."

"You're very welcome, young man."

She watched him go over to the elevators, change his mind, and took the stairs. *Such a handsome man,* she thought. *Oh, to be young again.* She sighed.

Peyton took the stairs two at a time. When he reached the second floor, he did a turnaround, checking to see which hallway led to Administration. He followed the signs to office number 205. Once there, he stood and stared at the door. He hasn't been through a job interview in over twelve years. He wasn't quite sure what to expect anymore. He wasn't afraid to admit that his nerves were working overtime. He took a deep breath and opened the door. He walked up to the reception desk.

A pretty brunette with dark-rimmed glasses greeted him. He glanced at her name plate on her desk. "Can I help you, sir?" She smiled up at him.

"Yes, Miss Dougal," returning her smile, "I'm Peyton Tre-Vaine. I have an appointment with Dr. David Sawyer. I apologize for being a few minutes late."

She checked her appointment calendar. "Yes, here you are, and no worries. Dr. Sawyer asked that you fill out this application, and when you are finished, bring it back to me, and I will inform him that you are here." She handed him the application. "You can have a seat over at the desk."

He gave her another smile. "Thank you."

"You're welcome."

Peyton sat down and looked over the application. It didn't look too complicated. He answered all the questions with breakneck speed and handed it back to Miss Dougal. She looked over his application. "Everything looks good. If you will have a seat, I will inform Dr. Sawyer you are ready."

He took a seat in a chair along the wall. He watched as Miss Dougal knocked, went into Dr. Sawyer's office, and closed the door. When she came back out, she took a seat at her desk, glanced over, and politely said, "He'll be out shortly."

He nodded his head to confirm and wondered how long shortly meant. As he looked at his watch, fifteen minutes later, his nerves began to shatter. He wanted to get up and pace but held himself back. Five minutes later, Dr. Sawyer opened his office door. Peyton stood as an older gentleman with silver hair, average height, dressed in a grey pin-striped suit, came up with his hand extended and introduced himself. Peyton shook his hand.

"Hi, I'm Dr. David Sawyer, and you must be Peyton."

"Yes, sir," he answered nervously.

"If you'll step into my office, we'll proceed with the interview."

Peyton followed him in and took a seat in front of his desk, while Dr. Sawyer sat down in his chair. "I've looked over your application and see that you have served in the army for a little over twelve years."

"Yes, sir," he answered.

"It states here that you were in search-and-rescue for your final tour in Afghanistan."

"Yes, sir. My team and I along with my military dog served on many missions while serving overseas."

"Your time as a helicopter pilot is pretty impressive."

"Thank you, sir. I love flying the choppers and want to make it my mission to continue if the opportunity is still available."

"Yes, the job is still available. I have one more candidate to interview, then I will make my decision. Let me go over the job description with you, and if you have time, I'll take you up to the roof and show you the landing pad and one of the helicopters we use to fly patients in and out of the hospital. At times, there is a search-and-rescue mission that comes up. If you are selected, you will go through a training course in emergency situations, along with search-and-rescue. Do you have any questions so far?"

"Not at this time," he answered, "but I'm sure I will as we go along."

The interview took a little over an hour. When they went up on the roof, Peyton took one look at the medical helicopter, and the adrenaline started coursing through his veins with the thought of getting it in the air.

Dr. Sawyer watched as Peyton walked around the chopper, looked inside, and he could literally see the excitement on his face viewing the aircraft. He had a good feeling about Peyton. "Is this up to your expectation, Peyton?" asked Dr. Sawyer.

With a big grin on his face he returned, "Man, is it ever! I'd love to get this in the air!"

"I can see, and you may get that chance. Let's head back down." When the elevator opened on the first floor, they stepped out. Peyton turned to shake his hand and thanked him for the opportunity to pursue the job he was offering. Dr. Sawyer retuned with, "I'll be in touch."

Peyton caught a cab and directed him to the airport. It was already after four o'clock, and he wasn't sure when the next flight out to the island was. When he arrived, he rushed in through the doors and up to the counter. He glanced up at the flight schedule. His eyes caught on a flight back to Oahu at six p.m. He asked the attendant if there was a seat available. When she checked, she answered, "Yes, there is one seat available, but it's at the back of the plane."

"I'll take it."

CHAPTER 12

It was 7:30 when Peyton exited the plane. He sent a text off to Helen to see if she had dinner yet. A text came back, *I had something light after work, but could eat something.*

Do you want to eat out or would you like me to pick us up something? he returned.

How about Mexican? she answered back.

Sounds good, need to check on Justice on my way to get the food, I'll be there within the hour. Helen sent back a "thumbs up" sign. Peyton hurried over to his SUV, where it was parked in one of the airport's lots. Arriving at Mark's, he went in only to find Justice wasn't there. He searched the house but came to the conclusion that he must be with Mark. He hoped so anyway.

He sent a text off to him. *Hey bro, is Justice with you?*

It took a few minutes for him to answer. The restaurant must still be busy. *Sorry bro, just saw your text. Yes, Justice is with me, didn't want to leave him at home. He's been a hit here with the waitresses and staff. He's in my office. Mike is just about to leave. Do you want him to drop him off?*

No, can you keep him there? I'll meet you at 11:00, he returned.

No problem, I'll see you then.

Peyton put his cell phone back in his pocket and headed to the Mexican restaurant up a few miles from Mark's.

When the doorbell rang, Helen rushed to open the door. Peyton came in with bags of Mexican food in his hands and set them down on the counter. He turned and pulled Helen into his arms, squeezed her body close to his, and kissed her passionately. She returned his kiss and decided she wanted to skip dinner and take him to bed. She pulled away from him. "How about we eat later?" she purred.

"You read my mind," he breathed. He picked her up and carried her back to the bedroom. The clothes came off, and an hour later, they came back out into the kitchen. Helen warmed up their food while Peyton pulled out some plates and silverware along with a bottle of wine from the fridge. He poured them each a glass and they settled down at the counter to enjoy their dinner. "Everything tastes so much better after good sex, am I right?" asked Peyton with a gleam in his eyes.

"You are so right!" she returned with her own gleam in her eyes. "How did your interview go this afternoon?"

"It went well. I think I have a shot at it. One of the medic choppers Dr. Sawyer showed me was the top of the line. I'd love to get it in the air, see how it handles. He said he would be in touch. I should know one way or the other in a few days."

"That's wonderful, Peyton. I hope you land it."

"Me too. It will be an adjustment, but it will feel good getting back into the work force." He hesitated for a moment. He caught her eyes. "I'm going back out to the marina tonight with my brothers."

Helen, taken aback, "Peyton, this is police business. It's not for you to decide to go back out there."

"Listen, Helen, I need to find out if there is a bomb planted on that boat. I could be wrong, but my gut is telling me otherwise. I'm going to take Justice with us."

"How are you and your brothers going to get on that boat to check it out?" she inquired.

"I'm heading over to the restaurant to meet my brothers at eleven. We are going to work on a plan before we go out. We need to come up with a way to get this Rodrick guy off the boat and distract him long enough for Justice and me to get on the boat and check it out. If there is a bomb, Justice will find it," he returned.

She looked into his eyes with determination. "I'm coming with you."

Jenna was just getting ready to head out the door to see Mike when the doorbell rang. She rushed over to the door, along with Cuddles at her heels. She picked her up and opened the door. There in the doorway stood Mike. Jenna, caught off guard, exclaimed, "Mike, why aren't you at the restaurant?"

"I came to see you; we need to talk."

"Actually, I was just about to head out to see you. Come in." Mike came in and closed the door behind him. Jenna put Cuddles down. When she came back up, she searched his eyes and couldn't help herself. She rushed into his arms. He crushed her to him. After a moment, he released his tight hold on her but kept his arms around her. She gazed up into his eyes. "Mike, honey, I'm so sorry for storming out this afternoon. I'm sorry I wasn't willing to listen to you. It's just that when you told me what you and your brothers were going to do, it scared me. It still scares me, but I am willing to listen now. Can you tell me what this sting operation is about?"

Mike released her and took her hand in his and pulled her over to the couch. He sat down and pulled Jenna onto his lap. He wrapped his arms around her and bent to kiss those sweet lips of hers. His kiss grew more intense as his feelings for this woman came out of him. He lifted his head and kissed her soft lips one more time before he began to explain. "Jenna, love, about this afternoon, I want you to know that I wasn't trying to keep anything from you. I was going to tell you later at dinner, but I still wasn't sure what plan the police departments were going to implement until Zack came in and informed us what would be going down tomorrow night, just before I came to see you." He went on to explain the plan, and what role him and his brothers were going to play in it. After she listened to him, she felt a little better, but still had an uneasy feeling about it.

"What about tonight?" she asked.

"Me, and my brothers, along with Justice, are going out to the marina to see if we can get on that boat. Peyton feels there could be a bomb placed on it. Justice reacted when they got near the boat yesterday when he went out to scope the area. It could be drugs, but he wants to make sure. If there is a bomb, a bomb squad will have to be called in."

"How do you plan on getting on that boat?"

"We're to meet at eleven at the restaurant to go over a plan before we go out."

Jenna quickly sat up. "I'm going with you!"

"No, Jenna, you're not!"

"But I have a great idea, Mike!" she exclaimed.

"Jenna…"

"Mike, honey, will you please listen?"

Mike searched her eyes and sighed. "Okay, shoot."

Jenna went on to explain how she could sidetrack the man, then Peyton and Justice could get on the boat. Mike had to admit it was a good plan, but it was risky. "Are you sure you want to do this?" he reluctantly asked.

"Yes. After all, I was the star in our junior play in high school!"

He chuckled and shook his head. "Okay, but I'll be close by if I need to take him out." With the look that he gave her, she knew without a doubt he meant every word. She gave him a fierce hug.

"I just need to change my shoes, and then I'll be ready."

"It's still early, have you eaten dinner?" he asked.

"No, I've been so uptight that I hadn't thought about it."

"We'll go back to the restaurant and get a bite before Peyton comes in."

"Okay." She went to get up, but he pulled her back and proceeded to kiss her senseless.

When he lifted his head, "Hmm…maybe we should just stay here, forget the world, and lose ourselves in just us," she purred.

He groaned. "I would like nothing better than to do just that, little one, but I'm afraid my brothers would be disappointed if I didn't show up tonight." He sighed. "Go change your shoes, and we'll get going."

Jenna gave him one last kiss. She came up from his lap to go and change into her tennis shoes. After she left, Mike sat for a minute, put his hands through his hair, and wondered how she talked him in to this little plan of hers. It was going to be nerve-racking. She came back from the bedroom as Mike got up from the couch. He took her hand in his. "Ready?"

"Ready," she affirmed.

It was almost nine o'clock when they arrived back at the restaurant. Mike went to put their order in, while Jenna went to a corner booth to sit and wait for Mike. Tammy came up and asked if she wanted anything to drink. "Just two coffees with cream. Mike will be joining me shortly," answered Jenna.

Tammy went to get their coffee as Mike came and sat down in the booth beside Jenna. "Have you seen Mark?" she asked.

"No, not yet. He must be in the office with Justice. He brought him to work when Peyton wasn't back from his interview this afternoon."

Tammy brought their coffees and set them down on the table. "Can I get either of you anything else?" she asked.

"Palani is fixing our meal. Check with him, and when it is ready, could you bring it out to us?"

"Yes, I'd be happy to."

He turned to Jenna. "Sweetheart, did you want a salad with your dinner?"

"No, I don't think so, whatever you ordered will be fine." She smiled.

Mike turned back to Tammy. "I will have a dinner salad, with the Hawaiian dressing with mine."

"Sure thing," she replied.

When she left to get his salad, Jenna entwined her arm with his and smiled up at him. "Do you think it's slow enough that Justice could come out here with us?"

Mike took a look around the bar. It was clearing out, but he wasn't able to see into the Hawaiian room or the lanai. "Maybe by the time we have our dinner we can bring him out."

"Okay, I can't wait to see him again!" Jenna caught a glimpse of the new general manager walking in from the lanai. "How is Jack getting along?"

Mike glanced over to where Jenna nodded her head. "He's doing a great job. Both Mark and I are very pleased at how fast he is catching on. We should be able to leave him on his own in a couple of weeks." He wrapped his arm around Jenna and squeezed her close. He smiled down at her; with his eyes glittering, he whispered in her ear, "Just in time for our wedding and honeymoon."

She returned his smile. "Yes, I can't wait to be Mrs. Michael TreVaine."

He bent and gave her a sweet kiss. His salad came, and the kiss was broken. He released her and smiled up at the waitress. "Thank you, Tammy."

Jenna sat there eyeing his salad. He was just about to take a bite when he glanced over at Jenna. With pleading eyes she asked, "Can I have a bite?"

He chuckled and shook his head. "You said you didn't want a salad."

"I know, but it looks so good!" He took his fork of salad and placed it in her mouth. "Hmm, good!" she said as she was chewing.

"I can have Tammy bring you a salad." He chuckled.

"No, no, I'm fine. I just wanted a bite."

As he continued to eat his salad, out of the corner of his eye he could see her watching him take every bite. When Tammy brought out their dinners, she set them down on the table. Mike looked up at the waitress, and asked, "Tammy, could you please bring Jenna a salad with the Hawaiian dressing?"

"Sure thing." She smiled.

When she left, Mike turned to his wife-to-be. Jenna stopped him before he could say anything. "Mike, you didn't have to order me a salad."

"I felt guilty the whole time I was eating mine!"

With a gleam in her eyes, she chuckled. "I'm sorry. Thank you for ordering it. I'm hungrier than I thought." By the time they finished their dinners, the restaurant had pretty much cleared out. "That was delicious!"

Tammy came to refill their coffee cups and take their plates away. She came back and asked if either one of them would like dessert. Mike glanced over at Jenna; she shook her head no. "No thanks, Tammy. Could you bring me the check?"

"Sure, I'll be right back." She came back with the check and set it on the table.

As she started to walk away, "Hang on a second, Tammy." He picked up the check, took a look, threw some bills on the tray, handed it back to Tammy, and with a smile, "Keep the change."

"Thank you! Enjoy the rest of your night."

Just as Tammy left to go see what needed to be done before she left the restaurant for the night, Mark came into the bar with Justice. He saw Mike and Jenna in a corner booth. Justice was anxious to go to see them. Jenna saw them first. She nudged Mike. "Justice and Mark are on their way over, can you let me out?" Mike slipped out of the booth so Jenna could greet Justice. She got down on her knees and held out her hand. Justice greeted her with a sniff, and then a lick. Jenna placed her hand on top of his head and began to pet him down his back. Justice snuggled up against her, to revel in the attention he was getting. Mike and Mark watched as Jenna talked softly to Justice, and in return the dog licked her face. They were both amazed at how the dog was adapting to different people, along with his new environment, since coming back to the States.

As Jenna continued to fawn over Justice, Mike and Mark took a seat in the booth. "I see you and Jenna settled things between you," Mark inquired.

"Yes, she understands why we have to do this. She's even come up with a plan to get on that boat tonight, but it's making me nervous as hell."

"Seriously? What is the plan she came up with?" he asked.

Mike was just about to tell him when Justice perked up and started barking. Jenna, concerned, asked, "What is it, Justice?" She turned to see what he was barking at and realized it was Peyton and Helen coming in through the bar. She let him go to greet his master. Justice ran up to Peyton, with his whole body wiggling and tail wagging. Peyton bent down and embraced him, started running his hand down his side, as Justice lay down on his back for a full belly rub.

As Peyton rubbed his belly, he softly said, "Have you been a good boy for Mark and Mike?" Helen, watching the two of them together, knew that her dad made the right decision in retiring Justice early. You could see the bond between them was unbreakable. Peyton rose and turned to Helen. "Helen, meet Justice."

Helen bent down to put her hand out so Justice could sniff it. She then came down on her haunches and petted him. "Hi, Justice. I see you are such a handsome boy. I've heard a lot about you." Justice began licking her face. "Aww, I like you too!" She chuckled.

Peyton smiled as she came up from the floor. He glanced over to where his brothers and Jenna were sitting. He headed over there, with Helen and Justice trailing behind. Mike, Mark, and Jenna watched as the three of them came over to their booth, Mike wondering what Helen was doing here. They all greeted each other. Peyton gave his dog a signal, which Justice immediately obeyed, to lay down beside the booth.

Mike spoke up and asked, "Would you two care for anything to drink before we get started?"

"I'll have a black coffee," responded Helen.

"Make that two," answered Peyton.

"Mark?" asked Mike.

"Bring me a coffee as well. I have a feeling it's going to be a long night."

Mike went over to the coffee urn and filled up a carafe with coffee, grabbed three coffee cups, some cream for Mark, some spoons, set them on a tray, and headed back to the booth. As he was sitting the tray on the table, Jack, their new general manager came up behind him and asked if he could speak to him.

"Sure, what can I help you with?" asked Mike.

"I just have a few questions about cashing out the bar register. I just finished up with the main register but have not cashed out the one in the bar before."

Mike turned to his brothers and the women. "Excuse me for a moment. I'll be right back." Mike followed him over to the bar register and proceeded to show him how to cash it out.

As they each poured themselves a cup of coffee, Mark glanced over at Jenna. "Mike tells me you have a plan for getting this Rodrick sidetracked long enough for Peyton and Justice to get on the boat."

Surprised, both Helen and Peyton set their coffee cups down and stared at Jenna. Jenna, a little taken aback, wondered if Mike had already told Mark about it. She glanced over at Mark. "Did Mike already explain the plan to you?"

"No, he said you just had a plan."

Peyton spoke up, "Let's hear it."

Jenna went on to explain what she wanted to do. When she was through, she looked over at Mark. "I'm going to need two half bottles of wine, and we'll need to stop at the drug store on our way out."

Mark, stunned, looked at her like she had grown two heads! "Are you sure Mike is in agreement with this plan of yours?"

"Yes!"

Mike came back to the booth and slid in next to Jenna. "Sorry. It took longer than I thought. Just wanted to make sure all the drawers and receipts were locked away in the safe. What did I miss?"

Mark glared at his brother. "I can't believe you are in agreement with this plan your fiancée wants to implement! Do you have any idea how dangerous it is! We don't know how this Rodrick guy will react!"

"Look, Mark, I am not happy about Jenna being involved, but we will all be in the background. I for one will make sure she's safe! Can any of you come up with a better plan?" he asked irritably.

Helen was silent while everyone was conversing but couldn't help but speak up. "Listen, guys, I can see where Jenna is going with this." With determination she glanced over at Jenna. "Let me be your backup."

Peyton sat forward. "That's an excellent idea! If this Rodrick guy tries anything, Helen will know what to do to take him down. And don't forget, we also have Justice." Justice sat up with his ears perked up at the sound of his master's voice.

Mark and Mike studied each other. Mike glanced back at

Peyton and Helen, then he turned to Jenna. "Are you sure you want to do this?"

With determined eyes firing back at him she said, "Yes!"

Jack chose that time to let them know that all the employees have gone home and the restaurant is set up for tomorrow night. "Thank you, Jack," replied Mark. "We're just getting ready to leave, we'll lock up."

He nodded and left.

Peyton looked around the table. "Are we ready to do this?"

In unison, "Let's go!"

Lieutenant Kevin Andrew was sitting at a desk in his hotel room, going over the plans for tomorrow night's sting operation. He was just informed of the changes that were made over an hour ago. He sent a text off to Detective Fred Zealand to come and join him, so they could go over the plan to make sure everything goes smoothly on their end. He also sent one off to Detective Stacy Rayland but hadn't received a response yet. The knock on the door let him know that Fred was outside waiting. He went to the door to let him in. "Hey, Fred, come on in. I just called down to have some coffee and rolls sent up. I just received the update from the police department, and we need to go over the changes that were made regarding the sting operation. I sent a text off to Stacy but haven't heard back. Have you heard from her today?"

Fred hesitated. He had received a text from her just recently, letting him know she was going out to the marina with Peyton and his brothers to try again to get more information on the boat. After the last time she went off on her own, the lieutenant wasn't happy. Did he go ahead and tell him, or play like he hadn't heard from her?

"Well, sir..."

"Okay, Fred, you have been standing here debating on whether to inform me of something, or not. Tell me where she is," he demanded.

Shit! he thought. *The lieutenant could always read people. I better let him know what's going on, or my ass will be in the sling!* "She went out to the marina with Peyton and his brothers."

"SHE DID WHAT?" he yelled. The lieutenant started pacing. "What in the hell does she think she's doing? I did not give her orders to go out there again! Doesn't she know she could blow this case if something goes wrong?"

"They have a plan, sir," Fred tried to explain.

Kevin stopped in the middle of his pacing and glared at Fred. "A plan? What kind of plan?"

Fred opened his mouth to tell him when Kevin interrupted, "Never mind! We're going out there and stop this plan of theirs!" Kevin went to grab his keys.

"What about the coffee and rolls, sir?" asked Fred.

As mad as Kevin was, he stopped, gave Fred the stink eye, and said, "What in the hell do coffee and rolls have to do with this?"

"Well, I just thought that since you ordered them we should at least take some with us!"

Kevin just shook his head and headed for the door. The minute he opened it, there stood a waiter, ready to knock, holding a tray with coffee and rolls. With his frustration at a boiling point, he backed up and let the waiter in. He set the tray on the table, handed the lieutenant the tab for him to sign, and rushed out the door. "Well, Fred, you got your wish! Grab us each a coffee and some rolls. I'll meet you out in the car!" With that, he walked out of his hotel room and slammed the door behind him! Fred jumped.

Geez, thought Fred, *this is going to be one hell of a long night, with me at the brunt of the lieutenant's temper*! Fred poured them each a coffee. Good thing they had brought to go cups. He grabbed some of the rolls and headed out the door. He didn't need to keep the lieutenant waiting. Not a good plan!

Out at the marina, everyone quietly got into place. Peyton and Justice were one boat down from the *Millie Ann Dream*, hunched down on the dock just behind the boat. Across from him were Mike and Mark, also hunched down on the dock behind a boat. A light was on in the cabin of the *Millie Ann Dream*, so they knew the guy Rodrick was still awake. All the other boats were dark. All three men watched as the scene was about to take place.

Down under the stairs, Helen and Jenna were getting the bottles of wine ready. Helen put the sleeping pills in the bottle that Jenna held in her left hand. The right was clean. Jenna took a few swigs of the wine in her right hand. Helen, watching her, said in a stern voice, "Hey, go easy on that. You have to remember which one has the drugs in it," she whispered.

"Oh, right!" she whispered back. Jenna took another swig. "Jenna!"

"Just making sure I'm in true form! Oh! Can you ruffle up my hair and pull my shirt out?" she whispered. "I need to look the part." Helen did as she was asked. When she was done, she had to admit, Jenna sure looked like a woman drunk.

"Are you ready?" asked Helen.

Jenna giggled. "Ready!"

Jenna and Helen came out behind the stairs. They took a look around. All was clear. Jenna started up the steps, with Helen close behind. Helen had her Glock pulled and was ready to defend them if she needed to. When they reached the top, Jenna took another swig just to build her confidence. She was wondering now what got into her head that she could do this.

"Jenna," whispered Helen, "are you going to be able to handle this? If you're not comfortable, we can stop right now." Helen was concerned, with all the alcohol she's consumed already, whether or not she could pull this off.

Jenna turned back to Helen. "I'm fine, just getting into form. Let's do this!" Jenna started off towards the boat, while Helen slipped down on a dock across from the boat and waited. When Jenna got close, she started laughing, and hollered, "Maggie…! Maggie…! Where are you?" she slurred.

Down in the galley, Rodrick Kevina was looking over some plans for tomorrow night's drug heist, when he heard someone yelling up on the dock. *Son of a bitch*, he said to himself. He hid the plans and started up the stairs to the main deck to see who in the hell was yelling at the top of their lungs. Some people do live on their boats!

Jenna, trying to see down into the cabin of the boat,

"Maggie...!" she slurred. "Are you down there having a party without me? I have your wine!" Jenna staggered back a little, then moved forward. She was feeling a little dizzy. Maybe she did overdo it with the wine. *Keep your head on straight, Jenna*, she said to herself. "Maggie, I'm coming on board!" She was just about to crawl over the side of the boat, when a man with a scowl all over his face approached her.

"What are you doing out here?" he growled.

Jenna jumped! She stood and stared into angry green eyes. He was a big man, wearing faded jeans and a T-shirt, a rough-looking character that she felt stemmed from a life living on the edge. "Oh! You scared me!" she giggled. "I was looking for my friend. I seemed to have lost her. I have her wine, you see." She held up her left hand. "I saw your light on and wondered if she was having a party with someone without me. Is she down there?" she slurred. She started to climb over the side again when he caught her by her upper arms.

"Now hold on there, miss! She ain't down there!" he yelled.

Jenna's lips started to quiver, and tears started down her cheeks. "She's not?" she hiccupped.

He shook his head. "No."

The tears started flowing. "You gotta help me find her, sir! I hope she hasn't fallen into the water and drowned! I don't know what I would do without her. She's my best friend!"

Rodrick was always a sucker for a woman's tears. And what a beautiful woman she was. As his eyes roved over her body, he could see in the dim light she had pretty brown eyes. With her long dark hair disheveled, and a figure to boot, she was one sexy broad. Maybe this was his lucky night! His face softened. "Why don't you come on board, and we'll see if we can straighten this whole mess out about your friend."

Jenna wiped the tears from her face and sniffed. "You mean it?" She watched his eyes turn to lust as he helped her onto the boat.

"Sure, we'll have some of your wine. Then I'll see what I can do to find this friend of yours," he said slyly.

Mike and Mark watched as the man called Rodrick took a weeping Jenna down into the cabin. Mark nudged his brother. "Hey, Jenna's a pretty good actress. If I didn't know any better, I would say she really is drunk!" he whispered.

Mike turned and glared at his brother. He was already beside himself with fear and anger over that man having his hands on her! As he had watched her performance, knowing Jenna, he was wondering if she really was drunk! They continued to watch as Helen silently came out from the dock and climbed on board. Peyton and Justice were on red alert for the signal for them to come aboard the boat.

Helen positioned herself at the top of the stairs, ready to take him out if anything goes array. She listened.

"Why don't you have a seat over here at the table, miss…?"

"Sally, my name is Sally," she slurred. She took another swig of her wine and set the other bottle on the table.

He slid into the seat beside her. "Sally… such a nice name. Let's you and me get to know each other better before we go searching for your friend," he drawled.

Jenna noticed he was practically foaming at the mouth

with lust as he placed his arm around her. Jenna tried to keep her scruples about her. She knew Helen was up there in case this guy went too far. "Well, handsome," she purred, "let's have some wine, and maybe I could be persuaded to forget all about my friend. After all, she did leave me out here all alone," she cooed.

Rodrick's eyes roamed over her breasts and down to her abdomen. He wanted his mouth on those breasts and him deep inside her. He picked up the bottle she set on the table and smiled. "To a night of getting to know each other."

Jenna picked up her bottle and clinked it to his. "To a night of getting to know each other." They both took a drink, Jenna just a sip, as she knew she already had too much wine. Rodrick, on the other hand, guzzled a good portion of his. Jenna hoped the sleeping pills would take effect soon. He bent to press his lips next to hers when she stopped him. "Oh, sugar, we can't kiss until I know your name. You know mine, tell me yours. Then let's have another drink, I'm so thirsty."

He grinned, picked up his bottle, and took another slug of his wine. As he again leaned down to kiss her, he was feeling a little out of himself. "My name is…Rod…" He slumped down into Jenna's lap. Jenna, sitting there with this big oaf lying across her, yelled up to Helen.

Helen came running down the stairs, still with her gun pulled, and took in the situation. "Nice work, Jenna!"

"Thanks, now can you go get the men so they can get this guy off of me?"

Helen put her gun back in her holster. "Sure, be right back!" She ran up the stairs and ran right smack into the lieutenant. Shocked, "Lieutenant!" she exclaimed. "What are you doing out here?"

"I might ask you the same question. Didn't I give you direct orders not to come out here again until this case is wrapped up?" he snarled.

"Listen, Lieutenant, I will explain everything to you," she hissed in a soft voice. "But right now we have a situation going on here, and I need to alert the men. We have a small window of time to accomplish what we came out here to do."

Lieutenant Andrew huffed. "This better be good, Rayland, or I have a good mind to take you off this case right now!"

"Please, just bear with me, sir." Fred stood in the background as he watched his partner fly off the boat, only to arrive back several minutes later with all three TreVaine brothers, and a dog.

Mike was the first one down the stairs to find Jenna with Rodrick, slumped across her lap. He pulled him off of her and dragged him over by the bed. Mark, following his brother down, saw him trying to maneuver Rodrick onto the bed. He grabbed his feet and, between the two of them, placed him on the bed. He was out cold. Mike rushed to Jenna's side. "Sweetheart, are you okay?"

"Yes, honey, I'm fine. I'm feeling a little woozy, though. Did I ever tell you that I'm a cheap drunk?" she giggled.

He chuckled. "No, I don't think you have. Come on. Let's get you up top and into some fresh air." He pulled Jenna out of the booth. She slowly slid down his side, as she tried to walk beside him. He hauled her up on his shoulder and climbed up the stairs. Jenna felt like a sack of potatoes. When he put her down, the breeze from the ocean grazing across her skin felt good.

With her arms around him to hang on, she smiled up at him. "How did I do?"

"You were great, sweetheart." He kissed the top of her head.

"I told you I could do it!" as she passed out in his arms.

Peyton and Justice were just heading down into the cabin when Mike stopped him. "Listen, Peyton, give me your keys. I'm going to take Jenna back to your vehicle. I'm afraid our little star has had too much to drink." Peyton ginned as he took the keys out of his pocket and handed them to his brother. "Don't be long, Peyton. We don't know how long this guy will be out."

"No worries. If there is a bomb on this boat, Justice will find it in short order." Mike nodded, hauled Jenna up in his arms, and started to carry her off the boat.

Watching, Lieutenant Andrew asked, "Do you need any help, Mike?"

"Thank you, but I can handle it. If you and Fred could keep watch to make sure no one comes around, that would be a big help."

"No problem," answered the lieutenant. *When this is over,'* he thought, *someone is going to get a real reaming out.* Traipsing back to Peyton's SUV proved to be more of a challenge than he thought. Carrying Jenna in his arms, through the woods, he finally made it back to the vehicle. As he put Jenna into the SUV, he sighed, *I knew we should have brought two vehicles.*

Peyton gave Justice the signal. "Okay, boy, let's go to work." Justice immediately started sniffing all around. He sniffed in every nook and corner of the cabin. Suddenly, he stopped. His hair stood on end as he let out a low growl. Peyton looked down where Justice was pointing. There were two steps down into the front of the cabin. Peyton went down and felt around on the floor. He could see where the carpet was cut. He pulled it back. There in front of him was a secret compartment. With his heart pounding, he pulled on the latch. He fully expected to see a bomb set up but instead found drugs. There look to be at least a couple hundred thousand in street value. He heard a groan coming from the back of the cabin. Peyton hurried and closed the door of the compartment, put the rug back, and headed back up the stairs. He grabbed the two bottles of wine on the table and took off up the stairs, where Lieutenant Andrew, Helen, Fred, and Mark were waiting, with Justice right behind him. "Okay, we need to split now! He's starting to wake up!" They all hurried off the boat and down into the marina. It wasn't long before they were back at their vehicles.

When Peyton and Mark got into his SUV along with Justice, Mike sat forward with Jenna, still passed out in his arms, and asked, "What did you find?"

"It wasn't a bomb, it was drugs," said Peyton grimly.

Over an hour later, Rodrick was trying to sit up. His head was pounding. At that moment, he realized that that cheap brunette had put something in the wine to knock him out. He would find her and make her pay! As he stood up, staggering a bit and feeling woozy, two people who he thought appeared to be men came down the stairs into the cabin. One he recognized as one of Manchez's guards, the other was in a face mask, so he couldn't tell who he was. Rodrick, taken by surprise, exclaimed, "Hey, guys. What's going on?" The guard pulled out a forty-four Magnum pistol and aimed it at Rodrick's chest. Terrified, Rodrick tried to talk some sense into the guard. "Hey, what do you think you are doing? I'm on your side!"

"Sorry," said the man with the gun, "but we have our orders."

Rodrick tried to argue. "From who?" he asked angrily.

"You don't need to know from who!" he shot back! Two shots were fired into his chest. With his eyes bugged out, Rodrick fell back across his bed in a pool of blood. The one with the face mask went down the steps into the front of the cabin. The person reached down, pulled the carpet back, and opened the compartment. "Man! Did we hit the jackpot!" his partner yelled up, taking the drugs out of the compartment and placing them into a large handbag. While his partner was getting the drugs, he searched the drawers of the cabin until he found the device he was looking for. He grabbed it out of the drawer, as his partner came up from the front of the cabin. "Let's get out of here before the cops show up!" They both took flight and got the hell out!

After Peyton dropped his brothers and Jenna off at the restaurant to retrieve their cars and head home, he headed back over to Helen's. When Helen answered the door, he found Lieutenant Andrew and Detective Zealand sitting at the small table in the dining area, discussing what transpired out at the marina. Helen had already put coffee on and asked her if he could help her put it out on the table. As they worked together, they soon brought out a tray with coffee and rolls to set on the table. Peyton poured them each a cup, then took a seat beside Helen. "So it wasn't a bomb, it was drugs?" asked the lieutenant.

"Yes," answered Peyton. "Justice led me to a hidden compartment down in front of the cabin. When I opened the latch, I fully expected to see a bomb, but it was drugs. And not just a small amount. I would say the street value was at least a couple hundred grand."

Fred whistled. "So, you think this Rodrick guy was skimming off the top?"

"More than likely, Fred," explained Peyton. "My guess is every drug heist he handled, he'd take a bag or two, then turn around and sell it on the side."

Helen, listening, glanced over at Peyton. "You know, Peyton, the one thing that still bothers me is the fact that Marco specifically asked Rodrick if everything was in place if something went wrong with this drug deal. He wanted to make sure no evidence was tied to him or his organization. Could Rodrick have placed a bomb somewhere else, maybe in the warehouse?"

Peyton turned to Helen and caught her eyes. He wished he had an answer for her. "I don't think so, Helen. Justice would have detected it. He was specifically trained in drug detection or bomb modules. When we walked by the warehouse, he would have sensed something was in there." Justice, who was lying by the table, perked his head up when he heard his name. Peyton smiled. "Go back to sleep, boy. You've worked enough for tonight." Justice laid his head back down and promptly went to sleep. They all chuckled.

"Is he always on the alert?" asked the lieutenant.

"Yes," he replied. "When we were working together over in Afghanistan, we had to be ready, day and night. It will take a while for Justice to adapt."

Kevin looked at his watch. It was after three in the morning. "Well, Fred, let's head back to the hotel. We can't do anything more tonight. We all need to get some sleep." He glanced over at Helen. "I'll call you if there are any updates for tomorrow night." Both Kevin and Fred rose up from the table and headed for the door, with Helen and Peyton following. Kevin turned back to Helen. "Let me know how tomorrow goes at Manchez's office. Be on the alert. We don't know after tonight's stunt that your cover wasn't blown."

"Yes, sir," she replied. After they left and Helen closed the door, she turned to Peyton. "The lieutenant isn't very happy with me. I'm lucky he didn't take me off the case."

Peyton put his arm around her. "Let's get to bed. It's been a long night. Things will look better after we've had some sleep." At least he hoped so. There were a lot of things that still plague his mind, like if and where a bomb could be placed to get rid of the evidence. Once he hit the pillow it wasn't long before he fell into a deep sleep.

CHAPTER 13

He was inside a NATO training center. Hidden back away in the dark, he watched as a Taliban insurgent military jeep came crashing into the front of the building. There was an explosion with fire and smoke. The explosion caused fire to break out in different parts of the building. As the smoke cleared, Taliban rushed into the building, firing at anyone and anything they could see. He and his men and several of the Afghan allies rushed out firing back. They took out several of the Taliban insurgents, but not before Jeff, one of his teammates, was shot down along with several others. The anger overtook him as he came out fighting, killing more of the Taliban insurgents. A fog seemed to surround him, as he watched in horror as some of the Taliban that were left started to drag his teammate and the dead out of the building to a hole just a ways from the building. He watched as, one by one, they continued to throw his men into the hole. Peyton tried to get the Taliban to stop, but he was always an arm stretch away. He watched as it happened over and over again, with no end in sight. He started screaming for them to stop.

He opened fire, but they never seemed to die. Someone was trying to get to him, when suddenly he woke up.

Helen woke up with Peyton tossing and turning, moaning for someone to stop. Justice was on the bed, licking his face trying to wake him up. "Justice, down!" commanded Helen. Justice jumped off the bed but turned around and laid his head on the bed beside his master. Helen shook him. "Peyton. Peyton, wake up! You're having a nightmare!"

Peyton sprang forward in a sitting position, sweat pouring off his skin, shaking uncontrollably. With his breathing heavy, he turned to Helen. "I couldn't save them. They're gone and I couldn't save them!"

"Peyton," she assured him, "it was only a nightmare."

He lay back down on the bed. "It was so real," he breathed.

Helen brushed her hand across his brow. "You're okay now. Can you tell me about it?"

As Peyton's breathing returned to normal, he pulled Helen down next to him and held her close. She put her arm around his chest and waited. She felt his body relax a little as he started to tell her about his experience overseas. He told her about the car bombing, how he lost one of his teammates and another seriously injured. "We were told that Taliban insurgents were seen heading in the direction of the NATO training center and to be on the alert. A week had gone by, and nothing. Then it happened. I still feel like I could have done more to prevent the deaths that night."

"Peyton, none of what happened is your fault. You did what you could under the circumstances."

Peyton hugged her closer to him as he felt the tension release from his body. He kissed the top of her head. "Thank you for listening."

Helen lifted herself up and tenderly ran her hand along the side of his face, his beard caressing her hand. "Peyton, if ever you need to talk, I'll be here."

As he gazed into her eyes, he reached up and ran his fingers through her hair and placed it behind her ear. He knew in a heartbeat he was in love with this woman. He had no idea how it would be between them after tonight's sting operation, but he was going to do everything in his power to convince her that they were meant to be together. He pulled her head down and gave her a kiss that showed her what he was feeling.

When she lifted her head, she gazed back into his eyes. "Wow, that kiss was incredible."

Peyton pulled her back down and place her head on his chest. He wasn't ready to talk about that kiss. "Let's try to get back to sleep; we are going to have to be up in just a few short hours." Helen snuggled down on his chest with her arm wrapped around him. He held her tight against him. Lying next to him, she felt his hold on her relax. His breathing slowed, and she knew he had fallen asleep. She thought about what he had told her, about his experience overseas. As she closed her eyes, she wondered how anyone could come to grips with what they saw and dealt with while serving their country.

The next morning Mike was awakened by his cell phone. Still half asleep, he answered, "Mike TreVaine."

"Mike! Zack here. Can you and your brothers meet down at the police station ASAP?"

Mike sat up, careful not to wake Jenna. Alert, he asked, "What's going on?"

"There's been a homicide out at the marina, and word has it that you and your brothers were out there last night. I need you, your brothers, and anyone else that was with you to come in for questioning."

"Can I ask you who was murdered?"

"Rodrick Kevina. The guy that works on Manchez's boat," stated Zack.

Mike sat stunned. He was alive when they left! "I'll get ahold of my brothers and we will be down there as quick as we can."

"Good, I'll see you shortly," he returned.

Mike turned to shake Jenna. "Sweetheart, it's time to wake up."

Jenna moaned. "What time is it?"

"It's just after seven."

She snuggled back down into the pillow. "It's too early, just let me sleep a little longer."

"No can do, little one. Zack just called and we have to go down to the police station. Rodrick Kevina was murdered last night."

As Mike's words sunk in, Jenna instantly sprang forward in the bed. She moaned. Her head felt like it was busting from all the wine she drank last night. "Did I hear you right? Rodrick was murdered?" Suddenly it hit her! "Oh, Mike, I've killed him! The drugs we put in the wine must have killed him!"

As Mike looked into eyes full of fear and shock at what he

just told her, he took his hands and placed them on her upper arms. "Jenna," he said with determination, "you did not kill him. There were not enough drugs in the wine to kill him. Something else must have happened after we left. You go shower and get dressed, I need to call my brothers." Jenna hurried and was showered and dressed in fifteen minutes flat. Mike followed suit, and it wasn't long before they were entering the doors of the police station.

Zack met them at the door. "Hi, Mike, Jenna. Thanks for coming so quickly. Mark and Peyton are on their way. They will be here shortly. Let's go back to the conference room. Lieutenant Andrew and Detective Zealand are with Lieutenant Fillmore and Detective Jenson. Follow me." Mike and Jenna followed Zack into the conference room and were greeted by the four men sitting at the table. "Have a seat. I'm going back out to the lobby to wait for your bothers arrival."

When Zack left, Mike turned to Lieutenant Fillmore. "Can you tell us what happened to Rodrick?"

"Sorry, Mike," answered Lieutenant Fillmore, "I would prefer to wait until your brothers get here so I'm not repeating myself. We need to ask all of you some questions, to clear up any misinformation that was given to us last night at the scene of the crime."

Mike nodded and turned to Jenna. He could see she was nervous as she fidgeted with her hands in her lap. Mike took one of her hands in his and gave it a gentle squeeze. She glanced up at him as he smiled down at her and whispered, "It's going to be okay." She gave him a slight smile and nodded her head. Zack came back into the room, with Peyton and

Mark close behind. Mike and Jenna greeted his brothers as all three men took a seat at the table.

"Now that we are all here, let's get started," stated Lt. Fillmore. "I've asked Lieutenant Andrew and Detective Zealand here as well, as they were out at the marina later, after your little escapade went down. What were you four doing out there, and what did you expect to accomplish by taking such a risk?" he asked.

Peyton spoke up first. "Listen, Lieutenant, this was all my idea. I wanted to see if there was a bomb planted on that boat. I wanted to make sure we weren't dealing with a bomb threat, along with handling this sting operation tonight."

"Didn't you know that this whole thing could have blown up in your faces? Suppose the people we are dealing with recognized you tonight?"

"As far as we know, Lieutenant," answered Peyton, "no one saw us. We made sure of it."

"So, what did you find?"

"After we knew Rodrick was out from the sleeping pills we had put in the wine, Justice and I went down into the cabin. Justice went on point looking down into the front of the cabin. I went down and found a secret compartment. When I opened it, I found drugs, a lot of drugs, instead of the bomb that I had suspected. When I heard groaning, I hurried to close it up, grabbed the two bottles of wine off the table, and got the hell out! We all left together."

"Did your brother tell you that Rodrick was killed last night?"

"Yes, but I swear he was alive when we left!"

"We searched that whole boat and there were no drugs found, not even in the compartment you are referring to."

"Sir, I swear to you on my honor that the drugs were there and I didn't take them."

Lieutenant Andrew confirmed, "He's telling the truth. He brought nothing up with him from the cabin, other than the two bottles of wine. Then we left."

Both Mike and Mark, who were listening, were getting impatient. Mike asked, "Can you tell us how Rodrick died?"

"Please tell us he didn't die from the sleeping pills," cried Jenna.

Lieutenant Fillmore glanced over at Jenna. "No, Jenna. He was shot with a forty-four Magnum pistol, twice, in the chest."

All three brothers and Jenna sat back in their chairs stunned. "None of us had a gun except Helen. No shots were fired while we were there," exclaimed Mark.

"Look, Mark," stated Zack, "none of us is accusing anyone of you with killing Rodrick, but we have to find out what exactly happened when you were out there. Let's take it one at a time. Let's start with you, Mark. Tell us from the beginning how you were involved and what happened while you were there."

Mark proceeded to tell him he had gone out there with his brothers and Jenna to get a scope on the marina and how it was laid out, and that they had also come up with a plan to get Peyton and Justice on the boat. "We were all hidden behind the boats, on the docks, but close enough to keep an eye on Jenna, to make sure everything went as planned. When

Jenna was able to get on the boat with Rodrick, Helen followed onto the boat and was there to make sure nothing happened to Jenna. Once Helen came back to notify us that it was safe to come on board the boat, we all rushed on and down into the cabin of the boat. That's when we saw Rodrick, passed out from the sleeping pills we had put in the wine that he drank. Mike and I lifted Rodrick onto the bed, and there is where we left him. Peyton and Justice went to work. Peyton found the drugs down in front of the galley, where he left them. When he came up from the cabin, he said we needed to get out of there as Rodrick was starting to wake up. We all left and headed back to our vehicles."

"Mike," asked Zack, "what is your take on this?"

"It is pretty much as Mark had stated. My only concern was to make sure nothing happened to Jenna. When we were able to get on the boat, I rushed down to make sure Jenna was all right and found Rodrick slumped over Jenna's lap. I pulled him off, then drug him over beside the bed, where Mark helped me lift him onto the bed. When I checked on Jenna, she said she was fine, which she was not, so I carried her up and out of the cabin, where she passed out in my arms. I asked Peyton for his keys. I took Jenna back to his vehicle, where we waited for everyone to return."

"We've already heard from Peyton," stated Zack. "Jenna, what was your role in all of this?"

Jenna, feeling a little intimidated, she had never in her life been interrogated before, looked up at Mike. He nodded his head. She noticed Craig taking notes as all of them gave their statements. Nervously, she looked back over at Zack, and began, "Well, Zack, just so you know, I came up with this harebrained scheme. When we all arrived at the marina, the men went on up to where the boats were moored and Helen and I went underneath the stairs to get ready. I had two half bottles of wine, one in each hand. Helen put the sleeping pills in the bottle I was holding in my left hand, the right was clean. Once that was done, I had Helen mess up my hair and pull my shirt out so I would look like I was drunk. I took a few swigs of my wine to relax me so I would make sure I could pull this off." She smiled. "I might have had a little too much wine!" They all chuckled as she continued, "I started up the stairs with Helen right behind me. I drank some more of my wine and started off. I played like I was calling for my friend who left me out there all alone. When Rodrick heard me, he came up from the cabin and approached me. He was not a happy camper. He was very angry at first. When I tried to explain why I was out there, he insisted that my friend was not down there with him having a party. I started crying. He felt sorry for me and helped me onto the boat, where he took me down into the cabin. I remember setting the bottle of wine I held in my left hand on the table and held on to the one on my right. I took another drink. I was starting to feel a little woozy but held on till I was able to get him to drink some of the wine on the table. When he passed out, I called up to Helen. She then got the men. Mike was the first to come down, and as he said, he pulled Rodrick off me, and he and Mark placed him on the bed. I remember Mike hauling me upstairs, and after that, I don't remember anything." Mike squeezed her hand to reassure her she did great. She glanced up and gave him a slight smile. She turned back. Zack was shaking his head.

"Jenna, this guy could have assaulted you. Weren't you afraid?"

"At first, yes, but I guess I drank enough wine to carry it through. It all worked out Zack. We were able to get the information we needed. There was no bomb on the boat!"

Lieutenant Andrew stepped in, "She's right, Zack. Even though it was one hell of a risk, at least we know we are not dealing with a bomb threat."

"What was the time of death?" asked Peyton.

"When we arrived at the scene, it was three in the morning. The coroner states time of death around two fifteen a.m."

"We all left shortly after one a.m.," stated Mark.

Lieutenant Fillmore went over all the information given and addressed the men and Jenna in the room. "Okay, I want to thank you all for your statements. We now know you are all in the clear, as the homicide happened after two a.m. If you have time, we need to go over tonight's plan, to see if it needs modification knowing what we know now. I am still waiting on Mick to give us the time and description of the vehicle involved in transporting the drugs. Helen is supposed to check in to let us know how things are going at her end."

While they were discussing the plan for that night, Lieutenant Fillmore got a text. He checked his phone; it was from Mick. He read the text. When he finished, he looked around the table. "I just received the text from Mick. We now have the time of arrival and the description of the vehicle." He went over the information with all of them, Jenna listening intently, as she wanted to make sure of Mike's role, and whoever was involved, would be safe.

When they were discussing how they were going to stop the truck without the suspects fleeing, Jenna perked up, and with a gleam in her eyes said, "Gentlemen, I have a brilliant idea!"

All the men looked her way. Mike, knowing Jenna, and seeing that look in her pretty brown eyes, firmly stated, "Jenna, no! Not this time!"

She turned towards him. "But, Mike, you haven't heard what I have to say!"

After listening to Jenna's statement, Lieutenant Andrew was intrigued. "Let's hear what she has to say, Mike."

Mike sighed; he wasn't sure he wanted to hear this.

Jenna went on to explain how they could stop the truck and how they could apprehend the drivers of the truck. Mike watched his bride-to-be explain how this plan of hers would play out and wondered if this was the same woman he fell in love with. She went from being totally against this sting operation to being totally involved! When she finished, she glanced over at Mike and peered into eyes wary of her plan. "What do you think?" she asked of him.

"What do I think? Jenna, this is too dangerous! I don't want to risk your life out there. Anything could happen to you!" he said in exasperation.

"But you and Mark will be with me in the shadows, along with some of the police officers!" she insisted.

Peyton, listening to Jenna's plan, and Mike's reaction, spoke up, "Listen, Mike, she did a pretty good job last night.

If Jenna feels confident that she could pull this off, it's worth a shot. Justice and I can be there for the initial shake down, making sure the drugs are on the truck before I head out to the marina."

Mike and his brother had a stare down before he turned and fixed his eyes on Jenna. With the utmost determination in her voice, she responded with, "I can do this!"

As Mike glanced around the room at the men seated at the table, waiting for his reply, he turned to the one woman he would give his life for and said, "Okay, but I don't have to like it!"

CHAPTER 14

Helen, who was sitting at her desk, tried to focus on her task for the day, but her mind kept wandering to the message she received from the lieutenant that morning about Rodrick Kevina being killed early this morning. Peyton had already left when she received his text. She knew the lieutenant and her partner Fred were at the police station going over the details of the homicide. She was anxious to know what happened. The drugs she put in the wine were not enough to kill him. He was alive when they all left. As she pondered over what could have happened, the doors to the elevator opened. Two men she had never seen before came into the reception area and up to her desk. Both were large men. As she stared at the two, the one on the right was bald with vivid blue eyes, and his facial features were set in stone. The other one had black hair, dark brown eyes, his skin color was dark brown, and he stood just a little shorter than his cohort. He too resembled the other man, with his facial features set in stone. Both were dressed in dark suits. "Can I help you, gentlemen?" she asked.

The one with the bald head answered, "We are here to see Mr. Manchez. Is he available?" he asked in a gruff voice.

"May I ask what this is concerning?" she countered.

"We have some information for him concerning one of his sporting goods stores. It's very important."

Helen broke out in goosebumps as she studied the man in front of her. She had a feeling that these two men had something to do with the homicide out at the marina early this morning. She composed herself as she asked, "May I ask your names, so I can inform Mr. Manchez of your arrival?"

"Tell him Bart and Stan are here to see him," he stated sternly.

Helen pushed the intercom. "Yes, Helen?"

As she eyed the man named Bart, she answered, "Sorry for the interruption, Mr. Manchez, but there is a Bart and Stan here to see you. They state it's important."

At his desk, Marco wondered what was happening to the men he hired. They know they are not to show up here unless called in. "Send them in," he answered irritability.

"You can go in now."

As the two men walked around her desk, she heard one comment to the other, "Let's hope the boss isn't too upset by us coming in here, or our heads could roll."

"Let's hope," the other said, as they entered Marco Manchez's office. This led Helen to believe there was more to it than just a problem at one of his sporting goods stores. She didn't know how long the men would be in Marco's office, so she hurried up and texted the lieutenant.

The two men sat down in the chairs in front of Marco's

desk. As they seated themselves, Marco with his hands folded, leaned forward, glared at the two men, and asked boldly, "What is so important that you had to show up at my office? You both know the protocol. You are to text or phone me unless I call you in here for a meeting!"

Both men looked at each other and wondered if it hadn't been a mistake by coming here. Both turned back to their boss. Bart spoke up, "We're sorry, Mr. Manchez, but we felt we should come here directly and inform you that Rodrick is dead."

Marco, shocked, sat up from his desk, "What? How?" he demanded.

"We went to check on him this morning, to make sure all was ready for tonight, and found police all over the boat and docks. Word has it Rodrick was shot in the chest sometime early this morning."

Marco sat back in his chair, stunned. He wondered who was behind this. Rodrick was supposed to see to it that if anything went array, he would make sure no one in his organization was implicated. "What else did you find out?" he demanded.

"I overheard one of the police officers tell the officer in charge that a compartment was found in the front galley of the boat. Word has it that there were drugs in that compartment. Whoever killed Rodrick knew where he stored them. After killing him, he took the drugs and left," Stan confessed.

Marco's blood started to boil. *So, Rodrick was skimming off the top. Good thing he's dead, saves me from killing him myself!* "Did they find anything else?"

"As far as we know, no, sir," answered Bart.

"Go back out there and let me know if the police are gone, then call me."

"Yes, sir." The two men rose and left the office, leaving Marco wondering who in the hell else knew Rodrick was stealing drugs. *Whoever it was knew there was enough there to kill for it!* Another problem he needed to deal with was to find out if the device Rodrick made is still on the boat. Without it, this whole thing could blow up in his face! It was too late to stop the drug heist, it was already in motion. If he didn't get this shipment to LA on time, he would be a dead man. He had too much on the line; his only hope in this going as planned was Mick.

Helen watched the two men leave the office and head down to the main lobby in the elevator. Oh, she would have loved to have been a fly on the wall so she could have listened to the conversation. She alerted the lieutenant, to give him the description of the two men. He informed her he would notify her partner Fred and the police departments involved with the case. If those two men were involved in the homicide, the police could pick them up for questioning. She would have to wait to hear back from the lieutenant with any news. The intercom buzzed. "Helen, come into my office," stated Marco.

"Yes, sir." She got up from her desk and opened the door to Mr. Manchez's office. "You wanted to see me, sir?" she inquired.

"Yes, Helen. Get Mick Southerland on the phone. Ask him to come into the office."

"Yes, sir." She closed the door and made the call.

A short time later, Bart and Stan drove into the marina. There were two police cars still parked in the parking lot. Stan, who was seated in the passenger seat, sent a text off to their boss that the police were still here. He waited for his reply. One of the officers who was coming down from the docks noticed a black SUV pulling into the parking lot. He radioed his men to stop what they were doing. "Listen, there's a black SUV parked out here in the parking lot. I'm going to see who it is. I need you down here to back me up."

Bart and Stan watched as the officer approached their vehicle. "What do we do?" asked Stan. "They saw us out here this morning."

"I'll tell you what we are not going to do. We are not going to stay here and be questioned by the police!" Bart backed up, just as the officer neared the vehicle, turned, and slammed his foot on the accelerator. Tires squealed as he tore out of the parking lot.

The police officer and one of his men jumped into their patrol car and raced after the black SUV. The officer radioed for more back up. "This is officer Rick Boyd, badge number two six seven. We are on a high-speed chase, going south on Highway Seven. The description of the vehicle is a black Ford Edge, license number H13580, traveling at a high rate of speed. Suspects may be armed and dangerous. Proceed with caution." Officer Boyd gained speed and was hot on his tail. With his lights flashing, his siren blaring, the suspects didn't stop. Officer Boyd pressed on the accelerator and pulled up beside the SUV. His partner next to him, through the PA system, informed the suspects to pull over. In his rearview mirror, Officer Boyd saw two other patrol cars coming up fast behind the SUV. Officer Boyd sped up and pulled in front of the vehicle. One of the patrol cars from behind, pulled up beside the SUV, and the other one stayed behind. Officer Boyd slowed his car and, between the three patrol cars, pulled the SUV off to the side of the road.

As the officers raced from their vehicles with their guns pulled, Stan turned to Bart. "Way to go, Bart. Now we're toast!"

Bart glared back at Stan. "We know nothing! Is that clear?"

At the police station, Officer Boyd and his partner hauled the two men into the station. Peyton, Jenna, and his brothers were just leaving the station as the men were brought in. Peyton turned to Jenna and his brothers. "You go on ahead. I'm going to hang back, to see what's going on here. I'll meet up with all of you tonight."

"Okay, Peyton, we'll see you tonight," replied Mark.

Mick entered the elevator that would take him to Marco Manchez's office. He received a text this morning from Detective Williams that Rodrick Kevina, a guy who worked for Manchez on his boat, was found dead this morning. He wondered if this was the reason he called him into his office, or if he was going to change course for tonight's drug heist. The elevator door opened. He walked up to Helen's desk. He took a brief look around. "Can you tell me what this is about?" he asked.

Helen shook her head. "Sorry, Mick, I have no idea, but

two men came into his office this morning. I think they may be connected to the homicide out at the marina early this morning," she said in a hushed voice. "I've already alerted the lieutenant and gave him a description of the two men."

Suddenly, Marco Manchez's office door opened, just as Mick was going to comment. "Mick, you're here!" he said in surprise. He then gave Helen a questioning look.

"Sorry, Mr. Manchez," Helen stated, "I was just about to announce him."

He glanced back at Mick. "Come into my office, Mick." Mick walked around Helen's desk and entered Marco's office. Marco closed the door, but not before he gave Helen a withering look.

Whew! That was close! she thought. She didn't like the look he gave her when he went into his office. This night couldn't come fast enough. She wanted to be done, and not keep wondering if her cover was going to be blown at any minute!

Mick, with his arms crossed and feet slightly apart, waited for Marco to take a seat behind his desk. "Have a seat, Mick."

Mick took the seat in front of his desk. He leaned forward and asked, "Is there something going on that I should know about?" he asked.

Marco stared steadily into Mick's eyes and answered, "Have you heard about a homicide that occurred out at the marina this morning?"

Mick knew he had to play dumb. So, with a surprised look, he answered, "I'm sorry, Marco, but I haven't even been out to the marina, since the drugs aren't to be delivered until tonight. Do you want me to go out there to see what happened and report back?"

"The homicide happened on my boat," he said disgustingly. "The guy was my first mate. What I've heard is that he had drugs stored in a secret compartment on the boat. Whoever killed him knew he had the drugs and where they were stored. How are you at navigating around the police?"

Mick shrugged his shoulders. "I can manage. What do you want me to find out?" he asked.

"I need you to go out there to find out if anything was discovered on the boat, besides the drugs missing, and report back to me." He had received a text from Stan that the police were still there. He answered his text and told him and Bart to stay away, but never received a text back to confirm. Now he couldn't get ahold of either one of them!

"Is this all you need?"

"For now. Text me back as soon as you find out. Is everything all set for tonight?"

"So far so good. I haven't met the other guards as of yet."

"They will be there two hours before the drugs come in, along with Victor." He opened his top drawer, pulled out a slip of paper, and handed it to Mick. "Here is the code to the warehouse."

Mick pulled a small pad of paper out of his front pocket of his shirt, along with a pen, and wrote the code down. He handed it back to Marco. He looked into Marco's eyes and asked, "Is there anything else?"

"Just make sure everything goes smoothly tonight." Mick rose from his seat; Marco followed suit.

"I'll make sure of it." Marco followed him to the door. As he opened the door for Mick to let him out, he glanced at Helen, then he watched Mick walk to the elevator. When the doors opened, he walked in, with the doors closing behind him. Marco glanced back at Helen. He wanted to make sure nothing was going on with the two. He was well aware that they were deep in conversation when he opened the door earlier. He closed the door and went back behind his desk. As he sat down in his chair, thoughts of what happened out on his boat swarmed in his head. *Who could have killed Rodrick? How much in street value did the killers walk off with?* It bothered him that one of his most loyal and trusted men would steal from him. Anyone working for him knew the outcome if any of them were caught stealing. Then, there was the other problem. He had to know if the device Rodrick made was still on the boat. He had to make sure that no matter what he wouldn't be implicated in tonight's drug heist. He looked at his phone. He slammed his fist on his desk! *Why in the hell haven't Bart and Stan retuned my message?* He took and rubbed his hands down his face. This day was turning out to be more of a headache than he planned!

At the police station, Peyton, sitting in front of a computer with headphones on, watched the two men sitting in the interrogation room. Both men glanced around the room not saying one word. He could tell that both men were nervous. One would look at the other, then look away, while one of them tapped his fingers on the table, waiting for the detective to come into the room. Peyton needed to know if by chance they had anything to do with the homicide this morning. He wanted to get a good look at the two, in case they were connected to Manchez's organization. Detective Williams was kind enough to let him sit in while they were being questioned. As he focused on the screen, Detective Craig Jenson entered the room. He sat down in front of the two suspects. With a pad of paper on the table and a pen in his hand, he stared at the two men before him. "I'm Detective Craig Jenson. I need to ask both of you some questions as to what took place out at the marina early this morning. Do either of you know a Rodrick Kevina?"

Neither one of them answered. Detective Jenson looked from one to the other. "We know you were both seen out at the marina trying to get information from one of the officers this morning. Who are you working for?"

Both men stayed silent.

Detective Jenson looked over at the one called Bart. "Where were you at two fifteen a.m. this morning?" he asked sternly.

"I was home asleep with my wife," answered Bart.

"Will she be able to verify that?"

"Yes!" he answered.

"If you were both sleeping, how would she know that you didn't wake up, slip out, and shoot Rodrick in the chest?" Craig demanded.

"I swear to you that I was not out there, and I did not kill him!" he asserted.

Frustrated, Craig turned to Stan. "And where were you this morning around two fifteen a.m.?"

"I was home as well, asleep," he answered.

"Do you have anyone who could vouch for you?" he asked.

"No, I live alone," he said bluntly.

Detective Jenson looked back over to Bart. "What made you take off when an officer approached you? The officer clocked you going a hundred miles per hour plus! What are you hiding?"

"Detective, I am not hiding anything. It was a stupid move, and I apologize to the officer."

"Well, your apology is not going to keep you from getting ticketed for reckless driving, and purposely ignoring an officer in pursuit. I should throw you both in jail for the latter one alone!" he insisted. Detective Jenson angrily got up and left the room. Peyton continued to watch the two men after the detective left. Both men leaned back in their chairs, looked at one another, and then stared at the door, wondering if someone else was going to come in.

Lieutenant Fillmore and Lieutenant Andrew were outside the room watching through the window when Craig came out. He walked up to the lieutenants. "We have to let them go; there is nothing we can hold them on. As you both have seen, they're not talking. They're working for someone, I know it!"

Lieutenant Fillmore continued to watch the two men. "You're right, Detective. I feel the same way; they're holding back," commented Lieutenant Andrew.

Zack walked up to the men; they all turned towards him as he began to go over the information he uncovered, "We checked them out with the information given, they're clean. Also, we couldn't get into their phones to see who they have texted or called, not much to go on."

Lieutenant Fillmore finally spoke up. "Let them go, ticket Bart, since he was the one driving, and I'll put another detective on to keep an eye on them. They are definitely hiding something. Maybe they will lead us to whoever they are covering for."

Mick pulled into the marina, parked, and got out of his car. He looked around the grounds and spotted an officer talking with a fellow officer near the stairs leading up to the docks where the boats were moored. He walked up, nodded his head, and introduced himself. "Mick Southerland. I heard there was a homicide here early this morning. I'm working on a case that may be connected to this one." He quickly showed the two officers his badge. One of the officers stepped up and filled him in. "Would it be possible for me to go up and check out the boat?" he asked.

"I don't see why not. We haven't uncovered much; we were just about to leave, but we can take you up there."

Mick followed the officers up to Manchez's boat. When they approached it, Mick saw it was taped off due to the homicide and continuing investigation. He asked, "Did you look through every drawer and compartment on the boat?"

"Yes," replied one of the officers. "We pretty much tore the place apart, but we didn't find a thing. The only thing that was taken was the drugs in a compartment in the front area of the galley. Everything else was left untouched."

"You didn't see anything unusual, maybe some type of device that would detonate a bomb?" Mick had learned from Zack this morning that Peyton and his brothers were out here late last night, to see if a bomb was planted on the boat. None was found. But that didn't mean that one could be placed somewhere else. They needed to cover all the bases.

"No, we found nothing that would resemble a detonator," the officer answered.

"Okay, thanks for all your help. I'm going to have a look around to see if there is anything I can uncover."

"Suit yourself. We're heading out." The officers walked back down to their vehicles.

When he heard the patrol cars leave, Mick went on board the vessel. He looked around the starboard and didn't see anything unusual. He followed the stairs down into the cabin. He went through all the drawers himself and found nothing. He next stripped the bed and lifted the mattress. Something appeared to be under the protective cover. He pulled it back. Underneath, he picked up what seemed to be some sort of map. As he opened it, he read what was inside. He quickly refolded it and stuffed it in his pocket. He put the bed back together and left the boat. He would need to get with the detectives ASAP. He texted Marco, to let him know that nothing out of the ordinary was found on his boat. As he walked down to his SUV, he glanced over at the warehouse. He checked his watch. *Well, this is as good a time as any to check out the inside.* He went up to the door, pulled the piece of paper out of his pocket, punched in the code, and walked in. There didn't appear to be anyone around. He started walking through the building. He checked out the areas behind the crates and the area where the boats were stored. He was bent down, looking underneath this one yacht, when he felt a barrel of a gun pressed against his head.

"What the hell are you doing in this building, and how did you get in?" the man behind him scowled. Mick's heart started racing, as the adrenaline started coursing through his veins. He raised his hands and tried to get up. He heard the click of his gun as the man pulled back the hammer. "Don't move if you want to live! Now tell me what you're doing here!"

"Listen, I work for Marco Manchez. He gave me the code to his warehouse and asked me to check around." Mick wasn't sure this guy was part of the drug heist tonight, so he didn't want to give him too much information. "You can call him. He will verify that I am Mick Southerland and that I am on his payroll." Mick tried to turn his head to see who held him captive.

"I wouldn't do it if I were you!" The man holding the gun pulled his cell phone out of his pocket to dial up his boss's number. When Marco answered, "Sorry to bother you, Mr. Manchez, but I have a man here that claims to be Mick Southerland. He says he's on your payroll." As Mick listened, "Yes, sir… Sorry, sir… Yes, sir." When the conversation ended, Mick felt the gun pull away from his head. He breathed a sigh of relief.

"May I get up now?" he questioned the man.

"Yes," he answered.

Mick slowly rose up from the floor, then turned around to face the man who had held the gun to his head. Mick thought the man looked familiar to him. He wasn't sure, but he thought he might be the officer from the sheriff's department.

He fit the description Detective Williams had given him several weeks ago. Staring into a pair of brown eyes, Mick inquired, "I take it Marco confirmed my identity?"

"Sorry, Mr. Southerland. With everything about to go down tonight, you can never be too careful. Go ahead and check out what you need. I need to finish up some paperwork, then I will be leaving."

"Thanks, Mr....?"

"Oh, sorry, Ben Gillard," he stated as he held out his hand to shake.

Bingo! *He is the slime ball from the sheriff's department!* he said to himself. Mick reluctantly shook his hand. "I won't be long, Ben," he said curtly.

"Take as long as you need, we need to make sure this drug heist goes smoothly tonight." With that, he turned and walked back to the office and closed the door. Mick watched him go in and sit down at the desk through the window of the office. Once he was busy on the computer, Mick went and finished checking out the warehouse. When he was done, he had a clear view of the layout of the building. As he was leaving, he glanced over at the office and realized Ben had already left. He wondered if he was going to be here tonight as one of the guards. He looked at his watch; it was already past three. He needed to get with the detectives on what he found on Manchez's boat. He headed out the door and into his SUV. He pulled up Zack's number as he pulled out of the parking lot. What he had to share was detrimental to how they apprehended the people involved in this drug deal.

"Detective Williams," he answered.

"Hey, Zack. Mick here. I just uncovered some information out here on Manchez's boat. It has to do with tonight's drug heist. You and all the department heads involved with the case need to see this. Where can I meet you?" he asked.

"Meet me and Detective Jenson out at the North Shore Park. We'll be there in twenty minutes."

"Right, I'll see you there."

Peyton was just about to leave the police station, when Zack came up to him. "Peyton, hold on just a minute." Peyton turned towards the detective. "I just got a call from Mick. He has some new information on the drug heist tonight. Do you have time to ride out there with us?"

Peyton checked his watch. He was supposed to meet Helen and his brothers at the restaurant in little over an hour. "How long will this take?" he asked.

"No more than an hour if we leave right now."

"Okay, let's go!"

Mick, sitting in his car, watched the kids swing on the swings and climb the playground equipment while he waited for the detectives to arrive. He didn't have to wait long before he saw them pulling into the parking lot. Zack, Craig, and Peyton exited the vehicle and walked up to Mick's car. Mick came out of his vehicle and waited as the men approached him. He shook hands with each of them. "Guys, I'm going to cut to the chase. We only have a few hours left before everything goes down tonight. I found this map between Rodrick's mattress and the protective cover underneath. You and the department heads need to take a look. It's a map of tonight's drug heist. It gives us a clear view of what will be going down tonight." Mick pulled the map out of his pocket and handed it to Zack. Zack pulled it open and placed it on the hood of Mick's car. All four men gave it a look.

Peyton was the first to speak. "This is going to help big time, as now we know where Manchez's men will be placed in and around the building when the truck comes in."

Zack, studying the map, returns with, "Let's get this back to the station. We need to go over it with the lieutenants," he stated. "Peyton, can you and your brothers and Jenna meet at the police station at seven p.m.?" he asked.

"That should work. We are having dinner at five thirty at the restaurant. Helen will be with us."

"Excellent, that should give us enough time to go over the final plans and be out at the marina before the shake down tonight. Mick, I will send over the plans to you in an email. Then I want you to delete it."

"Right," said Mick.

"Thanks for uncovering this, Mick. We'll be in touch." All four men got into their cars and exited the park. Mick decided to get a bite to eat, then he would head back to the warehouse to wait for Zack's email. After looking at the map, he would also try to figure out a way to set Victor up so they all wouldn't end up dead!

CHAPTER 15

Helen, sitting at her desk, was trying to figure out a way to leave early. She needed time to rush home and change before she met Peyton at the restaurant by 5:30. Jenna and his brothers would be there as well. After dinner, they would head over to the police station to go over the final details of the sting operation. She received a text from Lieutenant Andrew telling her that they had caught the two men she had described to him earlier but had to let them go due to the fact there was nothing they could hold them on. He also informed her that the police department put a man on to follow them, as they felt the two men, Bart and Stan, were holding back and covering for someone.

Helen signed out of her computer and shut it down. *Well, she thought, this is as good a time as any to see if I can leave.* She rose up from her desk, went over and knocked on Marco's door.

"Come in," stated Marco.

Helen nervously opened the door and took a deep breath. Marco looked up as she stood just inside the door. "Sorry to bother you, Mr. Manchez, but I was wondering if I might be able to leave early today. I have an appointment to get my hair cut. The hairdresser was only able to fit me in this afternoon."

Marco sat back in his chair and studied Helen. She seemed nervous. "Come and have a seat, Helen."

Surprised, she wondered what he wanted to talk to her about. She nervously walked into his office and took a seat in front of his desk. "How long have you been with me, Helen?" he asked.

"A little over four months, sir," she replied.

"How do you know Mick?"

Surprised by the question, "I'm sorry, sir?" she asked.

"I noticed that you and he were deep in conversation when I opened the door earlier. Did you know him before he came into the office?"

"No, sir. I had never met the man until he came in with Ralph several months ago. By the way, I haven't seen Ralph in quite a while, did he leave your employment?" she asked in return. She needed to throw him off track. She knew he was fishing for information, due to the fact that she didn't let him know right away that Mick had arrived. She also knew that Ralph was murdered. And it was suspected that it was one of Marco's men who took him out.

"Ralph had an unfortunate accident. He is no longer with us."

"Oh, I'm sorry, sir. Will there be anything else?"

Marco sat back up to his desk and leaned forward. "No, Helen. That will be all. You may go and enjoy your weekend. I will see you back here on Monday."

Helen rose from her chair. "Thank you, Mr. Manchez. You have a good weekend as well." Helen left his office and closed the door. She breathed a sigh of relief! Thank the Lord this night will soon be over! She grabbed her purse and headed down to the main floor in the elevator. When the doors opened, she hurried out of the main doors of the building. She couldn't get out of there fast enough.

Marco watched as Helen left his office. She appeared to be nervous as she sat down in front of him. He hadn't noticed her being nervous before in his company. He wondered… He picked up his phone and made a call.

Helen, back at her bungalow, hurried and changed into black jeans and a T-shirt. She quickly let her hair down and brushed it out. She had bought a black wig a few days ago, threw it in a bag, along with her make-up and some extra clothes. She would finish getting ready at the restaurant. She put on her shoulder harness and her ankle holster and placed her guns inside each holster. She slipped on her dress boots and a lightweight jacket and flew out the door. She noticed a hair salon on her way to the restaurant and decided to stop in. Just in case Marco put a man on to follow her. She didn't trust him after the conversation she had with him. She pulled into the parking lot and went inside. One of the girls was able to give her a quick trim. As she walked out the door, she looked at her watch. She was going to be a little late meeting Peyton. She would explain when she arrived. As she pulled out of the parking lot, she didn't notice the black SUV pulling out behind her. When she arrived at the restaurant, she looked around but didn't see a black sedan around and breathed a sigh of relief, just as a black SUV drove by. She went inside the restaurant to find Peyton, Jenna, and his brothers sitting together in a corner booth in the bar area. Justice was lying under the booth by Peyton's feet. She went over to greet them. "Sorry I'm late. I had to take a slight detour."

Peyton rose from the table to let Helen in. "Justice, come, boy," commanded Peyton. Justice came out from underneath the booth. While he waited for his next command, Helen slid into the booth, followed by Peyton. Peyton turned to Justice. "Back underneath the booth, boy," he commanded. Peyton, anxious to hear what kept her, asked, "What happened?"

Tammy chose that moment to come and ask her if she wanted anything to drink. "Just a black coffee," she answered. When she left, Helen started in, "I went to Marco's office to ask if I could leave early. Told him I had an appointment with a hairdresser. He asked me to come in and take a seat. When I did, he started asking me questions about whether or not I knew Mick before he started coming into the office."

With everyone listening, Mark asked, "Why did he want to know?"

Tammy brought over Helen's coffee and set it on the table in front of her. "Are any of you ready to order?" she asked.

Mike spoke up. "Can you give us a few minutes, Tammy? We'll let you know when we are ready."

"Sure, no problem," she answered.

When she turned to serve other customers, Helen glanced back at Mark. "Marco had called Mick in earlier. When he opened the door to his office, he saw Mick and me talking. Marco was quite upset that I didn't tell him Mick had come in right away. I'm sure he was trying to get information from me as to the conversation we were having."

"What did you tell him?" asked Peyton.

"I just told him that the first time I had met Mick was when he came in with Ralph, which was true. I turned the tables on him and mentioned to him that I hadn't seen Ralph in a while. He then told me he met with an unfortunate accident."

Mike huffed. "Well, we all know what that was!"

"Yes," answered Helen. "I asked him if that was all. He told me to go ahead and go, and he would see me on Monday."

"Fat chance!" returned Peyton. "After tonight, he'll be locked up for a long time!"

Next to Mike, Jenna shivered. "Let's hope so. That man is evil through and through!" exclaimed Jenna.

Mike looked over at his wife-to-be, worried over her part in the sting operation. "Are you sure you're ready to do this tonight?"

Jenna knew Mike was concerned; she was actually a little nervous about it herself, but she answered him with confidence. "Yes, Mike, I'm ready. No worries." *I might have to have a glass of wine, though, just so I can relax before I go out.*

Mark looked at his watch. "It's getting late. We better order if we are going to be at the police station by seven." Mike motioned Tammy over, and they each gave her their order. "Tammy?" he asked.

"Yes," she answered.

"Could you please tell Palani to make it quick. We have to be somewhere in an hour."

"Sure will, Mike."

Mike turned back to Peyton and asked, "What did you find out this afternoon, when Mick showed you and the detectives the map he found on Marco's boat?"

"Listen, bro, I'm not sure I want to discuss it here. Let's wait till we get to the station, and the lieutenants will go over everything with us then. But I can tell you this: it gave us a better picture of how it's going to go down tonight."

"Good. I'm anxious to review it."

"Just so you know." He looked at his brothers and Jenna. "It won't change your involvement," Peyton replied.

"Good to know," said Mark. Their food came, and they quickly ate their meal. Tammy came back and asked if they wanted any dessert. "No thanks, Tammy. Just the check," answered Mike.

Helen needed to get up and change into the outfit she brought with her. Jenna needed to get up as well. "I'll go with you." The men came up out of the booth to let the women out. As they went towards the rest room, Marco and his wife came into the restaurant.

There was a line up at the door. Marco looked to see if he could find Mark or Mike around and discovered all three of the TreVaine brothers sitting in a corner booth in the bar. They were dressed in jeans and T-shirts. Not the usual attire that they normally would wear. A man came up to him and his wife. He had jet black hair, dark brown eyes, and was of average height. "Good evening, how many are in your party tonight?" he asked.

"Just the two of us," answered Marco. "May I ask if Mark

or Mike are working tonight? I see them sitting over in the bar area."

Jack glanced back over to where the TreVaine brothers were sitting. "Actually, no. Let me introduce myself, I'm Jack Fleming, the new general manager." He held out his hand to shake. Marco shook his hand. "Mark and Mike are taking the night off and spending it with their brother Peyton and Mike's fiancée' Jenna," he explained.

"I'm Marco Manchez and this is my wife, Millie."

"It's very nice to meet you both. Do you have a preference as to where you would like a table?" asked Jack.

"We prefer the Hawaiian room, if there is a table available," answered Marco.

"Just give me a minute and I'll go check for you." Jack left to go check the Hawaiian room.

In the meantime, …Helen and Jenna were in the restroom. Helen was changing into the outfit she had brought with her. Jenna came out of the stall and waited for Helen to come out of the one next to hers. When she came out, Jenna was shocked! Stacy was dressed in tight leather pants, a black knit sleeveless sweater, black leather dress boots, and a matching black leather jacket. "Wow, Helen! Is that what you are wearing?" asked Jenna.

"Yes, I need to wear a disguise in case Marco had someone follow me. Also so no one else in his organization will recognize me. Can you help me with this wig, Jenna?"

"Sure."

Helen put her long blond hair up in a ponytail, and Jenna helped get the wig in position on her head. She tucked any loose ends underneath it. Helen went to work on her makeup, took a comb through the long black hair of the wig, and was soon ready to go out and meet up with the men. She looked at herself in the mirror, then at Jenna. "What do you think?" she asked.

Jenna, amazed at the transformation, grinned and said, "I'm not sure if Peyton is going to recognize you!" They both grinned and headed out the door of the restroom. They were walking down the hallway into the bar, but both stopped dead in their tracks! Both women quickly backed up. Marco and his wife were at the hostess station!

Helen tried to think. "Jenna, you go out and alert the guys. Make sure you all leave together. Tell Peyton I will be out shortly, and make sure he goes with you. Oh, and grab my purse!"

"Okay, see you shortly." Jenna came into the bar and up to the men. "I don't know if you noticed, but Marco and his wife Millie are waiting at the hostess station."

Mark spoke up. "Yeah, I noticed, but didn't want to say anything to draw attention to ourselves."

"Where's Helen?" asked Peyton.

"She'll be along in a minute. She asked that we all leave together. That includes you, Peyton, and Justice. She said she would meet us outside the restaurant."

Peyton didn't like that idea, with Marco standing right by the door. What if he recognized her even with her hair down and her glasses off!

Jenna could see Peyton hesitate when his brothers said it was time to go. "Peyton, Helen knows what she is doing," she whispered. Jenna grabbed their purses, hid one under her jacket, took Mike's arm, and led them towards the door. Peyton called to Justice and proceeded to follow them to the door.

"Let me handle this," Mike said under his breath.

"Good evening, Marco, Millie. How are you both doing tonight?" greeted Mike.

"Fine, fine," he answered. "I see you and your brother hired a general manager."

"Yes, with the restaurant getting busier, Mark and I felt we needed to bring someone in to handle the reins so we could take a little time to ourselves and work on other aspects of the business," replied Mike.

"It's the first Friday night we have had off together since we opened the restaurant." Marco chuckled.

"Well, he seems like a nice enough fellow."

"He is," replied Mike. "He's doing a great job for us." Mike heard a low growl behind him.

Peyton looked down at Justice. "Easy, boy," he said in a low voice. He gave him a command to sit.

Marco looked over at Peyton, and down to a black lab. He turned back to Mike. "When did you start allowing dogs into your restaurant?"

Mike was just about to answer, when suddenly Jack came up to Marco, to let him and his wife know that their table was ready in the Hawaiian room. Marco nodded his head and started to follow Jack to their table. As he passed Peyton and his dog, he heard another low growl. He turned to glance back at Peyton and his dog. "I don't think your dog likes me."

"Sorry, Marco," Peyton responded. "He's very protective of me. Justice and I worked together in the military. It will take time for him to adjust."

With Jack still waiting to take them to their table, Marco nodded his head, glanced back over to the men and Jenna standing by the door. "Well, gentlemen, Jenna, have a good evening."

"Thank you, Marco. You and your wife do the same." With that they exited the door. They walked a few steps from the door, stopped, and waited for Helen to join them.

Helen, tying to be patient, looked in the direction of the hostess stand. The men and Jenna stood talking to Marco and his wife. Finally, they left, and the new general manager led Marco and Millie to their table. Suddenly, Marco stopped, whispered something in his wife's ear, and was walking this way! Helen scurried back into the restroom. She took a minute to compose herself. Then, with confidence, she opened the door, just as Marco was passing by the restroom. She started walking, swinging her hips back and forth in a seductive stride. He smiled. She returned his smile as she continued to walk past him. He turned around and watched as her hips swung in all that leather! *She is one sexy broad*, he thought. *Too bad I'm married; I wouldn't mind having a go with her!*

Helen seemed to be taking her time coming out of the restaurant. "Listen, you go on ahead. Justice and I will wait for Helen, and we will meet you at the police station. It's already after seven."

"Okay," answered Mark. "We'll see all of you down there."

Peyton was getting frustrated waiting for Helen. He was just about to go back into the restaurant when a gorgeous woman with long black hair, dressed in black leather, came out of the restaurant. He stopped her. "Excuse me, miss. Did you happen to see a very good-looking woman, with long blond hair, dressed in black jeans and a T-shirt in the bar area of the restaurant, or possibly the restroom?" asked Peyton.

"Sorry," she drawled. "But I didn't see anyone in the restaurant that fit that description." She gave Peyton a wink. "Maybe you should forget about her. Let's you and me go have some fun!"

"Whoa, young lady. I already have a date for tonight. And she is right there in that restaurant!" he exclaimed.

Helen chuckled. "Peyton, it's me!" she cried.

Shocked, he asked, "Helen?"

"Yes. Now, come on! We're already late! And from now on, you are to call me Stacy."

Peyton, dazed at the transformation, watched her cute little ass going back and forth as she walked to the car in all that leather! She stopped and turned towards him as she realized he and Justice were still behind her. With a smile on those pretty red lips, she said, "Eyes up here, Peyton," as she points to her eyes. "Come on, we have to go!"

Peyton rushed up to her, pulled her into him, and kissed her hard. When he lifted his head, he breathed, "When this is all over, be ready for some intense lovemaking!"

Stacy felt the chills going down her spine as she responded, "Yes, but first we need to concentrate on tonight!"

"Yes ma'am!" he replied. "Come on, Justice!"

As they headed down to the police station, two men in a black SUV kept watch on the restaurant. Stan looked at his watch. "Look, Bart, I don't know what is taking this woman so long to come out of the restaurant, but we need to get going. We'll just have to tell the boss she is in the restaurant somewhere."

"He's not going to like that!" answered Bart.

"Well, he's not going to like us being late going out to the warehouse. After this afternoon's fiasco we don't want him to get any more upset than he already is! I'll text him. Just get going."

Bart started the engine, and they headed out. Marco heard his phone ding. He took it out of his pocket and read the text from Stan. He took a deep breath, looked over at his wife, and sighed. "Excuse me a moment, Millie. I need to go check on something."

"Is everything all right?" she asked.

"Nothing to worry about, I'll be right back." Marco wanted to check for himself, to see if Helen was somewhere in the restaurant. He got up from his seat and walked through the bar, looking on his way out into the lanai. He scanned the tables but didn't see her.

Jack came up behind him. "Is there something I can help you with, Marco?"

Startled, he turned toward Jack. "No, I just thought I saw someone I knew out here in the lanai. Guess I was wrong."

"Maybe I can help you. Can you give me a description of this person?"

"Well, it's a woman, actually. She's my receptionist. She has blond hair, and usually wears it on top of her head. She could have worn it down, and wears large dark-rimmed glasses. Did you happen to see her tonight?" Marco asked.

"Umm, no one who fit that description. But I did see a pretty blond woman sitting with the TreVaine brothers. But I didn't see her leave with them. She must have left on her own sometime tonight because she's not here now," answered Jack.

Marco, looking perplexed, didn't know what to think. "Thank you for your help, Jack."

"You're welcome, sir." Marco turned and started back to his table, stopped, then went outside to make a phone call.

"Stan here," he answered.

"I thought you said you didn't see Helen come out of this restaurant," he yelled into the phone!

"We didn't, sir. She has to be in there."

"Well, she's not!"

"Sir, we followed her from her bungalow to the hairdresser, then to the restaurant, and we never saw her leave! I can even give a description of her. She was wearing black jeans, black T-shirt, she wore her hair down, and she wasn't wearing her glasses."

Marco, stunned, thought about the woman Jack seen sitting with the TreVaine brothers. Could that have been Helen? "Somehow she slipped out without you two knowing it. Where are you now?" demanded Marco.

"We are just coming up to the warehouse, sir," answered Stan.

"I want you to give me an update every hour until the job has been completed!" he ground into the phone. "Do I make myself clear?"

"Yes, sir!"

Marco ended the call and stomped back into the restaurant. When he returned to his table, the food had been delivered, and it was cold. He ran his hands down the sides of his face. This whole day was not going as planned. He'd better be thinking about plan B, should things go south!

Peyton, Stacy, and Justice arrived at the station and were led back to the conference room. The two lieutenants, Zack, Craig, and his two brothers were leaning over the table looking at the map. "Where's Jenna?" asked Stacy.

All six men looked up from the conference table and stared at Stacy. "Nice outfit, Rayland!" commented Lieutenant Andrew.

Stacy grinned. "Thanks!"

"She's getting ready, she'll be out in a few minutes." Mike smiled. "Are all of us supposed to call you Stacy now?" asked Mark.

"Yes. Now that I am working with all of you tonight, it's important not to give my cover away till this is over."

Peyton and Stacy moved up to the table, just as Jenna walked in, wearing a red mini-skirt, silver sequined tank top, red high heels, and several colored bands around her left wrist. She had a matching silver sequin band around her head. Her hair was sprayed red and was piled on top of her head, with tendrils coming down around her face and neck. Her big brown eyes were heavily made up. Rouge adorned her cheeks, and a bright red lipstick covered her lips, to complete the character she was to portray. Everyone in the room turned to take in the woman that just walked in the door.

"Wow, Jenna!" exclaimed Mark.

Mike stared with unbelieving eyes at his woman.

She went up to him, smiled, and said, "What do you think, honey? Do you like my new look?"

Pulling her into his arms, "I'm not sure I want you leaving this building dressed in that outfit. Are you sure you want to do this?" he asked for the third time today. He was worried. He didn't want anything to happen to her.

Jenna placed her hand on his cheek. She saw the love and concern in his eyes. "Yes, I'll be fine. You'll be close by. We'll do this together, along with your brothers and the police force."

"Mike," encouraged Stacy. Mike turned toward Stacy. "I'll be right beside her. I'm to be her backup. I'll make sure she's safe." Mike half smiled and nodded.

"Okay," Lieutenant Fillmore started, "let's go over these plans and make sure we have everything covered." They all turned toward the table, as the lieutenant went over how the map was laid out and where everyone involved in the case were going to be positioned. "Police dressed in plain clothes will be over here, along with a few on the docks. Do any of you have any questions before we start out?" They all shook their heads no. The lieutenant looked at his watch. "Okay, the first phase is about to start. Let's head out."

CHAPTER 16

Out on Highway 7, there was an unmarked car a few miles from the TreVaine brothers, Stacy, and Jenna, along with Justice, to alert them when the truck with the drugs was getting near their location. On the other side of the road were two police officers lying on the ground in wait. Down in a ravine, the men were waiting for a radio call, while the women were standing along the roadside, ready for their role to begin. Aside from Jenna, everyone was dressed in black, so as not to be seen. All were wearing mini cams, and radio equipment, except for Jenna.

"Jenna," Stacy asked in a low voice, "how are you doing?"

"I'm not afraid to tell you I'm extremely nervous. I hope I can pull this off. I brought a small bottle of wine with me, just in case."

"Where is it?"

"It's in my purse," she responded.

"If you think it will help calm you, go ahead and take a drink from it before the truck arrives. We need this to go like clockwork."

Jenna reached into her purse and took the small bottle of wine out and twisted off the cap. She took a long draw of the wine, screwed the cap back on, and placed it back in her purse. "Okay, I'm ready."

"Just remember, I'll be right beside you."

She nodded her head yes.

Mike, never taking his eyes off Jenna, watched her take a drink from a bottle and put it back into her purse. He knew she shouldn't be doing this. He started to get up to tell her it's not too late to call it quits when Mark grabbed his arm. "What are you doing?" he whispered.

"I'm going to tell Jenna she doesn't have to do this before the truck arrives. She's already drinking from the wine she had in her purse. I don't want anything to happen to her!" he asserted back.

Mark listened as Peyton took the call. "It's already too late. The truck is on its way." Mike scrunched back down beside his brother, his heart going into overdrive as he was about to watch his love, and Stacy, do a performance of a lifetime! He sent up a prayer, just as the truck was slowing to a stop.

Driving north on Highway 7, Al and Dan saw two women up ahead trying to hitch a ride. "Hey, Al," said Dan, "do you see what I see up ahead?"

"Yeah, but we have no time to stop. We have a job to do."

"Oh, come on, Al! I haven't had a woman in a long time, and they look just right for the picking. Let's stop and give them a ride. We can always tie them up and gag them until the job is done. Then when we drop the drugs off, we get the hell out and go have a good time!"

Al thought for a moment, and grinned. "Okay, we are running a little ahead of schedule. Let's make this quick. If we are late at all with this load, we're dead men. Remember that."

As they came to a stop, "You take the one in black leather, Al. I'm going to take this cute little thing, all dressed up just for me."

Jenna's heart was racing as she tried to calm herself, when the truck pulled up alongside them. "I'm right with you, Jenna," Stacy whispered. "This won't take long. Remember, the men are not too far from us."

Jenna nodded as the man on the passenger side rolled down his window.

"Hi, ladies, you two need a ride?" he drawled.

Jenna noticed the man was practically foaming at the mouth. She let her tongue glide across her lower lip as she answered, "Yes, sir. You see, my car broke down a few miles up the road. My friend and I started walking back to town, as our cell service is bad, and we couldn't get ahold of anyone to come and help us."

The man's eyes roved up and down Jenna's body and stopped when he saw the top of her breasts peeking out from the sparkly tank top she was wearing. He glanced over to the woman in black leather. She too had a dynamite figure. He glanced back at Jenna. But this one, he thought, is going to satisfy the need he has in his loins. "Where are you two beauties headed?" he asked.

"We need to get to the marina. We were hired by a gentleman who owns a yacht for a party he's throwing. We are already late. Can you help us out?" she asked seductively.

Dan glanced back at Al and grinned. Al nodded his head. With both men looking towards the women, the officers began to get into place. "Well, young ladies, this is your lucky night. We are headed that way as well."

Jenna stepped in front of Stacy and up to the cab of the truck. "Really?" she exclaimed,

"Oh, this would help us out so much!" She turned back to Stacy. "Hopefully Mr. Rawlings won't be too upset when we show up a little late."

Stacy flipped her hand in the air. "No worries, Sally. We can sweet talk him around. You just leave that to me." She glanced up at the guy and gave him a wink. "Can you help us into your truck?" she asked.

"Sure, honey." Dan couldn't believe his luck. He couldn't wait for this job to be done. He was going to have one hell of a time with Sally, maybe both. He and Al could switch off. *Oh, this night couldn't have gone any better if we had planned it!* Dan opened the door and came down from the cab. When he went to open the door of the club cab, he felt a barrel of a gun in his back.

"Don't move! Put both hands in the air!" Stacy commanded.

Dan raised his hands as the men started rushing out to help the women. While Al was watching for Dan to open up the club cab so he could get a good look at the women they would be driving to the marina, he heard a click. He turned quickly to see a gun pointed at his face. He saw another officer behind him, with his gun pointed directly at him. He knew then this was a set up. *Damn Dan for wanting to pick up some women!*

"I want you to step slowly out of your cab and onto the ground with your hands up," demanded the officer. He stepped off the step railing and opened the door at the same time. Dan did what he was told. "Turn around and put your hands behind your back." His partner came and cuffed him. The first officer radioed for a car to come and pick up the suspects.

"Let's move around to the other side of the truck." When they came around, Al saw his buddy in cuffs, plus three other men and a dog. He knew they were sunk. *There's no use trying to make a run for it. The dog alone scares the shit outta me.*

Al gave Dan a scathing look, as he was taken up beside him.

Peyton and Justice moved to the back of the truck. He unlatched the door and pushed it open. Justice, with his tail wagging and eyes on the inside of the bed of the truck, was impatient to get in. "Okay, boy. Let's see what's in here." Justice jumped up and went to work. He soon found the crate. Sure enough, there was a star stamped on it. He opened the crate with a small crowbar he had brought with him. What he saw inside made his head swim. There were enough drugs in there to make someone quite wealthy. With his pocketknife, he put a small slit in one of the bags and tasted what was inside. *Boi.*

Mark came around the back of the truck to check on his brother. "Did you find the drugs?"

"Yes," as he was putting the top back on. He and Justice came down from the back of the truck and walked around to the side. He nodded to the officer.

The officer turned toward the two men in cuffs. "Did you two know you were carrying drugs in the back of your truck?" he asked. Neither one of them spoke. "Where are you taking them?" Silence. "According to these two women, you were headed for the marina. Who are you working for?" Still no answer. "Okay, maybe you'll talk when you've been locked up for a while. Read them their rights and take them down to the station, Officer Bowing."

As they were leaving, he turned to the TreVaine brothers. "Okay, you've got some time to make up, you need to get going."

Mike went over to Jenna. "You go with the officer. I'll meet you back at your apartment."

Jenna responded with fear in her eyes. "Mike, I want to go with you."

"No, Jenna, this is where I put my foot down. If you're with me, I won't be able to concentrate on what I'm supposed to do. Try to understand, Jenna. I need to know that you are safe. Please, go back to your apartment and stay there until I return. We will be fine. We have plenty of backup." His eyes pleaded with her.

"Mike, we have to go," insisted Mark.

Mike pulled her in his arms and gave her a kiss worth remembering. He pulled away and took her to the officer who was to take her home. "Make sure she goes inside."

The officer nodded.

As he turned to walk back to the truck, she called, "I love you!"

He turned back with eyes showing all that she meant to him. "I love you!" He turned to get into the truck, and within moments, they were gone. As she watched the truck pull out onto the highway, she whispered, *Be safe*. She sent up a big prayer, for the Lord to keep watch on all who were involved.

Peyton, at the wheel of the semi, drove as fast as the law would allow. Mike, Stacy, and Justice sat in the back of the club cab, while Mark sat up front. He looked over at his brother. "I was hoping I could drive this thing," stated Mark.

"Have you ever driven a semi?" Peyton asked his brother.

"No, but I took a quick online course the other night. It didn't look too complicated."

Peyton laughed and shook his head. "I'm afraid that is not the same as driving one, bro."

"Well." He chuckled. "I still think I could do it." They were silent for the rest of the trip, as each one was lost in their own thoughts as to how this night would turn out. Peyton looked in his rearview mirror at Helen, no, Stacy. He hoped he would keep her name straight. She seemed so calm for what was about to take place. He wondered how Mick was doing, if the officers were able to do their part. They would soon see.

In the warehouse, Mick was watching Victor as he paced back and forth through the building, checking his watch every so often. Mick sensed something was up and didn't trust him. He went over to the window and looked out over the back of the warehouse. He couldn't see much but knew there were officers out there waiting for the right moment to take out the outside guards. He didn't know what the plan was to accomplish this goal, but he hoped it worked.

Outside, a car with a local pizzeria sign drove into the parking lot of the marina. Zack, who was disguised as a delivery man, was wearing faded jeans with holes in them, a black T-shirt with a sleeveless matching vest. On top of his head was a knit cap, pulled down over his ears. His nine-millimeter Glock was tucked securely behind his back, inside his jeans, while the vest hid the top of his gun. The two guards in front were alerted as the car pulled in the parking lot and parked. They watched as Zack came out of his car. With the short barrel rifle hanging down from their shoulder strap, both guards pulled them up to their sides, ready to take out anyone suspicious. Zack pulled out three large pizzas from the back seat of the car. He walked up to the man guarding the door. He noticed the semi-automatic rifle he had pointed directly at him. With confidence he stated, "I have a pizza delivery."

"I didn't order a pizza. Did you, Ted?" he asked gruffly.

Ted shook his head no.

"These are compliments from a Mr. Marco Manchez. Said he wanted to make sure his crew out here was fed."

Ted walked up to Ned. "Well, that was nice of the boss. I'm starving! I'll go get the guys in the back."

While Ted went around the side of the building to get the other two guards, Zack asked the man called Ned, "How many are inside the building?"

"What business is it of yours, delivery boy?" he answered curtly.

"Mr. Manchez wanted to make sure there was enough for everyone."

"Four!" he yelled.

Zack knew this but wanted to make sure no one else was added that they weren't aware of. Ted came back around to the front of the building with the two men who Officer Boyd arrested earlier today for reckless driving and fleeing from an officer of the law. *Bingo! Now we know who they are working for.*

"Man! I can't believe the boss would send pizza out to us! Not after we talked to him just a while ago!" exclaimed Stan.

"Do you think we should take one inside?" ask Bart.

"Hey, you guys should eat this while it's hot! Once you have eaten your share, one of you can take some inside to the others. There's a picnic table over here. I'll just set the pizzas on it, and you guys can dig in!" Zack walked over to the picnic table, set the pizzas down, and started off to his car. He turned, and with a wave of his hand said, "Enjoy the pizza, guys. You all have a good night!"

Bart opened the first box and grabbed a piece. The others followed suit.

Zack, back in the car, watched, as officers surrounded the four men. "Don't anybody move or say one word. Now, slowly step away from the picnic table. Place your hands on top of your head."

Shocked, the four guards stepped back from the table as the officers surrounded them. "Now take your weapons and place them on the ground beside you!" Slowly, they slipped the shoulder strap off and the rifles fell to the ground as officers held them at gun point. Two officers took the weapons from each of the guards. "Now, put your hands behind your back." The officers cuffed each one. "Now, gentlemen, let's go for a walk." After reading their rights, four officers led the suspects down the road to the back of the woods, where cars were waiting to hall them off to jail, while the rest hung back and lined up on each side of the building. Zack got out of the car to join them. He met up with Lieutenant Fillmore and Lieutenant Andrew. His partner, Craig, was on the other side of the building with a couple of the officers from the sheriff's department.

"Great job, men," commented Zack. "I just gave a signal to Mick that the guards have been taken out, also to the Tre-Vaine brothers. Now, we wait for the truck."

"Will they make it on time?" asked Lieutenant Andrew.

Zack looked at his watch. "They got a late start, but Peyton was going to make up the time on the highway. They should be here within the next fifteen minutes."

"Let's hope so. We don't need the guards in the warehouse getting restless, especially Victor," stated Kevin.

Peyton, driving the short bed semi, turned to his brother Mark. "We are just a little ways out from the marina. We should just make it on time. We need to get ready."

Stacy, sitting back with Mike, noticed that Justice was panting heavily and whining every so often. Mike noticed it too. She wondered if he was all right. Stacy sat forward to inform him what was going on. "Hey, Peyton, Justice is acting funny back here. He's panting and whining. Is this normal behavior when he is working on a case?"

"Not usually, but the drugs are still on the truck. He may also be anticipating when we deliver them."

"What can we do to calm him? We can't have him acting like this when we get to the warehouse."

"When we get there, I'll give him the order to calm and

be quiet. In the meantime, just pet his back and try to soothe him. We'll be coming into the marina in just a few minutes."

Mark's phone vibrated with an incoming text. When he read it, he looked over at his brother. "The outside guards have been taken out."

Peyton took a deep breath. "Good, phase two has been successfully executed. Now let's pray phase three goes as planned."

The marina was coming into view. Peyton slowed the semi and turned down the drive to the back of the warehouse. He could see some of the police officers lined up along the wall as they passed. "Okay, we need to get in place. Stacy, Mike, get down in the seat." Peyton pulled up in front of the garage door, stopped, ready to back the trailer in. Peyton and Mark then pulled out their hats, slipped them down over their foreheads to keep from being recognized. Justice was still whining in the back. Peyton gave the order, "Justice! Quiet!" he commanded. Justice laid his head down on the floor.

Stacy, down on the floor with Justice, petted his head. "It's going to be okay, boy. It will all be over soon." He seemed to calm down but was shaking as Peyton started to back the semi into the warehouse.

Mick, watching out the window, saw the semi drive in. He went over to push the button for the door to open. As Peyton backed in, Mick glanced over at Victor. He was texting someone on his phone. He assumed it was Manchez; he in turn texted the men on the boat, sitting out in the harbor, waiting to come into dock. When the semi was fully in the building, Peyton cut the engine. Victor, with his semi-automatic short-barrel rifle, pointed it at Mick. "Close the door!" he demanded.

As he pushed the button, he thought, *So, he was to be taken out along with the others when they checked the drugs. Not if I can help it!* He glanced up at Peyton as he opened the door to get out of the cab. Mark followed suit.

Victor motioned to one of the guards. "Go check the front door; make sure it's locked." As the guard left to check the door, Peyton and Mark moved to the back of the truck, flipped the latch, and opened the door. Peyton pulled out the ramp attached to the back of the truck and set the one end down on the cement floor. The guard came back and nodded his head. "Okay, you two get up there and pull the crate with the drugs in it," Victor demanded.

The two guards and Victor stood behind the truck as Mark and Peyton climb up into the back of the rig. Mick stayed just to the side of the back of the semi, keeping his eyes on Victor. With Mark leaving the door slightly ajar, Stacy and Mike silently came out of the cab with Justice. With their guns pulled, they crept up to the front of the semi, jetted across, and hid behind some crates, while all eyes were still on the back of the semi. Slowly, they crept behind the crates until they were behind the guards. Justice, on high alert, was silent as a mouse.

Mike turned to Stacy. "I'm going across and get behind that yacht," he whispered. "I want to get closer to the guard on the right. You keep an eye on the guy next to him. It looks like Mick has got a bead on Victor."

She nodded. Stacy watched as Mike crept across the warehouse and got into place. Then all eyes were on the guards, as they waited for the right moment.

Peyton and Mark hauled the crate from the front bed of the truck to the rear. Peyton took the top of the crate off with the short-handled crowbar he had in the pocket of his jacket. Victor waved to one of the guards with his rifle. "Jake, get up there and check to make sure the drugs are in the crate and accounted for."

Jake went up the ramp, took out his pocketknife, and put a small slit in one of the bags. He tasted it. Nodded his head yes. As he checked the rest of the contents, Stacy and Mike moved in, with Justice moving slowly beside Stacy. "This is the police! Don't anybody move! Place your weapons on the floor!" demanded Sergeant Rayland.

Victor and the guards reacted. Just as they turned to fire their guns, Mike came up to the guard on his right and sucker punched him, grabbed his gun, and threw it across the building, while Mark turned and punched the second guard to take him out. While his brothers were handling the guards, Peyton and Mick both went after Victor, but not before he fired several rounds of ammo, flying towards Stacy. Stacy dropped to the floor, missing several bullets, with one hitting her left arm. She grabbed her arm as the pain hit her. She watched as Mick took a swing at Victor, knocking the gun out of his hand. Victor went after him, but not before Peyton turned him around and gave him a punch in the gut and then to the jaw. This hardly affected Victor as he lunged toward Peyton. Justice, watching his master being attacked, went into defense mode.

"Justice, no!" yelled Stacy. He flew out, and within seconds he was on Victor, grabbing his arm, growling and pulling him away from Peyton. Victor went down, rolling on the floor, yelling, "Call your dog off!"

"Justice, down!" Justice heard the command and backed off of Victor. "Stay!" he commanded.

Victor slowly got up from the floor, half dazed, holding on to his arm. Mick took over, and he pushed Victor up against the side of the truck. Peyton came up beside him and, between the two of them, cuffed Victor's hands behind his back and turned him around. Victor turned to Mick, with eyes as black as coals, his facial features in a rage. "I should have known you were a damn cop!" he exploded.

Mick, staring back at Victor, shrugged his shoulders. "Sorry, Victor, it's time you paid the piper for all the killings you and your boss have arranged throughout his drug dealings."

Glaring into Mick's eyes. "I give you fair warning, Southerland, watch your back, or you might just end up dead like the rest of them!"

"Threats don't intimidate me, Victor," as he pointed his gun in Victor's chest. "So, I suggest you shut your mouth before I put a bullet in your chest like you did poor Ralph."

As the words sunk in, Victor had the decency to realize that it was over.

Officers outside the building, hearing shots being fired, tried to get inside through the door. It was locked. Lieutenant Fillmore went over to the window, just on other side of the door. "Stand back!" he ordered. With the butt of his riffle, he broke the window, and the men rushed inside. What they saw had them immediately taking over. Mike and Mark had the two guards down on the floor, holding them at gunpoint. Mick was guarding Victor, with Peyton down on the floor with Stacy, holding her as she had been shot. Lieutenant Andrew ran up to Stacy. He went down on one knee as he examined his detective. Concerned, he said, "Rayland, how are you doing?"

Holding her arm, she glanced up at the lieutenant. "I'm fine. One of the bullets just grazed my arm."

"You'll need to have it looked at. An ambulance is on its way. Can you get up?"

"Yes, I think so." She winced as both Peyton and the lieutenant helped her to her feet.

Mike and Mark came up to Peyton as Mick along with the other officers took out the guards and Victor to their cars and down to the jailhouse. "How's she doing?" asked Mark.

"She's going to be all right. Just a graze in the shoulder. Thank God a bullet didn't hit her heart!" answered Peyton. He shuddered; just the thought of losing her made his heart ache. When he saw her lying on the floor, holding her arm, he rushed to her side. With his heart throbbing, he pulled her in his arms and instantly knew he was hopelessly in love with this woman.

Mike, watching his brother with Stacy, could see without a doubt he had lost his heart to her. Looking back at Justice, he also knew something was definitely wrong with his dog. "Hey, Peyton, I hate to interrupt here, but Justice is still acting weird. I'm going to go get his lead out of the cab of the truck. Maybe he needs to go out."

Peyton, looking over at Justice, was sitting by the middle of the truck wining with his head down. Something was up.

"Okay, Mike. You go get his lead. I'll go check on him." He gazed down at Stacy with eyes that showed all the love he held for her and placed a gentle hand on her left cheek. "I've got to go see what's bothering Justice. Will you be all right?"

She nodded her head. "Go, I'll be fine."

"I'll stay with her," responded Kevin. "Go check on your dog."

Mike went to get the lead while Peyton and Mark started walking up to where Justice was sitting. "Justice, come here, boy. What seems to be bothering you, huh, boy? What's going on?"

Justice, with his head down, came up to his master as Peyton knelt down on the floor. He petted his head, but Justice started whining again. Justice went back over by the semi and barked.

"Hey, boy, you've already found the drugs. Your work is done."

Justice continued to bark. Peyton stood up and went over to Justice, to see if he could figure out what was bothering him, when it suddenly dawned on him that he was trying to tell him that something was underneath the cab of the semi. He turned to Mark. "Can you go and find a creeper so I can get underneath the cab to see what may be under there?"

"Sure." Mark turned to go get the creeper as Mike came around with Justice's lead. Mike snapped it on his collar. The front door suddenly opened. Two people from the sheriff's department came into the building. Mark stopped when he saw guns pulled out, pointed directly at them.

"Good evening, gentlemen, Detective Rayland. Ben and I

are here to take the drugs off your hands." With a wave of her gun, she commanded, "You three go over and stand with the TreVaine brothers." When they were all standing together, "Very good, now I want each of you to take your guns out of your holsters, and slowly put them on the floor, then kick them over to us. And you keep that dog of yours on his lead, or I will kill him if he starts toward us."

They all did what was asked of them. As Stacy bent to put her gun down, she winced. Her left arm was killing her. When she rose back up, grabbing her arm, she asked in a stunned voice, "Gwen, why are you doing this?"

"Ben, pick their guns up and put them over in the corner of the building." Gwen turned to stare at Stacy. "Why, Detective Rayland, you ask? Well, I'll tell you why. You see, Ben here and I have been screwed over by Marco Manchez for a long time, and this is our way of getting even, you might say. We're putting the screws to him by taking his drugs, and we'll make the money. We already have a buyer for them."

"Listen, Gwen, you don't have to do this," Lieutenant Andrew tried to reason with her. "We have enough evidence on Manchez that he will be put away for a long time. How far do you think you are going to get before the police catch up with you?"

She glanced over at the lieutenant. "We have a one-way ticket out of here, Lieutenant." She pulled something out of her pocket. She held up a small device in her hand. "You see this? One click and it will blow this whole warehouse to smithereens, with everything and everyone in it." She started pacing as she continued, "So, you see, as long as you give us enough time to get off the island, you will all live; if not, I will activate the bomb that is underneath this truck."

Peyton grew sick inside. Sweat came out across his brow. Here he was looking for a bomb on the boat when it was on the truck instead! That's what Justice was trying to tell them all along! He wondered how much time they would have to deactivate it should she press the button.

She stopped her pacing long enough to give instructions. "Ben, go get the drugs and put them in this bag." She handed him the bag she was carrying. Ben went up the back of the truck and started loading the drugs into the bag. When he was finished, he came back down and stood beside Gwen. "Just for an added insurance, Rayland, get over here!" she demanded. "You will go with us to make sure we get off the island, and if any one of you follows us, she's as good as dead!"

Peyton, with fear in his eyes at the thought of them taking her with them, spoke up, "Wait a minute, Gwen. She has an injured arm, she needs medical attention." *What the hell is taking the ambulance so long to get here? They should have been here by now!* "Take me instead. I'll make sure you both get on the boat."

He started to walk toward them, when Gwen aimed her gun directly at him. "Stop right there! We will be taking Detective Rayland!"

Peyton and Stacy locked eyes. "It will be okay, Peyton. I'll go with them."

She started walking toward them when Kevin took her good arm to stop her. He looked her square in the eyes and said in a low voice, "I won't let anything happen to you!"

"No worries, I still have something up my sleeve," she whispered, as she looked down at her boot.

"Come on, Rayland!" Kevin, still holding her arm, "Don't do anything foolish. Remember we still have men up on the docks."

She nodded and started walking toward the door, holding her injured arm. Gwen came up behind her, as Ben took her arms and pulled them behind her back. She closed her eyes as she felt the pain shoot down her arm as he put the cuffs on her. With the barrel of a gun poking her in the back, Ben shoved her out the door, and then they were gone.

The men rushed over to get their guns while Lieutenant Fillmore radioed the men on the docks. "This is Lieutenant Fillmore. Ben Gillard and Gwen Sacks of the sheriff's department are in on this drug heist. They have the drugs and are headed your way. They took Detective Rayland of the state police as hostage. They are armed and considered dangerous. Gwen also has a device that will set a bomb off here inside the warehouse should they not succeed in getting on the boat. Lay low, and do not fire on suspects until Detective Rayland is clear of gunfire."

When the men had their guns in hand, Lieutenant Andrew went and handed Lieutenant Fillmore's gun to him. Peyton was beside himself. He needed to get to Stacy before anything happened to her. He turned to the lieutenants and his brothers. "I suggest we all get the hell out of this building. If Gwen decides to activate the bomb, I don't know how much time we have before it detonates to deactivate it and I don't want to take the time to find out. We need to get to Stacy. She has no way to defend herself against those two!"

"Peyton, we need to devise a plan, but you're right, we need to get the hell out, and now!" exclaimed Mark. All five men exited the building, along with Justice. Up ahead, they could see Stacy walking up the steps to the dock, with Ben and Gwen right behind her. Suddenly, Gwen turned around. All five men watched as she raised her hand.

"RUN!" exclaimed Lieutenant Andrew. As they all started to run for their lives, the building exploded into a ball of fire! All the men were thrown in the air and onto the ground, with debris falling all around them.

"Well." Gwen smiled. "That took care of that problem!" Stacy looked back with horror, wondering if any had lived through the explosion. Her heart grieved for Peyton and the rest. She wondered now how she was going to help take these two down. She knew there were officers ready to take them out, but she needed to give them access. *Focus, Stacy, focus!* she said to herself.

Ben was shocked, as he looked back at the burning building. "What the hell, Gwen! I didn't actually think you would detonate the bomb! Along with the drugs, we already have one murder on our hands, now we could have more! I didn't sign up for this!"

"He's right, Gwen. You need to give it up now, before it's too late!" pressured Stacy.

"Shut up! Now start moving! The sooner we get on that boat and get out of here, the better!"

Stacy needed to keep her talking. "Gwen, I never thought you of all people could be this devious. You, a police officer for the sheriff's department! How could you betray your own department?" she asked.

"When I found out Ben was working for Manchez as an informer and the debt he owed him was cleared while he was still sucking me dry on the loan I took out with him, I devised a plan to get even, and brought Ben here on it with me. We both had had enough."

"Why kill Rodrick?"

"Ben knew he was skimming off the top of Manchez's drug deals, so, at first, we were going to just get his drugs and skip town. We saw the little performance your friend made. Too bad he didn't stay out, but he woke up, so we had to kill him to take the drugs. We knew Rodrick had placed a bomb on the truck, so we took the device for insurance. Now, enough talk, get moving!" When Gwen shoved the gun into her back, she started moving.

Peyton, lying on the ground, groaned. He tried to move but felt glued to the ground. Every part of his body hurt. He remembered Stacy was in trouble. It gave him the power to move. He pushed himself up and shook his head. As he looked around, he saw Justice lying just a little ways from him. He crawled over to him. He was still alive. "Hey, buddy, how are you doing?" He lifted his head at the sound of his master's voice. "It's going to be okay, boy." He looked around. *Where in the hell are the first responders and the ambulance?* he wondered again. He heard groaning nearby. He got up to find his brothers and the lieutenants not too far from him. He pulled himself up and stumbled a bit, walking over to check on each one. All of them were alive, and it looked like they would make it. He pulled each one further away from the blaze as the building started to crumble. He went back to his dog. Just as he picked him up to carry him away from the building, he heard a rumble. He ran as fast as he could before another explosion hit. He went back down on the ground, covered Justice with himself, and waited for the debris to stop flying around them. He then went back to check on the men as they started to wake up.

Mike sat up. Dazed, he asked, "What happened?"

Frustrated, "Gwen pushed the button," answered Peyton. "Do you think you can get up?"

"Yeah, I think so."

"Come help me with the others. I'm going to call 911. I'm surprised they aren't here already. The lieutenant said they were on their way a while ago." After he called 911 and made sure the rest were waking up and were going to be all right, he said to Mike, "Listen, I'm going after Stacy."

Determined, Mike turned toward his brother. "I'll go with you."

"No, you stay here and wait for the ambulance, I'm going alone."

Mike searched his brother's eyes. "Okay, but be careful!"

"Always," he returned.

Mike watched as Peyton left. When he passed Justice, Justice raised himself up and let out a weak bark. Peyton knelt beside him. He put a gentle hand on the top of his head and ran it down his back. "Listen, boy, you can't go with me this time. You need to stay and watch over the men. I'll be back."

Mike came up behind him. "I'll make sure he stays with me."

"Thanks, bro." Then he was off.

Peyton ran down to the beach and went up a short flight of stairs that would lead him behind the two from the sheriff's department, and Stacy. As he crept along, he finally was able to see them walking along the walkway to where the boat was moored. He wasn't sure where the officers were located but knew they had to be somewhere around the boat that was to take the drugs to LA. With his gun pulled, he continued along the walkway. Suddenly, they stopped. Peyton ducked behind one of the yachts as Gwen turned around to check behind her. She thought she heard something, but she must have been mistaken.

She turned back around. "Keep moving. The boat is just up ahead." She nudged Stacy with the barrel of her gun. They started off. Peyton moved back out. Stacy was beside herself on what to do. She knew the officers were somewhere around the boat, but she didn't know where. She wondered if they had gotten the men bringing in the boat, off, and into custody. As they neared the boat, she couldn't see anyone around.

Gwen, with the gun still in her back, and Ben right beside her, demanded, "Okay, Rayland, it's time to board the boat."

Stacy took a deep breath, fell down on the walkway, did a tuck-and-roll, and slammed her boots into Gwen's knees! Gwen flew backwards, with her hands flying in the air, as Peyton came up behind Ben and took him down. Officers, flying out from in and around the boat, rushed in.

Just as Gwen was about to pull the trigger at Stacy, one of the officers yelled, "Drop it, Sacks! It's over! You fire that gun and you're as good as dead!"

Gwen dropped her gun and raised her hands. Officers surrounded her, hauled her up, and cuffed her. Peyton picked Ben up, handed him over to an officer, and rushed over to Stacy's side. "Honey, are you all right? You gave me the scare of my life!"

Stacy, shocked, said, "Peyton, you're alive! I thought you and the others were all dead!"

"No, sweetheart. When we saw Gwen raise her arm as you were walking up to the docks, we all ran for our lives. We all made it out alive."

"Thank God!" she exclaimed. One of the officers came up, bent down, and took the cuffs off her hands. Stacy winced as she brought her arms around in front of her. Her arm was really hurting.

"Nice job, Detective Rayland. You too, Peyton. Thanks to all of you who helped, we were able to stop this drug heist. Now we wait to hear if the detectives from the police department have arrested the man who arranged it."

Off in the distance they heard the sirens. It wasn't long before the ambulance and the fire department came into the marina. Peyton pulled Stacy in his arms and held her for a few minutes. He kissed her forehead. "Sweetheart, do you think you can get up, or do you want to wait till the medics come up here?" he asked.

She glanced up into eyes that looked lovingly down at her

and smiled. "I think I can make it down to where the others are. I'm sure the lieutenant is worried about me."

"Okay, let's take it slow." Peyton came up first, then helped Stacy up. With his arm around her, he helped her down into the marina, where the medics were already checking the men and the firefighters were working on the blaze as the building continued to crumble to the ground. They walked up to where the lieutenant was. She saw a gash in his leg.

"How are you doing, Lieutenant?" she asked. "Your leg looks pretty bad."

"I'll be fine. It isn't as bad as it looks, just sore. We were all lucky we didn't come out with more than we did. How's your arm?"

"The same, very sore," she answered.

A couple of medics came up to them. "We need to check all of you for injuries."

Peyton spoke up. "I'm fine, but these two need attention." He turned to Stacy. "I'm going over to check on my brothers and Lieutenant Fillmore to see how they are doing." He glanced over to where his brothers were. He saw Justice was by Mike's side looking over at him. Thank God his dog appeared to be all right, but he would have to be checked out by a vet to be sure. He turned back. "I'll be back."

She nodded her head in return.

Peyton walked up to his brothers. "How are you guys doing?" he asked.

"We're fine, Peyton. No worries," answered Mark.

"Justice has been anxiously waiting for you to come back,"

stated Mike. "I had a time keeping him here. He kept pulling on his lead to follow you."

Peyton bent down on one knee. He pulled his dog close to him. He let out a whimper. He pulled back. "Justice, where are you hurt?" He felt with his hands along his body and legs and didn't feel any broken bones, but when he touched his right shoulder, he whimpered again. "Okay, boy," soothed Peyton. "We'll get you to a vet and see what's going on." He came back up. "I'm going back to check on Stacy, then I'm going to need to get Justice to the vet. Any ideas on how to get back to town?" he asked.

"I made a call to Jenna, she's on her way. The officers are tied up with last-minute details of the night. I wasn't sure if any could run us back, and we are ready to get out of here," answered Mike. "Lieutenant Fillmore says he's doing fine. He is with the officers, and will head back with them when they are through with the investigation."

"Okay, I'll see how Stacy and Kevin are doing and where the medics will be taking them and be right back. Justice, stay here with Mark and Mike." He turned to head back to Stacy.

Jenna, in a panic, tried to stay calm. As she drove down the road to the marina, she saw all the lights flashing and the fire from the building. There was an officer blocking the road into the parking lot, so she couldn't get close. She informed the officer who she was, and why she was there. "You'll have to park here and walk down. I can't let you get close to the area with your car." She thanked the officer, shut the engine off, and came out of her car. She rushed down, away from the building, looking all around. She finally spotted Mike and Mark close to the docks with Justice. Where was Peyton? Mike said he was okay, but did something happen in the time he called? Her heart thudded as she ran up to Mike. Mike turned and saw his love coming up to him. He pulled her into his arms for a fierce hug. "I'm so glad to see you!" he whispered.

"Oh, Mike, thank God you're all right!" She pulled away from him and gave Mark a quick hug. "Thank goodness you are all okay!" She turned back to Mike. "Where's Peyton?"

"He's over with Stacy and the lieutenant. The medics are treating them and will be taking them to the hospital." She looked over to where Mike pointed. The medics were just heading this way with the two patients, with Peyton following them.

Peyton came up to them. "They're taking them to the Honolulu General. We need to get Justice to the vet. I'll catch up with them later. They both have minor injuries and will be fine." Peyton took Justice's lead. "Can you walk, boy?"

Justice came up on all fours and tried to walk. He limped as he went, favoring his right leg. Peyton picked him up and carried him to the car. Once everyone was inside, they started off. Peyton called ahead, and when they arrived at the veterinarian hospital, Dr. Giles was waiting for them. Peyton rushed in with Justice, then followed Dr. Giles back to a patient room, where Peyton laid him on a table. He examined Justice and found his right shoulder was dislocated. Justice yelped as he moved it back into place. Dr. Giles looked up at Peyton. "Justice is going to be fine, but I would like to keep him overnight for observation. I will give him some medication for the pain so he can rest, but he should be able to go home tomorrow afternoon."

Peyton breathed a sigh of relief. "You hear that, Justice! You're going to be just fine."

Justice looked up at his master with his big brown eyes and wagged his tail. Peyton petted his head and told him he would see him tomorrow. He held out his hand to the doctor. "Thanks, Dr. Giles. I appreciate all you have done for Justice and meeting us here so late tonight. I'll see you tomorrow."

"You're welcome, Peyton. Go home and get some rest, you look like you need it."

He gave his dog another pat on the head, nodded, and smiled at the doctor as he walked out the door. Even though his body was telling him that is exactly what he should do, he needed to get to the hospital. He needed to be with Stacy.

CHAPTER 17

Peyton drove to the hospital after Jenna and his brothers dropped him off to get his car. They were all going home to crash, but they would meet in the afternoon at the police department to give their account for the night. He pulled into the parking lot. He rushed through the doors of the emergency entrance and found Fred, Stacy's partner, sitting in the waiting room. Fred saw him and rose to greet him. He shook his hand. "Have you heard any word on how the lieutenant and Stacy are doing?" he asked.

"Not so far," answered Fred. "I'm not sure they have even been seen by a doctor yet. I can't seem to find out anything about their injuries!"

"Well, to ease your mind, they both have minor injuries and will be fine. Can I get you a cup of coffee while we wait? It looks like there's a vending machine down the hall."

"That would be great." Fred sighed. "I'll wait here in case the doctor or a nurse comes out to give us an update."

"Okay, be right back." Peyton left to go get the coffee and came back with two steaming cups, one in each hand. He handed one to Fred, then sat down and waited.

It seemed like hours passed before a nurse came out from the doors to the waiting area. "Fred Zealand?" she asked. Both Fred and Peyton rose.

"Yes," answered Fred.

"Both Lieutenant Andrew and Detective Rayland are doing fine. The doctor cleaned out their wounds and stich up the lieutenant's leg. The doctor is signing the discharge papers, and you will be able to take them home shortly."

"Can we go back and see them?" asked Peyton.

"Sure, follow me. I'll take you back."

Kevin and Stacy were together in one large room, with a curtain in between them. Fred went to talk to the lieutenant, while Peyton went to Stacy. She smiled when she saw him. He bent to give her a gentle kiss. He lifted his head and gazed into her pretty hazel eyes. "How are you doing?" he whispered.

She raised her good arm and placed her hand on his cheek, she felt the roughness of his beard against the palm of her hand. "I'm fine, just sore. The doctor said I will be as good as new in a few weeks but may have to go through some physical therapy."

He sat down next to her on the bed. He took her hand in his. "That's good news. The nurse said you and the lieutenant will be discharged soon. I'll drive you back to your bungalow."

Stacy gazed into his deep blue eyes. She knew she needed to distance herself from him. The lieutenant already told her he was going to book their flights back to LA the day after tomorrow. Once they wrap up their end tomorrow, Kevin wanted to head back as soon as possible. *Could one more night with him hurt?* she wondered. She would let him take her home. Then she would tell him. "Okay." she smiled. "That would be nice." The nurse came in with her discharge papers, along with some pain medication to take for three days, and instructed her that over-the-counter pain relievers could be taken after that if she needed it. Stacy signed the papers and handed them back to the nurse.

"Okay, Detective, you are free to get dressed and leave. I'll order wheelchairs for you and the lieutenant."

She nodded her head as the nurse left the room. She turned back to Peyton, and asked, "How is Justice doing?"

"He's going to be fine. He dislocated his right shoulder when he was thrown from the building exploding. Dr. Giles put it back in place and is keeping him overnight. We were all very lucky we came out of it with minor injuries."

Stacy, lifting her hand once again to a face that was covered in dirt, and red with the heat of the explosion, had tears coming from her eyes as she said, "I thought for sure when Gwen raised her hand and pushed the button, and I saw the building explode into a ball of fire, I didn't think anyone of you could have survived it. I'm so glad you are all right, as well as your brothers."

Peyton placed his hand over hers. "Stacy, when I saw that you had been shot, I thought my heart was going to come out of my chest. I want to tell you that I…"

"Here we are!" Two orderlies with wheelchairs came into the room. One of them went over to the lieutenant's side, to get him ready.

The other one pulled the chair up next to Stacy's bed. "I see you're not dressed yet," he commented.

"I'll give you a few more minutes and I'll be right back." He left the room.

Stacy turned to Peyton. "I guess I'd better get dressed. Can you hand me my shirt?"

Peyton got up off the bed, picked up her T-shirt and handed it to her. She slipped off the gown and pulled the shirt over her head. As she tried to put her bad arm in the sleeve, the pain racked her body. Concerned, he asked, "Can I help?"

She took a deep breath. "No, I've got this."

As she managed to get the shirt on, softly he said, "You don't always have to be strong, you know, you can lean on others, who care about you."

She stared into his eyes before she replied, "It's hard for me to do that, Peyton. I've lived on my own for a long time now. I don't know how else to be."

"Just know that I am here, whenever you need me."

She didn't know what to say but "Thank you." She slowly came off the bed and sat down in the wheelchair, when the orderly came back in. The curtain was rolled back.

Kevin was wheeled up to her. "Are you ready to get out of here, Rayland?" She was so tired all she could do was nod her head yes. "Then let's go."

Back at her bungalow, Stacy let Peyton help her get into sweats and a button-down shirt. When he got her settled on the sofa, he went and retrieved her pain medication and a glass of water. When he read the prescription dosage, he decided to make some sandwiches and hot tea. By the time he got back to Stacy, her eyes were closed as her head rested against the back of the sofa. He set everything on the coffee table. She looked so peaceful. As he gazed lovingly down at her, he leaned down and gave her a kiss on the cheek. She opened her eyes. "Oh, sorry, Peyton, I must have fallen asleep."

"You have nothing to be sorry about. You have been put through hell tonight." He sat down beside her. "Before you take your pain medication, you need to eat a little something. I made a sandwich and a hot tea for you."

Stacy held his eyes for a few moments. *How am I going to tell him I will be leaving the day after tomorrow?* She lowered her eyelids. She turned to reach for her sandwich. She took a couple of bites, then set the plate back down. She wasn't really hungry but made an effort to eat a little something. She took her pain meds. She hoped it would relieve some of the pain soon. She sat back against the sofa, slowly sipping her tea.

Peyton, watching her, asked, "You didn't eat very much, can you eat a little more?"

"Thank you, Peyton, but no. This was nice of you. Go ahead and eat your sandwich. Feel free to eat the rest of mine." As he ate his sandwich, he felt something was off between them. There was a coolness he hadn't felt before. Maybe he was reading too much into it. She's been through a lot tonight, and she needed rest. He finished his sandwich, then took the plates and empty cups into the kitchen. After he put them in the dishwasher, he came back into the living room, to find Stacy had stretched out on the sofa, and appeared to be sound asleep. He smiled. He went into her bedroom to get a blanket out of the closet. He covered her and placed a gentle kiss on her cheek. She moved a little, snuggling under the blanket. He turned out the lights, locked the door behind him, and left to go back to Mark's. He would check on her in the morning. He needed a hot shower and a good sleep himself.

On his way home, he was thinking how close he was to telling her that he loved her before they were interrupted. Maybe, it was just as well he didn't. He had a feeling her time here was limited. He had to figure out a way to make it work between them. Otherwise, he was going to be dealing with a shattered heart.

Outside Manchez's mansion, Detective Williams, Detective Jenson, and several other officers from the police department had arrived to arrest him. Detective Williams pounded on the door. "This is the police! Open up in the name of the law!" He pounded again. Detective Williams ordered some of the officers to go around to the back. There were no lights on in the house. He had a bad feeling. He broke the door down, and they all rushed in. They turned on lights, going through the entire home, only to find Manchez and his wife were gone!

Detective Jenson came up to him. "What are you thinking, Zack?" he asked.

"I think that, somehow, he got wind of what was going down tonight and fled the island! Our only hope is to catch him at the airport." He radioed some of the officers out patrolling the highway to head toward the airport. This may be their only chance at stopping him before he was able to leave the island. "Come on, men. Let's head out!"

At the airport, they met up with a couple of the officers he radioed in from the highway in the terminal. "What have you got?" inquired Zack.

Officer Brown responded. "We checked all the airlines, and he and his wife are not on the roster for flights going out. We've sent security out to find Manchez's hanger where he keeps his private jet. We've also asked the flight control tower to hold all flights coming in and going out for the next hour until we find out if he is hold up in his aircraft."

"Excellent! What is the quickest way out to get to the hangers?" asked Zack.

Officer Brown got a call on his radio. As he tried to listen, Zack could hardly contain himself as he could see Manchez and his wife slipping away. *Come on, come on, COME ON!* he said silently to himself.

Officer Brown looked up. "They found the hanger!"

"Okay, let's go!" They all filed out of the terminal and ran out onto the tarmac to where the hanger was located. The officers surrounded the building. Detective Williams and Detective Jenson were on each side of the hanger door. With his heart beating wildly at the thought he was finally going to nail this guy, the door to the hanger slowly raised. They rushed in with their rifles up and ready to take Manchez out, only to find the aircraft wasn't there! Zack, frantic, rushed out onto the tarmac. He tried to see if the aircraft might still be on the runway. He could see headlights way off into the distance. There were several police vehicles near the hanger. Zack motioned to Craig. They flew into one and headed down the runway with their sirens blaring and lights flashing to see if Manchez's jet was waiting to take off.

Marco Manchez was sitting in his private jet with his wife Millie, wondering why in the hell haven't they taken off yet!

"I don't understand, Marco. Why do we have to take off on a vacation in the middle of the night when we could leave first thing in the morning! You didn't even give me a chance to pack some clothes!"

"Listen, Millie," he said nervously, "I told you, I wanted to surprise you. We can get what we need when we get there!" Marco was chopping at the bit wanting to get the hell out of here! He looked out his window and saw in the distance police lights flashing. He unbuckled his seatbelt and turned to Millie. "I'll be right back. I need to see why the pilot hasn't taken off yet."

Millie sighed. "Okay, Marco."

He went into the pilot's cabin. "What's going on, Rick? Why haven't we taken off yet?"

"Sorry, Mr. Manchez, but all flights are grounded for the next hour. I think it has something to do with the police cars up ahead."

Marco's brow was beaded with sweat as he tried to think of what to do. He saw a police car pull out onto the runway and was headed this way. He panicked. He pulled out his gun, pulled back the hammer, and pointed it at Rick's head. "Get this thing in the air!" he yelled. Rick turned to see the barrel of a gun right in his forehead.

"But, Mr. Manchez, I'm not allowed to—"

"I said now!"

Rick wasn't going to argue with a gun pointed at his head, so he pulled the throttle back and started taxing down the runway. Marco sat down in the co-pilot's seat and buckled in. With his gun still pointed at his pilot, he watched as the police car came flying down the runway, heading straight for them! His pilot continued to build up speed. Marco was sweating it, as the police car was just a few yards from his jet; his pilot pulled the throttle down and the aircraft lifted into the air, just as the plane's wheels barely cleared the police vehicle!

Zack, in the car, slammed on his brakes, just as the plane lifted into the air! As Craig and he watched the plane climb high into the night sky, Zack slammed his fist on the dash. "Damn it, Craig! I can't believe he got away!"

Craig sat, stunned. "I can't believe we're still alive, with that jet coming straight at us!"

Zack looked over at his partner. He took a deep breath. "Sorry, I tend to get a little carried away when we're this close to catching this guy!"

Craig just stared at him in disbelief! "Well, if you have any more of these tendencies, warn me ahead of time! I almost shit my pants thinking anytime we were going to crash!"

The expression on his partner's face led him to smile. "You have to admit it, though, it was exciting!" Zack chuckled.

"Yeah, exciting, not when you're sitting in this seat!" Craig said in return. He didn't think this was funny at all. "Let's not do that again anytime soon. How about we go back and see what flight plan he filed, and maybe we can catch him on the other end."

"Right," as Zack turned the car around and headed back to the hanger; he couldn't see how that was going to happen. Once they are out of the country, it was going to be hard to track him. He also knew flight plans could be changed in the air.

Marco looked back out the window as the plane lifted into the air. He took a handkerchief out of his pocket and wiped his brow. He put his gun back into his shoulder holster. "Sorry, Rick, but we needed to get out of there."

Rick said nothing. As soon as he landed this plane, he was done working for Marco Manchez. As soon as the plane leveled out, Marco got up to go back and sit with his wife for the rest of the flight. He sat there, pondering what he was going to do. He'd wait to hear from some of his men. Then he would make his move.

CHAPTER 18

Stacy woke up early the next morning. She was stiff and sore all over. Her arm was killing her. She went into her bathroom to splash some warm water on her face and freshen up a bit. After she was done, she went into the kitchen to make a pot of coffee. While it was brewing, she put a couple slices of bread in the toaster. She poured herself a cup and buttered her toast. As she sat down at the counter to eat her breakfast, and before she took her pain medication, she reflected on last night's sting operation. She had her suspicions about Gwen but never would have guessed she could be a cold-blooded killer. She and Ben would be put away for a long time, along with the others. Once they wrap up today, and file their reports, her partner Fred along with the lieutenant and her would be heading back to LA, which brought her thoughts back to Peyton. He must have left after she had fallen asleep. She was going to tell him last night that she would be leaving in a few days, but she just couldn't do it. She would do it tonight, after they had dinner. She would make a clean break.

There was no way a relationship would work between them. *Him here, me there, it would be impossible.* She sighed. She finished her coffee and toast and took her meds. She put her dishes in the sink. She decided to take a hot bath, to work out the kinks in her body before she went down to the station to meet with all who was involved with last night's sting. After she ran her bath, she sank down into the hot water and felt her body relax. She didn't want to think anymore. She just wanted to forget all the turmoil of last night and how hard it was going to be to tell Peyton it was over.

When Peyton arrived back at Mark's, he took a hot shower before he crashed into oblivion. He slept in just a bit before he was up making phone calls. He called the vet, and was informed Justice was doing great. He was up walking and had eaten this morning. He called Stacy but couldn't get an answer. She might still be sleeping. He would try again a little later.

Mark came from his bedroom to the smell of coffee and waltzed into the kitchen. He was sore from head to toe. The hot shower he took last night when he got home didn't even put a dent in the pain. He would have some coffee and something to eat so he could take some ibuprofen. He looked around for Peyton. He saw him sitting in the living room on his phone. He poured himself a cup of coffee, took a sweet roll out of the fridge, and went to join him.

"Good morning, Peyton. Mind if I join you?" asked Mark. Peyton looked up from his phone.

"Good morning, bro. No, just making some phone calls. How are you feeling this morning?" he asked.

"Like the semi you drove last night hit me!" He chuckled. Mark set his roll on the coffee table and sat down across from his brother. "How are you feeling?"

"The same, pretty sore. We were all very blessed to get out of that explosion with minor injuries," he answered.

"I agree. Have you talked to Stacy this morning to see how she is doing?" he wanted to know.

"I haven't been able to get ahold of her yet. She must still be sleeping. I did get ahold of the vet. Justice is doing well, and I can pick him up this afternoon."

"That's great, Peyton." Mark took a bite of his roll and sipped his coffee. He asked, "I hope I'm not overstepping, but have you thought about when Stacy heads back to LA? Are you going to be able to deal with it?"

Peyton sighed. "I'm not sure, Mark. I'm in love with her. I want to see if we can make this relationship we started together work. I'm not real sure she wants the same thing. After we get through this afternoon, I'm going to take her to dinner, and then we'll talk."

"Is there any chance you would move to LA to be with her? Because long-distance relationships normally don't work out," he asked.

"I'm aware of it, but I hate big cities. I always feel trapped when I am in the city. I'm afraid I wouldn't be happy there."

"There's always a possibility she might come here. Have you heard anything about the pilot's job you interviewed for with Dr. Sawyer?"

"Not yet. But I really don't expect to hear from him until next week. That's another thing. The job would be a good fit for me. I love flying, and it would give me purpose to my life. If it's offered to me, I want to take it."

Mark looked into his brother's eyes. He knew the position was important to him. He would make one hell of a pilot for the hospital on the big island. "I hope you get it, bro; you of all people would deserve it. And as far as Stacy, well, I believe in all things working themselves out in time." Mark finished his coffee and roll. When he went to get up, he groaned. "I think I'm going to take some pain medication and take another hot shower. Hopefully, I will feel better before we join everyone down at the police station."

Peyton smiled up at his brother. "Hey, thanks for listening."

"You're welcome, bro. Anytime."

As Mark left to go take his shower, Peyton's thoughts returned to last night when he took Stacy home from the hospital. She was distant with him. Almost as if she was going to tell him something he didn't want to hear. He dialed up her number again. He listened to it ring, but she still didn't answer. He pushed the end button. Frustrated, he didn't know what to do. Should he go over there to check on her? Or wait till he sees her this afternoon? After he pondered over it, he decided to wait. He'd see her down at the station, and after that, they would talk. He got up off the couch and headed for the shower to get ready for this afternoon. He was afraid it was going to be a long one.

Stacy felt a lot better after her bath. Her arm hurt some, but the medication helped dull the pain. She checked her phone and saw Peyton had called her twice. Should she return his call or wait? She wasn't sure she could talk to him right now, as thoughts of breaking it off with him hurt too much. When she and the lieutenant were riding in the ambulance together, he told her he wanted to be back in LA the day after tomorrow. He missed his wife and kids. He wanted to close this case as soon as possible on their end. With the pain they were both in, she didn't feel it was the right time to ask if she could take some vacation time. Maybe she would approach him today, get his thoughts if they could get by without her. Fred could file the reports. She decided to text Peyton back, to let him know she was fine. She sent off the text, then went to finish getting ready for this afternoon's meeting.

After Peyton showered and was dressed, he came out and checked his phone. He saw Stacy had texted him. *Sorry I missed your calls. I will see you down at the station. Stacy.* As he re-read the text he thought, *Well, that was blunt and to the point.* He didn't care for this Stacy. He'd rather have Helen back. She seemed to be a totally different person in her real name. He thought of the nights they spent together when she was Helen. It already had him aroused. Could he get used to the real Stacy? He would soon find out.

Mark came from his bedroom. He walked up to Peyton and asked, "Do you want to ride down to the police station together?"

"Thanks, bro, but no. I have to pick up Justice after the meeting. Then, I want to take Stacy out to dinner. I have a feeling this may be our last night together."

Mark could see his brother was down. He wished he could find the words to make him feel better about the situation between his brother and Stacy. He sent up a prayer for the Lord to see him through this. "Okay, Peyton," answered Mark, "I'll see you down there."

"Right, I'll be there shortly." When he left, Peyton sat down at the counter and read Stacy's text again. Suddenly, he felt that his whole world was about to fall apart. As he left the house, he would soon see if what he felt held true.

CHAPTER 19

All who were involved with the case gathered around the conference table down at the police station. Each of them gave their account of what happened in last night's sting operation while an officer recorded all of their statements. Peyton couldn't keep his eyes off Stacy. She didn't greet him as he had expected and wouldn't look directly at him. She would glance his way, then she would turn her eyes away. He didn't understand. *How could she go from warm and tender to cold and aloof in one night?* he wondered. His thoughts were interrupted, as Lieutenant Fillmore took over the meeting.

Stacy tried to focus on what Lieutenant Fillmore was saying, but her mind kept drifting back to Peyton. She knew he had been watching her. She tried not to look at him, but her eyes kept wandering over to him. Her heart felt heavy as she thought about how she was going to tell him that she was leaving tomorrow. She glanced back over to him, and their eyes locked for a brief moment. Her heart started beating faster, as she took a deep breath. She needed to get through this meeting, then they would talk. She put all her effort into what the lieutenant was saying.

"I would like to thank all of you for your part in the events that took place last night. We were able to stop the drugs from leaving the island and arrest the main players in the drug ring, except for one."

They all sat forward. "What do you mean?" asked Peyton.

"I'm going to let Detective Williams fill you in on what happened last night. Zack, would you like to take over and explain what transpired when you arrived at Manchez's mansion?"

Zack rose from the table. He glanced around the table before he started. "When we arrived at Manchez's place, it was completely dark inside. Craig and I, along with officers from the police department, broke down the door and searched the house. When we discovered Marco and his wife were not there, we headed for the airport. When we arrived, the officers I sent on ahead of us discovered he and his wife were not on any of the commercial flights leaving the island. The security guards showed us where Marco's hanger was, only to find that his jet was gone. Craig and I got into a patrol car and flew down the runway to stop the plane from taking off. Off in the distance, we could see the plane was headed down the runway even though there was a stop put on all aircraft departing and arriving into the airport. As the plane came closer to us, and before we collided, we came to a screeching halt as the plane lifted into the air," explained Zack.

"And I don't mind telling all of you that being a passenger, and watching that plane coming at us, was an experience I personally do not want to go through again anytime soon!" exclaimed Craig.

They all chuckled as Zack continued, "So, the man who we have been trying to catch these past months got away. I'm sorry."

Mike could tell Zack felt bad about what happened. "Zack, you and Craig along with the other officers did your best. I just wonder how he got wind of what was going down that he fled."

Lieutenant Fillmore took it from there. He looked over at Mike. "We currently have an APB out on Marco and his wife. His flight plan revealed he was headed to the Cayman Islands. We have authorities on all three islands on alert. Once we finish interrogating the suspects, we'll have more information. Now, this is just my thoughts, I have a feeling since Ben and Gwen were trying to take the drugs and sell them, one of them tipped Manchez off to get him off the island, then they would have a clean sweep with no interference from him. Plus, they were also in on the sting operation. Once they knew Victor and the guards were taken out, the rest was easy for them. They just didn't know we had men waiting for them by the boat that was to take them to LA. The only problem for us was them taking Stacy as hostage. But between Peyton and Stacy, and the officers on board, we were able to apprehend the two." The lieutenant looked over at Peyton and then Stacy. "Good job, you two."

Jenna, listening, spoke up. "What would make Gwen kill somebody? She was an officer of the law. It amazes me that she played such a big part in all this, and to knowingly blow up a building, with the possibility of men being in there, floors me!"

"Greed does things to some people. We don't know all the circumstances, but you can rest assured Gwen and Ben along with the others will be put away for a long time. If there isn't anything else to add to the discussion, I think we are done. I know Mark and Mike need to get over to their restaurant." Lieutenant Fillmore continued, "Again, I would like to thank all of you for coming down here to give your statements, and a special thanks to the state troopers out of LA, Lieutenant Andrew, Detective Rayland, and Detective Zealand along with Special Agent Jason Hague, and the TreVaine brothers for helping us capture and arrest the suspects we have in hand. We couldn't have done it without your part in it." His eyes moved to Jenna, he smiled. "And for you, Jenna, for playing such an important role in helping us in this sting."

Jenna grinned back. "You're welcome. It was truly an experience." She turned to Mike with a gleam in her eyes. "We make a great team. Maybe we can do it again!"

Mike took her hand in his and gave it a squeeze. She caught his eyes. "I think not, I want you around for our wedding."

Everyone chuckled. With that, everyone rose from the table, shook hands, and started to leave the building.

Peyton waited by the door for Stacy. He was a little upset with her attitude towards him. He noticed that she waited for the others to leave before she approached him. Stacy's heart was thudding as she neared him. Nervously, she greeted him, "Hi, Peyton."

"Hi," he responded. He waited.

She stared into blue eyes that gave nothing away before she asked, "Can we go somewhere to talk?"

He nodded. They left the building together. When they were in the parking lot, he took her arm and turned her toward him. "What's going on, Stacy? Why the cold shoulder after all we have been through these last few weeks?"

She took a deep breath. Oh, this is not how she wanted to tell him she was leaving. "I don't know how to say this, but to just spill it. I'm leaving to go back to LA tomorrow at noon."

Peyton had a feeling this was what she was going to tell him. He knew she would be leaving soon. He didn't expect it to be quite this soon. Peyton took her hands in his. "Stacy, we knew this day would come. I admit, I didn't think it would happen tomorrow. I thought that, maybe, you would have been able to spend some time here after the sting was over."

"I wanted to ask the lieutenant for some vacation time, but he insisted I needed to go back, to wrap things up at our end. I'm sorry, Peyton, but I don't have any control over his decision."

"Okay." He could tell it was just as hard for her as it was for him. "I just have one thing I have to do, then we can go have dinner and enjoy the rest of the night before you have to leave in the morning."

"Do you want to have dinner at my bungalow?" she asked tentatively.

"Actually, that might work better. I need to pick up Justice from the vet, and with Mike and Mark both working tonight, I'll need to keep an eye on him."

"All right. I'll pick up a few things for dinner, and I'll see you later."

They both turned to go. Stacy thought she must be insane to put herself through this torture. *What happened to distancing myself from him?* she asked herself. She knew that when she left tomorrow, her heart would ache with thoughts of never seeing him again. *Can we make a long-distance relationship work?* As she headed to the market, she told herself to stop thinking. Just enjoy this little time she had left with him this evening. And that is exactly what she was going to do!

Peyton drove to the veterinarian hospital. He called ahead to let them know he was on his way. When he arrived, the receptionist greeted him, "Good afternoon, Mr. TreVaine. I'll let Dr. Giles know you're here to pick up Justice. Have a seat. It will only be a few minutes."

"Thank you." Peyton went over to one of the chairs and took a seat. Ten minutes later Dr. Giles brought out an impatient Justice, anxious to be with his master. Peyton noticed he was slightly favoring his right leg. Other than that, he looked great. With his tail wagging, Justice came up to him and lay his head down on Peyton's lap. He smiled and bent to give his dog a kiss on top of his head. He ran his hand down his head and back. "How are you doing, boy? Are you feeling better? Huh, boy?" he asked. Justice raised his head. With his tail wagging, he let out a big woof! Both Dr. Giles and Peyton chuckled. Peyton rose and took his lead.

"Justice had a good night. I did find a lesion on his belly. I cleaned it out and put some salve on it." Dr. Giles handed him a bag. "Here is some medication for his pain and some extra salve to put on his sore. Other than that, he should be as good as new within a week, so you're free to go."

Peyton shook his hand. "Thank you, Dr. Giles. I appreciate the care you have given Justice."

"You are welcome, Peyton." Peyton settled up his bill, and they were off. He stopped in at Mark's to pick up Justice's bed and some dog food. He left a note for Mark that he and Justice would be back in the morning. On his way to Stacy's, all he could think about was how he was going to convince her he was committed to their relationship and, somehow, it would work out.

Stacy was preparing dinner when she heard the doorbell. When she opened it, she greeted him with a warm smile. She looked down to see Justice was by his side. She glanced back up and met his eyes. "Come in." She closed the door behind them. She bent down beside Justice, and with both hands ruffled his fur and asked, "How's he doing?"

"He's doing great. The vet said he would be good as new within a week." He took the lead off his collar, to let Justice go to sniff out the territory. "I need to get his food and water dish out of the car. I'll be right back."

"Okay, I'll pour us a glass of wine."

Stacy went to the fridge. She pulled out the bottle of wine she had chilling. She poured them each a glass. She was checking on their dinner when Peyton came back into the kitchen.

"Something smells really good."

She turned and smiled. "It's roast beef with red potatoes, carrots, and pearl onions. I just have to make a couple of salads and warm up the dinner rolls."

"Is there anything I can do to help?" he asked.

She saw the dog food on the counter. "Do you need to feed Justice?"

"Yes," he answered. "It will only take a minute." He set about filling Justice's dishes with food and water. He set them down in the hallway, so they would be out of the way. Justice came and proceeded to devour every bit of it. When he came back into the kitchen, "Okay, what would you like me to do?"

As Stacy handed him his wine, his fingers touched hers and she shivered. Gazing into those deep blue eyes of his she wanted to say, *Take me to bed*! Peyton took a sip of his wine as his eyes roamed her body. She was wearing blue jeans with a light-blue, button-down knit top, and she was barefoot. Her long blond hair was gently flowing over her shoulders. Her pretty face was devoid of make-up. As his eyes continued to take her in, all he wanted to do was take her in his arms and just hold her. When his eyes focused on the bandage on her arm, it reminded him of how close he was to losing her last night. He set his glass down on the counter. He came up to her, took her glass from her, and placed it next to his. He pulled her into his arms and touched his lips to hers. Stacy responded as she wrapped her arms around his neck and pulled him closer. As the kiss grew more passionate, Peyton had all he could do to keep from stripping her down and making mad passionate love right here on the kitchen floor! But he needed to clear some things up between them. He finally broke the kiss. He pulled slightly away from her.

With her eyes full of wanting, and his heart pounding in his chest, he said, "Listen, Stacy, I would like nothing more than to make love to you right here and now, but I want to take this slow, make the night last. Let's have dinner and we'll talk."

With her eyes locking with his, she didn't want to talk, nor did she want to think about tomorrow. She wanted to spend the night in his arms one last time, even if it started on the kitchen counter! He released her. She continued looking into his eyes, trying to read what he was thinking. She dropped her arms from around his neck and nodded. "Okay," she resigned herself, "If you would like to make the salads, I'll put the rolls in the oven and set the table."

Peyton went to the fridge. He retrieved everything he needed to put the salads together while Stacy put the rolls in the oven. It wasn't long before they were sitting down at the table, enjoying the delicious meal Stacy had prepared.

While they were eating, concerned, Peyton asked, "How is your arm?"

Stacy looked at the bandage on her arm. "It's actually pretty good. It's not as painful as it was last night."

"That's good to hear." He put his fork down. He glanced across the table and caught her eyes. "Can I ask you something?"

"Sure," she responded.

"If we were to figure out a way to make our relationship work, would you be willing? I don't want this to be our last night together."

Stacy stared into his eyes but looked down as she started to answer him. "Peyton, of course I would be willing." She glanced back up. "But how long would it last? When I am put on a case, sometimes I work around the clock. If you land that job over on the big island, how would we schedule time to be together? As much as I would like it to work, I just don't see how it can."

"Would you ever consider working at one of the departments here, or on the big island?" he asked.

Stacy picked up her glass and took a sip of her wine.

"I know neither of the islands have a state police department, but would it matter?" he asked.

She set her glass down. Could she give up her job in LA? She has been with the force close to seven years. She worked hard to get the position she has now. She was up for a promotion. Looking across the table at his rugged features and those deep blue eyes of his, could she give it all up for him? She was definitely attracted to him. Every time they made love, it made her soar. She has never felt this sort of attraction with any other man in her life. This chemistry they have together, was it love? Should she consider leaving the post and pursue working in a different police department? It was something to consider. "I'll think about it, but what about you? Would you consider moving to LA?" she asked.

"I'm sorry, Stacy, but with the life I have lived most of my life, I'm afraid I would feel like a caged animal. Can you understand?"

Yes, she understood. She knew in her heart he wouldn't be happy living in the city. "Yes, I understand. When I think about you, I can only see you in wide open spaces. Let's not talk about it anymore. Let's just enjoy our dinner."

Peyton wanted to resolve this here and now. He didn't want to be left hanging. He loved her. He wasn't sure she loved him in the same way. They finished their meal in silence. The more Peyton sat trying to enjoy the dinner she prepared, the angrier he got.

Peyton came up from the table with his dishes. He placed them on the counter. He went back to the table and gathered up the leftovers to put them away. Stacy, watching him, knew he was upset. She wished she could give him the answer he wanted, but there were no guarantees if they tried to keep a relationship going it would last. She knew she had a problem with commitment. It totally scared her. But then her heart was going to be broken either way. Whether they tried and failed, or whether they ended it after tonight. She came up from the table with her dishes and walked up beside him by the sink. He took her dishes from her. He started rinsing and putting them in the dishwasher.

"Peyton, I—"

He shut the water off and turned to her. "Stacy, don't say anything. I will help you clean up. Then Justice and I are going to head out."

"You're leaving?" she asked, shocked. She didn't want him to leave! Knowing it could be their last, she wanted one more night with him!

"Yes, I think it would be for the best. I think we should say good-bye tonight. When you're ready to make a commitment to our relationship, you let me know." He finished rinsing the dishes and put them in the dishwasher. He gathered up Justice's dishes and called his dog.

He headed toward the door, when Stacy called out, "Peyton, wait!"

He turned back toward her, blue eyes flaming. She saw the anger in his eyes. With tears starting to form in her eyes, she pleaded, "I'm sorry, Peyton. Please understand."

His heart was torn. "I understand, Stacy, more than you know yourself. You're afraid to take a risk. You're afraid to take a chance on us! When you decide what you want, you have my number. Come on, Justice, it's time to go." With that, he turned, opened the door, and they were gone. Stacy stood staring at the door. She wanted to go after him, but instead crumbled to the floor. As tears flooded her eyes, she cried for what she had just lost. Damn him for stealing her heart!

Peyton stood outside the door. He almost turned around and walked back in. He was a little harsh, but damn it! If she had any feelings at all for him, she would have at least tried to talk things through. Instead, she cut him off. This is best, a clean break, he told himself. He helped Justice into his SUV and drove back to Mark's. He could only hope that his shattered heart would heal in time.

He let himself into the house when he arrived back. He got Justice settled, grabbed a beer from the fridge, then went to see what was on the TV. He was surfing through the channels when he heard his brother come into the living room.

"Hey, bro, what are you doing home so early? I thought you and Justice were spending the night over at Stacy's," he asked.

He glanced up at Mark as his brother sat down in one of the chairs next to the couch. "That was the plan, but plans change."

"What happened?"

"Nothing happened," he grunted.

Mark could tell his brother was angry and hurt. "You want to talk about it?"

Peyton took a deep breath and let it out. "Stacy and I are no longer seeing each other. She's leaving to go back to LA tomorrow. I thought maybe we would have more time, but it's not the case. When I wanted to talk about continuing our relationship, even if it was long distance, she cut me off and didn't want to talk about it. I got angry. We said our good-byes, end of story." Peyton took a pull on his beer.

"I'm sorry, bro. She wouldn't consider moving this way?"

"She said she would consider it, but my head says she won't." Peyton glanced over at his brother. "You know what, Mark? When she was Helen, she was the most warm, tender, loving person I have ever met. When I took her home last night from the hospital, Stacy, who I now have to call her, became a completely different person. She became distant. We had one kiss we shared before dinner tonight that reminded me of the chemistry we have together, but I stopped it before we went too far. Mark," he asked, "am I wrong for wanting to clear the air about us?"

"No, bro, you're not wrong. If I was in the same situation, I would want to know where we stood as well. Give it some time. I believe if it is meant to be between you two, it will work out eventually."

"Thanks, Peyton, I hope you're right."

Mark got up from his chair. "Would you like another beer? I'm going to go grab one for myself," he asked.

"Yeah, I feel like getting drunk."

Mark knew how he felt. He was drunk a few times when he and his ex-wife first broke it off. He took two beers out of the fridge, grabbed a bag of pretzels, and headed back to console his brother. This could take a while.

CHAPTER 20

The next morning, Stacy, her partner Fred, and Lieutenant Andrew were getting ready to board the plane to take them back to LA. Stacy cried most of the night after Peyton left. Her eyes were still red, and her nose looked like Rudolf's. She tried to cover it with make-up, but it still shone through. She kept checking her phone to see if Peyton had texted her. No messages. Well, what did she expect, he was pretty angry with her, and she couldn't blame him. She did suffer from commitment issues. As they boarded the plane and took their seats, Kevin turned toward her and asked, "Are you all right, Rayland?"

Stacy glanced over at her boss. "I'm fine." She half-smiled. "Just didn't get much sleep last night."

Kevin thought it was much more than that. He wasn't blind. "If you need to talk, I'm here." Stacy turned back to the window. She watched as the plane backed up from the terminal and headed for the runway. Once it was in position for takeoff, she heard the engines rev up. As the pilot pull down the throttle, the plane roared down the runway and lifted into the air. As she watched the island disappear behind them, and all she could see was ocean, she let the tears fall. Even though it was probably for the best, she wondered how she was ever going to get over him.

Peyton woke to a slight hangover. He and his brother were up until three in the morning talking. The alcohol dulled his brain, so when he crashed into bed, he was able to sleep. He looked at his watch. It was twelve thirty. His heart fell. She was gone, headed back to LA. He sighed. He didn't want to think. He got up out of bed and headed for the shower. He looked at himself in the mirror and decided to shave his beard off. When he was done, he showered, dressed, and went into the kitchen. The smell of coffee brewing lifted his spirit a little. Mark was sitting at the counter having a cup of coffee, reading the Sunday news.

"Good morning, Mark. Is there any coffee left?" he asked.

Mark looked up from his paper. "Good morning. I just made a pot. Help yourself."

Peyton took a cup out of the cupboard and poured himself a cup. He came over and sat down next to his brother at the counter.

"How are you feeling this morning?" asked Mark.

He shrugged his shoulders. "She's gone, Mark. How do you think I feel?"

"I'm sorry, Peyton. If I could fix this, I would."

Peyton glanced over at his brother. He could see in his eyes he was sincere. "I know you would. I'll get through this in time."

Mark, knowing that the two were very much in love with each other, wondered if either one of them would get over it.

"Say," asked Mark, "how about a round of golf to take your mind off things? I'll call Mike and Jenna to see if they can join us. After, we can come back here and grill some steaks. Do you think Justice will be okay while we're gone?"

Peyton wasn't really sure he wanted to go out. He'd rather stay here and sulk. Mark noticed his hesitancy. "Come on, Peyton, it will do you good."

Peyton took a deep breath. "Okay. Justice should be fine as long as it's just a few hours. I'll make sure he's taken care of before we go."

"Good. I'll go get cleaned up and text Mike while you take care of Justice." Mark came up out of his chair to put his empty cup in the sink. When he went back to his bedroom, Peyton sat there for a few more minutes. He couldn't help but think about Stacy, if she was thinking about him. He sighed. He was doing a lot of that lately. He slid off his chair and poured himself another cup of coffee. As he took a sip of his coffee, he wondered if it was only commitment issues she was dealing with, or was there a relationship she had in her past she was not willing to talk about that made her not want to get involved with him? He wished she would have at least tried to talk about it and not leave him doubting his own feelings about her. *Enough of this.* He went to get Justice settled.

He was just finishing up when Mark came down the hall into the kitchen. "Are you all set?" he asked.

"Just need to grab my wallet." As he went to get his wallet, again he thought of Stacy. Will the pain in his heart ever stop? Even though he was still angry, he remembered the way she made him feel, the way she felt in his arms. He shook his head. He needed to forget her. When he came back from his bedroom, he was determined to enjoy this time with his brothers and his future sister-in-law.

Mark asked, "Ready?"

"Ready."

Mike and Jenna were able to meet them at the golf course. They played eighteen holes of golf at a prestigious golf course on the west side of the island. Jenna had never played before, so it took a little bit before she got the hang of it. When they were done, Mark and Peyton picked up some steaks at the market before heading home.

Back at Mark's, they all pitched in getting dinner ready. The men grilled the steaks while Jenna put salads together and fried up some potatoes with melted cheese on top. She was setting the table, just as the men were bringing in the steaks. Mike came up and gave her a sweet kiss. "Can I get anything else out for you?" he asked.

She gave him a smile. "Well, I just need to put the potatoes on the table, could you grab the wine out of the fridge and pour it?"

"Sure thing." He gave her another kiss and went to get the wine. He poured them each a glass and set the bottle on the table. Jenna said grace. Then, they all sat down to enjoy the dinner they all prepared.

Justice was lying down beside Peyton's chair as they ate. He sensed he needed to be by his master. Jenna could see the bond between the two. It was like he knew what Peyton was feeling. She hoped he could get through this. Although, she didn't give up hope that somehow he and Stacy would eventually work things out between them. You could see even though Peyton had put on a good act today, he was miserable without her. Maybe a little nudge in the right direction might be appropriate. She would talk to Mike. She smiled to herself. Stacy gave her her contact information so she would stay in touch. She would give it a week, then she would call her. Give her time to finish up what she needed to do to close the case. Then she would see. There was always hope.

Four weeks later

Stacy sat in her office staring at the paperwork in front of her, not really seeing it. She finished closing up the case in Hawaii with her partner and was immediately put on another case. This one involved a homicide. Even though she was kept busy, her thoughts would always return back to Peyton. She'd reflected on their time together. The way he held her, how he made love to her long into the night. It still gave her tingles throughout her body. It's been four weeks. She hasn't received a call or a text from him. She missed him. She sighed; she couldn't blame him. She hurt him terribly. She hurt herself, too. It wasn't until she left the island that she realized she was in love with him. She didn't know if it was too late to make amends. He probably hated her.

Jenna had called her to see how she was doing. She put up a good front. She didn't want it to get back to Peyton that she was the most miserable person without him. She mentioned he got the job he interviewed for and was now working for the hospital on the island of Kona. She was happy for him. He's probably forgotten all about her and moved on. That made her totally depressed. It put the fear in her heart that it was completely over between them. *You need to stop this, Stacy. Didn't he say to you that when you're ready to make a commitment, call him? You need to reach out to him.* Was she finally ready to make a commitment to their relationship? She loved him. What if she did reach out and he rejected her? Her fragile heart couldn't take it. Her thoughts were interrupted when Lieutenant Andrew stood at the door of her office.

"Rayland!" he yelled.

She jumped and looked up at her boss. "Yes, sir?" she responded.

"Come into my office."

When they were both in his office, he motioned to her. "Can you please shut the door behind you?"

"Yes, sir." She closed the door and took a seat in front of his desk. She was not normally nervous when she was around him, but something in the way he addressed her left her feeling a bit uncomfortable.

Kevin, watching his detective, knew she hadn't been the same since she came back from Hawaii. He needed to get to the root of the problem, to see if he could help her through whatever it was she was dealing with. He had a hunch. "I called you into my office, Stacy, because you have been moping around the office for weeks. You seem to be able to handle your job, but it concerns me that you haven't opened up to anybody. You keep to yourself, and you've lost weight. Are you eating?" he inquired.

"Yes, but I'm not really hungry," she said without much enthusiasm.

He sighed and leaned back in his chair. He needed to handle this gently so he could get her to talk. "Stacy," he said in a soft voice, "can you tell me what's going on? I want to help you. I don't want to lose you to depression and an eating disorder. Tell me what's got you so down." He had a feeling it had to do with Peyton, but he wanted her tell to him so he could get her through this.

Tears started to form in her eyes, as she let the pent-up emotions come out of her these past weeks. The words came spilling out of her like a tidal wave. Tears were starting to flow down her cheeks as she began, "While we were in Hawaii, working on the case, I fell in love with Peyton. I didn't mean to, it just happened. I didn't truly realize it until we were on the plane headed back to LA. The night before we left, we were supposed to have dinner. It didn't go well. He wanted an answer from me, whether I wanted to try and have a relationship living so far apart. At the time I couldn't see it. I now regret telling him I couldn't see how it could work." She sniffed. Kevin handed her some Kleenex. She took them from him. She wiped her eyes and blew her nose. "I'm sorry, sir, I didn't mean to bring this all on you," she cried.

"I'm glad you did. Have you ever thought about looking into a job where he is at?" he asked.

She gave a half smile. "Peyton asked me the same question. I didn't know at the time if I could give up my job here."

"And now?" he wondered.

"I think I would be open to it, if I knew it was not too late for us."

"Tell you what," he stated, "let me do some checking for you. Do you know if he is still in Oahu?"

"No." She sniffed. "He has a job working at the hospital on the island of Kona, working as an emergency pilot," she answered.

"Okay, give me a few days. I'll see what I can do. In the meantime, you need to eat. I don't want you wasting away, and not able to handle your duties here at the post. That's an order," he commanded.

"Yes, sir, I'll try sir. I do feel better now that you coaxed it out of me."

He smiled. "Good. Now order us a pizza with the works. We'll have some lunch together." He wanted to make sure she ate something. Stacy rose from her chair to leave his office. When she reached for the door handle, Kevin stopped her. "Stacy." She turned back. "Yes?" she responded.

"I know this is hard. I too went through a time when I didn't know if Anna felt the same way I did. She had me all tied up in knots for weeks, but it all worked out. You might want to reach out to him, let him know how you feel. I will pray for you both that it will all work out in time."

She swallowed as she fought the tears. She nodded her head and said softly, "Thank you," as she left his office. She ordered the lieutenant's pizza, and pondered over whether or not she should call Peyton or text him. Would he answer her? She decided to call Jenna first, to see how he was doing, before she would brave calling him.

That night she called Jenna. When she answered, nervously she said, "Hi, Jenna. Stacy here."

"Stacy! How are you doing?" answered Jenna.

"I'm fine. Actually, I'm not fine." Jenna heard the tears as she tried to tell her how she was feeling. "I'm so miserable without him, Jenna. I love him so much. Can you tell me how he is doing?"

Jenna's heart went out to her. "Well, as far as we know, he's doing okay. Ever since he moved over to the big island and started his new job, we haven't heard from him much. Mike talked to him briefly a week ago, to make sure he got fitted for his tux. The wedding is only ten days away. Did you get your invitation?" she asked.

"Yes, but I'm not sure I can make it." She wanted to come, but she wasn't sure she could face Peyton.

"Oh, Stacy," cried Jenna. "You have to come!"

"I don't know, Jenna. I don't think I can face him. It would hurt too much." Her voice was a little wobbly when she asked, "What if he's found someone else?"

"I'm sure he hasn't," replied Jenna. She knew in her heart he was just as miserable as Stacy was. "You need to reach out to him," encouraged Jenna.

"I don't know if I can. What if he rejects me? I would break into a million pieces!"

"I know how you feel: Mike and I had our share of not knowing how the other one felt, but it all worked out in the end. I may be wrong, but I think you should try."

"Okay, Jenna, I'll think about it. You take care. Maybe I'll see you at your wedding. Bye." Stacy hung up before Jenna could tell her good-bye.

Mike, sitting next to her in a booth at the restaurant, had been talking to Mark while she was on the phone. He turned towards her. She looked pretty down after her phone call.

"Who were you on the phone with, sweetheart? You're not looking very happy right now."

"That was Stacy." She sighed. "She's miserable, Mike, and I don't know what to do about it."

Mark, listening in, answered her, "Well, I can tell you this, our brother is just as miserable. I keep in touch with him every few days to make sure he's okay. I even flew over there two weeks ago. I stayed overnight at his apartment. He's having a rough go of it."

"How can we get them back together?" she asked in earnest.

"We've done all we can, honey. We sent out an invitation to her. Hopefully, she'll come. We'll have to wait and see. It's up to the both of them to work it out." Mike put his arm around her. He squeezed her tight against him.

"Mike's right, Jenna. Peyton's waiting for her to make the first move. He told her when she left, it was her call."

Where had she heard that before? She nodded her head. She would pray for them. Then she would wait to see what the Lord would do.

After she hung up with Jenna, Stacy went back and forth over calling Peyton. She decided to text him, just to see how he was doing. Nervously, she punched out a text, *Hi Peyton, how are you doing?* She pushed send and waited. She sat there for five minutes, and nothing. She sighed. She put her phone down. She went into the kitchen to fix herself something to eat. She was going to follow the lieutenant's advice and not let herself get run down. She needed to keep her strength up, if only to keep her job. She would get over Peyton eventually. *Ha!* she told herself. *Not likely.*

Peyton had been called into work on an emergency flight. A patient needed to be airlifted to the Seattle Hospital for a liver transplant that couldn't be performed here on the island. The man was in stable condition. He would be taken to surgery as soon as they arrived. When he landed the helicopter, he helped the medics bring the patient out of the chopper and into the hospital from the roof. He decided to go down to the cafeteria and grab a bite to eat before he headed back. After he picked out his food at the different food bars, he paid the cashier and took a seat at a small table by the window. He looked out over the city. It was a clear day. He could see Mt. Rainer in the distance. It was one of the largest mountains in the country. All you could see was the snow that covered the mountain top. As he started to dig in, he thought back over the last four weeks when he got the call from Dr. Sawyer that the job was his. It couldn't have come at a better time. He needed something to take his mind off Stacy, and how they left things. He threw himself into learning all the aspects of the job and what it entailed. Along with taking care of Justice, it hardly gave him time to think. Only at night, when he tried to sleep, the memories would come rushing in. As he was sitting there, he decided he better check his messages. He pulled out his phone and was shocked to see one from Stacy! He read the short message. He huffed! How the hell did she think he was doing? It angered him to think that it took four weeks for her to reach out to him. He finally gave up after two weeks when he didn't hear from her. He poured himself into his job so he wouldn't have to think about her. He hated her for taking his heart and leaving it in the dust. While he sat there staring at his phone, he debated on whether to answer her or not. He went back and forth, telling himself that it was too late. But then she did reach out, even if it took a while. He finally punched in, *I'm fine,* and pushed send before he changed his mind. He finished his meal, put his tray on the conveyor belt, and headed back to his chopper. It was a five-hour flight back to the island, and with the time change, it would be late in LA when he arrived back home. He would see if Stacy responded to his text when he got home.

Before Stacy got into bed, she decided to check her phone one more time. She saw that Peyton did in fact text her back. It was short and to the point, but at least he answered her. Of course, hers wasn't any better. She climbed into bed and lay her head down on the pillow. As she closed her eyes, she would decide whether or not she would send another message tomorrow. She was just too tired to think anymore.

CHAPTER 21

The next day when Stacy arrived at work, Kevin called her back into his office. She stood at the door. "You wanted to see me, Lieutenant?" she asked.

"Yes, come in and take a seat."

Stacy went into his office and sat down. She waited. Kevin glanced up and handed her what appeared to be an airline ticket. She glanced back. "What's this?" she asked him, perplexed.

"After we had lunch, I made a few calls over to the big island to see if they had any openings in their police department. There's a position opening up for a detective in their homicide division. You have a three o'clock interview with Lieutenant Carlson, who heads up the division. You have just enough time to pack an overnight bag and catch the flight out to Kona. I reserved a room for you at a hotel near the airport. The information is in with the airline ticket."

"But, Lieutenant—" she stammered.

"No buts, Rayland. I'm going to hate to lose you, you're a good cop, but you need to go where your heart is, and it's not here. Now get going, you don't have much time."

"I don't know what to say."

"You don't have to say anything. I'll see you back here on Thursday. Have a safe flight, and good luck."

Stacy rose from her chair. As she was leaving his office, she turned back to the lieutenant. "Thank you, Kevin."

He smiled. "You're welcome. Now get out of here!"

Stacy flew home, stuffed some clothes in her overnight bag along with her makeup and rushed out the door. She barely made it on time. When she was seated in the aircraft, she relaxed as the plane started down the runway and lifted into the air on its way to the island. Once she was able to turn her phone on, she checked her messages. There was one message from Fred, wishing her luck on her interview, the lieutenant must have informed him, and the one from Peyton from last night. She frowned. He didn't expound on his message like she was hoping for. She sat there looking out the window at the blue Pacific Ocean and debated on whether to let him know she was coming over to the island for a job interview. She decided to wait to see if she landed the job. But then if she did get the job, would he even want her there? It's been a little over four weeks since she has had any contact with him. What if he is seeing someone else! *Oh, Stacy, you have to stop this train of thought*, she told herself. *You're getting yourself all worked up over if's!* She decided to get her laptop out. She would update her resume to keep her mind off Peyton. She hadn't applied for a job in a long time, and she wasn't sure if Lieutenant Carlson would want to see it. This kept her busy for the rest of the flight. When the plane touched down on the island, Stacy looked at her watch. With the time change, she had a little over an hour before her interview, so she took a cab to her hotel, got settled, and grabbed some lunch on her way to the police department.

Peyton was on his way to the hospital. His schedule was to pick up a patient at the hospital in Oahu and bring her here. He was at a stoplight. He glanced over to see a yellow cab next to him. There was a woman in the back seat. She was giving directions to the cab driver. She had her blond hair pulled back in a bun behind her head, and she looked an awful lot like Stacy! The light turned green, and the cab took a right turn into the city. A horn blared behind him. He shook his head and pressed his foot on the accelerator. Ever since her text yesterday, the memories came flooding back. He found himself wanting her in the worst way. Now he was starting to see visions of her, even though he knew she was in LA! He needed to forget her.

When he arrived at the hospital, he focused his mind on getting the job done. Depending on when he needed to have the patient back here, he would see if his brothers could meet him for coffee. He hadn't seen Mike since he moved here. Mark kept in touch, but he knew with the wedding next week Mike was far too busy. It would be good to see them both again. He missed spending time with them.

Stacy walked into the police station and was greeted by a Sergeant Smith sitting at the front desk. "Can I help you, ma'am?" he asked.

"Yes, Detective Sergeant Stacy Rayland, to see Lieutenant Carlson." She showed him her badge. "I have an interview with him at three."

"Have a seat. I will let him know you are here."

"Thank you," she replied. Stacy took a seat in the lobby. While she waited, she checked her messages again: nothing from Peyton. She didn't know what she was hoping for. She sighed.

The door opened, and a very tall, good-looking man came out to greet her. He was dressed in a dark pin-striped suit, worn with a crisp white shirt, and a blue-and-white striped tie. His hair was jet black, and his brown eyes shone as he shook hands with her. "Hi, sorry to keep you waiting. I'm Lieutenant Gary Carlson, and you must be Detective Rayland."

"Yes, it's very nice to meet you," she responded nervously.

"You as well," He smiled. "Let's go back to my office and we'll get started.

The interview took a little over an hour. "I'm very impressed with your resume and your answers to my questions. You came highly recommended by Lieutenant Andrew. How do you feel about transferring to a police department from working in a state police position? It will be a transition on your part."

"Well, sir, I know it will be a change from what I am used to, but I am up for the challenge."

"Can you start on Monday?" he asked. Stacy was shocked! She didn't think she would get the job this quickly.

Hesitantly, she asked, "You...mean this coming Monday?"

"Yes. One of my detectives retired last week, and I need to get him replaced. We're short staffed as it is."

"It doesn't give me much time." She thought about everything she had to do before coming over here. "Would it be possible for me to start on Wednesday of next week? I'm sure I can get everything settled back in LA before moving here."

He thought a minute. "Okay, be here Wednesday morning, and we'll get started."

Stacy rose from her chair and shook hands with the Lieutenant. "Thank you so much for this opportunity. I'm looking forward to working with you."

He smiled, "Same here, congratulations, welcome to the force."

Stacy left the police station feeling light as a feather as she headed over to her hotel room. She had a lot to do. After two hours of making phone calls, her stomach was telling her it was time to eat. She noticed a Ted's Bar and Grill in walking distance of the hotel. She slipped on her shoes, ran a comb through her hair, put some lip gloss on her pink lips, and headed out the door. The place was pretty busy, but she found a small table in the bar area. She took a seat and pulled out the menu. A waitress came up and asked if she wanted anything from the bar. She ordered a white wine. While she was waiting for her wine, she looked around. It was decorated with fish netting hanging down in different areas of the bar. A big swordfish was mounted above and behind the wraparound bar. Pictures of people with their big catch of the day were hanging on the walls. It was the first bar she had been in that didn't have TVs in the place. The waitress came back with her wine. She set it on the table and asked if she was ready to order. Stacy ordered a club sandwich to go with her wine. When the waitress left to put her order in, she pulled her phone out to check her emails. There were quite a few from her partner on the case they were currently working on, and one from the Hawaiian Arms Apartments. She had seen a sign outside their building with "apartments for rent" coming back to her hotel. She had called to see if they had any one-bedroom apartments for rent. She was on the phone with them when her sandwich arrived. She made an appointment to look at one within the hour. While she was eating her sandwich, she didn't notice Peyton and a woman come into the restaurant.

Peyton glanced around for a table. He and a medic came in to grab a bite after a grueling day. There were five major accidents, which three of them had to be air-lifted to the hospital. He saw a table coming available over in a corner of the bar. "Come on, Sammy, there's one opening up." They passed a table where a blond woman was eating her sandwich. Her body features were similar to Stacy's, only she was thinner. But he couldn't see her face with her hair falling down around it. He got a strange vibe as he passed her table. They took a seat at the table that had opened up. A waitress came up to them, cleared the table, and asked if they would like something to drink. They both ordered coffee. When she left to get their coffee, he looked over at the blonde sitting at the table. Her back was toward him, but there was something so familiar about her. The waitress came back with their coffee. When she set their coffee on the table, she asked if they were ready to order. Peyton ordered a burger with the works and fries, while Sam ordered the fish and chips. After she left to put their order in, he looked back over to the table where the blond woman was sitting. She was gone! He glanced over by the door and saw her walking out. She looked just like Stacy!

With his heart pounding, he got up off his chair and said to his friend, "Excuse me a moment, Sam, I'll be right back." As he was trying to get to the door, he bumped into a couple along the way. By the time he got out the door and looked around, he couldn't find her! *Damn! Was it her?* He couldn't be sure. He walked back into the restaurant and sat down.

"Is everything okay?" asked Sammy.

"I don't know, Sam, I thought I saw the woman I was involved with before I came to work here on the island, but I couldn't catch her. It's like she disappeared into thin air."

"I'm sorry. She must have meant a lot to you."

"She did. I hate to admit it, but I miss her." He smiled. "I think I'm starting to imagine she's here when I know for a fact she is in LA."

"How long did you know her?" she asked.

"Not long, but I fell pretty hard for her. She wasn't willing to make a commitment, to try and have a relationship living so far away from each other. I would have moved heaven and earth to be with her."

Sammy studied his emotions crossing his face and asked, "Would you have considered moving where she lives?"

He sighed. He looked into Sammy's eyes. She was a pretty thing. She had long brown hair, tied back into a bun at the base of her neck. She had blue eyes. Her complexion was fair, and she had a nice figure that showed even in her scrubs. She was a good medic. He enjoyed working with her whenever they were scheduled together. "I thought about it, Sam, but I know I in my heart I wouldn't be happy living in a big city. I just put in an offer for a little farm, twenty minutes from the hospital. It has forty acres, plenty of room for Justice and me. The house needs some work, but the barns are in good condition. I might even think about getting a couple of horses."

"That's wonderful, Peyton! You know, if things are meant to be between the two of you, maybe she'll come here."

"Yeah, maybe." He sighed. When their food came, it left Peyton thinking about the woman he saw today, once in the taxi and here tonight in the restaurant. Could it have been Stacy? If it was her, why hasn't she contacted him, just to let him know she was here? As he ate his sandwich, he couldn't help but think… He shook his head. No, it wasn't possible; after the way they left things between them, he doubted very much that she would move here for him.

Stacy met the woman at the Hawaiian Arms, and found the apartment was fully furnished, in a nice neighborhood, and fifteen minutes from the police department downtown. She signed a three-month lease. If things didn't work out here, she could always go back to LA. She went back to her hotel room feeling a lot more confident in getting moved in on time to meet the Wednesday deadline. But she still had a lot to accomplish in the next several days. At least she didn't have to worry about furniture. She would sublet her apartment, wrap up her work at the Post, pack her things up, and be moved in by Tuesday! All well said and done, she could only hope it will go smoothly. It was late when she finally finished making phone calls. She decided that she would wait until she was moved into her apartment here to contact Peyton. With thoughts of him swirling in her mind, she fell into an exhausted sleep.

CHAPTER 22

Mike and Jenna's wedding day finally arrived. It couldn't have been a more perfect day. The sun was shining. The temperature on the island was in the low seventies, but if anything could go wrong, it did! Jenna woke up with a slight headache, after she'd had a little too much wine at the party her friends had planned for her last night. She looked at the time. She was supposed to be at the church at nine to meet the florist. It was already eight fifteen! She sprang out of bed with her head reeling and jumped into the shower. When she was dressed, she knocked on Sasha's door. When she didn't get a response, she opened the door. Sasha was still out like a light. She, too, had a little too much wine last night. "Sasha, it's time to get up. We're due at the hairdresser at ten thirty!"

She moaned. "What time is it?"

"It's almost nine. I'm supposed to meet the florist at nine, and I'm going to be late!"

Sasha, lying there like a slug, only frustrated Jenna more! She was starting to panic, as all the last-minute details of the wedding swarmed in her head. "Sasha!" she yelled.

Sasha rose up in a sitting position, "Okay, okay, I'm up, I'm up! You don't need to yell; I've got a splitting headache!"

"Sorry, but I have to know you're up before I leave for the church, or you'll miss your hair appointment."

"Okay…" Sasha moaned. "I'm right behind you."

Jenna, watching her friend, wasn't so sure. "Sasha!"

"Yes?"

"Put your feet on the floor and stand up."

Sasha complied.

"Good." Jenna smiled. "I'll see you at the hairdresser."

As she left to go meet the florist, Sasha, with her right arm and finger pointing at the door, yawned and said, "Right!" as she collapsed back down on the bed.

Jenna was twenty minutes late arriving at the church, and the florist was not a happy camper. Inside, all of the flowers were set in the foyer of the church, with the florist looking at her watch. She looked up as Jenna walked into the church. "You're late! I have another wedding to set up yet this morning!"

Jenna, with her head beginning to hurt even more, said, "I'm sorry. I'm afraid I had a little too much wine last night and didn't hear my alarm, but I'm here now, so let's get started."

The florist sighed, and realized she was a bit too brisk with the bride-to-be. She had plenty of time. "Okay, I've already set up the wedding arch. I've placed the yellow and white Hawaiian hibiscus with green tropical foliage and baby's breath throughout the arch. I took some variegated orange roses and placed them in different areas of the arch."

Jenna looked over at the arch, which was placed in front of the altar. It was simply beautiful. As she looked around at the remaining flowers, she got to work. Between the two of them, they finished up in record time. When Jenna looked around, she was pleased with the results. On every pew there were a cluster of yellow sweetheart roses with white hibiscus and a single orange rose tied together with green satin ribbons. Placed on the altar was a floral arrangement, in an array of color, with a single candle in the center. On each side of the arrangement was a candle, with yellow hibiscus and baby's breath around the candle holder. It was beautiful. She thanked the florist as they both walked out of the church. When she checked her watch, she let out of breath. She was now late for her hair appointment! At the rate she was going today, she would be late for her own wedding! And she still needed to stop at the venue to make sure everything was set in place for the reception!

Stacy was on her way to Oahu for Mike and Jenna's wedding. She hadn't reached out to Peyton yet. With the move to the big island and starting her new job, she was non-stop. When she checked into the police department Wednesday morning, her boss immediately put her on a homicide case, which required all of her time. Sitting in the small aircraft, she thought about Peyton. She knew that the two brothers and Zack were standing up with Mike, with Mark being his best man. Stacy was a little apprehensive about seeing Peyton again. It's now been almost six weeks since she last laid eyes on him. *How will he react when he sees me?* she wondered. She hoped he didn't reject her. Her heart couldn't take it. Lost in her thoughts, she felt the plane land and come to a stop. She unbuckled her seat belt and exited the plane. When she stepped down on the tarmac, she took a deep breath. *Well,* she thought, *today is the day of reckoning.* She would soon find out if Peyton still had feelings for her, or if he's moved on. She hailed a cab to take her to the church. Looking at her watch, she should just make it on time.

Peyton, watching his brother Mike pace back and forth in a room where they gathered at the church before the wedding, wondered if he was going to be like this when he decided to get married. Thoughts of Stacy popped into his head. He hadn't heard from her since that text she sent him last week. He didn't expound on his text to her either. So where did that leave them? He still missed her. He wanted to see her again. If it took him moving to LA, he decided, he would take the chance and see if he could live in the city. He would make the effort as long as they were together. After the wedding, he would contact her, to see if she would be willing to see him. He would proclaim his love for her in hopes that she wouldn't reject him. He was still heartsick without her. As it grew closer to the time of the ceremony, Mike stopped his pacing and asked his brother for the fourth time today, "Peyton, do you have the marriage license?"

Peyton came up and put his hand on Mike's shoulder. "Yes, bro, I have the license. You need to calm down."

"What about the rings, do we have the rings?"

Mark shook his head. He didn't remember being this nervous at his own wedding. "Bro, the rings are with Cameron, tied to the pillow he will be carrying down the aisle. I'm sure Jenna made sure the rings were attached to the pillow. Take a deep breath and quit stressing!"

Just then the door opened, to let them know it was time. Mike took that deep breath, and, with his heart thundering in his chest, went to meet his bride, with his best man and the groomsmen following behind.

As the wedding procession started, Mike watched as the bridesmaids came down the aisle, wearing sleeveless gowns that hugged the bodice, with the skirt falling to the floor in a beautiful orchid color. A white silk sash around the waist was tied in the back with a bow, with silk ribbons flowing down the back of the skirt. The maid of honor followed, with the flower girl and ringbearer coming up behind. Jenna's niece, Brittney, was in a chiffon gown, the same color as the bridesmaids, with puffed sleeves and a white silk bow with ribbons flowing down in front of her dress. Cameron looked handsome in his tux, and so grown up as he carried the pillow with the rings beside Jenna's niece who was sprinkling orchid petals in an array of color on the white runner. When they were all standing in front of the church, the wedding march began.

Jenna, with her arm entwined in her father's arm, watched as her wedding party went down the aisle. As it got closer for the time for her to go, her dad looked at his beautiful daughter and smiled. "Have I told you yet that you are the most beautiful bride I have ever seen. I can't believe my baby is getting married."

She looked over at her dad with tears in her eyes and asked, "Am I doing the right thing, Dad?"

He gave his daughter a wink. "Well, it's a little late for asking that question, but to ease your mind, I like Mike, and he's a good match for you."

Jenna smiled as they stepped up to the entrance of the sanctuary. When she saw Mike, her breath caught. Dressed in a black tux with an orchid shirt and black bow tie, he couldn't look more handsome if he tried. When she caught his eyes from the back of the church, seeing the love he had for her, she knew she was doing the right thing. As the music for the wedding march began, the guests rose, and Jenna and her dad started down the aisle. A woman slipped into the back pew and watched as Jenna proceeded down the aisle with her father.

Mike, in awe of his beautiful bride, couldn't take his eyes off her. She wore a white satin dress with a scoop neckline, cap sleeves, with the bodice coming down to a V in the back to the waist. Two rows of pink pearls lined the neckline to the back, with pearl buttons going part way down the back of dress. An orchid satin sash at the waist came around to the back in a big bow. The full skit came down to the floor, with a medium train flowing behind her. She chose a traditional veil, with tiny orchid flowers that lined the outside of the white netting. It was attached to a tiara with pink pearls lining the front. The white netting in front covered her face. The veil hung down just below her shoulders. She carried a beautiful bouquet of flowers, in an array of color that went perfectly with her dress. As her dad took her hand and placed it in Mike's, the pair walk up to the altar, where Pastor Kingsley stood ready to marry them. Vows were spoken, and rings were exchanged. The two took a candle and lit the single one in the center, to signify the two becoming one. Mike lifted her veil. The kiss that they shared spoke volumes of the love and commitment they made to each other as a married couple. They turned to face their guests, as Pastor Kingsley introduced them as Mr. and Mrs. Michael TreVaine. The guests cheered as they walked back down the aisle, grinning from ear to ear, as husband and wife.

Stacy was purposely late for the reception. She didn't want Peyton to see her until all the formalities were over, when she could steal him away for a few minutes to talk. And if he rejected her, she would feel less embarrassed, and slip out without a lot of people noticing. She stood in the doorway of the reception hall. Peyton was over by the set-up bar, talking to a couple she had never seen before. She took a deep breath as she walked into the room. She just about jumped out of her skin when Jenna came up behind her and turned her around. "Stacy! Oh my gosh, you came! Has Peyton seen you?"

"Um…not yet." She looked in his direction and their eyes locked. "But I think he has now."

Jenna looked over where Stacy was staring, turned back, and squeezed her hand. "Good luck." She backed away, as Peyton started over.

Peyton was shocked to see Stacy here. She was a little thinner than he remembered. He had no idea that she was even invited to his brother's wedding. His eyes took her in as he walked slowly up to her. In a black cocktail dress with spaghetti straps, the dress hugged her body and fell just above her knees. Her firm breasts showed just above the bodice, and she wore a gold charm necklace to accent. Her hair was done up with soft wisps flowing down along the sides of her face. Gold studded earrings complemented her outfit. She looked absolutely stunning. His heart beat erratically as he walked up to her. "Hi," he breathed.

"Hi," she whispered back. Stacy was in awe of the man in front of her. He was ruggedly handsome in his black tux and bow tie. He was clean-shaven and her eyes couldn't get enough of him.

"What are you doing here?" he asked in amazement.

"I was invited. But to be honest with you, I purposely arrived late to the reception, in hopes that I could speak to you in private." Her eyes pleaded with him.

The music started up, and a slow song began to play. His eyes burned into hers as he held out his hand to her. "May I have this dance first?" She held his eyes, then placed her hand in his. They walked out onto the dance floor. He took her in his arms. As he held her close, Peyton never felt more at home than he did right now. He gazed down into her hazel eyes and poured out what he was feeling. "Stacy, I miss this. I miss holding you and loving you. I miss your sassiness, I miss us working together. I miss everything about you! Could there still be a chance for us?" his blue eyes pleading.

"Oh, Peyton, I've missed you so much! I've been so miserable since I went back to LA. Yes, if you'll still have me, I would like that." She smiled up into his eyes.

His eyes turned serious as he said, "I've been thinking. I'm willing to come to LA if that's what it takes for us to be together. I'm not sure how I will like it, but all I know is I don't want to lose you again."

"Really?" she asked with questioning eyes. She was surprised that he would consider moving to a place she knew he would come to hate, after a time in the city, for her.

He smiled down at her. "Yes, really!"

She giggled.

"You think this is funny?" he asked curtly, pulling away from her slightly.

"I'm sorry, Peyton. I have some news of my own. When Lieutenant Andrew saw how miserable I was, he arranged an interview for me at the police department on the big island of Kona. There was a position open in the homicide department. I interviewed and got the job the same day! They wanted me to start this past Wednesday, which only gave me a week to move and get started. I wanted to call you to let you know that I was on the island, but when I arrived, my boss put me on a homicide case right away, and I have had no time to contact you. I wanted to be with you, Peyton, but I was also scared. Scared you might have moved on."

He was shocked to find that she had been on the island for a full week and never ran into her. Then it dawned on him that the day after she had texted him, he thought he saw her twice that day but couldn't be sure. "Was your interview the day after you texted me?"

"Yes," she responded.

"And were you at Ted's Bar and Grill having dinner that evening?"

Surprised, she asked, "Yes, how did you know?"

"I thought I saw you there, but I wasn't sure. When I saw you walk out the door, I tried to run after you, but you disappeared. I was missing you so much that I thought I was hallucinating."

"Oh, Peyton, I never saw you! I wished I had. I was going to text you that I was there on the island, but it was late, and I had so much to do that I thought I would wait till I moved, but it didn't work out the way I wanted. Can you forgive me?"

Peyton slammed her body into his for a fierce hug. He let her go slightly, to bend his head down, to deliver a kiss that sent both their hearts on fire. He lifted his head. "Stacy, there's nothing to forgive. Yes, it would have been nice to know you were on the island, and not far from me, but I understand how rushed you must have been, and then to be put on a case right away! Stacy, I love you with all my heart, and I'm hoping you feel the same way about me."

The music had long stopped, but as she gazed deep into his eyes, she let go. She wasn't afraid of commitment anymore. Not as long as he was by her side. She lifted her hands to his handsome face and declared, "Peyton TreVaine, I love you with all my heart, and I'm not afraid anymore to make a commitment to our relationship." She reached up and kissed him with all the love she held in her heart for him. He pressed her body close to his as he returned her kiss, and knew in his heart he was finally home.

EPILOGUE

Mark, sitting at one of the tables during Mike and Jenna's wedding reception, sipping on a beer, glanced around the room. He was happy that his parents were able to come over for the wedding. He and his brothers hadn't seen their parents in a few years, so it was nice catching up on all the news of their retirement and what was going on in their community. He glanced over to his brother, who was talking to his sister and one of his cousins that were able to make it over for the wedding. He then turned to see Stacy standing in the doorway of the reception room. She was one beautiful woman. He looked back over at his brother to see Peyton walking towards her. There was no doubt in his mind that his brother was still in love with her. When he glanced back at Stacy, he could see she felt the same. He watched as the two danced together to the slow rhythm of the music. He could see another wedding in the future. While he sat there, he thought about his own wedding eight years ago. He was so young, fresh out of the service. He had met Sherry six months before he was discharged from the Air Force and fell madly in love with her. They were married one month after he was discharged. His brother, Mike, approached him about investing in a restaurant with him. He took the challenge and invested his time and money into making the restaurant the success that it was today, but not without a lot of sacrifices. Cameron was born a year after he and Sherry were married. He tried to divide his work/life balance, but there always seemed to be something that would take his time away from his family. If it wasn't the restaurant, it was the online courses to finish his degree in marketing, with a minor in accounting. It took its toll on his marriage. Looking back, he could forgive his wife for having an affair. It still hurt, though. Their divorce was final a couple of weeks ago, and it seemed like an end to an era for him. For Cameron's sake, he would try and remember the good times, the bad not so much.

His sister came up and approached his table. "May I join you, dear brother?"

He smiled up at her. "Do you need to even ask?"

She laughed and took a seat beside him. His sister was an attractive woman. She stood about five-three, with dark brown hair and brown eyes, which she inherited from their mother. She was a stay-at-home mom, raising her and her husband's two rambunctious boys, even though she had a BA degree in education. "I noticed that you seemed lost in thought when I came up to you. How are you doing, Mark?" she asked with concern. "Since the divorce, I mean."

"Funny you should ask. You know the divorce was final a few weeks ago."

"Yes," she answered.

"I have my regrets, but it was for the best. Right now, Cameron is my focus, along with the restaurant. I want to make sure his life is stable and know that he is loved by the both of us even though we live apart."

She smiled and put her hand over his. "Someday you will find that special someone that will make your heart dance, and the love that you will share will be greater than the one you shared before."

He returned her smile. "Thanks, sis, I hope so."

"You will, you are far too handsome not to!"

The next morning, Mark and his son Cameron took his brother Mike and Jenna to the airport. They were spending two weeks in Paris for their honeymoon. When they saw them off, he turned to his son and asked, "What would you like to do today, son?"

He glanced up at his father. "Gee, Dad, I don't know." He thought a moment, and his eyes lit up! "Could we go to that cool ice cream parlor downtown? We could get one of those big ice cream sundaes!"

Mark chuckled. "Do you think you could eat one of those?"

"Well, Dad." He grinned. "If I can't, I know you will!"

Mark laughed. "Okay, you got me. Let's head over there!" Mark settled his son in the back seat. He walked around his car and climbed into the driver's seat. He drove downtown and found a parking spot near the parlor. As they came out of the car and started walking toward the ice cream place, he heard his name called. He turned around to see Zack coming up fast, with Tammy, one of his waitresses, following him.

"Mark! Wait!" yelled Zack. Mark waited until Zack and Tammy came up to him.

Tammy, with a look of fright and tears coming down her face, cried, "Mark! Can you help us! I can't find Bethany!"

Alert, Mark turned to Zack. "What's going on?"

"Tammy was in the store over there. Bethany was by her side. She looked away for just a moment to talk to the clerk. When she turned around, Bethany was gone! I was just walking by when she came running out of the store screaming!"

Just then, they heard another scream! Seemed to come from the parking lot across the street! Mark and Zack looked at each other, then Mark turned to his son. "You stay here with Tammy. We'll be right back!" He turned to Zack. "Let's go!" They both ran across the street, dodging traffic as they went. They heard another scream, followed by, "Let me go!" They saw a guy, a few cars down, trying to get a little girl in the car. Both men ran up to the man, but not before the little girl kicked him in the shins, making the man grab his leg, jumping up and down. The little girl started running.

"Bethany!" Zack yelled. She stopped, turned around, as Zack came up to her, holding out his arms.

She ran into them with tears in her eyes and cried, "He was going to take me! I was so scared! I kicked him in the shins! He wouldn't let me go!"

"You did good, honey. He's not going to hurt you ever again." As he looked over to where the car was parked, he saw the man run off with Mark on his tail. Mark grabbed his shirt from behind, turned him around, and gave him a punch to the gut and then to the jaw! He went down. Zack hurried up to them with Bethany still in his arms. "Nice work, Mark!"

"Thanks," as he shook his hands out.

Zack turned to the little girl. "Bethany, can you go with Mark? He will take you back to your mom. I'm going to take this guy to the police station so he can't hurt you or anyone else again." She nodded her head yes. He smiled and handed her off to Mark.

"I'll stay till you get him cuffed and call for backup."

"Thanks, Mark."

Zack went and turned the guy on his stomach, pulled his hands behind his back, and put the cuffs on him. He radioed for a car to come and take the suspected kidnapper to jail. When he started coming to, Zack pulled him up in a standing position and hauled him over to his car. The man shook his head. "What happened?"

Zack smiled and nodded as Mark took Bethany back to her mother. "You ran into a bulldozer!"

Mark handed a frightened Bethany to her mother. "Oh, Bethany, are you all right?" Tammy squeezed her daughter tight to her. Bethany had her arms tightly around her mother's neck in return. She let go of her mom and wanted down. Tammy went down on her haunches. She gazed into her daughter's eyes.

"I'm all right, Mommy, but I'm afraid I might have hurt the man trying to take me when I kicked him in the shins!"

Tammy brushed the hair from her daughter's face and smiled. "Whether you hurt the man or not is not the point. He was a bad man, and you are one brave little girl! I would have done the same!" She stood up and took her daughter's hand in hers.

Cameron, with his eyes big as saucers, took in the situation. "Gee, Bethany, I'm not sure I would be brave enough to do that!"

Bethany looked over at the little boy. With a toothless smile, she asked, "Sure you could! What's your name?"

"I'm Cameron, and this is my dad." Cameron proudly looked up to his father.

"Thank you and the other man for saving me," she said shyly.

Mark beamed down at her and smiled when he said, "You are welcome, young lady."

Tammy in return exclaimed, "Yes, Mark, thank you, I don't know how I will ever repay you and Zack for saving my daughter's life!"

He stared into a pair of liquid amber eyes, and suddenly had an instant urge to protect her, and her little girl, come over him. He never really noticed her before, other than being an employee at him and his brother's restaurant, but suddenly his eyes fell on her petite figure, dressed in tight jeans and a tank top. She was pretty, and something inside him wanted to get to know her better. He smiled. "Cameron and I were just heading over to the ice cream parlor. Would you two care to join us?"

Bethany, jumping up and down, looking up at her mother, asked, "Can we, Mom, can we?"

Tammy, gazing down at her daughter, responded,
"Oh, I don't know..."

"Pleeease?" she pleaded.

Tammy looked up into deep blue eyes, and caught her breath. At work, she always admired how handsome he was but would never let herself react to the chemistry she felt for him. He would never date her. His rules about dating employees were set in stone. His eyes smiled into hers, waiting for her to respond. "Are you sure?" she asked.

He grinned. "Yes, I'm sure."

Her heart beat a little faster as she said, "Okay."

Both kids jumped up and down, and yelled, "Yay!" as they all walked down the street toward the ice cream parlor.

WILL MARK BREAK THE RULES TO FIND LOVE? LOOK OUT FOR THE NEXT BOOK IN THE HAWAIIAN TRILOGY, **HAWAIIAN EMBERS**, COMING SOON.

[handwritten note: ↑ Got from Library]